THE REGULARS

In the Fabulous Fifties, they were
the kids who Bopped and Strolled on the
TV show that had all America dancing.

Reunited twenty years later
for a TV special, they played out the
drama of their secret passions
as millions watched!

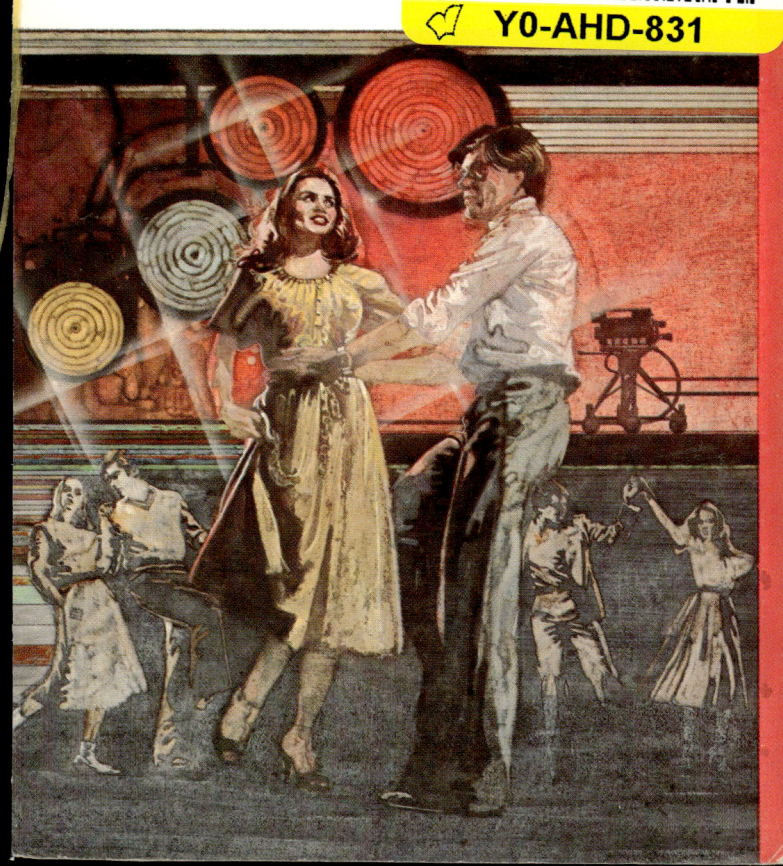

STEPHEN LEWIS

"Spectacular success as a writer of sexy bestsellers pegged to the news!"
—*Boston Herald American*

"His readers number in the millions... they're getting a peek at the way things are."
—*Washington Star*

"Stephen Lewis is an indefatigable wordsmith..."
—*New York Times*

"Lewis' fresh, fast-moving style... will certainly expand this young author's already considerable following."
—*Atlanta Journal-Constitution*

"All of his books seem to turn into bestsellers!"
—*Bestsellers*

Novels by Stephen Lewis

THE CLUB
NATURAL VICTIMS
BEACH HOUSE
SOMETHING IN THE BLOOD
THE BEST SELLERS
THE LOVE MERCHANTS

THE REGULARS

Stephen Lewis

LEISURE BOOKS ∞ NEW YORK CITY

This is a work of fiction, and all characters (with the exception of public figures) are fictitious. Any similarity between these characters and real people in name, description, occupation, or background is purely coincidental.

A LEISURE BOOK

Published by

Nordon Publications, Inc.
Two Park Avenue
New York, N.Y. 10016

Copyright © 1980 by Stephen Lewis

Original Lyrics Copyright © 1976, 1977, 1978, 1979, 1980 by Stephen Lewis, used by permission

All rights reserved
Printed in the United States

**THIS IS DEDICATED—
TO THE ONES I LOVE.**

THE
REGULARS

Book One

1.

THE CUSTOMARY CHORUSES OF "GOOD mornings," some of them sincere but most of them from apple-polishers, greeted Kay Duvane from the time she entered the TBS Building on Sixth Avenue (*nobody* referred to it by its official name of Avenue of the Americas: that was strictly for tourists and stationery) to the moment she made her way into her private office on the tenth floor. She met them with her professional smile, carefully cultivated from twenty-two years of on-the-job practice.

The fact of the matter was that there was nothing "good" about the morning at all: it had started off badly, and it would probably get even worse in the hour and a half left before noon.

Even before she'd left her apartment on Central Park West, she'd been upset. Mimi, the Siamese and heaven-knew-what-else cat who'd been her roommate ever since she'd found her as a stray, shivering kitten nine years before, was either getting old or sick, but finicky to the point of concern. It wasn't just that Mimi had refused to eat the Salmon 'N'Egg catfood she'd been fond of for a near-record three weeks. If anything, Kay admired the animal's independence, so much like her own, and after years of experience she was well aware that Mimi's tastes changed with no more reason than whim.

This time, though, it was different. For four days, Kay had set out every flavor and brand of food in the house—canned, dry, and semi-moist—and Mimi had done nothing more than nibble.

"What's the matter?" Kay had asked. "Don't you watch the commercials?"

But the joke fell flat, and not even the piece of liver she'd picked up at the butcher's, then broiled and cut into tiny pieces, had worked. Always before, it had been a foolproof way of getting Mimi to eat, and a peace-making treat when a bad day or a bad week made her shun the cat's occasional demands for attention.

Kay had left the apartment wondering whom she was really upset with: Mimi for being so damn aggravating, or herself for caring more than she liked to admit. "One more day," she warned the cat, "and you're going to the vet!"

Her spirits had brightened on the way to the Park Lane. The Women's Broadcasting Breakfast Club was an exclusive bunch, and she was a charter member. It had started years before almost informally, a natural alliance of a minority group... women executives in the male-dominated world of television. Its reputation had grown over the years, particularly under the spotlight of press attention the group had received as a result of the feminist movement.

The biggest names, brightest minds, the "shakers and movers" within the industry—male and female—were honored to be invited to address the monthly meetings. Being nominated for membership (all new candidates had to be sponsored by members) was a status symbol within the industry, and even being invited to a meeting as a guest carried clout.

Kay had wanted to take Sheila Granger, her assistant, but things at the office had been too hectic and someone had to be there to cover. As it turned out, she'd have appreciated the company, if only because it was something that misery naturally loves.

It wasn't just that the eggs had made her think of Mimi or that the croissants were cold. The real problem was the issue that had been the topic of the speech Nat Gallin, one of the biggest agents in the business, had made.

"The Coming Network Crisis," it was called, and aptly so.

Nat, to his credit, was a pro. He'd started off with a few clever jokes and a couple of anecdotes about the old days, days that some of the women in the room, Kay among them, remembered. But fond recollections of the days when the medium was young had been only a jumping-off place.

As he continued, Nat had painted a frightening picture of television as a medium that had grown old before its time... at least *network* television. Video was certainly alive and well. That was the problem. The Beta and VHS videotape systems were thriving. The public, in spite of a generally gloomy economy, was buying the systems up as fast as the manufacturers could come out with new models. Videodiscs, too, were a hot item—so hot there was a waiting list of thousands at the few stores where the machines had been test-marketed.

Instead of the problems of incompatibility that some had predicted would carve the home video market into tiny, inconsequential pieces, it appeared that those who were into the new technology were into it in a big way. The actual TV set, it was clear, was like a stereo receiver. Just as consumers bought a cassette deck, a reel-to-reel recorder, and a turntable for a "complete" system, they appeared more than eager to buy videotape decks, videodisc players, TV games, and anything else that came on the market... including the home computers that were only a few years away.

When you added the reality of cable systems that gave small, independent stations a dramatically wider audience, and the reality of pay TV offering first-run movies and increasing numbers of sports events and specials, the facts were frightening.

The major networks hadn't just enjoyed dominance of the airwaves (for so many years they were taken for granted); they'd had sole domain. Of course public television received a lot of attention from the critics, who were continually holding its "achievements" up as examples of what the medium was capable of. In truth, however, the ratings showed it to be almost insignificant. There was no disputing the fact that Dick Cavett was an articulate, intelligent interviewer who often had fascinating guests. But the American viewing public, by an overwhelming majority, preferred Johnny, Merv, Mike, Dinah, and Phil when it came to preferences in talk show hosts. *Masterpiece Theatre* and the other British imports were hailed as triumphs of artistry—but the public preferred *Three's Company*, *Mork and Mindy*, and other such half-hour sitcoms to multi-part adaptations of the classics.

If public television posed no real threat to the networks, independent stations—those unaffiliated with ABC, NBC, CBS, or TBS—were more of a nuisance than a real threat. Their budgets, compared to what the networks spent on programming, were minuscule. As a result, they offered viewers a mixture of old movies, reruns of old network series now in syndication, and an occasional special... usually one the networks had passed on. True, the independents sometimes came up with a dynamic newscaster or talk-show host who made an impact, and they often made deals with home teams that attracted those viewers who wanted to catch every game the local baseball or hockey team played. *Local* was the key word, though: the independent stations were no real threat to the networks. Like their share of the market, the advertisers they attracted were small. Mail-order records and kitchen equipment, local stores, businesses, and used-car lots were the bread and butter of the independents. Major advertisers, the national-brand products and corporations who spent the big money at Madison Avenue agencies, bought network time for their commercials.

Ever since the beginning, the networks had thought of the ever-increasing number of television sets in American homes (the Bureau of Statistics had announced, to the networks' delight, that more homes had TV sets than bathtubs) as outlets for their product. Competition for the viewers' attention and loyalty was intense, but the number of competitors was clearly established and strictly limited.

At least that was the way it had been.

In his talk, Nat Gallin had restated the new realities that were causing panic and havoc within the network offices and conference rooms.

Times had changed.

The party, decidedly, was over.

Viewers had more options, and they were eager to exercise them. Network television had gone from being the only game in town to being one of a growing number of alternatives. To make matters even worse, the alternatives were often more attractive than any programming network TV could offer. New movies (uninterrupted by the lifeblood of commercial advertising that kept TBS and the others in business, and uncensored by a network standards and practices expert), four-letter, hardcore sex, and blood-and-guts violence that the FCC was always complaining about, along with religious and special interest groups—that, Nat had told his listeners, was just the tip of the iceberg.

15

"I've done a lot of business with most of you," he'd said, his eyes sweeping the room as he stood behind the lectern. "You know that television and I go back quite a ways. We've grown together, and I'm sincerely grateful: a man doesn't go from a one-room office on West Forty-sixth Street to the presidency of a major talent agency with offices on both coasts without help.

"Because I'm grateful, I'm sorry to have to tell you that the problem is going to get worse. Where is the product that these consumers will watch coming from? The movie studios will supply some of it. They dominate the market in pre-recorded cassettes and discs at the moment. But you people will have your share, too. Assuming your legal departments have their way—and they usually do—your networks are going to be able to sell some of your programs and specials in this new market. Of course that means you'll have to get going: already, pirated tapes are big business.

"You'll have to confront the problem of reruns, too. Let's suppose you sign a Cher, or a Barbra Streisand, or a Sylvia—who is a client of mine, by the way—for a special. Do you rerun it, or sell the tape to the home market? Or will the consumer already have taped his own copy from your first run, and cut out the commercials?

"I represent a wide range of talent, as you know. Writers, directors, performers—all the elements that make your series and your specials happen. They're often a frustrating bunch, to be sure, but many of them are smart. So smart they're beginning to ask why they should continue to work in television as all of us in this room know it. They're aware that it's just a matter of time until independent production swings around from filling the needs of network programming to catering to the growing home market.

"In summation and in short, my friends, the crisis is coming. It's already here, and it will get worse. As an agent—a flesh-peddler, a ten-percenter if you prefer—I can't afford to neglect reality. I have to look at figures, and advise a client like Syliva, just for the sake of argument, of the best and most lucrative career opportunities.

"Will she, in a few years, be doing specials for your networks? Or will she be making tapes that will retail for ten or twenty dollars—videotapes with the same appeal of her albums, though with a higher retail price and therefore a better royalty?

"You see my point, and I see your problem. I wish I had an answer, but I don't. Like it or not, the public medium we've worked in together for so many years is going private."

And like it or not, Kay thought, remembering the speech as she sat at her desk, *my ass is on the line. Mine and that of every woman in that room and everybody else in this business.*

"You work and work to get to the top and then you have to work even harder to stay there," Kay said, gazing out the window.

"Pardon?"

Kay glanced up, swiveling in her chair, realizing that she'd spoken aloud, and that Sheila Granger had come in from her adjoining office, the smaller of the two in the suite they shared.

"Don't mind me," Kay said with a wave of her hand. "Just a cheery little thought that came to mind."

"How was the meeting?" Sheila asked.

"Great for inspiring cheery little thoughts. Actually, it was more like a funeral. They should have held it at Frank Campbell's."

"Who died?" the younger girl asked.

"Television," Kay answered drily. "Now fill me in on what's been going on here."

All in all, the morning had been fairly quiet. Sheila had

taken Kay's calls; they shared a secretary, but in the year and a half they'd been working together, Sheila had been given an increasing amount of responsibility. There were certain things that Kay and Kay alone had the authority and expertise to handle, but many of the calls from writers, producers, and directors involved questions that Sheila could answer and deal with. She logged them and reviewed them with Kay, making sure her boss got the important messages quickly. The practice left Kay free to make the dozens of outgoing phone calls that were part of her daily routine, and to attend the meetings and conferences that were part of her job.

It was the same with the mail. Unless letters were marked "PERSONAL," and few were, Sheila opened them, separating the invitations to movie screenings and theater productions, the proposals and scripts, the contracts and correspondence about projects in the works or under consideration.

The urgent letters demanding Kay's attention went on her desk, arranged in order of importance. The more routine matters were handled by Sheila, who dictated replies which were typed by Helen, their secretary, and placed in a folder on Kay's desk for her signature.

The relationship between the two women was a good one. It had been that way from the start, and it had gotten even better with time. Sheila's real job, as they both saw it, involved freeing Kay from as much paperwork and as many little details as possible ... and acting as a sounding board for Kay's major problems and projects. Professionalism and respect were at the core of their relationship, along with an equal amount of trust.

Unlike some executives, Kay Duvane was secure enough to recognize her assistant's ambition and talent without being threatened by them. Instead, she encouraged Sheila to get fully involved, to use her drive and intelligence to their mutual advantage.

It's going to be easier for her than it was for me, Kay thought, as Sheila gave her a rundown on the morning.

Two decades earlier, when Kay had started out in the business, there'd been no women in positions of real power. The men who held them had viewed her as a threat, a freak, or—when they were being their most pleasant—an amusing curiosity. She'd had no sense of mission when she hired Sheila, but the younger woman's determination and intelligence had impressed her. Unexpectedly, Kay had found herself in the role of mentor, with Sheila avidly savoring every tip, every insight and piece of advice she gave.

Me playing Good Morning, Miss Dove? she thought from time to time, amused by the relationship. *Well, anything that helps a girl get through her forties—and it does beat* Goodbye, Mr. Chips.

Within a half-hour of her arrival in the office, Kay had gotten through the morning calls, the mail, and the inter-office memos.

"I've done some summaries and evaluations on the 'magic mountain,'" Sheila said, using their private term for the mound of scripts and outlines that never seemed to really diminish. Writers, producers, and agents knew better than to submit anything but their best concepts for specials to Kay Duvane, but all the same the number of submissions was staggering. The "magic" factor was the way the pile never shrank, no matter how determinedly the two women attacked it. Kay had taught Sheila early on that each and every submission should be considered on its own merits. A seasoned pro with a shelf of Emmys in his den was capable of coming up with something horrendous, and an unknown was capable of creating something fantastic.

"We should go through them, I suppose," Kay sighed, "but we're not going to. I've got one property right here that's giving me a headache." As she spoke, she opened the lizard-skin satchel she carried in place of an attaché case. She withdrew a script and dropped it on the desk with a thud.

Sheila Granger knew what the property was even before she glanced at the title page.

AMERICAN DREAMERS

A Television Drama by

Will Brandt

"You're having lunch with him today, aren't you?" Sheila asked.

"Don't remind me!" Kay pleaded, rolling her eyes.

"But I thought you liked him. What's the matter? Isn't the script any good?"

Kay paused. "It's not good, Sheila. It's great. It's brilliant and sensitive and touching. I read it three times, and it got better and better. If I was the type, I'd have cried my eyes out."

"Great! We've been looking for dramatic specials. It sounds like you've finally found one. And it's nice that it's by a writer you like so much—"

"Put the brakes on," Kay interrupted, bringing her hand down on the script with a force that surprised both of them. "Sorry," Kay apologized. "It's one of those days, I'm afraid. You're right, Sheila. I do like Will. And I love the script. But I'm going to have to pass on it."

Confused, Sheila brushed a strand of honey-blonde hair back from her face. "I must have missed something. I thought you said it was a great script—"

"That's just it. It's *too* damn good for us. Forget all that crap the publicity department put out about *TBS Playhouse* being a return to the golden age of television drama. Sure, the network is looking for prestige, but the name of the game is ratings, and we both know it."

She lifted the script with both hands, waving it as she

continued. "This is about a dying woman who has nothing left but a little time and the land she's lived on all her life. It's a small farm she doesn't work any more, and there are oil deposits under the ground. She knows that someday the whole place will be torn up, but she doesn't want to see it."

"Oh," Sheila said softly. The pieces were falling into place. As a "prestige" series of specials, *TBS Playhouse* had attracted sponsors seeking to improve their corporate image. The two plays scheduled for the season had been sold to one of the oil companies.

"It's not just the sponsor thing," Kay said, as if she was reading Sheila's mind. "If that was the only problem, I'd still be able to use the script, or I'd pass it over to Barry and ask him to consider it as a TV movie.

"But people don't want to see stories about dying old women—even if they're noble. Everybody has a mother or a grandmother or an aunt who's dying. True, the reviews would probably be fabulous. But the ratings would be disastrous."

"I'm sorry, Kay."

"You and me both, sweetie. Will Brandt is a good writer. He's just had a bad streak of luck, and he needs a break. Now I have to tell him I can't give it to him. Hey—how about doing me a favor, Sheila?"

"Sure. What is it?"

"Lunch is going to be pretty rough. If you'd come along, it might make it a little easier. Will's been seeing this old face of mine for years. At least we can give him something pretty to look at while I give him the verdict."

"Fine," Sheila agreed.

"Good. Ask our darling secretary to confirm the reservation, will you? The Four Seasons at twelve thirty, and make it for three. I've got calls to return and the usual crap..." As Sheila left the office, Kay called after her. "Hey—is that a new dress?"

Sheila nodded, pleased that Kay approved of the

lime-green St. Laurent she'd got on sale.

"It looks smashing, sweetie. Leave it to you to be able to wear that color. I'd look like Harriet Hepatitis if I tried it."

The image of Sheila Granger remained in Kay's mind's eye even after the younger woman had gone into her own office.

She's a nice girl, Kay thought. Nice—and a damn good worker, too, that was for sure. From the start, when her former assistant had gone over to NBC to work in Daytime Programming, Kay had decided against hiring another man as a replacement. Mark had been bright and pleasant enough on the surface, but she'd always sensed that he resented having to work under a female superior.

Sexism was one problem she didn't need any more of, Kay had told herself; she'd had to contend with it, fight against it, and succeed in spite of it from the very beginning of her career. There hadn't been any women in positions of real authority then, and the few who were working in the industry—mostly in the soap operas that had been "translated" from radio—were always called "girls," no matter how old they were.

Men made decisions. "Girls" followed instructions. Men made big moves in the network hierarchy, with titles and offices to match. "Girls" got small raises, and their behinds pinched in the elevator.

Kay had seen several women try to accomplish what she herself had done over the years, and she'd watched casualties fall by the wayside. Some just didn't have the smarts and the stamina the business demanded. Others couldn't hack the chauvinism and went to the magazines or book publishers where a woman had a better chance. And some, out of frustration, turned to the comforts of alcohol, or pills, or affairs with men in positions of power, in the misguided search for recognition.

Well, nobody could accuse her of having screwed her

way into her position. She'd earned it and fought for it, hanging in and hanging on. Along the way, she'd made her share of enemies. Kay knew what they said about her behind her back. She was the "Iron Maiden," tough as nails, a bitch. So what? You didn't make it from a secretarial position in the publicity department to a vice presidency by winning popularity contests.

For Sheila, Kay thought, it was going to be easier. Not as easy as it would be for a man, but a hell of a lot easier than it had been for her. In the first few weeks after Sheila had come to work for her (she'd easily been the best of the applicants personnel had come up with, and she certainly was being wasted in her previous slot with the public service department), Kay had been surprised at the unexpected emotions she felt.

There was no question that she'd made the right choice. Sheila was bright, attractive, eager to please and more than willing to learn. She picked things up fast, was more efficient than Mark had ever been, and she'd volunteered to take scripts and proposals home at night and on weekends, doing the evaluations on her own time to catch up on the backlog.

But looking at Sheila, Kay had seen something frightening... something like a ghost of herself as she'd once been. Not that they looked at all alike. She'd never been as model-thin as Sheila, and she'd never had that perfect complexion or those blue eyes or that natural blonde hair. Still, she'd gotten her share of pinches back in the old days, and like Sheila she'd had a sense of style—admittedly a more tailored look, but one that had always suited her.

The thing Kay recognized was the ambition, the drive. One extra-large order of I'm Going to Make It, come hell or high water. What she'd resented, startled by the feeling, was Sheila's relative innocence. She was no babe in the woods—she'd been at TBS for a couple of years, certainly long enough to see that dirty pool was one of the games you had to play at times—but she didn't yet see how dirty it could get.

It was the nature of the beast, the way the business worked. It took and took and still demanded more. The rewards were there—money, power, satisfaction—but the price tags were hidden. Nobody told you that the moment you ceased to be useful or, worse, started to be a problem, you got kicked out on your ass without any warning.

Lee Dean, the host of *Dancetime, USA!*, TBS' answer to ABC's *American Bandstand*, had been the fair-haired boy back in the old days when Kay had worked in publicity. Then the payola mess came up, and he went off the air for good. Nicholas Kahn had been a crackerjack anchorman on the news and one hell of an interviewer. Granted, it hadn't been too smart of him to go to a gay bar in the first place, and it had been even more stupid to try to get pushy with the cops who raided the place. But still, it could have been hushed up: didn't six years on the nightly news count for something better than getting fired?

The casualties in the entertainment division were obvious to everyone—including the public, who did the actual deciding about who made it or didn't. Each year, Kay had seen it happen. The new shows were touted as the greatest things since the discovery of fire. The new stars were given the big buildup at the annual affiliates meeting, and the publicity department pulled all the stops out promoting them in the papers and magazines and on the talk shows. Then, when the ratings came in, only the numbers mattered—the ratings separated the winners from the losers, the renewals from the cancellations.

No show or star was really ever safe. A situation comedy could be a hit one season and a flop the next, if a competing network put something really powerful in the same time slot. Back in the days when variety shows had been popular, TBS had held first place in the Nielsens with it's back-to-back lineup on Wednesday nights. Then the other networks had attacked with westerns and detective shows, and the whole picture changed. The variety-show hosts had contracts—they got their checks, but they didn't get on the air.

Behind the scenes, on the side of the television screen the public didn't see or seem to even care about, it was even worse. You were only as good as your last credit, only as valuable as whoever happened to be in charge thought you were. (And God help you when there was a major shakeup in your division or, worse, on the top two floors that housed the presidents of the various departments and divisions and the chairman of the board!)

Hot producers went cold. The demand for directors lasted as long as the shows they directed were hits. And writers like Will Brandt... well, there was a case in point.

He'd had three hits on Broadway and offers from Hollywood, but he'd believed that TV was more "pure" than motion pictures. During the mid-1950's, he'd been one of the medium's most acclaimed writers, along with Paddy Chayefsky and Rod Serling. The Golden Age of live TV drama was flourishing, and he was part of it. On *Playhouse 90* at CBS, and on TBS' own *Video Premiere Theater*, his scripts were outstanding, bringing him praise, awards, and recognition.

The Golden Age had faded to the dross of situation comedies, westerns, and general escapist fare. The Cold War, and economic pressures at home were among the factors that changed public taste. Then, too, the popularity of the medium was rising. TV sets were no longer a luxury item for a wealthy segment of the market: more and more people were buying them, people who wanted to be entertained rather than stimulated by heavy fare.

Will Brandt had gone back to Broadway, and the result was disastrous. The same critics who'd hailed him as an "innovative genius" just a few years before attacked his return. The first time back, they called him "stilted and too mundane," suggesting that "Mr. Brandt seems to possess a talent better suited to the little box than the big stage." His next effort, an evening of three one-act plays, fared slightly better in the reviews, but did terribly at the box office. The theater-going public wanted big, splashy musicals or light comedies.

Suddenly, and almost unbelievably, Will Brandt couldn't find a Broadway producer. That sent him into a depression, followed by a nervous breakdown. By the time he recovered, he was old news at the networks that had once fought for him. There were a few highpoints over the next fifteen years—his first play was turned into a movie, as was one of the original dramas he'd done for TBS. Several revivals of his early work were done in various repertory theaters around the country. A new play by Will Brandt opened Off-Broadway to generally favorable reviews and a moderate box office.

But Nancy Brandt, the woman Will had married in 1954 who'd stuck by her husband through the ups and downs of his career, had cancer. Her death made Will's nerves crack again. He spent nearly two and a half years going back and forth between bouts of drinking and periods of drying out at Silver Hill.

Now he was finally back in New York, certifiably "well" again, and the news that TBS was launching a prestigious if limited series of original dramatic specials for television had excited him. Kay, who'd known him and followed his work for years, had met with Will and his agent, and she'd been encouraging. Today she would have to dash the hope he'd clung to.

The phone buzzed, and Kay recognized Sheila's familiar signal.

"Time to go already?" she asked, wishing it wasn't. "Okay, let me just touch my face up and we'll get it over with."

In front of the mirror in her private bathroom, Kay

Duvane examined her face as she applied a fresh coat of lipstick. Not bad for forty-eight, she decided, but the wear and tear, the constant struggle to survive, had left its signs. She'd always been too smart to ruin her skin by baking it in the sun the way some women did every chance they got, but there were still those lines and crow's feet around her eyes. She'd been lucky enough to inherit her mother's high cheekbones (thank God!), but her neck was beginning to sag. Maybe it was time for a visit to the plastic surgeon. She could have the lift done on her next vacation—TBS liked its executives to look youthful and attractive.

Dabbing on a touch of Chanel and applying a new coat of powder, Kay thought of Sheila. She was so eager to make it, so dedicated to a career. There was no point in telling her that there were times when you ended up asking yourself what the goddamn point of the whole thing was. Times when you wondered if maybe you wouldn't be happier if you had the kind of lives the demographics profiled—the lives of women who spent their days at home with the kids, the washing machines and the stoves, with the game shows and soap operas for company. They didn't have to worry about hanging on to a job they'd spent their whole life fighting for—or about the most painless way to bruise a brilliant dramatist's already battered ego...

"Is the old war paint on straight?" Kay asked Sheila, as they met in the reception area.

"You look terrific, Kay."

"I swear, you have a sinfully convincing way of lying, sweetie. It's a shame you never thought of going into politics."

They laughed as they waited for the elevator, but Kay's eyes were on Sheila's. No, she thought, there was no point in telling her that the whole business was ugly: she'd see its cruelty soon enough for herself. And there was nothing to be gained from trying to explain that maybe, just maybe, she'd be a lot happier in the long run if she concentrated on finding a nice guy instead of dedicating herself to a career.

Hell, Kay reminded herself, she'd once been as young and determined and certain of her purpose as her assistant was now. And if anyone had told her how tough things could get, it wouldn't have stopped her for one second.

2.

AFTER THE CROWDED CONFUSION OF Bloomingdale's, the crush of bodies in the subway, and the hectic rush of East Siders pushing and shoving their way along the sidewalk in their eagerness to get home, the silence of the apartment was a refuge.

Sheila Granger leaned against the door the moment she was inside, double-locking it out of habit. The shopping bag that held the Calvin Klein jeans she'd been determined to buy for the last three days slipped to the floor. Suddenly they weren't important any more—nothing, Sheila decided, was important except relaxing, getting the tensions and pressures of the day and the city and the TransAmerican Broadcasting System out of her mind... if only for a little while.

Closing her eyes, Sheila took several deep breaths. "Clearing the mind," the instructor had called it at the introductory session of the weekly TM class she'd gone to once and planned to continue. But that first lesson was as far as she'd gotten: the following week, instead of learning the secrets of total relaxation and finding her "center," there'd been a meeting at work that lasted till well after nine. The following week, Sheila had found herself in a loft in SoHo—*Off*-Off-Broadway—watching a boring play by an author the network was considering for a development deal.

By then, she'd decided, it was too late. Everyone else in the class would have already been well on the way to mastering TM, and she'd still be back at square one.

Thank God you don't need lessons to relax in a tub, Sheila thought to herself. She picked up the Bloomingdale's bag and walked slowly through the living room, trying to view it as objectively as she could...as if it weren't her apartment, but someone else's.

"Not bad," she said aloud, smiling, pleased with herself.

For as long as she could remember, having a place of her own and decorating it exactly the way she wanted to had been one of her dreams. Her favorite toy as a girl was her dollhouse, and she'd loved 'redoing" it, pasting wallpaper (wrappings from Christmas presents; illustrations, and sometimes samples of real wallpaper) inside the miniature rooms. Her mother had been pleased with her interest: caring about a home, Dorothy Granger reminded her daughter, was an important quality in a woman. Since Sheila had an obvious knack for it, her mother had advised, maybe she should study interior design—it would be a nice hobby, a "little something to do," as she put it, until Sheila got totally involved with the *real* business of life, which of course meant looking after a home and family of her own.

It had been hard—nearly impossible for a time—for Sheila to explain that decorating, the whole idea of "a little something to do," and the goal of finding a husband and starting a family weren't the things she wanted from life.

"Don't you *want* a home of your own?" Dorothy Granger had asked her daughter when Sheila, in her junior year of high school, finally announced that she wanted to have a career... and a career in television at that. The look in her mother's bewildered eyes made it clear that Sheila might just as well have announced her plans to become the first woman astronaut. Even Sheila's father had been surprised—so surprised that he clicked the remote control that muted the sound of the football game he'd been watching on television in the family room, to follow the conversation between his wife and daughter instead of the play-by-play narration.

"Of course I do, Mom," Sheila had answered as tactfully as possible. She knew the pride her mother took in every phase and facet of what she referred to as "keeping house." It was a series of rituals, small crises and major triumphs. An endless war against dirt and dust, a constant search for the perfect arrangement of furniture, and a cover-to-cover recipe search in the new women's magazines that arrived in the mailbox the first of every month.

"I mean, everyone wants a home," Sheila had continued, noticing that her mother had stopped working on the needlepoint pillow on her lap. "Everyone wants a place to come back to at the end of the day. But I'd like my days to be... well, full of excitement."

The moment was awkward. Sheila saw the hurt in her mother's eyes even before she spoke.

Dorothy Granger had sighed. "I just don't understand," she said, confused. "You see my life, Sheila—aren't my days full? I shop. I clean. Granted, having Teresa come in every day to do the heavy work is a big help, but a maid is a maid. Her idea of clean and mine aren't the same. Then there are the Art Museum Committee, the Friends of the Library, the Cleveland Woman's Club—"

"Please, Mom," Sheila pleaded, hugging her mother, desperately wanting to convey the love she felt and erase the hurt she hadn't meant to inflict. "I know how busy you are all the time. Your life makes you happy, and I'm glad. I admire you. I *love* you, Mom."

"Then what is it?" Dorothy asked. "What's so important about a career? And why *television*, of all things? I always thought you'd go to a junior college, Sheila. Take some art courses, some decorating..."

"And have a nice little hobby," Sheila said, more sharply than she'd intended. "But that's not what I want, Mom. It's not what I need as a person. Television is loaded with opportunities. When we studied it in communications class, I got excited in a way that I'd never been excited before. I've talked to my guidance counselor, and I've read everything the library has. I *need* to try it, Mom."

Dorothy's philosophy of life, Sheila knew, included a cooling-off period during which problems and "unpleasant subjects" were given a chance to "blow over." Her mother had gone back to her needlepoint, her father had turned the volume of the TV back on, and Sheila had gone up to her bedroom to do her homework and finish the biography of Edward R. Murrow, on whom she was writing a term paper.

Just as she was getting ready to go to bed, her father had knocked on the door.

"Talk a minute, princess?" he asked.

Sheila nodded eagerly, smiling. The pet names Fred Granger used for her always made her think of the Anderson family on *Father Knows Best*.

"You've really got your mind set on this TV business, haven't you?" he asked.

"Daddy, I'm sorry. I didn't mean to upset Mom. But she has everything worked out for me... the way *she* wants it to be, I mean."

"Now honey, you know your mother means well—"

"I know she does," Sheila agreed. "But I want to make my own choices. I'm not a little girl any more. I've got to start my college applications, Daddy. I *have* to make choices. And I want to make the ones that are right for me. Is it wrong to feel that way?"

Ten minutes later, just before he kissed her goodnight, Fred Granger and his daughter made an agreement. Sheila wouldn't force the issue: she'd apply to one junior college, just for her mother's sake. At the same time, she'd apply to the schools that offered the communications and media majors she'd need for a career in broadcasting. In the meantime, Fred would gently work on convincing Dorothy that Sheila knew what she needed to pursue for her own happiness.

Over the next year and a half, time had flown, but the progress Sheila and her father made with Dorothy Granger had come slowly. Of course her mother was proud when Sheila was accepted at UCLA, NYU, and Emerson—her first choice, and the school that had offered her the biggest scholarship as well. But her pride had been tempered with repeated warnings that television—and business in general—was a "man's world." A woman's place, her mother reminded Sheila over and over, was in the home.

Still, when her father had taken her to hear Walter Cronkite speak at a Chamber of Commerce dinner and then (wonder of wonders!) even arranged for her to spend a few treasured minutes with the nation's most admired newscaster (who'd told her that there were more opportunities for women in the industry than there'd ever been before, though broadcasting was still male-dominated), Dorothy Granger hadn't argued. Nor had she voiced any objection when her husband introduced Sheila to a newcomer at the advertising agency that handled the account of the dairy-products company where he was sales manager.

Sheila had been thrilled to meet Lynne Casey—she'd

actually worked as a copywriter at NBC in New York, and had an endless supply of stories and advice to share over the Saturday lunches that quickly became a habit. Dorothy actually approved of the friendship, because while Lynne had gone to New York, she'd "come to her senses" and married, moving to Cleveland where her husband worked as a reporter for the *Plain Dealer*. Besides, Lynne was pregnant—"expecting," as Dorothy put it. Once she had her baby, she'd do the sensible thing, put all that television and advertising business behind her, and get down to the *serious business* of caring for her family.

In Lynne's example, Dorothy felt, there was hope for Sheila.

By the time Sheila left for Boston, Dorothy and her daughter had come to an uneasy truce. Emerson, Mrs. Granger convinced herself, would be "an experience," a phase that Sheila had to go through. She'd get it out of her system in time... and at least she'd be in Boston, where there were Harvard men, not to mention a host of brilliant potential husbands at MIT and other schools.

Her father, Sheila realized when they said their tearful good-byes, had fulfilled his promise.

And college more than lived up to her expectations.

The courses she took were more than interesting—they were fascinating. She felt as if she'd been transplanted into the world she was destined for, and at the same time as if she were an explorer studying territory that most people didn't even recognize.

Most people simply took television for granted, turning it on and off when they wanted to be amused, informed, or offered a means of escape from their problems. It was a companion to the housewives who watched game shows and soap operas, a babysitter for the children who'd watch almost anything, the best seat at sporting events, and the cheapest, most convenient form of entertainment available.

But to Sheila Granger, the fact that there were a hundred million TV sets in more than seventy million homes was staggering. Americans, on the average, watched six and a quarter hours of TV each day. The power of the medium overwhelmed her. It sold soap powder and soda. It reflected life like a giant (if sometimes distorted) mirror. It shaped dreams—and it could change lives.

The more she learned, the more she realized how much she wanted to be a part of the medium. But *which* part—that was the question. At Emerson, she took speech and acting courses because everyone else did. To her surprise, she found that she possessed a natural ease and talent, and she considered going into the on-camera side of the business, daydreaming about becoming another Barbara Walters. In writing classes—both practical courses that taught her how to write publicity releases and reports and the more creative ones, too, where she learned the fundamentals of writing an actual TV script—her grades were high and her instructors encouraging. After such a beginning what was to stop her from someday winning an Emmy for Best Original Drama?

It wasn't until her third year that Sheila decided that production was what really excited her, and the decision came about in a way that would have made Dorothy Granger despair.

There'd been a few initial forays during her first year in Boston into the world of "mixers" at other schools, but Sheila had quickly decided they weren't for her. The fraternity/sorority world struck her as an extension of high school social life . . . and she wanted to grow, to move ahead, not to relive the past. Though Harvard and Radcliffe had liberalized their admissions policies, accepting more minority students and paying more attention to academic performance than to whether or not an applicant's family had the right last name, the marriage of Ivy League sons and daughters of the Seven

Sisters was still intact. The BU men she met, for the most part, seemed to be going to college because they were supposed to: they had no firm plans, no fixed goals. And MIT... well, Sheila found the technology of television science enough.

No, her mother wouldn't have approved of her real friends, particularly Jason Browder, the man she saw the most of. One look at his long hair, sometimes held back with a headband but more often wild and curly, would have made Dorothy Granger wince. And if his hair hadn't done it, there was the matter of his clothes—dirty jeans, worn, scuffed boots, wrinkled shirts and tattered sweaters. "A hippie," Dorothy would have pronounced, making it clear that hippies were a major part of what was Wrong with the World Today.

Looks didn't matter to Jason—and his looks didn't matter to Sheila. It was his mind that attracted her more than anything else—and his talent. Everyone agreed that his ability as a director was amazing. In workshops, he guided student actors into extracting every nuance of a scene, every laugh from a Neil Simon comedy, every subtle emotion from Ibsen, every shade of meaning from the more avant-garde works. He saw a performance in his mind, and had the ability to translate his vision to everyone involved. Rather than forcing his actors to read a line his way, he helped them understand the concept the playwright had in mind as he, Jason, interpreted it, and if an actor had a different idea, Jason had an open mind.

Sheila loved hearing Jason talk about directing, though like her mother he took a dim view of her interest in television. It was "trash," he told her, "a big load of corporate crap" that catered to the lowest common denominator of taste. She found herself arguing about public television's merits, and the networks' serving the function of reflecting popular taste, with a logic that surprised her. Jason was a senior, and his friends accepted her readily and respected her opinions. Art versus mass popularity was a frequent topic of conversation. Some students admitted that they wanted fame or money: they planned to go to Hollywood or New York, to make movies or work on Broadway or in television. Others, like Jason himself, were dedicated to art and to preserving the classics, to making sure they didn't get lost amid the "garbage" that the public usually preferred.

When Jason directed *The Cherry Orchard* as his senior project, Sheila found herself helping and observing. Producing—putting together the dozens of details that went into a finished performance—fascinated her. She found herself observing and remembering and making mental notes: this wasn't just theory from some textbook, it was *real*. True, there were vast differences between stage production and television production, but Sheila became convinced that production was the job for her. And if there were only a few women who produced for television... well, in time she would add one more name to that list, the name of Sheila Granger.

Jason's production of the Chekhov play wasn't just a success. It was a triumph. As usual, news of an exceptional talent at a school with Emerson's reputation spread. From New York and other places, powerful figures in the media industries came to see the play at the invitation (and on the advice) of friends on the faculty. The school's television department worked with Jason on staging a videotape production, and Sheila eagerly sought the assignment of production assistant.

When Jason rejected the offers from two Hollywood studios and several New York producers, accepting instead a resident directorship with a new repertory theater in Toronto, Sheila was sad. She knew she'd miss their talks... and she'd miss the quiet times, too, the nights they spent in each other's arms, either in the small, perpetually cluttered room of Jason's, or in the off-campus apartment she shared with a speech major who spent a lot of time with her lover, an assistant art professor at Radcliffe.

But as it turned out, there wasn't much time to feel sorry that Jason would soon be leaving.

Another, far more serious tragedy was in store.

Sheila found the message waiting when she came home from classes, scribbled in her roommate's familiar hand.

Urgent! it said. *Call home! Your Aunt Helen called three times. Hope everything's okay—I'll be at Larry's.*

Instinctively, Sheila felt a chill. She called Cleveland regularly every Sunday. Only a few days before, she'd spoken to her parents and everything had been fine. Nothing was said about Aunt Helen, her mother's sister, who lived in Omaha: why was she calling now, and what was she suddenly doing in Cleveland?

Her hand shook as she dialed the familiar number. It wasn't her mother who answered—or Aunt Helen either, but her Uncle Dick.

"You'd—you'd better get here as soon as you can, Sheila," he began, trying to break the news gently. "Your father had...well, they call it an accident—"

"Accident! Daddy? What kind of accident? The car—"

"They call it a cerebral accident," her uncle explained.

"Oh God, no!" Sheila cried. "That's a stroke. Not Daddy—"

"I'm afraid so, Sheila. Of course Helen's with Dorothy at the hospital, but...well, it doesn't look good. I'm sorry. How soon can you get here?"

The trip from Logan Airport to Cleveland seemed to take forever. Sheila alternated between numbness and guilt, thinking of the letters she'd meant to write but hadn't gotten around to, the times she'd meant to call home but had been too busy. *Let him be all right,* she prayed silently. *Please, God, let Daddy be all right, and I'll make it all up to him and Mom...*

Uncle Dick was at the airport. He filled her in on the

details as they drove to the hospital. It had happened quickly, he explained, in her father's office. His secretary had just taken some dictation and gone to the coffee wagon. When she came back, less than a minute later, Fred Granger was slumped over his desk.

"The doctors say he probably didn't feel any pain," her uncle said.

"The doctors? But what about Daddy? What does he say?"

Uncle Dick looked at her, then forced his gaze back to the road.

"He—he isn't conscious, Sheila. I wish there was an easy way to say it, but there isn't. They don't expect him to regain consciousness. It was a massive stroke. I'm sorry."

Sheila felt her heart sink.

The small lounge off the intensive care unit was decorated in soft blue tones, but they did nothing to lighten the mood. Dorothy Granger fell into her daughter's arms, sobbing hysterically.

"Calm down, Dot!" Sheila heard her Aunt Helen say, still, after all the years, an older sister accustomed to giving orders. "They gave her a tranquilizer," Aunt Helen explained, "but I'm going to ask the doctor to give her another one."

Uncle Dick went with her, leaving mother and daughter alone.

"I can't believe this happened," Dorothy sobbed. "This morning was just like any other morning. I made some cinammon rolls yesterday—you know how your father loves them—and we had them with our coffee. Then he kissed me and left for the office. And now...now—"

She broke down again. As Sheila held her, patting her mother's back and trying to hold her own tears in check, a thought flashed through her mind. So many times as a child it had been the other way around: she was the one who'd cried, while her mother did the comforting. Now, strangely, their roles were reversed.

Aunt Helen and Uncle Dick returned with a balding physician in tow. "Miss Granger? I'm Dr. Kendrick. I've ordered another Valium for your mother. If you'd like to see your father—"

"Yes. Yes, please," she answered, getting to her feet.

In the hallway, the physician was gentle but candid.

"Your father isn't in any discomfort, Miss Granger. I can assure you of that. He isn't aware of any sensation. Frankly, it's a matter of time. The damage was massive and I'm afraid it's irreparable. We could use extraordinary life-support measures, and if there was any possibility of even a partial recovery, naturally we'd do all we could. But in situations like this, it's customary to see that the patient is comfortable until nature takes it's course."

"There's no hope?" Sheila asked, already knowing the answer.

"I'm sorry," Dr. Kendrick told her again, guiding her into a room. Six beds were in a semi-cricle, divided by thin curtains. "This is Mr. Granger's daughter," the doctor told the nurses monitoring the machinery that was keeping track of the patient's vital signs.

Sheila steeled herself before looking at her father.

When she did, the sight surprised her. There was no trace of pain or discomfort on his face. His features appeared calm, the familiar lines of character relaxed. There was now something almost childlike, and certainly younger, about her father's face. It seemed strangely at peace.

"Daddy?" Sheila whispered, reaching for the familiar hand. She took it in both of hers, squeezing it as if to imbed the love she felt into his flesh. "Oh, Daddy, I love you so much. You know that, don't you? You've always known.

"You—you did the right thing when you let me go to Boston, Daddy. I can't remember if I ever told you that ... if I ever thanked you enough. I'm going to make you proud of me, Daddy. Wherever you are."

Sheila bent over the guardrails at the side of the bed, brushing her lips against her father's cheek. His skin, she would always remember, was cool.

One hour and fourteen minutes later, Fred Granger died.

The next week was a blur of mingled shock and pain, but there were many loving people to help. All his life, Sheila's father had been a man who believed in taking care of details and tying up "loose ends." He'd taken the time to make sure that when he died, everything would be in order.

His attorney arrived just a few minutes after Reverend Hathaway, their minister. Fred Granger had left his wife and daughter well provided for: there were stocks, insurance, savings, and the house itself... more than enough to guarantee that there would be no need for Dorothy Granger to worry. Several years before, he had spoken to his minister about the kind of funeral he wanted: a simple service, a brief eulogy, a burial in a plain coffin in the cemetery plot he'd already selected.

"Isn't it just like your father to have thought it all out?" Sheila's mother asked, her voice shaky.

At the grave, mother and daughter stood close together, their hands clasped tightly.

'Someday," Dorothy Granger whispered, "I'll be there beside him."

Then Sheila eased her mother away from her father's resting place, toward the waiting limousine.

There were friends and relatives—a seemingly endless stream of them—throughout the next week. They came with cakes and casseroles, comfort and conversation... necessary and appreciated variants on the theme that life had to go on.

Amid the demands of courtesy and the open wound of loss, Sheila sensed her mother's unspoken question: *how?* How did you go about transforming a life that had been half of a partnership into a solitary existence? Aunt Helen, with her natural affinity for taking charge, spoke of "all the things that had to be done." There were thank-you notes to be written for the flowers and the condolence cards. And there were decisions to be made: did Dorothy want to stay in the house, with its constant reminders, or sell it, move to an apartment or perhaps leave Cleveland and go to Omaha to be near her sister?

At night, sleeping in the room where she'd spent so many years, Sheila wrestled with the conflicting obligations that tore at her. She had left home and gone off to school as the first step in making her own life. Continuing on that course, pursuing it to success, was a pact she'd made with her father's memory. But now her father was gone. Her mother was alive and suddenly alone and lonely.

Come home! Dorothy Granger's eyes said, when Sheila looked into them. *Come back! It can never be the same as it was when your father was here, but it can be close. At least we have each other...*

"It's been a week," Aunt Helen said one morning at breakfast. "Shouldn't you be getting back to college?"

Sheila pushed two sausages and a scrambled egg around the plate, pretending that she was eating the food her aunt had insisted on preparing.

"I don't know what I should do," she confessed.

"Well, I do. I'm going to stay here another week or so, then I'm taking Dorothy to Omaha for a rest. She needs it. When she's feeling better, she can start to make her plans. As for you, you're going back to Boston. Your father was very proud of how well you're doing in school, Sheila. He'd want it that way."

"Thank you, Aunt Helen," Sheila said, her eyes filling this time with tears of gratitude rather than grief. By the time her mother, who'd been taking the sleeping pills Dr. Kendrick prescribed, came downstairs, the matter had been settled and Aunt Helen had booked a flight for her niece.

Glancing around the living room of her own apartment five years later, Sheila Granger shook her head. It was hard to believe that her father had been gone so long.

She had worked hard at school, because work was a way of coping with the pain, a way of forgetting it for a little while, anyway. She called and wrote to her mother often, sensing the loneliness and the difficulties in adjusting which Dorothy found it hard to verbalize.

I have a life to look forward to, Sheila thought often. *Mom just has a life to look back on.* It was a concept that brought out her tenderness and compassion, and at the same time reinforced her determination to make a different life for herself, a life that wouldn't hinge on children who would leave and a husband who might suddenly die and a house that would seem empty without them.

During the summer after her junior year, Sheila went home to Cleveland. Her mother had decided to sell the house: it was too much work keeping it up just for herself, and she'd found an apartment complex where there were other women like herself... widows, friends to play bridge with or have over for dinner. Anything to help pass the time.

Once—and just once—Sheila suggested that maybe her mother might want to think about getting a job.

"What kind of job could I do?" Dorothy snapped. "I know how to keep house. I know how to cook the kind of roast you like best, and I can bake a ham with the raisin sauce your father loved so much. I can arrange flowers and make grocery lists and clean out closets, and I'm fifty-four years old. Exactly what kind of job does that qualify me for?"

An instant later, Dorothy apologized.

"I'm sorry," she told Sheila, hugging her tight. "I don't

mean to sound like a witch. It's just that I feel so...so useless sometimes. So empty."

The move had been a good idea. Sheila had returned to Emerson for her final year, and that June her mother flew in for her graduation, insisting on accompanying Sheila to New York and getting her "settled" in an apartment.

"First things first," Dorothy Granger insisted, when her daughter suggested that it was more important to go on job interviews than to spend her time shopping for pots and pans and furniture. By agreeing with almost all of her mother's opinions and deferring to her tastes, the process of apartment-hunting and "setting up housekeeping" was accomplished in two weeks. Then, with her mother safely back in Cleveland, Sheila had gone about the business of finding a job.

Her professors and the professionals who'd come to school to speak had warned her of the realities of the world she wanted to enter. Television was competitive to the point of being cutthroat. Getting started on the ladder to the top meant beginning at the bottom, and this was even harder for a woman than it was for a man.

She had interviews at all the networks. And in spite of having been warned, Sheila felt a sense of rejection each time, when none of the personnel people seemed overly impressed with her enthusiasm and her excellent record at Emerson. There were more interviews with independent production companies, where the prospects were somewhat brighter. While most of the companies that produced the situation comedies, the action series, and the game shows were located in Los Angeles, others producing commercials, documentaries, and programs for classroom or industrial use were located in Manhattan. Sheila got two offers from these, and while neither was what she wanted, they were at least a start.

She was on the verge of accepting one of them when TBS wrote a letter asking her to call if she was still interested in a position. TBS wasn't the biggest network—

in fact, it was having a bad year. But, Sheila reasoned, that might be a point in her favor: that meant she'd have greater opportunities for advancement—if she was lucky.

And she *had* to advance. The "position" turned out to be floating secretary, filling in for the vacationing secretaries while they took their vacations. But it was network TV, a chance to get her foot in the door, and she'd taken it.

That had been four years ago ... four years that passed with dizzying speed. She wasn't a secretary any more, but assistant to Kay Duvane, vice president of special programming. The work was hard and demanding, exhausting at times, but there were compensations, not the least of which was working for and with a woman Sheila respected and admired.

There had been regular raises, enough to let her give up the studio apartment her mother had helped her find and move into the spacious (if you didn't count the tiny kitchen) one-bedroom in an East Side highrise. She'd been able to get rid of the furniture and the dishes she'd agreed to for the sake of pleasing her mother, and to buy things she liked.

Tonight, glancing around the living room, Sheila tried to see it through her mother's eyes.

Dorothy Granger would no doubt observe that the off-white shag rug wasn't practical, because light colors "showed all the dirt." She'd probably say that the beige suede sectional sofa "wouldn't hold up"; and that the Dali lithographs displayed on the pale sand walls weren't her "cup of tea" and certainly not *nearly* as nice as landscapes. Smiling, Sheila imagined her mother sticking a finger into the soil around the pair of potted palms in front of the windows and commenting that they were getting entirely too much (or too little) water.

Still, while the room wasn't furnished in anything that even approximated her own taste, her mother would have to admit that it did have a certain sense of style and a "pulled together" look. Even if their tastes were entirely different, her mother would be pleased at what Sheila had accomplished.

Best of all, she had accomplished it herself... the apartment and the decor and the progress she'd made at the network, where she was definitely on the way up.

"If only Daddy could see me," Sheila said aloud, 'he'd be proud, too."

Before she took her bath and cooked the lamb chops she'd taken out of the freezer before leaving for work, she decided she'd call her mother... just to say hello, and to tell her again that she loved her.

3.

THE RADIO DEEJAY ANNOUNCED THAT THE air quality was poor, that the 101 degree heat wave was "hanging in tough," and that it was "another groovy LA day in spite of all that stuff."

Lee Dean shook his head in a mixture of amusement and annoyance, reaching forward to lower the volume as he drove down Sunset Boulevard. Some things, he told himself, never changed: Los Angeles had to be one of them.

Styles changed in LA, of course, maybe faster than any other place else in the world. It was a matter of status rather than design, trendiness rather than taste. Being able to keep up with the latest looks promoted by the exclusive shops and boutiques on Rodeo Drive, Beverly Hills' answer to Manhattan's Madison Avenue, was a sign of success. Having the season's "hot" caterer do your parties, getting your flowers from the shop that was in current favor among the "A" list of partygivers, booking the right table at the right restaurant—these were all symbols of power and position, as important as driving the right car and knowing the right people.

Time had taught Lee that it was really all veneer. Beneath the tinsel of Tinseltown there was only dross. Los Angeles was the land of Eternal Hype and Endless Dreams. Image City. The "big" deal was always in the works. The check was always "in the mail." The lies—big and little—came easily when people talked about themselves and each other, so easily that the natural distinctions between myth and reality, fact and fiction, disappeared.

There were, of course, those who didn't have to exaggerate their importance of their place in the power structure.

The billboards along Sunset Strip celebrated celebrity, and Lee always noted them. Olivia Newton-John had another hit album out, and so did the Village People. Jack Nicholson and Jane Fonda were starring in new movies. Sylvia was appearing in Las Vegas in a special "in concert" engagement in the main showroom of the Diplomat.

Lee stopped for a light, studying the billboard that depicted her, full-figure and larger than life. Her slim, seductive body was sheathed in skin-tight silver lamé. The clinging gown was slit from both the neck down and the leg up, and her bronze skin looked golden. Her hair was brushed back from her face, then blown out behind her, accentuating the high, sculpted cheekbones, the big almond eyes, the sensuous mouth that were as distinctively her own as the voice that could go from a husky growl to a soft, heart-rending fragility.

Was it really possible, Lee asked himself, that the woman on the billboard, a superstar in concerts, on records, and in movies, had once been a skinny little kid in a trio? And if Sylvia had gone from being the lead singer with The Fantastiks to becoming a symbol of success and glamour on a par with Cher, Diana Ross, and Donna Summer, where had he gone wrong?

It was hard to believe, but once he had been bigger even than Sylvia. Once, she had needed him. He had never had her talent of course. He couldn't sing or act. But he'd had the right look, the right style, the image that TBS had been looking for. He'd been in the right place at the right time, and for a little while he'd stayed there...

The funny part was that he'd been almost ready to give it up when the big break came. His family hadn't been enthusiastic about his staying in New York, or about his going there in the first place. What was wrong with Toronto, they'd demanded? What was wrong with being a Canadian and staying where he belonged? There were plenty of jobs, and good jobs, too—not "foolishness" like television.

He'd tried to explain it to them, but he didn't fully understand it himself. From the first time he'd seen a television set, he'd been drawn by something almost magnetic. He'd wanted to be part of it; he'd *had* to. After graduating from high school, he'd gone to New York against his family's wishes, knowing that his father wanted him to follow in his footsteps and go into medicine—or at least "something serious." New York, Lee had argued, was where it was all happening.

And where it was going to happen for him.

But reality had hit him hard as soon as the excitement of Manhattan, the novelty of it, wore off. There were hundreds, thousands, *millions* of people, it sometimes seemed, with dreams like his own. He was tall and good-looking, but so what? Every actor who lined up at an open call was good-looking. Every hopeful who left his picture and résumé with the agents and managers had a dream. And most of them had training and experience— things Lee knew he lacked.

"Come home where you belong," his father wrote regularly.

He thought about it, but always there was a chance dangling just close enough to tantalize him, to make him believe a little bit longer. The Off-Broadway show he'd gotten a walk-on part in had closed the same night it opened, and the reviews hadn't even mentioned him, but it was a credit. The modeling jobs he occasionally got... There were hundreds of other young men with his same clean-cut look, but those jobs proved he was a professional. And along with the money he made as a writer, they helped him scrape along. Voice-overs... radio spots... audition after audition.

Then there'd been the two weeks on *Search for Tomorrow*—a real job on a real network show! True, he didn't have many lines or many scenes. But it was network TV all the same, the thing he'd wanted most. He'd always imagined going on something big like that, if not as an actor than as an announcer or maybe even a game-show host.

From the soap opera, he'd gone back to a year of waiting on tables, waiting in lines at cattle-call auditions, waiting for hurried appointments with half-interested producers and directors and casting people. *Waiting*... always waiting.

The call from Nat Gallin, one of the dozens of agents he visited regularly, had taken him by surprise. Nat had always been friendly and understanding—he was getting started too, he'd told Lee often—and he'd promised to "do what he could." There'd been a few readings and auditions that had come to nothing, but at least Nat was willing to listen, even to be encouraging, when Lee stopped by the office.

"I think I might have something for you," Nat told him when Lee returned the call answered by his service. "It's a long shot, but you know how this business is—what the hell? It's over at TBS. They've decided to try to give ABC a run for their money with a show for the kids. That 'music'—pardon the expression—they like. You ever watch Dick Clark?"

Lee *had* watched Dick Clark's *American Bandstand*— and he'd watched Clark's career with envy. From the time ABC had taken the show, which originated in Philadelphia, *Bandstand* had been more than a phenomenal success: it had been news. For years, rock and roll had been decried from the pulpits by hell-and-damnation ministers, and from the Tin Pan Alley offices of music publishers accustomed to dealing with composers who provided catalogs of show tunes and enduring popular hits with the potential of becoming standards.

The record companies, too, were in a furor: overnight, it appeared, American musical taste was changing. Unknown boys from Memphis were becoming hip-shaking sensations. Teenagers, with more social and economic power than ever before, were determining what songs radio stations played and what releases the record stores ordered. At first, the giants of the industry had said that rock and roll was just a fad—every generation had its share of novelty tunes and nonsense songs, but Americans weren't going to take such mindless noise seriously...

But the "fad" had lasted—and grown into an industry. As the giants, the "club" of major labels, watched in stunned amazement, new companies formed in basements and garages emerged. Unheard-of groups and single artists suddenly had top hits—and producers who had the formula kept turning out one hit after another, cutting into more and more of the market. Distribution, publicity, influence with the wholesale buyers—the giants tried to block rock and roll everywhere they could, but the newcomers and the new sound grew. Scare tactics didn't work: it was easy to convince parents that rock was responsible for juvenile delinquency, but it was impossible for parents to stop their sons and daughters from tuning in the radio stations that were playing the music that attracted listeners.

Until Dick Clark, television had been a bastion of mainstream sound and old-guard taste. Marriages had been affected years before within the industry, back in the days when radio had been the network media and television just an idea. The networks and the major labels weren't merely allied corporately (NBC with RCA Victor; CBS and Columbia); they were allied in purpose. It was a matter of talent: the big record stars made viewer-attracting variety-show hosts and guests. Nobody wanted to rock the boat... particularly with a medium growing so rapidly.

Then, in 1957, things changed. ABC, the third-runner in the network race, noticed that WFIL-TV had a local hit in *American Bandstand*, and a potential national star in Dick Clark, its handsome, personable host. The format of the show wasn't unique: basically, it was a televised record hop, with Clark as deejay. Records were played, kids danced, and artists with a new release to promote were interviewed after they lip-synched their number for the cameras.

In Philadelphia, the show was a phenomenon. Teenagers lined up for blocks to get in. Dick Clark was young enough to appeal to them—and mature enough to reassure their parents. He was, after all, "in charge" of those young people, and the kids who danced on *Bandstand* were well-groomed. Maybe *that* music wasn't so horrible after all, even if it *did* sound awful...

When ABC took the show network, *American Bandstand* became a smash, and Dick Clark emerged as an articulate national figure. In interviews and articles, he spoke to teenagers and their parents, acting as a bridge between the generations. He defended both the new music and traditional values in a way that was intelligent, polite, and reassuring. Local TV stations across the country—

those affiliated with other networks—copied the show for their own markets.

"TBS," Nat Gallin told Lee, "wants to do it in a big way. And they want to move fast. They're looking for a young host—"

"They must have lots of their own people to pick from," Lee suggested.

"That's for sure," the agent agreed. "But they want an unknown. Someone they can exploit as an 'overnight success.' That's the angle in this whole rock thing. They want a personality they can push in the teen magazines and the Sunday supplements. Dick Clark wasn't exactly a nobody before *Bandstand*, you know. He was a radio personality in Philadelphia—a popular one, too. That's how he got the show when it was local.

"TBS wants to go for contrast instead of comparison with Clark. As it is, the show itself is going to be a carbon copy of his."

"But can they do that?"

Nat Gallin laughed. "Come on, boy, in this business that's the name of the game. It always has been. In pictures, on Broadway, in radio, everybody gets in on a good thing. Only with television, it's more cutthroat and a lot faster. One season mysteries are big. Then it's westerns for a couple of years. A guy on a horse—who can tell one from the other? And this thing, playing records and having kids dance . . . well, it's a hit and nobody can argue with a hit. But *Playouse 90* it's not.

"Give it a shot, Lee. Who knows? You might be just what they're looking for."

The agent arranged the interview, and Lee Dean tried to act calmer and cooler than he felt as he sat across the table from the TBS personnel who would pick the host of *Dancetime, USA!*. Their questions about his experience, Lee knew, were a device: they already had his résumé and were really after a chance to size him up, to see how he talked and looked in person.

When he was dismissed with the familiar "Thank you, we'll be in touch," his spirits sank. It had been a "shot" as Nat said, and he'd taken it. But he'd missed. Too young, perhaps. Not the right look. In any case, off target.

"Don't get your hopes up, kid," Nat Gallin warned him three days later, "but TBS wants to see you again. They liked you. They're seeing everyone in town, and the way I hear it, there are quite a few call-backs..."

What did it matter how many there were, Lee asked himself. He was one of them! And he felt lucky.

The lucky feeling persisted through the first call-back and the second. It stayed with him during the camera test, where he read a commercial, announced several records, and conducted an ersatz interview with a girl from the network publicity department playing the part of a singer.

And when Nat Gallin called him and said, "You got it, Lee! You got it!" Lee Dean was convinced that since luck had finally found him, it would never, ever leave.

For a time, he seemed to be right.

TBS launched *Dancetime, USA!* with a furor and a fervor—and a promotional campaign—designed to capture a major share of the increasingly lucrative teenage market. The publicity department, the advertising department, and the full force of the network mechanism went into the effort to see that, every day, hundreds of thousands of teenagers went to the TV set to watch the Lee Dean show.

Promo spots and newspaper ads promised viewers "the top teen show with today's new beat! Live from New York City—where the action happens first!"

"More stars, more fun, more hits—faster—from the city that rocks all the time"... the hype teased and lured. The publicists fed items to Dorothy Kilgallen, Leonard Lyons, Earl Wilson, and Ed Sullivan about a "feud" between Dick Clark and the newcomer about to invade his territory. Everyone in the business, of course, knew the truth: the move was a risky one for TBS.

Bandstand had its audience—and it came on the air a full hour before *Dancetime, USA!*. But *Life Is a Long Time*, TBS' most popular soap opera, had been a fixture in the programming schedule for years. It was too popular to shift, and *Yesterday's Cares*, the *Queen for a Day*-like hard-luck story which followed it at 3:30, had also built its audience with the help of the soap's strong lead-in.

TBS' hope was that since ABC took the second half-hour after *Bandstand*'s 3:00 network start for *Who Do You Trust?*, a game show hosted by a newcomer named Johnny Carson, *Dancetime, USA!* had at least a chance. It was a recognized fact that a certain share of the audience would remain loyal to the competition. But, the marketing people pointed out hopefully, there were plenty of kids who didn't get home in time for *Bandstand*'s first half-hour. *Dancetime, USA!* could offer them an hour of start-to-finish programming. If they didn't feel they'd missed anything, the thinking went, the kids would build up a loyalty to the show.

Dig, *Teen*, *Screen Stars*, and the other fan magazines gave Dick Clark as much space as the stars he presented. Lee Dean found himself posing for layouts at Coney Island, "at home" in the lavish apartment the network rented for him, and in recording studios and restaurants with Sal Mineo, Tommy Del, Jerry Lee Lewis, and Alice Lane... his "friends," the stars.

Staff writers turned out articles with his byline for *The Saturday Evening Post*, *Coronet*, and other magazines in which Lee Dean advised parents that "There's Nothing Wrong with Our Kids," and that "Rock 'n' Roll Is Good for Us!" The differences between Lee Dean and Dick Clark were played up. Besides their physical dissimilarities (Lee was light-haired and taller) the fact that the host of the new "all-American" teen show had been born in Canada was hyped heavily.

Look ran a story that made it sound as if Lee was an immigrant who'd hit it big in the best Horatio Alger tradition. The New York papers ran pictures and pieces about how much the man from the other side of the border loved his new adopted home. And, they ran copy about the search for The Regulars—those lucky teens who'd be on *Dancetime, USA!* not just when they were fortunate enough to get tickets, but every day. TBS was promoting the contest heavily, counting on it to give the show a strong launch in the crucial New York market. *Bandstand*'s regulars had found their place through popularity and fan mail after the show made its debut. *Dancetime, USA!* had no time to lose, so it was decided to go on the air with a resident core of lucky teens who'd been chosen "on the basis of poise, personality, and danceability," with whom the viewers could identify.

Their personalities, it was hoped, would attract a loyal female audience. They'd show the folks at home the latest dance steps, and they'd wear the latest styles, courtesy of the manufacturers. They wouldn't be paid (the idea of using young professionals had been considered, but rejected because of viewer credibility), and they would come from all over the city. They'd be just like the kids who watched the show... only lucky enough to be The Regulars...

The thousands of entrants between the ages of fourteen and eighteen were narrowed down, newspapers cooperating. The publicity department saw to it that Lee Dean was photographed at parties and baseball games, and set him up as a guest celebrity on all the network's game and variety shows.

Then, on the first of January, 1958, the big moment came. The shock of getting the job, followed by the whirlwind of pre-production conferences, run-throughs, interviews, and promotion all seemed to hit Lee Dean at once as he walked from the makeup room into the studio itself that first day. The set was simple. There was a podium where he would preside as host, backed by a large bulletin board that displayed photographs of Elvis

Presley, Tommy Sands, and other teen idols, along with an array of high school pennants and the *Dancetime, USA!* logo in sparkling three-and-a-half-foot gold letters. There were bleachers, already filled with a small fraction of the nearly four thousand teenagers who'd lined up outside, starting at dawn. Even with the hundred and fifty seats filled, the crowd of teenagers, bored after the holiday excitement and celebrating the last day of freedom before returning to school, lingered outside. Patrolmen and cops on horseback struggled to contain them.

In the studio itself, a TBS photographer was busy already, commemorating the pre-show warmup conducted by the director.

"Remember now," he was telling the kids, "the cameras are going to do their job. You do yours, which means staying behind those tape lines on the floor. Everyone in the country is going to get a good look at you—I promise. So don't push in front of the cameras, okay? We're going to start dancing in another couple of minutes, and we're all going to have a good time. But right now, I want you to meet the host of our show. He's just as excited as you are about this being the first day of our show, so let's make him feel really welcome, huh? After all, we're all in this together. Here he is—Lee Dean!"

The cheers, whistles, and applause made Lee clench his fists as tightly as his smile as he stepped center-stage.

"Thank you," he said. "And thanks for coming down today. I need all the help I can get. We've got a great show for you—we're really gonna have a good time."

More clapping, more cheers.

"We're going to show the people who watch us—today and every day—that the music we love is here to stay!"

The yelling kids stomped their approval.

"If you've been reading the papers, you know that we've found our Regulars," Lee continued. "I'd like to introduce them to you now. Later, on the show, we'll introduce them to the people at home. Come on up here, you guys..."

They ran from the first row of the bleachers, Sandy, Bobby, Connie, Dennis...the whole dozen of them, eager and proud and nervous in spite of the run-throughs. The camera men had been told to focus on the Regulars frequently: they, in turn, had been instructed to act "just like everyone else," unless they were being interviewed by Lee or featured in a spotlight dance. The group now huddled close together in a group centering around Lee.

"Okay," he said, "let's dance! The Regulars will start things off, and the rest of you come on and join in. We'll be on the air before you know it."

He bounded up onto the podium. A technician hurriedly adjusted the two microphones (one that would amplify his voice in the studio, the other for the air) and tested one final time the line linking the podium with the control booth.

"Let's start with a new release from a guy who's made himself at home on the charts time after time. The man is Ricky Nelson—and his new release is 'Waitin' in School.'"

The engineer in the booth, following his own copy of the playlist, started the record. The Regulars began to dance, and slowly, then more quickly, other couples from the bleachers joined them.

"Great," Lee said, when the number was over and the kids turned toward him. "Now let's hear a real winner from The Champs. It's a brand-new release called 'Tequila.'"

There were two more songs, then the theme—a fast instrumental. The dancers sensed the mounting excitement as Lee told them, his amplified voice overriding the music, that the show was about to begin.

"Here it is!" the announcer said, from inside the booth, "the big music show with the big-city beat! It's time for

Dancetime, USA!. And here's that real cool guy from up north, Lee Dean!"

As they'd been instructed during the warmup, the dancers turned to the podium and applauded. Lee smiled broadly into the cameras. "Thank you," he said, glancing at the happy faces looking up at him, aware that the closest camera was pulling back. Then, as it rolled in again for a closeup, he directed his attention to it again. "And thank you for joining us today. We hope you'll be with us every day here on TBS for the latest, greatest sounds and steps..."

The show was on.

One hour later it was over.

Five hours later, at a party at the Starlight Roof in honor of the show, Lee Dean realized that he was a success at last, a celebrity, a star in his own right. The network officials, the account executives who'd bought air time for their clients' products, Nat Gallin, and a host of celebrities congratulated him over and over again. This time, he wasn't a guest at someone else's party—the party, Lee realized, was for him. He was certain that the party, like his luck, would go on forever.

The reviewers and the trade press seemed to agree that there was nothing particularly original about *Dancetime, USA!*, but they agreed that Lee Dean was a "personable" host. The network didn't care what the reviewers said—the kids liked the show and that was what counted. *Dancetime, USA!* was a hit, and if the fan mail that poured in for Lee and for The Regulars and various artists who guested on the show was any indication, the audience was growing every day.

For Lee, it was a dream come true—only better than a dream. In spite of his determination, he had never imagined getting so much so quickly. It was as if the struggling, hungry years had never happened; now they were only a memory. Suddenly he was on top, a household word, sought after for interviews, lectures, and guest spots.

He began to wonder if there had every really been a time when he'd been lonely, when he'd sat in a tiny room worrying about his future. Now he couldn't accept even a third of the invitations sent to him. Lunches at the best restaurants. Dinners. Parties. Suddenly there were so many people eager to be his friend—the promotion men from the record companies, producers, agents for singers and acts. They'd do anything to win his favor.

The power he felt was intoxicating.

He wasn't the producer of the show, but *Dancetime, USA!* was his show, and it was a powerful force within the industry. He didn't pick the records or book the acts, but he could recommend them, and his suggestions were always followed—after all, wasn't Lee Dean the man who understood what "noise" the "silent generation" wanted to hear?

There was nothing wrong in doing his new friends favors, Lee told himself. Especially since they were more than willing, hell, they were *glad!*—to do anything they could for him. They beseeched him to accept their gifts, from cars to watches, from clothes to gold-and-diamond cuff links. If he wanted to get away for a weekend, there were plane tickets, reservations, all expenses paid. A favor for a favor...that was the way the game was played, and he was a star player. His show had impact and influence. A guest shot could boost a troubled career, launch a newcomer, keep a hit act on top. Granted, a record that didn't make it wasn't going to become a hit just because it was played on *Dancetime*, but a song with a shot at the charts could break nationally when Lee Dean played it.

Besides the promo men, there were the girl singers whose managers and agents encouraged them to sleep with Lee to "help their careers." Everyone he met, it seemed to Lee, was eager to fulfill his every wish and desire.

When he walked down the street (he didn't do that too much—the inevitable requests for autographs made it difficult to appear in public) his face looked back at him from magazine covers...from *TV Guide* to *Teen*. The cola company that was the show's main sponsor had signed him to a personal contract for advertising, and so he was often on the back covers as well, the focal point of a print ad for the soft drink.

It was a dizzying, dazzling circuit of success and celebrity—and just when he was beginning to feel really comfortable in this brilliant new milieu, the foundations of the world Lee Dean had come to think of as his natural home were shaken.

The first tremors had been felt over two decades earlier. For years, ASCAP, the American Society of Composers, Authors, and Publishers, had been the only music-licensing organization. Its membership was tightly controlled, and the music publishers who held the reigns of the industry until radio came along weren't about to turn over their exclusive rights of passage through Tin Pan Alley. Throughout the 1930's, the publishers, musicians' unions, and record companies tried to block radio's right to play records, insisting that the public wouldn't pay money for a product it could hear for free...the products being records and sheet music.

1939 saw the radio broadcasters strike back with BMI—Broadcast Music, Incorporated. The new licensing organization encouraged new talent. The black writers, the "hillbilly" composers, the ethnic groups and newcomers who found themselves unwanted by ASCAP quickly responded to BMI's welcome. Tin Pan Alley's stranglehold on the music business diminished—but the fight went on for years, each organization representing a clear faction.

BMI was identified with the "new" sound: ASCAP with show tunes and standards. By the 1950's, the mixture of changes in taste and technology brought the conflict to a head. The 78 "shellac" was being replaced by the 45 single. "LP's," at 33⅓ rpm, were another factor, as were the technological improvements in sound in both radios and record players. Too, there were tape recorders for home use. And there was also rock and roll.

Radio had changed. More and more stations kept playing the most popular songs over and over: "Top Forty" was an increasingly popular programming format. Many of the country's biggest hit songs were written by "amateurs"—in the eyes of the old guard. And if the simple three-chord rock sound could sell records, who needed the sheet music?

The fight was on, with Ira Gershwin, Alan Jay Lerner, Frank Sinatra, Bing Crosby, and Steve Allen attacking rock in the press. The two licensing organizations fought it out in court, then even in the chambers of the House Judiciary Committee, where chairman Emmanuel Celler of New York, presiding over the BMI-ASCAP anti-trust actions of 1956, announced that rock indeed had a place, "particularly among the colored people." It was "a natural" expression of their emotions," he said. But Elvis, "with his animal gyrations," was "distasteful."

Not even the House of Representatives could stop rock, and in the fifties, people paid a lot of attention to what House committees did. There'd been the House Un-American Activities Committee, and the McCarthy investigations. There'd been the Hoffa hearings, and the Estes Kefauver hearings, and the Dodd Committee on TV violence. In 1958, there were investigations of the quiz-show scandal when it was discovered that the contestants on the networks' big money games were coached and prompted.

The word "payola" was heard for the first time.

To some, the idea of using cash or gifts to prompt a

deejay to play a particular record (or a particular company's releases on a regular basis) was no sin. It wasn't bribery: it was business, "promotion" rather than graft. To others, particularly those opposed to the rise of rock, it was scandalous, sinful, and shocking...a conspiracy to undermine American tastes and values.

To Lee Dean, it was a way of life from the start.

But as he sat across from Frank Henning, TBS vice president for daytime programming, he denied it.

"I don't like asking you this, Lee," the vice president said, "but I have to. Right now they're going after radio. They're starting slow, but it's going to build up big. I'm sure that over at ABC, they're asking Dick Clark the same thing—and everyone knows he's as honest as the day is long. So if anything's been going on, I'd like to hear it from you. Now."

Lee had looked at Nat Gallin, sitting beside him on the Danish modern sofa. "There's nothing, Frank," he insisted.

"Good," the executive said, offering a handshake. He spoke into the intercom on his desk. "Ask Miss Duvane to come in with those releases."

A young woman in her early twenties entered. Lee recognized her as one of the people from the publicity department.

"Miss Duvane is coordinating daytime publicity for me now," Henning informed them.

"Coming up in the world. Congratulations," Nat Gallin said. Lee forced himself to echo the words as Henning handed him two pieces of paper.

"We've done a lot together, Lee," he said, "and your word is good enough for me. I just want you to see we're behind you all the way."

Reading the publicity releases, Lee felt his gut tightening. The first, a statement from the network, informed the reader that TBS had the utmost confidence in the honesty and professionalism of its *Dancetime,*

USA! production staff, and particularly in "a man whose influence as a positive factor on the moral values of his fans, today's youth, goes without question—Lee Dean."

The second release quoted Lee himself as "deploring" the practice of payola as being "against the principles of decency, free enterprise, and artistic integrity."

From that day on his comfortable world began to fall apart, TBS was behind him, just as ABC was behind Dick Clark. There were lawyers to stall off investigators, but when there were "voluntary" interviews, Lee heard himself lying. What else could he do? he asked himself over and over. Say that he'd been too stupid to realize what he was doing? Explain that he'd simply been told it was all right to take the gifts and so he'd believed it?

Dancetime, USA! was pulling in a better than ever share of the market. The Fantastiks, a black girl trio from Harlem, had been launched on the show (God, he'd taken gifts for that favor, he realized), along with dozens of other acts. Maybe, just maybe, his friends would cover for him.

But his friends were in trouble themselves. Record companies panicked as their books were examined under the scrutiny of Congressional investigators. Promotion men squirmed as they were called on to give statements under oath.

Lee found himself praying for the first time in years. *Let it blow over*, he begged. *Let the country's attention focus on something else, and let this all blow over...*

But the investigations went on and on. The forces behind them, the conflicts within the music industry, were too powerful. The opportunities for publicity (after all, this was show business) were also appealing for Congress. Rock and roll was on trial—and Lee Dean knew he was guilty, though he hadn't meant or planned to be.

He watched, trembling, as Dick Clark went through his testimony before a House Special Subcommittee on Legislative Oversight of the Committee on Interstate and

Foreign Commerce. The Subcommittee was good copy: they'd exposed presidential assistant Sherman Adams' vicuna coat, as well as the quiz-show scandal. The hearings on "Payola and Other Deceptive Practices in the Broadcasting Fields" promised to be even more exciting.

Unlike most Americans, however, Lee Dean wasn't following Dick Clark's appearance before Chairman Oren Harris from a favorite armchair, but from a chair in his suite at the Hay Adams Hotel, across Lafayette Park from the White House. He himself was to testify next. Dick Clark's testimony, though the investigators tried to goad him, was cool, intelligent and articulate. Under oath, he answered questions about the interests in record and publishing companies he'd held before voluntarily divesting himself of them. In spite of the committee's self-serving publicity-seeking, he came through with an untarnished image—and with the grudging respect of his adversaries.

But Dick Clark had been guiltless.

The day after his major competition finished on the stand, Lee Dean was sworn in in the New House Office Building. Within three hours, during which the committee produced evidence from the people who'd been his "friends" which indicated that he'd accepted gifts, "consultation fees," and trips, his career was over.

If Dick Clark was the good guy, Lee Dean was the devil. He'd done much worse than fool America—he'd lied! And after coming from "another country," too, to influence our young people... The once-so-friendly press attacked with a vengeance. The soft drink company cancelled his contract, and TBS cancelled *Dancetime, USA!* after a two-and-a-half-year run.

From being a national hero, Lee Dean became a national disgrace. He tried taking out roadshows for a while, but the top name acts didn't want to be associated with his tarnished name. After seasons of traveling across the country in buses with also-ran acts, he'd gone to

England, then to Europe. Buying and selling rights to songs, booking acts for tours...it had been one long, frustrating hustle.

Then he'd gotten the offer that had taken him to Australia. At first he'd been frightened...Australia was so damn far away—but he was a Canadian, a British subject, even if his disgrace in America had made him feel like a man without a country to call his own.

Within a few days of landing in Sydney, his doubts were allayed. It wasn't just that TV was new in Australia, or that he was back in front of the cameras hosting a variety show. The spirit of the country was strong and vigorous, and contagious as well. Even in Canada, Lee had thought of Australia as remote, cut off from the rest of the world. It came as a suprise—and a pleasant one—to discover that news of the payola scandal had preceded him Down Under...and nobody gave a damn! It was a country, and a people, with firm beliefs in the second chance.

He'd had one, too. The moment he heard Kristy Kiley sing, the moment he'd seen her step on stage in that club in Melbourne, he'd known she had *it*...that quality that could make her an international star. Peter Allen, Olivia Newton-John, Helen Reddy...superstar talent had become one of Australia's major exports, and Lee was sure, *positive*, that Kristy could shine with the best of them. Working with her, he came to admire her as a woman as well as a talent: she was dedicated, quick to accept new ideas if they were good, and determined to defend her own artistic convictions when she knew she was right.

But she was uncertain of what to do about Lee's determination to make her a star in the States. She was loyal to her homeland—and making it there was enough for her. Neither of them had anticipated that the closeness developing between them would turn into love—and it was emotion rather than career motivations that finally convinced her to return to the States with him.

That was two years ago.

Kristy had gone back home. Lee's dream hadn't come true. The contacts, the old friends who owed him favors—they hadn't paid off as he expected. People remembered him, but none seemed to remember what they owed him.

All he had from the old days was memories, he realized the morning after Kristy flew home. But lots of people shared those memories. Now America was nostalgic for the 1950's, and *Dancetime, USA!* was an important part of that past. For weeks he tried to find an angle, a pitch, a formula that would let him capitalize on the past he'd been so much a part of.

Then, at last, he got it. Today it was neatly typed up in the attaché case beside the rest of his luggage in the back seat as Lee Dean pulled into the car return lot at LAX, ready to catch a flight to Vegas, hoping that this time the favor he had to ask would be granted . . . just for old times' sake.

4.

"THANK YOU," SYLVIA SAID, STRETCHING HER arms toward the audience as if to return the ovation. "We do thank you so much."

The response to her Dinah Washington medley, as usual, was overwhelming, and when it showed no sign of subsiding, she stepped back with her left foot, pitching her body forward from her waist, arms outstretched as if she were diving.

The "signature" bow filled the circle of light from the spot. Sylvia held it for a long moment, listening as the audience responded. When the applause was at its peak, she broke the pose, leaping up, turning, stretching her hands out to extend the moment to the orchestra behind her.

"Our wonderful band, ladies and gentlemen, Mr. Lloyd Dugan and his orchestra!" She turned back to face the tables in the packed showroom, the lighting changing with her movement.

The circle of light grew smaller and deeper in color as

Sylvia stepped downstage. A piano played softly behind her, repeating the same two bars over and over. With another few steps only her head was lit, the rose pinspot playing over the familiar features and dark hair, drawn back and fastened at the back of her head with an elaborately carved ivory comb that resembled a crown. At last the audience was quiet.

"I want to thank you, too," Sylvia told them as the piano continued softly. "For coming here tonight, for being so very wonderful, and for your support over the years." She paused, as if trying to remember something. Then she laughed softly. "Damn, I knew there was something else: I almost forgot to thank you folks for making our new record such a success. The album is called *Don't It Take a Woman,* and so is our new single which I'd like to do for you now."

She began to sing.

*"You're the kind of man
Who's kind of scared to stay.
You only come so close,
Then you back away.
Then you're on the move,
And you're on your own,
And you're tryin' hard
Not to feel alone...*

The full orchestra came in behind her.

*"But don't it take a woman to show you,
How much of a man you are?
Don't you need her shining eyes
To feel like a star?
Don't it take a woman to tell you,
All the things you need to hear?
Someone to hold onto
When you feel like the end is near.
Don't it take a woman to show you,*

*Just how good it can be?
Don't it take a woman,
A woman like me?"*

The lighting and the arrangement grew fuller as she began the second chorus. Singing, she slowly crossed the stage, back and forth, ending up in the center as she finished the number. The orchestra continued to play and she bowed again as the curtains closed.

The first half of the show was over. Waiters and waitresses were already hurrying to take orders and deliver drinks: part of her contract with the Diplomat specified that no service would go on during the show itself.

Thunderous applause followed as she stepped offstage, stopping just long enough to let the stage manager hand her a glass of water. She sipped gratefully, handing it back as the familiar figure walked toward her. Sylvia protested as Libby blotted the sweat off her bare arms and shoulders with a towel.

"I want to get to that dressing room and rest." she protested as the other woman patted her body.

"And I say you're goin' noplace till I get done. Want pneumonia or some damn thing?"

Sylvia sighed and let the woman who'd been her maid, confidante, companion, and surrogate mother for more than a decade have her way as usual. The ovation continued, though the audience knew very well that there was no chance of Sylvia's returning. It was only the first half of her show that was over.

"What do they want?" Libby asked, annoyed, cocking her head toward the applause. "An encore at halftime."

Sylvia turned her back to let Libby unzip her magenta gown, then gratefully stepped into a robe of thick, camel-colored velour.

"It's when they don't clap that we start worrying," Sylvia said in her dressing room, as she sank down on the sofa. "I swear, that damn disco number's gonna get the best of me yet."

"It's too much for you," Libby said. "I told you that from the gitgo—"

"It's *divine*," another voice said. As he spoke, a tall, thin man with light skin patted the chair in front of the makeup mirror. "Come on, Miss Star. We've got work to do..."

"Pierre, *please*," Sylvia pleaded in a mock whine. "We've got lots of time. They'll hustle the drinks for a good half-hour."

"Twenty minutes," he corrected her. "And we have eyes to put on, remember?"

"You just let her be for a minute, hear me?" Libby challenged him, hands on her hips. "And you keep that sassy answer you're workin' up right in your head!"

"Yes'm," Pierre answered, shuffling away because he knew that always provoked her.

"He's right," Sylvia said with a sigh. The Diplomat wouldn't waste any time getting drinks on the tables. The eye makeup Pierre had designed to go with the silver gown *did* take time, and there was her wig...He'd manage it all, the way he always did. It was hard to believe that he'd simply appeared in her life one day, coming backstage after a show at the old Copa, her first big date after leaving the act.

"I think you are fabulous," he'd told her then, "but I can make you even *more* fabulous. I was born to do your makeup and hair."

Out of surprise more than anything else, she'd given him a chance. He'd been with her ever since, a fixture in her life like Libby. The endless hotel suites were more a home to her in terms of time spent in them than the house she'd bought in Bel Air, and Libby and Pierre were more like her family than the flesh and blood relatives who only came around when they wanted free tickets to one of her concerts, or loans, or some other favor.

"That's a good girl," Pierre said approvingly, as she got up to sit in front of the mirror. Pierre knelt behind her, studying the reflection of her face—framed by a square of bright lights—with a critical eye.

"Excuse me," a voice said. The captain, in his formal uniform, stood in the doorway. "A gentleman asked me to bring this note back—"

"Tipped you, you mean!" Libby challenged him, grabbing it. "Didn't they tell you that nobody is to bother us during the break? We got things to do, costumes to worry about—"

"It's all right, Libby," Sylvia said. "Thank you," she told the captain. He bowed and backed out of the room, closing the door behind him.

"Well?" she asked, as Libby took the silver lamé gown from the rack, studying it carefully for signs of wear and tear. The design, by a teenage girl Sylvia had discovered in a Watts workshop and was sending through art school, was stunning. It worked as well onstage as it did on her new album cover, and on the huge billboard on Sunset Strip that the hotel had taken to announce her engagement. There were two duplicates for backup, and rotating them allowed the garments she wore to be dry-cleaned after every performance. But Libby took a pleasure in strengthening weak seams by hand, and a pride in making sure that hooks and snaps were secure before they could pose problems.

"Well what?" the older woman asked gruffly, annoyed at having to shift her attention from the costume.

"Don't I get to see that note?"

"Why bother?" the maid asked. "It's just from some fan or other. They always are."

"Must have been some fan with half a meatball to get that dude to bring it back," Pierre offered, reaching for the note which Libby had tossed on the coffee table. He passed it to Sylvia as he reached for a jar of the emmolient cleansing cream he blended personally for her.

Sylvia, it read, *Can you really top that last number? I'm looking forward to the second half of your show, and to seeing you afterwards. Hard to believe I was there when it started. You're "fantastik!"* It was signed *Lee Dean*.

"Lord, it's been years," Sylvia said, more to herself than to anyone else. "It's from Lee Dean, remember him? The dude that had *Dancetime, USA!?*"

"White fella?" Libby asked.

"Yes, a *white* fella," Sylvia answered, matching Libby's tone.

"Never heard of him," the maid said.

"Well, he's gonna be coming back after the show, so have them send some champagne, hear? We used to work that show all the time—he was real good to us back then. We went out on the road with him, too. It was after the show went off, and we hadn't had a hit in a while..."

"And you're not going to look like a hit tonight either, unless you let me get to work," Pierre pleaded.

Sylvia settled back in the chair, her eyes closed as Pierre dipped and sponged and patted.

Lee Dean... It had been years since she'd seen him. Sylvia wasn't sure of just how many, but she knew it was more than she cared to count. But the memory of the first time she'd seen Lee, the first time the Fantastiks had appeared on network television, was coming back to her.

Amazing, she thought: it was startling how vividly the emotions she'd felt that day were reawakened in her mind. Maybe it had something to do with what one movie critic called her "natural gift for raw feeling." But movies hadn't even been in her dreams that Friday afternoon in 1958.

At first, when they were told they'd been set for the show, she and Virgie and Dee had been thrilled. Short of taking an ad in the *Amsterdam News*, they'd done everything they could to spread the latest measure of the success they were certain they'd been destined for from one end of Harlem to the other. Why not? Harlem was full of groups with dreams of making it big in music. Girl trios like themselves, boys who copied the sound of Frankie Lymon and the Teenagers, or The Silhouettes, mixed groups patterned after The Platters... Any summer night—and most of the rest of the year too, for that matter—you could walk down Lenox or Amsterdam Avenue and hear them practicing on stoops and street corners.

Most of them were good, and some of them were great.

But *their* trio, they were something else. Maybe part of it came from the fact that they'd been singing together so long. Even before they started in junior high, Sylvia, Virgie, and Dee always stood next to each other at choir practice and Sunday services. But the young people's choir of the Mr. Calvary Baptist Church was just for hymns.

After school and on weekends they'd get together and sing for themselves, for the sheer pleasure of singing. They'd copy records, playing Dee's brother's collection with one ear half cocked for the sound of his sudden arrival home. His records were his pride and joy, and he'd warned all three of them about what would happen if he caught them touching the records or the record player again.

When Curtis was home, there was always another house to go to—and if there wasn't a record player, someone always had a radio. They listened to blues and gospel, top bop tunes and ballads, picking up melodies and lyrics with an ease that made it all the more enjoyable. Their harmonies, too, were natural and instinctive. Sylvie, as everyone had called her then, sang the lead: she had the biggest range, and the clearest, purest tone. Dee took the top harmony, while Virgie filled in below.

Over and over they practiced, because it was something to do and because they sensed, without ever really speaking of it, that there was something special about them. They weren't just working on songs: they were working on their *future*...

"Don't blink, darling," Pierre instructed, bringing Sylvia back to the present. "Keep them closed, just like that." She felt him gently peel away the set of false lashes she'd worn for the first show (uppers only—her bottom lashes had false supplements semi-permanently affixed). He dabbed the adhesive away. "We'll let that dry for a few seconds. You can open now."

Sylvia blinked, glancing at her reflection. The years had been good to her. In many ways, her face, without the lashes, was still a girl's. She watched as Pierre dotted a deep red blusher on her cheekbones, stroking it upward. When he completed each cheek, he used a lighter blusher, going upward from her brow to her hairline. Then, with a cream darker than her own skin, he contoured the hollow of her cheek and the space from above her cheekbone to her brow.

"Lashes," he informed her, and Sylvia closed her eyes again, her mind returning to the old days.

They hadn't worn makeup then—not when their mothers were looking, or when some nosy relative or neighbor could rat on them. But sometimes when they practiced, on those rare occasions when they had a chance to close a bedroom door without having to keep an eye on a younger brother or sister or, better yet, when they had an apartment to themselves for a few hours, they'd experiment with lipstick, eye shadow, and new hairdos.

"When we're famous, we'll be beautiful," Virgie used to say.

"We'll have gowns and jewelry, like they do at the Apollo," Dee would add.

Sylvia couldn't remember what she said. Always, it seemed to her, she'd been the practical one—the one who realized that singing at school assemblies or local club meetings was a far cry from the Apollo, the theater on 125th Street where the top black acts in the country played. Getting there was the task at hand, she'd realized. Once they made the Apollo, the rest would fall into place.

School talent shows, variety shows, social club entertainments, they performed every chance they got. They watched other performers, too: aspiring groups like themselves, and the professional acts they envied.

The Apollo was the place to catch acts from the Platters to old-time comedians who'd had their heyday during the years when the "chitlin circuit" could keep a black performer busy for a full season. True vaudeville had died with the advent of movies, but the Apollo still offered a stage show—the movie was only an added attraction.

For Sylvia and the girls, the best night of the week was Wednesday when, in addition to the regular show and the movie, the Apollo held its traditional amateur night. Anyone could sign up and have a chance on stage. Often the audience (and the Apollo audience was one of the toughest to please anywhere) seemed to prefer the acts with minimal talent, taking more pleasure in booing until the MC's long hook reached from the wings to yank the luckless performers offstage. But there were other moments, too, moments when the usually noisy audience would grow completely quiet—the ultimate compliment for a singer or dancer or group who might be appearing on a "real" stage for the first time.

Someday, Sylvia had sworn to herself, *it's gonna be us up there... someday...* When that day came, who knew what the future would hold? They'd be asked to play a full week at the Apollo, she was convinced, and from there they'd go on to other theaters, like the Howard in Washington. There'd be records, personal appearances, *stardom!*

That was the core of the dream that bound them together. Sylvie and Dee and Virgie. It was the goal that drove them through endless hours of practice, songs at first, then a few dance steps as well—"routines," just like the name acts had.

If they were really going to be an act, they knew when

they signed up for amateur night, they needed a name of their own. Finding one had preoccupied them for weeks. "Here they are, Dee and Virgie and Sylvia," sounded sloppy and unprofessional—they agreed on that much, but not on much more. Dee wanted them called The Dupris Sisters, which sounded French and therefore classy. Virgie wanted them known as The Hit-Makers, which Sylvie said sounded conceited. They hadn't even made a record, let alone a hit.

Some groups were named after cars or even animals, like The Cadillacs and The Colts. There were The Hearts, The Rays, and The Robins. There were The Cleftones and the Mellowtones, The Mello-kings and The Midnighters. There were also local versions of big-name acts who patterned their sounds and acts after their famous counterparts.

Sylvia was able to talk the other girls out of that—after all, she'd reasoned, nobody got to the big time by being a copy of something else.

"We're *us*," she'd insisted. "And we're special."

"Hey, how about that? How about The Specials?" Dee had suggested eagerly.

But just as quickly, Virgie had shot down the idea. "No way, girl! It sounds like we're somethin' marked down. Might as well call ourselves The Bargain Basement—"

Sylvia had agreed, but something in her mind clicked. *Special* wasn't right, but it was a step in the right direction. Their group was one of a kind—"unique"—but there was another group, four boys who sang together, who already had that name. They were good, they were great, they were fantastic—

"That's it," Sylvia had announced one day after school when the three of them met. "The Fantastiks, with a 'k.' How does that sound?" Her heart pounded as she watched Virgie and Dee react. Everyone was tired of arguing.

"I guess it's okay for now," Virgie said finally.

"All right with me," Dee agreed.

"Fantastic!" Sylvia had said, and they'd hugged and laughed.

A few months later, though, there was nothing to laugh about. Virgie, a senior and the oldest of the three, had a boyfriend named Billy and she also had a problem: she was pregnant. Dee and Sylvia were a year behind in school, but the street had its own way of teaching everybody and sex was an elementary lesson.

"What are you gonna do?" Dee had asked.

"Do?" Virgie boomed. "What the hell do you think? I'm gonna get rid of it, that's what. I'll tell Billy and he can set it all up."

The next day, though, Virgie was in tears. Instead of offering to find an abortionist and pay for his services, Billy told her that she couldn't prove a thing and that for all he knew, he wasn't even the father.

"Don't cry," Sylvia heard herself say. They were sitting in her living room, and her mother would be returning from her downtown cleaning job any minute. Tears would involve an explanation. "We've gotta figure out how to do something."

"My sister told me about a woman on 128th Street," Dee offered. "I think she's had it done a couple of times. This woman used to be a nurse. Trouble is she has to get a hundred bucks up front. Cash money."

"A hundred dollars!" Virgie wailed. It was more than any of them had ever had.

"There's a prize at the Apollo, isn't there?" Sylvia asked them.

"What about it?"

"We're gonna win it—*that's* what about it."

They'd talked about amateur night hundreds of times, but they'd always planned to wait until Sylvia and Dee were seniors. Dee's family didn't pay much attention to her show-business aspirations, but then they didn't pay much attention to Dee. Virgie considered herself lucky to be able to finish school: her father had made her sister quit at sixteen to get a job. She never discussed plans for the act at home, concentrating instead on the money she'd be able to make thanks to the typing and shorthand courses she was taking.

Sylvia's mother knew that her daughter wanted to go into show business—and she'd made it clear, from the first time Sylvia announced her ambition, exactly what she'd thought of the idea.

"No way!" Grace Jackson said with fire in her eyes. "Get those thoughts right on out of your head. You're gonna be something to be proud of, a nurse or a teacher or something like that. I lost your Daddy in Korea, Sylvie. Your brother's gone off lord knows where. I'm not about to sit back and watch my little girl—the only thing I have left in this world—turn into one of those tramps..."

"Open them... open your *eyes,* Sylvia!"

"Huh? Oh, I'm sorry, Pierre," she apologized, as he studied her with a critical eye. The lashes were thick and dark. Instead of mascara, he used vaseline to make them shine. "Ready for the wig?" he asked.

"Ready as I ever am," she answered. He'd already taken the comb from her head, and her hair was already secured from the first half of the show. Sylvia leaned forward as Pierre checked the pins, then took one of the three "cover picture" wigs from its stand, carefully removing the hot rollers he'd used to set it. Only when it was on her head did he brush it out, duplicating exactly the style she wore on the Sunset Strip billboard, on the cover of her album, and in the new publicity pictures taken at the same time.

"Coming together," he announced. "Now for the mouth."

"Coming on time to get dressed," Libby, annoyed, reminded him.

"Just hold on, Mama," Pierre said.

"I ain't your mama, Sister Boy..."

There'd been no dressing room that night at the Apollo—not that the old theater's dressing rooms were much of a prize anyway. Instead, they'd huddled nervously together backstage, Virgie worrying about the abortion, Dee struggling with a case of stage fright, and Sylvia feeling guilty about having lied to her mother, who thought she'd gone to Dee's to study for an English test.

Their black skirts didn't match, but they came closer to it than their shoes. They'd bought pink rayon acetate blouses from one of the bargain stores on 125th Street, telling each other that they'd look "glamorous" and a lot more expensive than $2.98 which they cost. They'd teased their ironed hair, and they'd set guiches, using tape to keep them close to their faces until they were dry enough to spray with lacquer.

After hours of arguing—almost as many hours as they practiced, they worked out what they wanted to sing.

They would open with a cover of Clyde McPhatter's "Treasure of Love," then do The Platters' (their favorite group) hit, "He's Mine." The Hearts' "A Thousand Miles Away" would be their third and final number—unless there was an encore, in which case they prepared a female version of The Cleftones' smash, "Little Girl of Mine," changing the lyrics to "boy."

Preceding them on the program were a a horrible girl singer—too fat and too offkey—followed by an effeminate light mulatto imitation Johnny Mathis. A so-so group had sung a so-what song. An oldtimer (the Apollo audiences *loved* oldtimers) had done a terrific soft shoe, to tumultuous applause.

Then, to their own surprise, the Fantastiks were on. "Here they are, ladies and gentlemen," the MC announced, "three little girls from right here in Harlem. They call themselves The Fantastiks... Let's give them a nice hand."

Midway through their first number, the stomping and

cheering had begun. Huddled around the microphone, their bodies pressed together not only to insure the right blend of sound but out of fear and the need for body contact, the girls—without missing a beat of the lyric—looked at each other and smiled. Sylvia had felt tears welling up in her eyes.

They were good! As good as she'd always known they could be. And this time, *finally*, this time other people knew it, too!

When their set was over, they floated offstage. Even the drag queens who traditionally held court in the boxes of the theater on amateur night stopped posing long enough to cheer them. The impressionist and the dance act who followed them on the bill didn't have a chance.

It was a charmed night. There was the first-prize money (the audience had liked the oldtimer, but he'd already had his day and theirs was just beginning), and there was more. The applause was still ringing in their ears when a smiling middle-aged white man pushed through the crowd of musicians congratulating them backstage. He gave them his business card and told them how much he'd enjoyed their performance. They had "potential," he said: with original material and a little direction, there was no telling how far they could go. And as the owner and president of Manhattan Records, he, Harry Silverman, was in a position to provide both—if they were serious about careers and interested in a contract.

Serious? They were dedicated, committed. In that brief space of time, those few minutes onstage, they'd been transformed.

They weren't Dee and Virgie and Sylvia any more. They were The Fantastticks, and they would be forever...

"*Now* you're Sylvia," Pierre proclaimed, stepping back, admiring his own work.

"It sure looks that way, don't it?" she asked, drawing her glossed and lined lips back to make sure that none of

81

the new tangerine lipstick was on her teeth. As usual, the job was perfect. Pierre had done his work well. The wig was brushed out into a sea of flowing hair that framed her face, and it moved when she did.

"You gonna get dressed?" Libby demanded.

"Yes'm," Sylvia answered, as the five-minute call came over the intercom in the dressing room. She slipped out of the robe as Pierre discreetly went into the bathroom to wash out his makeup brushes. Libby had two towels ready, one warm and moist and the other dry, to sponge Sylvia off before she stepped into the body stocking that matched her skin tone. The silver lamé came next and, as if on cue, Pierre was back to dust her exposed skin with shiny translucent powder flecked with tiny metallic silver glints.

Sylvia obediently closed her eyes as he squeezed a fine mist of perfume in her face to set her makeup, and sprayed her wig with lanolin for more shine. She leaned against the slant board as Libby slipped her feet into silver sandals and handed her the familiar bottle of her favorite perfume.

Joy, Sylvia thought, smiling as she dabbed the fragrance on lavishly, *the most luxurious perfume in the world*. She bought it and used it by the case.

"We sure are a long way from Harlem, huh?" she asked nobody in particular as she began to make her way toward the stage, followed by Libby and Pierre.

The musicians were putting out their cigarettes, and the backup singers were in place.

"Hey, beautiful," Lloyd Dugan said.

"Hey yourself," Sylvia answered, smiling at her music director. "There's somebody I want to introduce during the trio thing, so cover it, okay?"

"Sure, babe. You wanna change a cue?"

"No. Just keep the vamp going. I'll pick up the line."

He nodded. The "musical memory" of her days with The Fantastiks was a staple of the act, and had been for years. The visuals—slides and film clips projected behind her as she reminisced—were timed, as was her seemingly extemporaneous monologue.

The house lights dimmed. Lloyd, in position, counted down the beat for the abbreviated overture—a mixture of Sylvia's recent hits and songs from the old days with the trio. Behind the curtain, she stepped carefully to the center of the stage, thanking the stage manager as he tucked the body mike into the patch specially sewn into the halter of the gown, and guided her hands to the strips of cloth that had been sewn to the curtain.

As the familiar music played, Sylvia grasped them, mouthing "later" to Libby and Pierre, who were backing away. The moment was approaching. The stage manager nodded, letting her know that the lighting man was ready: the spot would hit the instant she pulled the curtains apart. Lloyd was watching her as he conducted, smiling as she let the music build. She gave him the signal, aware that the stage manager was watching him.

In an instant of pure theater, the music stopped as Sylvia snapped the heavy curtain open and stepped through it into a pool of light. There was a gasp of admiration and envy at the sight of her, posed with one hand on her hip to maximize the effect of the revealing gown. In that second before the audience had time to react, she let an expression of mock bewilderment flash across her face.

"What y'all lookin' at?" she asked the sea of staring eyes. "This is just some tacky old thing I found in the closet!" She laughed and they went wild, and she went into her first number.

Five songs and twenty-two minutes later, Sylvia spoke to the audience again.

"You know," she began, "sometimes I still feel funny being out here alone...kind of like something or somebody is missing. It's like—like I half expect that the curtain is going to open—"

It did, but the stage was dark. The audience wouldn't see the three adjoining screens for another moment, until the images flashed.

"And I'm going to see some familiar faces..."

The stage-left screen was filled with an image of Dee from one of the trio's first publicity photographs.

"Like that one—" Sylvia said as the audience applauded.

The right screen flashed a picture of Virgie.

"—and that one!"

A picture of Sylvia, taken twenty years before like those of the other two girls, filled the center screen. Turning to the audience, Sylvia appeared to be stunned, her eyes wide.

"Now who the hell is she?" she asked.

The orchestra softly played "The Way We Were" as the pictures of The Fantastiks were replaced by a movie.

"Harlem," Sylvia said, narrating to the views of those familiar streets. "It's a city within a city...a world within a world. It's where I came from, and the first thing I remember is somebody singing..."

The backup singers sang bits from children's songs, hymns, and blues. Onscreen, the camera moved down 134th Street, heading toward a particular tenement.

"That's the street I lived on and the house I grew up in," Sylvia said. "The apartment house, I should say. Dee Phillips and Virgie Kendrick lived in the neighborhood. I can't recall a time when I didn't know them, or a time when we weren't singing. It was fun, and it was free.

"We'd hear a song on the radio, or on a record, and we'd copy it...We never had any kind of lessons. I sang the lead because I was the loudest. I'd sing, and then Virgie and Dee would come in. Heck, I can't explain it in words. I guess the only way to do it is the way we did it then."

The band played a 1950's rhythm and blues intro, and

the medley began. Images of the trio flashed onscreen as Sylvia, accompanied by the unseen backup singers, began the series of The Fantastik's biggest hits. The arrangements were copies of the originals: the sound, twenty years later, was surprisingly like the original. As they sang, stills and films of the girls filled the screens. They were shown onstage, in recording studios, performing on *Dancetime, USA!*, and at the Apollo Theater. There were shots of marquees showing their name in lights, footage of them in London at the Palladium and on tour in Japan. Publicity pictures, magazine blowups, and candid shots changed to the beat of the music.

The girls wore skirts and slack outfits, gowns and minidresses. Their hair was styled in bouffants, French twists, sleek Cleopatra styles and geometric cuts. The montage ended with a picture of the group at the height of their fame; Sylvia in the center, her head thrown back, Virgie on the left, and Dee on the right.

As the medley ended, their images disappeared, leaving a shot of Sylvia alone. The band played more softly.

"Those were wonderful years," she told the audience, "filled with wonderful memories. Maybe you noticed that someplace along the way, we put a 'k' in Fantastik—we always could sing better than we spelled. And maybe you also noticed a TV show called *Dancetime, USA!*. That show was a first for us, and a big break. A special friend is here tonight—Mr. Lee Dean, the host of that show. Lee, where are you?"

She scanned the audience until she found him, standing at a side table. Sylvia blew him a kiss, and led the polite applause.

"Yes, we made some good friends along the way," she continued. "And then that way came to an end. Why? I guess it's like the man said—all good things have to. I wanted to do other things..."

Now the screens were filled with a montage of scenes

from Sylvia's movies, shots of her onstage, blowups of concert posters and album covers.

"You have to go forward in life—but sometimes it's nice to go back. And you know what? If you take some of those old songs and dust them off a little bit, they don't sound half bad."

The musicians began a driving, contemporary-beat version of "Mama Made Do," one of the biggest hits the trio ever had, and one of the last. This time, Sylvia sang alone.

The applause, when she finished, was deafening. The show wasn't over, but people at various tables were standing. They were clapping, Sylvia knew, for The Fantastiks and for the memory that triggered memories of their own.

"Hey!" she called out, quieting them, "you don't want to hear any *more* old stuff, do you?" The response was overwhelming. "Okay! All right—tell you what..." She turned and cupped her hand. "Grace? Linnie? Get out here, girls!" She introduced the backup singers.

"Now, this is gonna be *sort* of like the old days... but not the days you remember. See, there were lots of girl groups up there with us. Martha and the Vandellas... yes! The Marvelletes! The Ronettes... The Shangri-Las, Diana Ross and The Supremes! Well, I don't have to tell you that those ladies had some *hits*. And don't you think for a minute that we weren't a little jealous. There was enough success to go around, but we never got a chance to sing some of the greatest songs ever." She put one arm around each of the girls' shoulders, grinning. "That is, I never had the chance—until now."

Another medley began, Sylvia leading it off with "Don't Mess with Bill." Then they moved into "Walking in the Rain," "Leader of the Pack," and "Dancing in the Street."

"Miss Grace Helms and Miss Linnie Webster, ladies

and gentlemen!" Sylvia shouted, bowing to each of them as they backed away, offstage.

"You've been so nice," Sylvia said to the audience, after the applause died down. "So very nice—not just tonight but for so many years. I wonder if I can ask you all a favor? One more memory, one last request, one more time for all the good times..."

She sang The Dells' "Stay in My Corner," giving the number a sensual urgency. Her voice seemed to flow not only from her throat, but from every muscle of her body. The instant the song was over, she bowed in her inimitable way and the stage went black. Two encores and twelve minutes later, she was back in her dressing room, stretched out on the sofa.

The silver dress was in Libby's hands; the wig in Pierre's. There were four hours before the midnight show. A full twenty minutes passed before the knock on the door. Libby started to open it, but Sylvia, drawing on a reservoir of energy, waved her back, pulling her robe tight around her as she hurried to welcome her friend.

"Lee! I was beginning to think you forgot about coming back."

"I thought you'd want some time to relax," he told her, returning her hug. "You were fabulous."

Sylvia laughed. "Just a working girl tryin' to make a living. You got to give the people what they want, right? How about some champagne?" It was iced and waiting, and Lee opened it, pouring glasses for both of them.

"Here's to you," he said. "You were—fantastic. And those things you did about the group... they were really something. For a second there I thought I was going to cry."

Sylvia took a sip from her glass. "It plays nice enough, even if that isn't exactly the way it came down."

"You ever see the girls?"

"Are you kidding? Dee's okay. She was pissed at first, especially when that girl they got to replace me got strung out on drugs, remember? But she's out of the business now. Married a security officer and havin' babies. I got a card at Christmas."

"And Virgie?" he asked.

"Mean as a snake. Hates me, or so I hear. She got hold of my phone number a few years ago. Hell, I can't even remember who I was married to! Anyway, she'd call late at night, drunk or high and cursin' me out to beat the band."

"Too bad," Lee said.

Sylvia shrugged. "I guess so. Hey—how many years has it been, Lee? Since we've seen each other...?"

"I won't count if you won't."

"Deal!" she said. "Didn't I hear you were in Australia? And you came back with some terrific singer?"

"Kristy Kiley," he answered. "I was trying to launch her."

"Trying? What do you mean? You know everybody in the business. You don't have to *try*."

"That's what I thought," he told her.

"I'm gonna be back in a bit 'less you need me," Libby said. She and Pierre had been so quiet that Lee hadn't even been aware of them.

"Go on," Sylvia told her, and Pierre left too. She turned her full attention to Lee. "What happened?"

"You don't want to hear this..."

"I *do*," she insisted, patting the spot on the sofa beside her.

For the next ten minutes he poured it out. The unreturned calls, the unfulfilled promises, and the increasing frustration. The tension that had mounted as Kristy, homesick for Australia, watched the man who'd been a star Down Under become a flop in the States.

"You and her were... well, more than business, right?" Sylvia asked.

He nodded. "She wanted me to go back with her. She

said she didn't like the business anyway, not the way it is here. Australia is so...so different, Sylvia."

"Different how?"

"It gives you a chance. Here, everybody's out to knife you. There, they give you a shot. Even help you take it sometimes."

"If it's so nice, how come you didn't go back with the lady."

He stared into her eyes with a determination she recognized: it was so much like her own.

"Because I made it here once, and I'm going to do it again. I have to. I don't know why, but I have to. And I have an idea. It can't miss. It's like you said about giving people what they want. See, it's a TV special..."

He outlined it for her, and Sylvia listened, interested and impressed.

"Sounds like it's a natural," she told him. "Good luck, Lee. I mean it."

"You can do more than that—if you want," he said softly. Before she could question him, he poured it out. "Sylvia, this is my last shot. The only game I can play. I'm broke. Sure, I could go back to Australia, I guess. But I want to make it here again, just one more time. It's been a long time since I did the show. Twenty years, almost. TBS might go for the special in spite of the way I got bounced. But if you'd do it—you and the girls—they'd bite for sure—"

"Hey, hold on!" she said, putting her hand up in a stop signal. "I'd like to help you, Lee. But I told you. We don't talk—"

"But what if you did? What if you did for just one night? I'm not just asking for a favor, Sylvia. I'm pleading."

She shook her head. "The girls would never go for it. Dee's out of the business for good. Virgie hates my guts—"

"Let me try!" Lee begged. "Let me talk to them. And if they say yes... would you?"

She looked at him for a long time before answering. Her agent would have a fit, and her manager would scream. Not that the girls would ever consider it anyway. But there was Lee Dean—the man who'd given them a break when they needed it—down on his luck. Practically down on his knees, begging. The business, as his Australian lady friend observed, stunk: everybody wanted to be in on a good thing when you were hot, but when you were at rock bottom, nobody even wanted to know you.

"What goes around comes around," she said.

"Say what?" Lee asked.

Sylvia laughed. "Hey, what're you tryin' to do? Talk colored?" She held her glass out, and he refilled it. "What the hell?" she asked. "Like I say in the show, 'One more time for the good times.'"

"I thought it was the old times."

She smiled. "Well, something like that..."

5.

THE "UP AND OUT" THEME MUSIC PLAYED AS THE END flashed across the screen.

"Thank God," Kay Duvane whispered to Sheila, as the lights in the screening room came on. "Let's get while the getting is good—"

It was too late. Before the two women could make their escape, Donna Hatcher headed them off.

"Wasn't it marvelous?" she asked.

Kay cleared her throat. "It was stunning—in the truest sense of the word."

The publicity woman looked mortally wounded. "You mean you didn't like it? Pauline Kael said she thought it was very compelling, and Andrew Sarris called it an 'arresting film—'"

"Donna, save it, will you?" Kay asked. "I'm glad you're getting good reviews because, sweetie, you're going to need them. As a *film*, it may be the sleeper of the season fresh from Cannes, but as a movie, it's a dead dog—and strictly from hunger. We've got to run."

"I'll call you!" Donna promised.

"And she means it, too," Kay told Sheila as they hurried toward the elevator. "Remind me not to take her calls for another few days."

Traffic on Fifth Avenue was worse than usual. Kay rolled her eyes, as if asking heaven to send her a Checker with a police escort.

"Come on, we'll walk. It's faster," Sheila suggested. The two women fell into step, then suddenly Kay stopped in her tracks.

"*You* didn't like it, did you?" she asked.

"I thought it was pretentious—"

"Arty-farty," Kay corrected her. "And I don't give a damn what Pauline Kael said. It's never going to make it in Peoria."

Sheila agreed, and a quick smiled played over her face.

"Don't tell me there was a joke in there! Did I sleep through it?"

"No, Kay," the younger woman answered. "I was just thinking of something one of my neighbors said. We were both in the laundry room, and we started talking about movies. I told her about the screenings—"

"Let me guess," Kay cut in. "She oohed and ahed and told you how exciting it must be to see all the new movies as part of your job, right?"

"That's about it."

Kay laughed. "If they only knew!"

It had been a long time—*years*—since she'd actually been able to watch a movie for the pure pleasure of it. Instead, she viewed them with a professional eye, replacing her own sensibility with that of the Typical American Viewer. What she thought of a picture as an individual was sublimated. How a movie would translate into prime-time television was the important consideration.

For a time, the major studios had tried to hold their ground against television. The battle of the big and small screens had been fought with a variety of weapons. Some—like the cheap china given away on free-dish nights at local movie houses—were staples for a slumping box office that had been used since the Depression. Others, such as Cinemascope, PanaVision, and the other wide-screen processes, were technological innovations that made the small black-and-white TV screen seem even smaller.

But by the early 1950's, the writing was on the wall and the message was clear. Television wasn't a novelty item that would fall out of favor with an afffuent few. It was a "monster" growing by leaps and bounds. The home viewers didn't realize that movies were a form of entertainment, while TV was essentially an advertising medium. All that mattered to them was that they could sit home, relax, and watch programs of increasing diversity and technical quality "for free."

The party was over as far as the Hollywood majors were concerned, and the theater owners panicked. True, people would still pay to see an all-star cast in a lavish production, but the habit of going to the movies had been broken—or rather replaced—by TV watching. Programmers, the bread and butter of the old days, were a thing of the past. The public was suddenly selective.

With its constant demand for product, television turned naturally to the very studios it threatened. Their backlogs offered the potential for hours and hours of pre-produced programming. The first sales were of old westerns, B mysteries, and serials... the stuff that Saturday afternoon matinees were made of. Hopalong Cassidy became a star all over again, and a marriage of convenience was forged, even though the surviving movie moguls felt that selling their movies to the networks was consorting with the enemy.

In time, the failing studios found themselves relying on the new medium that threatened their very existence. Their own production schedules were trimmed drastically: either they had to diversify and get into TV production like Universal, or lease empty sound stages for television production, or go broke. The networks' ready cash for old features was an increasingly important factor in profit-and-loss statements, and a sure thing at a time when seven-figure budgets for new features were fast becoming the rule rather than the exception they had formerly been.

Warner's, Columbia, MGM, Paramount, 20th Century-Fox—the studios had sold off "packages" of old movies to the networks, forcing them to take the good with the bad, the failures with the winners. Like a carnivorous animal, television fed on feature films, buying up everything available. By the 1960's, when color was a fact of broadcasting life rather than the idea it had been little more than a decade before, there was no longer a backlog supply to meet the demand.

The movie business never really recovered: it only managed to survive. The studios sold off their backlots and even their warehouses of props and costumes under the guidance of the corporate accountants hired by the conglomerates they belonged to. They began selling the networks the television rights to their product more quickly. By the mid-1970's, with cable TV companies offering to subscribers unedited current movies that were still playing at the local drive-ins or grind houses, the networks became even more competitive. Prices for features became astronomical. Bids were made before pictures had a chance to succeed or fail at the box office—and in some cases, a network would insure itself the inside track by providing up-front financing for a film.

There were "movies for television," ersatz features that never made it to the American movie screen (though they were often released to theaters in foreign markets, where movies were still big business and exhibitors were hungry for product). Produced with a feature-film look, neatly scripted with scenes conveniently timed for commercial interruption, they became a major factor in TV programming.

But nothing guaranteed a good rating as emphatically as the first TV run of a smash hit—a picture such as *The Godfather,* or *Rocky*, or *Love Story*. The prices paid for the big pictures made them special events.

At least, Kay Duvane thought, considering it all, she didn't have to pass judgment on the features TBS bought for the two weekday nights when movies were the focal point of its prime-time programming. All she had to worry about, she reminded herself (smirking at the *all*), was special programming.

Increasingly, the problem was that the viewers were expecting every night to be special, and the advertisers were demanding that "special" be defined not as "of exceptional quality," but as "of wide viewer appeal." The numbers, the ratings, were the only things that mattered.

"Back to the salt mines," Kay said, as she and Sheila entered the TBS Building. "We survived the walk, unfortunately—"

"Come on, Kay. It's not *that* bad, is it?"

"That's what *you* think," Kay answered, pacing as she waited for an elevator. "You didn't have the pleasure, pardon the expression, of being at that meeting this morning. The affiliates are getting hard to handle. You know how independent they are these days. They want everything prescreened, and if they don't like a show, there's nothing we can do to make them carry it. If they don't like us—if we don't come up with the right numbers—they'll move over to another network. It's a new day, Sheila, and you know what? The weather is lousy."

Sheila didn't answer. She hadn't worked in television during the old days that Kay spoke of so often, but she was aware of how things had changed.

Each of the networks was allowed by the Federal Communications Commission to own and operate five stations. The networks, naturally, picked the major markets for their O and O's (owned and operated). But that still left plenty of territory. Back in the days when TV was new, anyone who acquired a license to operate a station immediately sought affiliation with a network. It was the only way to go, with the networks providing virtually all programming. In return for bringing in Pinky Lee, Milton Berle, and Lucy, along with the messages from their national sponsors, to his market, a station owner sold time for local commercials.

As TV grew, so did the number of local advertisers and their power. The advertising agencies and businessmen who bought local time for their clients didn't have the budgets that their national counterparts on Madison Avenue did, but they had the same purpose—buying advertising time that would expose their clients' products and services to the widest possible audience.

Network affiliates, even in markets with a couple of independent stations, commanded the highest prices. And the station affiliated with the top network at a given time commanded the best price of all.

There'd been a time when affiliates had no choice but to stick with their network through thick and thin, good seasons (and years) and bad. As they felt their power increase, however, things had changed. The local station owner could no longer be taken for granted by the network. If he didn't like a particular program, whether because he felt it might offend his viewers, or because it expressed a point of view in opposition to his politics (or those of an influential friend), he'd refuse to air the show, substituting a movie from his library, or a special he'd bought from an independent supplier. If he felt that the network he was affiliated with wasn't offering him the best shot at the highest dollar for his local commercial time, he'd change to another network, given the chance.

Losing a station was a disaster for a network, no matter how small the market it represented was. Besides the dollars-and-cents loss that a defection meant in national terms, there was a loss of prestige within the industry. And a loss of morale within the network itself.

"It's half past two," Kay informed Sheila, as they stepped off the elevator and walked toward their offices. "I've *got* to make some calls before the meeting. Can you handle things?"

Sheila nodded. "Of course, Kay. I've got letters and reports—"

"Don't we all, sweetie. Well, if anything wonderful happens, let me know. Otherwise, I'm locking myself in my cage. We'll go up together at five, okay?" She turned to the secretary, who was holding out a small sheaf of messages. "Give them to Sheila. And the calls, too. Don't put anything through if you can help it, okay?"

"Yes, Miss Duvane."

Kay walked into her office and closed the door.

God, how she hated the sweeps!

It was hard enough to come up with specials that could attract an increasingly hard-to-please national audience... and harder still to do it within the confines of her budget, which never seemed to increase fast enough to keep up with mounting production costs and the outrageous demands of the stars.

The seasonal things, holiday-themed specials that featured a familiar, well-liked star hosting a variety hour, weren't so bad. Buying a big movie to show on a big night, one when TBS was counter-programming one of the other networks, or trying to show its stuff in the Nielsens, wasn't that serious a problem, either, provided she had the market-research reports and box-office figures that could get an eight-figure purchase approved.

But the sweeps were something else.

Each year, in February, May, and November, the Chicago-based A. C. Nielsen company conducted a special four-week rating service for local stations... in addition to carrying on business as usual.

Nielsen homes, the approximately, 1,200 of them across the country which composed a representative sampling of the American viewer, were equipped with an Audimeter, a small black box attached to the television set that recorded what station was watched at what time. In return for a few dollars per month as compensation, along with a partial reimbursement for TV repairs, the monitored Nielsen homes—though they represented only about .0017 percent of the 70,000,000 households with television in the country—provided the information that was collected and compiled as "the numbers," the ratings. The fate of a new program or an old favorite, the rates for commercial time and the CPM (or cost per reaching each 1,000 viewers) were determined by the ratings.

Nielsen's services were varied. A fraction of Nielsen homes in New York City, Chicago, and Los Angeles were wired directly to computers. These sets determined the overnight ratings. The Multi-Network Area Report, or MNA's, measured the number of households using television (HUT's) by quarter-hours, and broke down the viewing patterns of monitored households by age and sex. The MNA's represented about 65 percent of the national audience, and were drawn from the seventy most populated cities in the nation.

In 1973, the company began the Storage Instantaneous Audimeter service. Telephone wires linked every Nielsen Audimeter with the company's computer in Dunedin, Florida. The SIA's gave the networks rating information and an audience breakdown within thirty-six hours of broadcast time.

The blockbuster—and ultimate last word—was the biweekly NTI, or Nielsen Television Index. Its extensive demographics broke down the viewing audience for any given quarter-hour in the preceding two weeks by age, sex, education, income, and general viewing habits. It showed how many households had their sets on at a given time; which program they turned on; which program they turned off or switched the dial to. In addition to the number of viewers within a household who watched a particular program, the service measured the Share of Audience—the percentage of viewers who watched a particular program, choosing it over the competition. The show that did the best in the busiest time period (prime time) was the number-one show of a given week.

The Nielsens were enough to contend with normally, but during sweep periods, Kay cringed.

Instead of a few homes or a few stations in a major market, the sweeps were complete ratings that measured viewer habits in relation to every station in the country. It wasn't a matter of little black boxes and computers: instead, Nielsen canvassers provided selected homes with diaries in which viewing habits were recorded by the family. The data, when analyzed, provided local stations with the information they needed to raise (or lower) their local advertising rates. It showed the popularity of one local newscaster as compared with another, and of one local entertainment or public service show as opposed to the competition.

Within the industry, at the networks, everyone said that the diary technique was unreliable: people made mistakes when they wrote their choice of programs and channels down, or sometimes forgot to fill their diaries in until the last minute, when they turned to *TV Guide* or the newspaper's Sunday TV listings to try to reconstruct or even invent the week's viewing.

But in local markets, the sweeps mattered—and what they really measured, in the minds of affiliates, was what kind of job the network was doing. In some areas, those large enough to support several stations, an affiliate had no choice but to stick with his network even if it was in last place. That, however, hinged on all of the networks being represented within the area. There were many markets, however, where not all the networks were represented by a strong local signal.

A station owner might decide that he'd be better off with TBS than CBS, or that an affiliation with ABC would give him more lucrative programming (and more profitable local advertising rates) than NBC.

Much as the networks disliked the sweeps, they programmed for them, loading their schedules with blockbuster movies, preempting weak or marginal weekly series with specials, and even hyping regular series by running episodes that featured big-time guest stars. All the stops were pulled, all the big guns fired in an effort to do as well as possible. If the viewer was the loser, confronted with a choice between several attractive specials all on at the same time, after weeks of reruns and pilots that hadn't made it for the coming season ... well, there were always reruns.

The sweeps were business, *big* business. A run for the money and, Kay thought, a run for your professional life as well.

The job of picking which specials to program during the sweeps was always an ordeal. There was no prestige that mattered except the final numbers, so the quality ideas were shelved for four weeks. Classical music or drama, documentaries about anything except sex, tours of foreign art museums, "intellectual" dramas—they were all the kiss of death.

The goal—and the impossible task—was to come up with programs that appealed to the widest possible audience, then to run promo spots plugging them until the viewer, ideally, would stay away from his own mother's funeral to watch them. On top of that, the schedule had to be kept as secret as possible until the last minute, when it was "revealed" ... another impossibility, since in addition to all the talk and gossip that went on in the industry, each of the networks had "sources" at the others.

"Sweet Jesus," Kay said, thinking about it all. She scanned the list of calls she *had* to make, preferring the expediency of dialing the numbers herself rather than going through her secretary. Her first call was to the producer of TBS' big country-music special, *Charlie Rich: At Home in Memphis.*

"Bob?" she asked. "Kay Duvane here. How are things coming...Oh? Great...he did? That's terrific. What good news. Fine, I'll look forward to it. Thanks—and thank Charlie and Margaret Ann for me, will you?"

Country music had moved into the urban markets, and scheduling an appropriate special, from the start, had been a good idea. Charlie Rich, as a top country star with crossover appeal in the easy listening market, had been Kay's first choice. Luckily she'd been able to get him. The special had been one of those rare charmed projects that had worked out perfectly in every way.

Margaret Ann Rich, Charlie's wife, was a talented songwriter: a segment of the special was devoted to following a song through the process of transformation from an idea to a finished single. Kay was certain that she had at least one hour of programming that would draw a good share.

The Cardboard Kingdom was another matter entirely.

The whole concept of a mini-series was risky. If you were lucky and caught the audience with the initial segment, you might be able to hold them all the way through, no matter what the competition offered. Word of mouth might even attract some viewers who missed the first episode or two, and a brief summary of what had happened "so far in our story" was designed to fill in newcomers. But if the plot, production, or performances didn't maintain initial quality, you were stuck with four or five nights that not only kept the other networks busy while the mini-series was on, but detracted from the rest of the lineup.

TBS had tried the idea with varying degrees of success, and when it came to the sweeps, *Revolution!*, a four-part series about a family caught up in the War of Independence, had been the top brass' first choice. It was a well-crafted concept, Kay had agreed, and everyone associated with the proposed project was topnotch talent. She had admitted that it could bring the network a lot of prestige, just as *Roots* had done for ABC and *Holocaust* for NBC.

Viewers, she'd said adamantly, were another matter. In her opinion they would stay tuned, all right—to the competition.

'No matter how good the story is," Kay had argued, "everyone's had it with the subject matter. The Bicentennial took care of that. If you had Liz Taylor and Ted Kennedy in the leads, it still wouldn't get a decent share. Maybe in another couple of years, but now now."

The package had its supporters, but ultimately Kay's opinion had been accepted. As a result, the pressure had been on her to find a better idea. Once the word got out that she was looking, she'd been deluged with scripts and proposals that included *The Tyrones*, a four-part adaptation of Eugene O'Neill's plays about a family like his own, which had been promising enough to warrant a development deal. But there had been problems about the rights, and the script had been too downbeat, Kay had decided with regret.

The Cardboard Kingdom, Ellie Loring's sizzling bestseller, had seemed like the best possible choice. The critics hated her thinly disguised novels about real show-business personalities, but the public loved them. They'd put her in a league with Harold Robbins and Jackie Susann, and *The Cardboard Kingdom*, like her other books, had held the top spot on *The New York Times* list of hardcover bestsellers for months. It had still been in the top fifteen titles when the paperback came out, selling 6.3 million copies in its first three months.

If the property had the advantage of being presold to the national audience, it also came with built-in problems. The rights had cost a couple of million dollars, but that was just the beginning. The only reason Ellie Loring had even considered selling her novel to TBS was that she'd hated the movie versions of her previous two books. TBS had agreed to give her script approval, and to bill the mini-series as "Ellie Loring's *The Carboard Kingdom*."

Kay had instructed Allan Jeffries, the project's producer, to see that the script was as faithful to the book as possible. Still, Ellie had refused to approve the first two drafts. Kay had found herself begging and pleading, trying to make Ellie understand that while the panoramic view of Hollywood—as seen through the eyes of a living legend afraid and unwilling to let herself face the fact that she'd grown old—made a great book, certain changes were necessary to translate it to television.

Not only were certain scenes simply too sexy to be shown in any form, Kay had tried to point out as tactfully as possible, it was essentially a woman's story. That was fine—but to keep the male viewer interested in the story it was essential to beef up the role of the studio czar, and to put greater emphasis on the business aspects of the plot.

Once Ellie had finally been placated on the script, there'd been casting problems. Just as the Nielsens measured which programs had the widest audiences, TV-Q rated performers on the basis of familiarity to viewers and "likability." Kay and Allan Jeffries had tried to utilize performers who had commitments to the network: soap-opera stars who demanded a movie of the week before they'd agreed to renew their contracts; comedians who wanted to do "serious" parts; actors and actresses under exclusive longterm TBS contracts. Everyone who was right for a role was committed to something else for the time they were needed, and those who were available weren't right. In the end, an expensive all-star cast had been assembled, with Anne Bancroft in the lead.

Now the mini-series was in post-production, and the standards and practices people were fighting with Allan Jeffries over crucial scenes they felt were *still* too hot for the home screen. Jeffries, in turn, was fighting with his director.

"Allan...will you listen to me, goddamn it!" Kay demanded, as he filled her in on the latest episode of who-said-what-to-whom. "Look, I don't have time for this. Get it cleared and do it fast! I don't care *what* he says. Tell him that *I* said to get it reedited, or I'll have someone else do it... What? Who the hell does he think cares? I don't give a damn if his name is on the credits or not—and they sure as hell don't care in Peoria."

She slammed the phone down, mad at herself for not vetoing Allan's choice of a director from the start, as her instincts had told her to do. Ted Shadden might be hot in movies or he might be lucky—he'd had two hits in a row, but they were the full extent of his feature work, and it was too early to tell. It was clear, though, that he thought he was doing Allan Jeffries, TBS, and television in general a favor by condescending to direct *The Cardboard Kingdom*, and it would be a cold day in hell before Kay worked with him again.

With a sigh, she crossed Allan's name from her list... another call out of the way. An hour later, only one more name remained on her list, and there were several pages of scribbled notes on her pad.

"Lee Dean," Kay said aloud, tapping her nails against the glass desktop. Talk about a name from the past! He'd been the last person she expected to get a proposal from—hell, the last time she'd heard of him, he'd been halfway around the world in Australia.

She had three boxes on her desk, "IN," "OUT," and "HOLDING." Though she knew every word of it, she reached into the HOLDING box and took out the presentation, looking at the title page.

DANCETIME, USA! The Twentieth
Anniversary Reunion

A Television Special
Conceived by Lee Dean

It was a good idea—there was no doubt about that, Kay knew. And it meshed so perfectly with one of the specials already in the works for the first Sunday night of the November schedule.

The 1950's were back, as *Grease* had proved at the box office and *Happy Days* and *Laverne and Shirley* demonstrated in the ratings. TBS had been inundated with imitations of all three properties, and variants on the basic idea. One series idea had gotten as far as a pilot, but it hadn't been scheduled: as often happened, an idea that looked good on paper didn't work when shot.

The pilot would end up filling a half-hour role in the summer schedule, but TBS had been determined to cash in on America's 1950's nostaglia one way or another. Teenagers discovering the period for the first time, adults in their thirties who wanted a trip down memory lane...the potential audience was too big and too attractive to ignore. Everyone agreed that there had to be a way to cash in—but nobody was sure how to do it.

For days, Kay had tried to come up with a fresh concept. Then, one morning, the idea was in her mind when she woke up, so obvious that she was amazed that nobody had thought of it before. The one thing everyone remembered about the 1950's, the single common denominator of the period, was the music. Rock and roll.

Hadn't *Dancetime, USA!*, one of the first shows she'd worked on when she'd joined the network as a publicity girl, been a hit for TBS while it lasted? Seeing a good thing, hadn't the producers of the network's slumping variety shows brought in rock acts in the hope of attracting younger audiences via guest stars? All those old shows were on kinescopes, somewhere in the TBS archives. Then, too, there was lots of film around on everyone from Elvis to The Fleetwoods.

If the right editor could be found—someone who knew the period and understood music—an exciting program could evolve, one that would attract a wide share of the audience.

The Rockin' Fifties: The Stars, the Songs, the Sounds! had been accepted almost instantly after Kay typed up a one-page concept. She'd been congratulated for bringing in an "in house" project that could use (and test) the talent of staff producers and technical people. There was a young editor named Carl Zimmer who had been widely praised for *Disaster!*, a montage of newsreel footage he'd put together for a news special. He not only loved music, but was a bona fide fifties buff.

The Rockin' Fifties was set, scheduled, and nearly finished. Still, there'd been a problem.

Viewers would get up and change a station to see a show—especially a series—they particularly liked, unless competing programming was clever and attractive. New series in which a network had a big investment were always scheduled to follow shows that were proven winners providing a "built in" audience for the newcomer. When a situation comedy clicked with the public, schedules were lined up accordingly in the hope that the viewer would stay with the network for two whole hours of prime-time laughs.

Programming had decided that *The Rockin' Fifties* would be ideal for a Sunday 7:30-9:00 period. The man at the head of the Typical American Family, the thinking went, would have watched football all day. The Typical American Housewife would be ready for a change, and the Typical American Kids would get their two cents in. As a result, the Typical American Home would turn to TBS—and the special.

What to follow it with was a problem that had plagued Kay and been the subject of several meetings. A big movie with a 1950's setting would have been ideal, but the network didn't have one. For a time, the decision had been in the air. A variety hour starring contemporary teen idols had been a possibility, but the preteens who were their biggest fans would be in bed. The news division had suggested a treatment of the big stories of the 1950's as a continuation of the theme, but nobody liked news, even *old*, nostalgic news, if there was such a thing—in prime time during the sweeps. Besides, it would mean too much black-and-white programming at one time, since there was next to no color footage from the fifties.

A two-hour TV movie had been a compromise solution, a story about a young would-be rock star's attempts to make it in the 1950's. It was a shameless ripoff of *The Buddy Holly Story*, without the talent that had made that picture so good. Ronnie Keller, a nineteen-year-old who'd drawn a big following in *The Unteachables*, TBS' classroom sitcom, had starred. Nobody was overjoyed with the result. Ronnie's agent had insisted that he do his own singing, which was hardly spectacular. Outside the familiar classroom setting, he seemed stiff and wooden. On another night, the movie might draw a good rating, but following the film clips of real stars at their peak, it was a definite letdown.

There'd been no better idea, though, and the movie had been tentatively scheduled. Then Lee Dean's proposal had come in.

Of course! Kay had thought immediately.

It made perfect sense. *Dancetime* was the ideal thing to follow *The Rockin' Fifties*. Everyone remembered *Dancetime* and The Regulars. The kids who'd danced on the show day after day had been the idols of every teenager who'd watched the show. More than idols, really, since they had no particular talent except the ability to dance and project personality on camera. But the viewers had identified with them, the teen magazines had written about and photographed them, and TBS' publicity department had plugged them for all they were worth. When the show went off the air, The Regulars went into obscurity, back to "real life."

Reuniting them, having them talk about the old days,

would be a wonderful human interest concept—particularly with Lee Dean as host. The whole idea was good, including his plan to have the performers with the top three hits twenty years before singing them on the special. Lee apparently had a commitment from Sylvia to appear with The Fantastiks, which as a group hadn't been seen in ages, Kay knew; Sylvia herself rarely deigned to appear on television. As for doing the show live, as Lee suggested, on a replica of the original set... that made it even better, and would be good for a lot of PR within the trade.

There was only one problem, one factor, that had kept her from passing the project along, fighting for it, with her unqualified approval.

Network television was extremely image-conscious. Lee Dean and *Dancetime, USA!* hadn't just left the air under a cloud: they'd been washed away in a downpour. How would the corporate policy-makers feel about reminding the public of the payola scandal—in the person of no less a veteran than Lee Dean himself?

On the other hand, time was a great healer. Payola wasn't a household word any more, and besides, who really gave a damn? The happy times, the fun of it all, was what people remembered and what they wanted to be reminded of. Hadn't television made plenty of its own mistakes? None of the networks was proud of the McCarthy years, and the way any performer even accused of leaning too far to the left had been blacklisted without a chance to defend himself or clear his name. CBS had fired one of its top radio stars, John Henry Faulk, after he was listed in *Red Channels*, the bible of who was and was not approved during the period. He'd sued the publishers and he'd won a libel settlement, but by then he'd been off the air.

To its credit CBS had at least admitted its culpability in a dramatization of the Faulk case—but that had taken two decades, and then some.

If they can do it, can't we? Kay wondered. Couldn't TBS forgive and forget—especially if there was a good rating involved? And what the hell was she doing sitting on a great idea because she was afraid that pushing it would ruffle a few feathers? God, had she worked so hard for so many years only to be afraid of trusting her instincts?

"Come in," Kay called, responding to the knock on the door. "Oh, Sheila—is it five already?"

"Ten to. I thought you might want to go over the status reports for the meeting."

"Smart girl," Kay said, reaching for the folders Sheila was holding. In return, she passed her assistant Lee Dean's proposal. "Better look at this again."

Sheila glanced at the title page, then at Kay. "You've made up your mind?" she asked. "Are you going to recommend it?"

"No," Kay said. "I'm not going to recommend it. I'm going to make certain we do it!"

6.

"...SO ANYWAY, WE'RE DOING THE SPECIAL. and Kay gave *me* the job of coordinating the whole thing. Not just a talent coordinator, Mom, but—"

"Is there a difference, dear?" the voice on the other end of the line asked.

"Of course there is! A talent coordinator just books the guests. My job—" Sheila braked her enthusiasm. Her mother would never understand, so why bore her with details. "Anyway, it's a big break for me, Mom. Just what I've been waiting for. I'm really excited about it, and I wanted to tell you."

"That's sweet, Sheila," Dorothy Granger told her daughter. "As long as you're happy, dear. Still, it sounds like an awful lot of work to me, and you know how important it is to get your rest. You *are* getting enough sleep, aren't you?"

"Yes, Mom," Sheila said, feeling her face masque tighten.

"And you lock your door, don't you, Sheila? There was

a terrible story on the news the other night. All about some girl in New York who left her door unlocked, and—" As Sheila braced herself for the grisly details, the sound of a doorbell ringing on her mother's end of the line cut the conversation short. "That must be one of the girls," Dorothy Granger explained. "We're playing bridge tonight—it's my turn to be hostess. They'll be so excited when I tell them you called."

"Say hello to your friends for me, Mom. And have a good game."

"Of course, they'll probably think you called to tell me you've met a wonderful man. There are other things in life besides television, Sheila—" The bell rang again. "Good-bye, dear. And good luck with . . . well, whatever it is you're doing."

"Thanks, Mom. We'll talk soon."

As she replaced the receiver, Sheila had to smile in spite of herself. Nothing about television, not even an Emmy, would impress her mother. Every time they talked, every time Sheila tried to share her career, Dorothy Granger made it sound as if her daughter was watching TV rather than helping make it happen. And after all these years, her mother was still pushing the Wonderful Man.

She means well, Sheila reminded herself, grateful that her mother's company had arrived in time to spare her the latest news depicting Manhattan as a Terrible Place Where Young Women Get Murdered. No doubt her mother would include the newspaper version, clipped from the local paper, in her next letter.

It was time to rinse the masque off. Sheila turned the taps of the bathroom sink until she got the right degree of lukewarm. She'd meant to have a facial, but there hadn't been time the last few days. Work had been hectic, and Kay had been on the warpath until word came down that the Lee Dean special had been okayed.

Odd, Sheila thought, rinsing her face. She opened the medicine cabinet and scooped some moisturizer out of a jar, massaging it into her skin as she went back to the bedroom. Several times before, she'd seen Kay get worked up when a program she believed in had trouble getting final approval. But this time was different. It wasn't just a matter of professional judgment, Sheila decided. Instead, Kay had made it a personal crusade.

Sheila hadn't fully understood what the problem was. Tempted as she was to ask for an explanation, she hadn't wanted to risk a blowup. Two days before, the call had come and Kay's mood changed from irritability to triumph.

"I got it!" she announced, sweeping into Sheila's office. "I know I've been a dragon, Sheila. Forgive me. I promise not to be mean any more. God, isn't it wonderful?"

For ten full minutes, Kay—as excited as Sheila had ever seen her—had gone on about the special. It would be fabulous, a critical success as well as a hit with the viewers. The publicity would be a "goldmine" for TBS and for everyone involved.

"And that includes you," Kay had said, winding up her fillibuster.

"Me? I don't understand—" Sheila answered.

"Let me take you to lunch and I'll explain it. Besides, it will help me make up for having been such a bitch."

Kay had taken her to Orsini's on purpose. It was primarily a watering hole for the fashion crowd, and there'd be no people from the other networks, or even TBS, to accidentally-on-purpose overhear their conversation.

What it came down to, Sheila learned, was that while the special had been approved, there were at least some people in top management who had mixed feelings about the project. As a result, every phase of production was going to be, as Kay had put it, "sensitive." The network had only agreed with the provision that the whole thing be done in house—and under Kay's personal supervision.

"Won't Lee Dean be disappointed?" Sheila had asked. "Wasn't he looking for a production deal?"

Kay had paused for only a second. "Lee will be producing, more or less. Look, Sheila—he's been away for a hell of a long time. Nobody knows more about *Dancetime, USA!* than Lee, but TV has changed a lot. He'll get it his way, but it will be done by us."

Over their veal picata, Sheila had pieced it all together. The network, she understood, realized that the concept was great. Lee Dean, as host of the original show, was the natural choice to host the reunion special. But the taint of the scandal he'd left with hadn't been totally erased: TBS was willing to forgive, but it wasn't about to forget. Nor was it going to give Lee Dean *carte blanche* to produce—and possibly embarrass the network.

"The contact work, the publicity, *everything* is going to have to be very carefully handled," Kay explained. "Lee's been around enough to know that's the way the network wants it, that's how we have to play the game. And *we* own all the rights to the show—not Lee. The important thing is that we're going to do it, Sheila. And you're going to coordinate the whole thing... with credit, of course."

Sheila felt her heart pound.

"Now don't worry," Kay advised before Sheila could say a word. "I'm going to help you, and you know you can always come to me with any question or problem. To tell the truth, I'd love to bring this one in myself, but I just can't take the time away from everything else. You'll keep your office, of course, but I'm going to start interviewing for an additional assistant. Hell, kid, smile! This is what you've been waiting for—the big break. Want dessert?"

Sheila shook her head.

"Me either. Let's skip coffee, if it's okay with you. I have a meeting." Kay signaled for the check, then leaned across the table, her hand grasping Sheila's arm.

"You're good," Kay said. "In fact you're better than

good. I trust you, Sheila. I know this is a lot of responsibility, but you're the woman who can do it. And don't think it won't lead to other things—"

"But I don't know anything about the 1950's. There must be somebody around who does—"

"There are *lots* of people who do, but what does that mean? Sheila, you see the demographics. The median age in the prime market segment is getting lower all the time. Sponsors want to reach the young people, the couples and the singles like you. They're the ones who have the disposable income. We have to make the 1950's interesting to them—and they don't remember it any more than you do.

"Besides, how many programs were there a couple of years ago about the Bicentennial? Darling, I may look it now and then, and feel it more times than I'd like to admit, but not even *I* can remember the American Revolution. You'll have research—it's all in the files—and you'll bring a fresh approach. It will be divine ... and marvelous for your career, I might add."

"What do I do? Where do I start?" Sheila heard herself ask, still amazed and confused.

"Well, this one doesn't exactly follow the textbooks, does it? The first thing we have to do is track down The Regulars. God only knows where they are. Then they have to be talked into doing the show. We're going to have to do the usual budgeting and all that crap, but Public Relations already knows that my office—*ours*, I mean— is going to handle the campaign on this. We'll map it out and they can do the contact work.

"Lee will be coming in next week. I've got an office for him on the fourth floor. You'll be working with him. And since you're so damn young..." Kay smiled to let Sheila know she was teasing, "...you'd better familiarize yourself with the show and the period. Okay?"

Okay? It was better than okay. It was wonderful! It was the chance she'd hoped for, and it had come sooner than she'd expected. There were no hard and fast rules in any business: it was her luck, and Kay's confidence, that had given her a chance on a network special where she'd be involved in every phase of production. She swore to herself that she wouldn't let down Kay, TBS, or her chances for her own future.

Climbing into bed, Sheila reached for the stack of material she'd brought home from the office. Videotape hadn't been in existence, much less in use, when *Dancetime, USA!* was on the air. Kinescopes deteriorated with time and use, so she'd given the network's film library the assignment of finding the best surviving records of the show and transferring them to video cassettes. Later, once The Regulars were located and the guests set, someone could go through all the kinescopes to find the film clips that would be used in the special itself. It would be a few days till the tapes came up.

In the meantime, Sheila had done her own research, digging through dusty files ("1958?" the man in Publicity had said, amazed when Sheila asked to see the clip file on the show. "You've got to be kidding!") stored in cardboard boxes. She'd been amazed at how much publicity Lee Dean had generated, considering that he didn't sing, or act, or tell jokes. The whole idea of a disc jockey appearing on TV and playing records while kids danced seemed so simple and innocent, yet in the late 1950's it was a new idea.

Dig, Teen, Rock 'n' Roll, TV-Record Stars... how dated they seemed. Propping herself up with a pillow, looking through the fan magazines which devoted pages to Lee and to The Regulars, Sheila had to smile. The ads alone were funny. OFFICIAL JAMES DEAN MEMORIAL RECORDS.... 1,000 PHOTOS OF ELVIS, SAL, FRANKIE, FABIAN, AND ALL YOUR FAVORITES, JUST $1.00... 10 DRESSES BY MAIL! 55¢ EACH!... ELVIS CHARM BRACELET...

The hottest story during the old *Dancetime* days, Sheila noted, was the Liz-Eddie-Debbie triangle. *Motion*

Picture devoted a cover to it, and so did all the other movie magazines. Dorothy Malone, Natalie Wood, Diane Varsi, and Molly Bee...Tab Hunter, Ricky Nelson, Tuesday Weld, and Sandra Dee—the magazines offered their "secret loves," the never-before-told tales of their heartbreak, their answers to the Ten Questions Teens Want Answers To.

The magazines were crammed with advice from Dick Clark, Lee Dean, and the stars. Everyone, it seemed, had his own idea of "The Teen Commandments," or his rules for "Being a Teen Today." It was as if a whole generation had been looking for advice.

DANCETIME DIARIES! one of the magazines promised. *The Regulars Tell Their Secrets.*

Sheila giggled, shaking her head as she studied the unfamiliar images. *It's a Dancetime Slumber Party!* the blurb proclaimed. *Join Sandy, Connie, Cathy, Lorraine, and Donna and share the fun—and secrets!!!* She read the story.

> When the show's over on the set of *Dancetime, USA!*, the fun goes on.
>
> All the gang are friends, even though they were strangers until they met on the show that has teens all over the country rocking. The Regulars sometimes have a soda or sundae after the broadcast, but during the week they hurry home (all in different directions) to their families, to supper, and to hit the books.
>
> Lee Dean, host of the daily hop, insists that The Regulars keep their grades up, or else!!!
>
> Still, there's always the telephone for girl (and *boy*) talk. Best of all are weekends, when those lucky teens who dance for the cameras and get to meet the likes of Bobby Darin, Tommy Del, and Dion can take a homework break and concentrate on majoring in fun by the ton.
>
> Like teens everywhere, those groovy *Dancetime* gals like nothing better than a slumber party. They do the usual fun things, from trying on clothes to making fudge.

Of course, being in the spotlight, they also compare the fan letters that pour in every day, and try to answer as many as they can.

Girls will be girls—so the conversation always comes around to boys. And that means Dennis, Bobby, Don, Andy and Hank ... those (sigh) *sooo* handsome guys who are official partners for our lucky sorority.

Sometimes the gals exchange diaries, sharing their secret thoughts and dreams. We were invited to come along on a recent Friday. While our photographer snapped these exclusive candid pics, we sneaked a peak at the diaries, and asked if we couldn't share a few of the secrets we learned with you.

Cathy, the long-tressed blonde, reveals the beauty secrets behind her popularity.

"Dear Diary," she wrote. "So many teens write to me or stop me in the hall at school to ask for beauty tips. Of course it's trial and error, finding out what works best for you.

"But some teens tend to overdo it, and too much makeup (especially when you are under 16) is worse than none at all. It looks so cheap—and gives people (boys!!!) the wrong idea.

"I hate to see girls who could look so much better if they'd take the time to wash their hair daily and *really* scrub their skin. It gives you a natural glow, and helps keep blemishes away.

"Good skin and hair care are my beauty secrets. And easy-going on the makeup to make the most of your looks."

Connie (hostess for the slumber party) confides her secret dream.

"Dear Diary," she begins, "Ever since I was chosen to be one of the lucky teens who are Regulars on *Dancetime, USA!*, I've had a dream. Seeing so many stars in person has made me realize that I want to go into show business myself. My friends on the show tell me I have a natural sense of humor (funny—Mom and Dad didn't laugh at my last report card!!!). Maybe I do.

"I asked Lee Dean for some advice. He understands

teens so well, and always has good ideas. Lee told me that the best way I could make my dream come true is by finishing high school, a *must* for any career. And by making the most of my teen years... easy to do, with such good friends.

"After graduating, I'll take my chances. Who knows? Maybe someday I'll make it to *Dancetime, USA!* as a guest star!"

Pert 'n' perky Sandy (known as the Girl with the Streak in Her Hair) reveals the secret of her popularity with the boys.

"Dear Diary," she wrote, "I've learned that the best way to be popular with boys is to be a good listener. They don't gossip as much as we girls do, but boys do like to talk about themselves. Sometimes a girl has to start the ball rolling, but there's nothing wrong with that. After all, it's 1958!

"Bringing a boy out of his shell is easy if you ask the right questions. Bone up on sports (just enough to ask a question or two—who wants to talk about *that* all evening?) or cars. Once you've started things going, you'll find what you have in common and become friends.

"Girls and boys don't have to date to be buddies. Everyone thinks that Bobby and I are going together because we dance on the show. The true story? Well, that's another secret!"

Lorraine, the dark-haired, dark-eyed girl, tells what it's like to get letters from fans all over the country.

"Dear Diary," she said, "I just can't believe the change being one of The Regulars has made in my life. I still have my friends (a couple of the girls at school told me they were afraid I'd get stuck up... guess I didn't!) but I have so many new ones. People who see me on TV write letters.

"It's been going on for months now, but it's still thrilling. I guess it's something you never get used to. Knowing that somebody took the time to sit down and write a note makes me feel so great. Sometimes girls write to ask me about a hairdo or a problem.

"Most letters, though, come from boys. A few are

awfully fresh! Most of them are nice and friendly. I don't know what to write back when they ask for dates. Some of them sound cute (and some send me snapshots that prove it!), but I live in the Bronx. Makes it kind of hard to date a boy in Kansas, Florida, or California. Oh well, it's the thought that counts.

"Dad says it's a good thing that the show pays for postage!!!"

Last but far from least, resident redhead Donna confesses her secret fear—for herself, her friends, and gals everywhere.

"Dear Diary," she writes, "I've seen it happen, so I know it's true. The worst thing that can happen to a girl is losing her reputation.

"Respect counts, not only with boys but among friends. Some girls are so eager to get attention that they don't care how they go about it. They peg their skirts, wear blouses that are too sheer, and put on cheap jewelry by the ton because they think it's glamorous. I had a friend at school who dressed like that against all advice, and boy! Is she sorry now!

"She'd hoped that a guy on the football team (she had a gigantic crush on him) would notice her and ask for a date. Instead, people began to talk. One boy who wanted to sound tough made up a story... naturally, a few others followed. It wasn't long before these vicious rumors spread all over school.

"I felt bad. My friend was a *nice* girl who'd made a mistake. She kept on making it, too. First, she used her eyebrow pencil to make a fake beauty mark. Then, at Christmas, she sewed bells into the hem of her slip.

"The principal sent her home, and *that* story spread. She finally couldn't take it anymore, and broke down. She told me she wasn't being asked to parties or on dates. She couldn't stand all the gossip. Her plan had backfired. Finally, she asked her Dad to transfer her to a school across town. Guess she'll miss her junior prom and everything!

"This lesson has taught me how important it is to

protect your reputation. And to think twice before spreading rumors that aren't true, no matter how things look."—THE END

Laughing to herself, Sheila Granger studied the pictures that accompanied the text. Just as a TBS publicist had written the story supposedly penned by "Eve Steele," one of the network's photographers had taken the pictures, setting up every shot. The five girls posing in their latest outfits, listening to records and practicing dance steps, sharing a magazine with Lee Dean on the cover, and dressed in pajamas, writing in their diaries, *couldn't* be for real.

She tried to remember exactly how she'd felt at seventeen. Everyone in high school had been involved in politics, and there'd been an anti-war demonstration on Memorial Day. In classes, people had talked about poverty, discrimination, and women's rights, the issues that were affecting the country. Had it really been so different in the 1950's?

Had there ever been a time when all that mattered was having fun? When "boys" and "reputations" were the focus of your whole world... when learning the latest dance steps and being first on your block to learn how to put your hair up in a French twist were the major events of life? Were those the only things that had mattered to the girls in the story she read? And what about the boys?

Had they been equally uncomplicated, interested only in their cars and favorite teams and dating at the drive-in on Friday night?

Was that the way it had really been in the "Fabulous Fifties?" So simple and easy? Was that what the whole nostalgia thing was about—or had it all been a kind of game, a way of forgetting your own problems and the world's?

Sheila Granger knew she had to find the answer.

7.

"GOOD?" KAY DUVANE SAID, AS THEY WALKED down the hall. "She's great, Lee. The best. To tell you the truth. I don't know how I'm going to get along without her. I have a million things... Well, you know what it's like."

Lee Dean nodded, searching the offices and the faces of people they passed in the corridor for a familiar smile. "Everybody's so—young," he said.

She laughed heartily. "They're so young it's scary, Lee. And they know so damn much. They didn't find it out the hard way, by being there when it happened. Many of them majored in television in college, can you believe it?"

He shook his head.

"Now Sheila—we'll meet her in a minute—is an example of the best. She's bright, efficient, and... Jesus, I sound like a press release! But you'll see what I mean. Of course some of them think that a diploma and experience are the same thing, and we both know that isn't so. We're meeting Sheila in the screening room. I thought it would be better there, since we won't be interrupted. So tell me, how does it feel to be back at TBS?"

"Better than it felt when I left," he answered frankly.

Kay recalled the quick, clean break the network had made when it exiled him, and had to look away.

"The important thing is that you're back here now, and we're going to create a fabulous show. I really feel it, Lee. The moment I read your proposal, I *knew* it was right on target."

"I was beginning to get worried, to be honest," he said. "I thought you might not want it."

Kay waved the idea off. "Not at all. It's just that these things take time. Remember the way it was in the old movies with Judy Garland and Mickey Rooney, where somebody says, 'Let's ask Dad for the barn and we'll put on a show!'? Back then it was instant-decision time."

"And now?"

"Now it's numbers. Demographics. Budgets. Projections. Sometimes I feel like an accountant. We make development deals left and right. But take a pilot. Once a pilot is shown, it has to be tested and retested. They don't cast for talent any more. It's all type and 'likability,' pardon the expression.

"They don't just take a test audience's word for it, either. They wire them up and actually measure emotional response to entrances and exits—"

"You're kidding!" Lee said, incredulous.

"The hell I am! They feed the results into a computer, and what comes out determines the lineup. Cross my heart—"

They had reached the screening room, but the sound of raised voices made Kay stop short. She'd never heard Sheila raise her voice before—what could have happened to make her so angry?

"... not my fault, Miss Granger," a man was saying. They must've thrown a lot of them away a long time ago.

The producers of the rock and roll special took a bunch of the kinescopes to use for film clips—"

"We're talking about a couple of two-and-a-half-minute film clips," Sheila cut in. "That leaves fifty-five minutes of an hour show, commercials included. What did they do with the rest of the film? Didn't you get it back?"

"Hey, I'm not a messenger. I guess they cut what they wanted and threw the rest out—"

Kay walked into the room.

"What seems to be the problem?" she demanded.

"Oh... Miss Duvane, it isn't my fault. I pull the file films out. That's my job. The person who signs for them has the responsibility of returning them. It's network policy."

Kay stared at the long-haired young man. "I'm quite familiar with the internal policies of this network, thank you," she said, and turned to Sheila. "What is he talking about?"

Sheila explained, simply and calmly. After waiting a week and a half (instead of the promised few days) for the old shows to be located, she had just been informed that there were a grand total of eleven kinescopes of *Dancetime, USA!* in the TBS film library. That meant only twelve hours, less commercials, of material from the old days from which to choose the clips to be included, interspersed with live material, in the upcoming two-hour special.

Kay whirled on the young man. "Go and check it out. Do it *now*. I don't give a damn what your job is. I want to know where those missing shows are. I want to know if the producer who signed for them still has them or if, as you're suggesting, he threw them out. I'd also like to know how your department can allow such a thing to happen—and I'm sure there are several other executives who will be equally interested. I want a report on my desk by tomorrow noon, and preferably sooner."

"Yes, Miss Duvane," he said, backing out of the room.

"And close the goddamn door!" Kay yelled as he left. "Christ, what stupidity!"

The silence lasted nearly a minute. Then, more composed, Kay went to Lee and led him to Sheila, taking his arm.

"Not exactly the cozy little introduction I planned," she said, "but at least you can see how committed Sheila is to the show. Lee, meet Sheila Granger. Sheila, Lee Dean."

They shook hands, Lee more awkwardly than Sheila, then took their seats. "I'm sorry about the flare-up," Sheila apologized, "but I was counting on that material."

Kay, Sheila realized, was purposely taking a back seat, letting her run with the ball. She'd be working with Lee on a daily basis, and it was important for them to have the right chemistry and relationship.

"Nobody else would have copies, huh?" Lee asked.

"I'm going to check with the coast," she explained. "You never know what will turn up in the library out there, even though they're always calling us for the older things." She saw the opportunity for a transition to a more pleasant subject, and grabbed it. "We did a lot better with the publicity material. Of course they don't have everything, but there's lots of old stuff—candids, magazines, newspaper clippings. Besides using some of the material as visuals, you know, blowing up the shots of the regulars and things, we could have a montage made up. It might be the perfect lead-in for the special. The old theme music over the montage at first, to trigger the memories of the audience. Then a cut to a clip of the old show, then a quick cut to you today in the replica of the old set—and in color."

He didn't react.

"It's just an idea," Sheila apologized, afraid she'd come on too strong.

"And a good one, don't you think, Lee?" Kay asked.

"What? Oh, sure. It sounds very good. I'm sorry, Miss—"

"Sheila," she said. "It's Sheila Granger."

"Sheila. I guess it's just thrown me, the whole thing of being back here."

"I can imagine," she answered.

Lee looked at her, studying her face and trying to decide if she really could imagine what it was like to go from the top to nowhere in one easy motion. Then, twenty years later, try to step back up.

"I'd planned to go through the material and familiarize myself with it," Sheila offered, "but as you heard, we just got the tapes. I've been doing a lot of reading, though—*Dig, Teentime, Beat*."

For the first time, Lee laughed. "My advice to teens, right? And variations on the theme."

Sheila laughed, too, glad to have broken the tension at last. "Not to mention The Regulars' secret romances—and everything else imaginable. The last thing I read last night was excerpts from the girls' diaries."

"Very juicy, I'll bet."

"Oh, *sordid* stuff!" she said. "The dangers of sewing bells in your slip at Christmas, how to talk to boys, very racy going."

Lee laughed again. "You know, it's amazing. Those were the days when everybody was talking about juvenile delinquents, and the kids didn't know half of what they do now. If you were just a little older than they were and spoke to them halfway decent, they were fine. They used to have to wear ties and jackets on the show, and the girls were told to dress the way they would for a school dance. We never had a problem."

"Imagine what it would be like now!" Kay interjected. "The mind boggles."

"What do you think changed?" Sheila asked. "Was it the times or the people?"

Lee considered the question, then pointed to the

wide-screen TV set on a table in front of them.

"It was that," he said. "The box. The tube. The television set. It set standards and examples. It taught everyone to want the same things. It hypnotized people slowly, until they didn't even know it was happening. All of a sudden it was part of the family—the kids' babysitter, the newspaper, the housewife's best friend.

"As for kids... well, it made them grow up at the same speed. Do you know what I mean? They didn't develop at their own rate anymore. They were conditioned to want to be like an image rather than themselves."

The two women looked at each other, surprised at the intensity of Lee's response.

"But wasn't it like that then?" Sheila asked softly. "Television may have been fairly new, but there were movies. They were examples, weren't they?"

"To a degree, I suppose," Lee answered. "But movies were about exceptional things, exceptional people. TV pretended to be about average people. That's what it came down to. When you went to a movie, you didn't get involved on the same level. You knew you weren't John Wayne or Bette Davis. They were literally larger than life.

"With TV, it was different. Maybe because the people were small, the images. I'm not sure. But you got confused. You really identified with the people in shows and commercials. If you didn't use the same soap they did, or the same brand of ketchup, there was something wrong."

Sheila was puzzled. "But you just said that the kids on your show were easy to handle—"

"Sure, because it hadn't happened yet. We were delivering the real thing back then."

"What—what was it really like, Lee?" Sheila asked.

"It's hard to put into words, but I think it was—a feeling." He paused, then pointed at the TV set. "Can you put one of those cassettes on?"

Sheila smiled as she loaded the tape deck and pushed the wide-screen Sony's power button.

Lee Dean grabbed his arm rests as if he were on a plane about to take off, bracing himself for the journey into his past.

"I can't really tell you what it was like, Sheila," he said, as the familiar theme music came up. "But that screen can show you..."

For the next sixty minutes, they watched the screen transfixed.

Frozen in living black and white were the faces of a vanished decade, the idealized images of a time gone by. The boys with their hair carefully greased, either long or crew cut... black pants, white sox, and Cuban-heeled shoes or loafers... The girls in white blouses with Peter Pan collars... chiffon scarves at their necks... circle pins... clips in the shape of poodles securing angora and cashmere sweaters... felt circle skirts... bobbysox and Mary Janes.

They bopped and strolled and slow-danced to the sounds of Tommy Del, Bobby Darin, and Connie Francis... The Drifters, The Fleetwoods, and The Fantastiks... They clapped after every song, turning to Lee Dean, young and confident at the podium, waiting for him to spin the next platter, announce the next guest star, show the crazy card some kids in Des Moines had made and sent in.

They rocked and rolled, showing off just a little bit and smiling, proud and a little self-conscious, when they knew the camera had caught them.

All of them, Lee Dean and The Regulars, so young and so happy that it seemed the beat wouldn't last for an hour—it would go on for the rest of their lives...

Book Two

1.

"I'LL GET THE DOOR, TERESA," BUFFIE Pendleton Bradshaw told the maid. "You check the food—and *do* try to remember not to stack."

"Yes m'am," the maid answered, hurrying back to the relative safety of the kitchen. The bell rang again. Buffie took a quick look in the foyer mirror, then opened the door.

"Darling!" Miriam Sanders gushed.

"Miriam, dear!" Buffie responded.

The two women leaned toward each other, their cheeks almost touching as they made kissing noises. The guest stepped inside, then put her finger to her chin, studying her hostess' jumpsuit.

"My, aren't we smart! Last month's *Bazaar*, isn't it? Calvin Klein?"

"It's this month's *Vogue*, Miriam," Buffie corrected her friend with transparent ease. "And it's Don Kline." *Bitch*, she thought silently. *You just wish you were thin enough to wear it! Who did that tent you're wearing? Omar of the Desert?*

"And that cinnamon polish on your toenails, too! Only you could carry it off, Buff. I always said you had tremendous panache."

"Aren't you divine," Buffie cooed. *I'd just like to hear a tenth of what you say behind my back!*

"What is it, dear?" Miriam asked, as Buffie led her into the living room. It was all oak and fieldstone, with a beamed cathedral ceiling and a solid wall of glass that looked out over the lawn to the Great South Bay. Miriam tossed her bag, then herself, onto the sectional sofa, and Buffie gave silent thanks for the strength of mind that had resisted the decorator's urging for velvet, demanding a sturdier flannel.

"I beg your pardon?"

"You know, dear, your girl... your maid. She didn't quit on you, did she? Oh, Buffie, no! Not another one!"

"Darling, you make it sound like we go through maids like Kleenex. I told you what happened. Dominique got homesick for Haiti and went back. We couldn't hold her prisoner, now could we?"

Miriam sighed. "Who can understand their minds? Homesick for what, I'd like to know."

"Anyway, Teresa is working out just beautifully. Of course it does take time to train them—"

"Isn't it awful? It takes just enough time for them to learn everything before they go off and leave you for a better—I mean another—job. Or to go back to wherever they come from. Be an angel, will you? Run and see if what's-her-name has a little teeny something to nibble on... just to hold me over until lunch. And maybe a tiny little vodka and something to wash it down."

As if you needed another morsel of food, Buffy thought. "Of course, darling. But Miriam, I thought you were doing so well on that new diet. Stillman, isn't it?"

"Atkins. Six pounds already. But I'm entitled to cheat just once in a while, like when I'm visiting my dearest friends?"

"Of course you are, angel," Buffie agreed. *It's your funeral—and your fat.* "Vodka and what was that again?"

"Vodka and vodka will be fine. Over a little ice."

Buffie hurried toward the kitchen. Hadn't she told Teresa to have the stuffed grape leaves on a tray in the living room? If she couldn't get the damn hor d'oeuvres right, how would they ever get through lunch?

The bell rang as she was berating Teresa, who immediately hurried toward the hall.

"Never walk away from me when I'm talking to you!" Buffie barked. "Miriam—Mrs. Sanders—will get it."

She hurried to greet the new guests, just in time to hear the tail end of some comment Miriam was making about "another new girl."

"Janet! And Phyllis! How *are* you, darlings. It seems like ages."

"I was sure we'd see you and Dennis at the club on Saturday, Buff. It was too divine. Stefanie Matheson got smashed!"

"What else is new?" Buffie asked, leading everyone back to the living room. "Actually I'd planned on going, but Dennis got stuck in town at the last minute. Working late on a brief or something."

"Or something," Miriam repeated, softly but pointedly. "Just teasing, darling. I don't know how such dreadful things come out of my mouth!"

Neither do I, Buffie longed to say, as Miriam wolfed down a big bite of grape leaf. *I'm surprised they have enough room.*

"You know that nobody admires Dennis more than I do, dear," Miriam added. "Why, he's come so far—"

She stopped short, Buffie's cold glare clearly indicating that she was again on the verge of going too far. Teresa appeared, and Buffie called for a pitcher of martinis and glasses for Janet, Phyllis and herself.

Twenty minutes and two drinks apiece later, the country club dance had been dissected in detail. They'd moved on to a wide but familiar range of subjects—doctors, hairdressers, children, and general gossip. It was going to be another typical afternoon in Bellport, Buffie told herself—lunch with the girls. But at least she wouldn't have to play hostess for another couple of weeks. She'd be able to go to Miriam's house and drop sticky grape leaves on *her* sofa. God, how would she ever get that oil stain out of the flannel? Maybe talcum powder. She braced herself as the telephone rang four and a half times before Teresa answered it.

"Someone's on the phone, Mrs. Bradshaw," the maid said.

"No!" Buffie gasped. "Actually I assumed as much. When it rings, one usually expects that someone is on the other end, Teresa. Take a message and I'll call back."

"But it's the TV, Mrs.—"

"What?" Buffie asked, confused. Nothing was wrong with any of the sets that she knew about. If Dennis or the girls had called the repairman...

"Some lady from the TV station. That's what she said."

Buffie sighed and excused herself. It was probably some dumb survey, or yet another fund-raising drive for the local PBS station. If it was, she'd tell the fund-raiser that they'd made two donations this year already, and it was not her duty or personal mission to bring culture to Long Island.

Her "hello" was anything but warm, but the caller didn't seem to mind.

"Mrs. Bradley? Mrs. Dennis Bradley?" the voice asked.

"Yes," Buffie answered. "To whom am I speaking?"

"This is Sheila Granger at TBS-TV. I'm so glad I've finally tracked your husband down..."

Buffie felt every nerve and muscle in her body tense. She pulled the library door closed without even glancing in the direction of her friends, and sank into the leather sofa.

It couldn't be! It wasn't possible! Not after all these years!

Yet it was, and the more her caller went on about it, the more upset Buffie became. God, would she ever be able to live it down? Hadn't she suffered enough?

Why did Dennis have to get involved with that terrible show in the first place?

Dancing on some dreadful television program when you were in your last year of high school... *really!* All right, so he'd come from a poor Staten Island family. So what? It wasn't exactly a social plus, but being poor didn't mean you had to make a spectacle of yourself either.

The show had been out of his system when they met at the University of Michigan in his last year, and her first year, of college. She'd never watched the show—there'd been no television at Miss Sheffield's, in Sheffield Farms, Maryland—and when one of the girls in Ann Arbor, well into their romance, told her that Dennis used to be on television, she had refused to believe it. They never even went dancing, she'd pointed out. Dennis was much more the bookish type, intent on making the grades that would get him into a decent law school on a scholarship. Surely the girl was mistaken.

But another classmate told her the exact same thing, and a third party confirmed it. She'd had no choice but to ask Dennis himself. To her stunned surprise, he not only said it was true, but didn't seem the least bit embarrassed.

"You make it sound like being on *Dancetime* was a crime," he said. "And a capital offense at that."

"I don't know what that means, Dennis," she answered, "but we don't know anybody in show business."

Good God! Mummie had already invited him to visit in Darien over the Christmas holidays! And she'd written to Miriam and all her friends about him. Of course he was almost *sinfully* handsome, and he looked marvelous in crew-neck sweaters. He was charming and dependable, too, and just about everything else a man was supposed to be... except rich, of course. *Born* rich.

Show business ran neck and neck with Lack of Social Background. Buffie had tried to drop each bombshell as casually as possible, considering their weight, in her phone calls and letters home to Darien. Mummie didn't waste any time: the second time Buffie even mentioned Dennis' name, there was a question about how "suitable" he was.

Buffie had glossed over Dennis' being a hardship case and concentrated instead on his scholastic achievements and his aspirations. After all, he *had* received a scholarship, and he was going on to law school... Harvard Law, if he could work it out. That was sure to be good for a few points with Daddy, an attorney himself.

Things had been going so well, Buffie told herself. Dennis liked her a lot: she was almost surprised. Of course everyone knew that if you flirted the right way and wore the right outfits, men could be absolutely *devastated*. Still, Dennis wasn't like most of the men on campus. Instead of viewing college as a fun way to kill a few years with the assurance of a draft exemption, he was dead serious about it.

There were a few girls who were definite intellectual types, the kind you were more likely to find in the library bent over a book than in the drawing room of a sorority. When she and Dennis first started dating, Buffie had wondered if those big brains were her competition. There was no way she could hope to make any kind of inroad if there were—she hated studying, loathed every course except Art Appreciation, and planned to stay in school only until she accomplished her unofficial major... Finding a Husband.

Sometimes Dennis lectured her about taking her work more seriously, but she knew he did it half-heartedly. She suspected he actually envied the casual way she treated her courses. Hadn't he called here "a breath of fresh air?"

Everyone said they made a beautiful couple. During class, when she should have been taking notes, Buffie Pendleton let her imagination run free. If she married Dennis, her name would be Buffie Bradshaw. She was pleased with the way it looked when she wrote it down, happy with the double B monogram she designed over and over again.

If she married Dennis . . . they'd have a long engagement of course. Otherwise they'd miss out on all the parties that mattered, and people might get the wrong idea, besides. She wasn't going to find a more attractive man than Dennis, she felt sure. Since he would soon be graduating, that would give her a perfect reason to leave school. She could take courses or something in Boston, or get a little job to keep busy with, but there'd be no more history or philosophy or dreadful required subjects like biology. Daddy could "help" Dennis with school and, when he graduated, take him into Dyer, Callahan, and Pendleton.

It was *too* perfect . . . until she found out about *Dancetime, USA!*.

That revelation had posed a whole new set of problems. How was she going to build Dennis up as a poor but brilliant young man determined to better himself? Mummie and Daddy would go ape if they heard he'd spent his last year of high school dancing on a TV show.

When she spoke of her parents' attitude, Dennis did his best to reassure her.

"Does it really matter, Buffie?" he said. "It was four years ago, after all. The show isn't even on any more."

"Even so," she said, "it's going to haunt our marriage—"

She hadn't meant to say the word: Dennis hadn't brought up marriage, though they talked around it a few times. But everyone knew the man was supposed to bring it up first. Dennis had stared at her, wide-eyed, and she'd had to cry, embarrassed for herself as well as for him. Maybe he wasn't even serious about her—who knew what went on on Staten Island?

"You mean that you—you'd marry me?" he'd asked.

"Of course I would," she'd answered through her tears. "If you wanted me—"

"I do. More than anything. But I was afraid to ask you. I told you how it is. I don't have any money. Even on a full scholarship, I'll have to get some kind of job to squeak by financially—"

"There's always Daddy," she replied, the tears stopping as she shared the plan she'd worked out so many times.

The ring she showed her parents wasn't impressive but it *was* a diamond. And later on, when they were married and Dennis was making money, he could always replace it with something bigger. He had good manners, he wasn't thrown by the fish and salad forks on the table in the big Darien house, definite points in his favor, Buffie thought. She was playing gin rummy with her mother while Daddy took Dennis into his study for an after-dinner brandy and a "talk."

"What do you think?" Buffie asked her mother, discarding a six of clubs because she knew Mummie needed it.

"Just my card!" Betty Pendleton exclaimed, picking it up with delight.

"*Mummie!* I mean about Dennis..."

"At least he isn't one of *them*," she answered. "Did you hear about Pammie Clark? Engaged to someone named *Goldstein*!"

"No!" Buffie replied, genuinely shocked.

"I'm afraid so, dear. Says he'll convert, of course, but still... it's no wonder they went down to Lyman Key for the holidays. Poor Lynne is heartbroken—"

The study door opened, and from the way the two men

emerged, Daddy with his arm around Dennis' shoulder, Buffie had known it was going to be all right.

"A fine young man," Harris Pendleton said, smiling at his wife and daughter. "Dennis here has a real head on his shoulders. Just the kind of fellow we could use at the firm, once he gets through Harvard."

The wedding a year and a half later, had been divine. Of course Dennis' people hadn't fit in with Buffie's people—but it wasn't as though they'd have to see that much of them. True to his word, Dennis didn't mention the *Dancetime* days, and when a few guests who recognized him, or thought they did, brought the subject up, he sloughed the questions off. Just as she'd known he would, Daddy had seen to it that Dennis had more than enough money to ease the financial pressures, and a summer job with the firm at a somewhat inflated salary. They'd searched through Westchester for a suitable first house (she'd done the searching, glad of a reason to skip her classes at B. U., while he concentrated on his work at Harvard Law), and they'd found a place in Rye that was close enough to Darien for frequent visits. At first Dennis was reluctant about letting her father put up the down payment, but Buffie had made him look at the practical side of things. It was just a start, another loan if Dennis insisted.

That was seventeen years ago.

For the most part, the years had been good. Dennis had gone to work for Daddy; after five years he'd been made a partner. They'd not had the boy and girl Buffie wanted, but two daughters, which was close enough. Carrie and Melissa were both attractive. The house in Bellport (Westchester had skidded downhill, with an influx of the Wrong Element: Long Island was the best alternative) was lovely, particularly after the recent redecoration.

The worst jarring note, over the years, the one that had sounded repeatedly, was that damn *Dancetime, USA!*. At first, Dennis had kept to their bargain, never mentioning the program. But then someone at the country club recognized his face as a Regular.

To Buffie's horror, Dennis had admitted it. What's more, he seemed pleased. When they got home, he actually dug out an old scrapbook, one she'd never seen before (and certainly hoped never to see again) filled with photographs and clippings.

Talking about it at home was bad enough. But Carrie had overheard the conversation, then told her friends at school. And that was the end of the secret in Dennis Bradshaw's past. A suitably gruesome climax took place one night when Dennis had one too many at Miriam and Chester's New Year's Eve party.

The band had played some "oldies but goodies," and Dennis, somewhat loose in the joints, had led a series of partners through the bop and the stroll and those other dreadful dances. Buffie was appalled.

Hadn't she been through enough? Buffie thought, her head pounding as the TBS woman went on and on about some "upcoming special." *Haven't I done enough suffering?*

"I hate to interrupt you, Miss—"

"Granger."

"Miss Granger. Do forgive me. But I don't think my husband is interested. He's now a corporate attorney... and well, it was all so long ago... What? No, Dennis hasn't seen or spoken of those people in ages. I'm afraid you'll have to count Dennis out..."

"I *beg* your pardon? Of *course* I intend to tell him! No, there's no need for you to bother him at his office. I'll discuss it with him tonight... Very well, Miss Granger, I'll have him get back to you personally, but I can tell you right now that you shouldn't count on him at all."

Buffie slammed the phone down.

"Go away!" she said, to Teresa's timid knock and tentative "Mrs. Bradshaw?"

She took a cigarette from the onyx box on the library table, lit it, and began to pace.

Damn! She'd have to tell Dennis, or that horrid Granger woman would call him at work. How had she ever tracked him down? And why did they have to do a stupid special about the 1950's?

Well, she would talk to Dennis—no, she'd simply *tell* him not to do it. Granted, they'd had their ups and downs. What couple didn't? And if their marriage wasn't exactly at its highpoint right now, if it had been more weeks than she wanted to count since they'd last made love, that didn't matter, either. They still had a very good social image, and she wasn't about to see it ruined just so he could have one night of auld lang syne—on national television, no less.

She would put her foot down. She would tell him that he owed it to her. She would warn him of the terrible damage such a show could do to his career. Carrie and Melissa would be ostracized and ridiculed. Their friends would laugh at them. Miriam alone would have a field day!

"Buffie? Darling, whatever is the matter?" Miriam called out not bothering to knock but striding into the library. "I don't mean to disturb you, dear, but you *do* have guests. And your girl is in a state. Some crisis in the kitchen..."

"Nothing wrong, Miriam," Buffie heard herself say. "It was—it was just an old friend from out of town. Her husband works at one of the networks, and they're here on business. She—she called me from the office, and I couldn't put her off."

Miriam's raised eyebrows told her that the story was pretty good but not convincing. Still, Buffie was determined to brazen it out.

"Let me see about lunch," she said, putting her cigarette out.

"You had us so worried, dear," Miriam told her,

following her into the kitchen. Looking frightened, Teresa stood in front of the oven, wringing her apron.

"Well, Teresa, what *is* it?"

Teresa didn't answer, but looked sheepishly instead at the closed oven door. Buffie opened it and stared in horror. She whirled on the maid and screamed, "The microwave, you idiot! I told you to put it in the microwave!"

As Miriam glanced at the collapsed salmon soufflé, tears poured down Buffie's cheeks.

"Oh, what a shame—" Miriam began.

"You'll have to excuse me," her hostess wailed. "Please. Tell Janet and Phyllis. I—I must lie down. I have a terrible migraine."

She ran from the kitchen, knowing full well that by noon the next day, *everyone* who mattered would know about her terrible disaster at lunch.

"Isn't Mom going to eat?" Carrie asked.

Dennis explained that Mom was in bed with a migraine. Melissa, thirteen, gave him a strange look before saying, "What—again?"

After dinner, he sent the girls to their rooms to do their homework or watch TV or whatever. Buffie had pitched another full-scale tantrum. He hoped the Valium he made her take would calm her. For the time being, he felt relatively safe in the library. The house was finally quiet.

An outsider looking at his life would probably envy him. It all looked perfect, as classic as a page from one of the magazines that dictated Buffie's taste. *Town and Country, Architectural Digest, Vogue*... It was the kind of life he'd thought he always wanted, the kind of life he'd worked for. But there were times now when he felt it wasn't his life at all, but a setup, a magazine layout he'd wandered into.

If he hadn't had to work so hard at school, it might all have been different. But with his father on a veteran's pension, crippled since Anzio, and his mother caring for him, there had never been enough money. The scholarship to the University of Michigan had been a godsend, like the show—an escape from Staten Island, and the first step toward the future he envisioned.

Buffie had been a welcome change in his life. Like a strange specimen in zoology class, he observed and studied her. Her habits and interests and natural environment—the world of coming-out parties, charity luncheons, and the Right Thing to Do—was so different from his own. And strangely tempting, too.

The last thing he'd planned to do was marry her—or anyone. That would come later, when he'd established himself and could afford a wife. Then, before he knew what had hit him, they were engaged. To this day he couldn't remember exactly how it had happened.

But suddenly he was meeting the Pendletons for the first time. He remembered the house in Darien, and the snow-covered grounds—clean, white snow, the way snow was supposed to be. Not the gray slush that passed for snow on Staten Island. He remembered the polished fruitwood of the dining table, the heavy silver, the course after course silently served and cleared by the Pendletons' staff. He'd had to glance at Buffie to know which fork to use.

Dennis knew exactly what was at stake.

First, the old man had grilled him about his goals. "I'm a Yale man myself," he'd said, when Dennis told him about going to Harvard the following year. Buffie was a highstrung girl, her father said. She took after her mother. Naturally both he and Mrs. Pendleton would feel better if Buffie's future was "settled," and Dennis was certainly a bright young man with a future. As an attorney and partner in a conservative corporate firm with a client list that read like the *Fortune* Five Hundred's top twenty (Dennis had checked it out thoroughly), he was in a position to help. There could be a place for Dennis in the

143

law firm, and a partnership in time... if he loved Buffie, that is, and wanted to marry her...

"I love your daughter very much, Mr. Pendleton," Dennis heard himself say. "And I'd like to marry her with your permission."

Studying had kept Dennis so busy that there'd been little time to question the plans that were set in motion. If he sometimes had doubts in his room (he couldn't study at Buffie's because she was always interrupting him; and besides, she was determined to wait until her wedding night before "going all the way"), he forced them out of his mind.

Buffie, he found, was shallow and boring if taken in long doses. It wasn't just that she couldn't talk about anything except clothes and gossip and the Right Thing to Do; she couldn't even listen. In spite of himself, Dennis found himself remembering Sandy, recalling the way she'd hung on his every word, sharing his dreams as if they were hers. Sandy had been willing to work at two jobs to help him through school, willing to give herself to him fully, her body as well as her heart, and to trust him completely...

After the *Dancetime* shows, when he walked Sandy home they would plan. The distance between Ann Arbor and Manhattan didn't matter at all, he explained. They'd write every day. He'd come home whenever he could, and she could go to Ann Arbor for weekends.

She was so eager to please him, so anxious for his approval. He found himself wanting to touch her all the time. In the studio, on the dance floor, he'd turn his head to find Sandy beside him. She'd be in Bobby's arms, but Dennis would maneuver his partner so that their bodies touched. The softness of her skin, the clean smell of her hair, aroused him automatically.

When they were watching a movie or having a Coke, he had to struggle against the urge to simply reach over and cup her breast, needing the warmth and firmness of her always. It was only sex, Dennis tried to tell himself, the same kind of sex his friends talked about when they compared notes (and boasts) on who did and who didn't go all the way. In his heart, though, he knew that this wasn't the same at all.

His friends looked at sex as a sport: once a partner gave in, they moved on to new conquests. For him, though, there was nobody but Sandy. Twice, worried that he was feeling something different from the guys he knew, something perhaps not normal, he'd forced himself to take girls who "did it" out. He'd done it with them, but he hadn't seen their faces or bodies at all. Closing his eyes, he'd conjured up Sandy's image—the trusting brown eyes, the brown hair with its blonde streak.

From their first time with one another—her first time with any man—their lovemaking had been addictive. The more they made love, the more they wanted each other.

He'd felt older with Sandy. That last summer before college, they had mapped each other's bodies and charted each other's responses. She had learned to slowly rotate her hips beneath him, extending first one thigh and then the other so that he could feel the muscles taut beneath his legs. He sensed the exact moment when she wanted to feel not only his lips on her nipples, but the teasing play of his teeth as well.

"Nice" girls let sex be done to them. In the beginning, his conditioning had made him feel guilty for "spoiling" a nice girl. But Dennis had come to realize that her need matched his own. If he had led her to the portals of ruin, she had stepped—no, *run*—through them gladly, a willing partner...

When that last summer ended, Sandy had cried at the train and held him.

"You'll forget me," she sobbed. "You'll meet another girl—"

"No, I won't," he promised. "It's going to be like we said."

But it wasn't.

In college, he had to work and study more than ever before. More and more of her letters went unanswered. Sandy had an after-school job working as an assistant bookkeeper in an insurance company. Ann Arbor weekends were out of the question. The picture of her he carried in his mind, the image of her he saw in the dreams that made him change his sheets, embarrassed, afraid someone would see, wasn't that of a girl like the girls on campus, but a woman. No older in years, perhaps, than the girls who wore pearls over their cashmere sweaters and who carried their books clasped to their breasts, but older in a way that had nothing to do with age at all. Her body, he came to think, was a secret he had learned too soon. Even if he had the money, even if transportation wasn't a problem, she wouldn't fit in at Ann Arbor.

Several times they talked on the phone, or tried to. The conversations were frustrating. Sandy would press him for details of his life at school, about fraternities and term papers and coeds, and he was surprised to find himself short-tempered when he had to explain what everyone else in the world seemed to know. Her stories of co-workers bored him. Inevitably, he'd apologize for not having written and urge a quick hang-up before she went broke. Sandy would answer that it didn't matter; she'd rather talk to him that eat. Her sincerity was as hard to deal with as his desire. It was as if he had to deny her and his need of her in order to be able to live without her.

The more she tried to remind him of her presence and her devotion, the more he resented her efforts. Sometimes when he opened one of the familiar pink envelopes, a few dollar bills would fall out, or a five with a note stapled to it telling him to "buy a new shirt." She knew he had no money—they'd discussed it for months. But instead of being gratified, he saw the crumpled bills as a painful reminder of his situation, a way of staking her claim on him. He came to hate the scent of the perfume she dabbed on her stationery, and the way she dotted her "i's" with circles. Finally, he stopped reading the letters.

When, early in November, Sandy had called him, frantic and crying, he'd had to struggle to control his own annoyance as he calmed her. She was in a phone booth at Grand Central: she'd come from a doctor's office. She had missed two months. He had to come home, she implored him. He had to help her...

I won't get away from her after all, he thought. Ideas rushed through his mind. Perhaps they could marry and get an apartment off-campus—but a baby? A wife? More responsibilities?

He could do the "right thing:" marry her, give up school, and get a job—doing what? At minimum wage with no future? Forget becoming a lawyer?

Knowing that he wouldn't, he promised to see her that weekend and to call her before.

Thursday night, after four beers, he dialed her number. "We'll have to get rid of it," he said, loathing the coldness he forced into his voice.

"Oh God, no..." He had to make himself stop her before the sadness in her cry broke his heart.

"I have to go, now, Sandy. I'll get the money, Sandy. I don't know where, but I'll get it. You have friends. Call someone. Ask around. Find a doctor or... or somebody else who does it. Find out how much it's gonna cost..."

Every time the phone rang in the dorm, he expected to hear his name called. Every day he searched for the familiar pink envelope in his mail. No call or letter came, and Dennis forced himself not to write or call her, the effort growing less as the days, then the weeks, passed by. The student employment office found him a job repainting classrooms over Thanksgiving. Dennis was grateful for any excuse that would keep him from having to go home.

When he finally went at Christmas, his family had heard nothing from Sandy. Christmas Eve, he took the ferry from Staten Island to Manhattan, then a subway crowded with holiday shoppers. The wind was whipping around corners as he walked from the train up her block, stopping to buy a box of candy, a Whitman's Sampler, at a drug store. Her building was filled with the smells of holiday cooking.

Sandy's mother finally answered his knocking. There was liquor on her breath, and he felt embarrassed by the stains on her housecoat as she held on to the door for balance.

"Well, if it isn't Sandy's little boyfriend!" she said.

"Is—is she here?" he asked, wondering what he would say—*could* say—to her.

The woman laughed. "Aren't you a little late? Sandy's in Texas."

"Texas?"

"With *Bobby*," she answered as if he were a child. "They got married. Didn't she let you know...?"

Dennis felt age shoot through him like a pain as he turned away, an older age than he'd ever imagined.

Back in Ann Arbor, studying was a way of losing himself, of not thinking of Sandy. When he eventually met Buffie, he decided that loving her or not loving wasn't really the point. She could help him get what he wanted. There would be freedom, luxury even. There'd be steady, sure advancement. Safety.

The society pages announced the marriage of Mr. and Mrs. Dennis Bradshaw. The bridegroom would join the well-known firm of Dyer, Callahan, and Pendleton, after the couple returned from two weeks in Bermuda. They'd be "at home" in Rye...

But Dennis hadn't been at home there, or in the office, or in his own life, which wasn't his any longer, but something Buffie had constructed with the same detail she brought to arranging flowers or seating plans for dinner parties. Her friends and his co-workers were cordial to him, friendly and accepting. But the places they'd been, the people they knew, the lives they'd lived were different from his. Like an actor playing the same role night after night onstage, he'd grown comfortable with his part. But always, under the surface, there were constant reminders that he'd married the boss' daughter and was, professionally and socially, in on a pass.

The right friends, the right parties, the right time to have children and the right time to move to Bellport—Buffie's sense of what was proper and suitable was so imperative that he'd always gone along. There were rewards, to be sure. He realized that he was a hell of a lot further along in his career than he'd have been without Buffie or her father. His wife certainly blended well with the wives of his clients and associates at business dinners. They spoke the same language. His future was set and secure, and for the life of him Dennis couldn't understand why Buffie's insistence that he never let anyone know he'd been a Regular on *Dancetime, USA!*, that he block out those few marvelous years of his life, seemed like such an exorbitant price to pay.

Her attitude was ridiculous, of course. He seriously doubted that their friends gave a damn, and he often didn't care if they did. Still, maybe his own thinking was as out of line as hers.

One thing he knew; he had been happy with Sandy. Hard as he tried, he couldn't stop himself from thinking about her. Sometimes, he thought, it grew worse over the years. He wasn't a young man anymore. Shaving, he'd look at his reflection, seeing the gray in his hair and the lines. Holding the razor in midair, he'd watch as Sandy's face appeared beside his, her hair falling against his shoulder. For an instant, the time of a memory, his own face would change. Instead of seeing a thirty-eight-year-old man, he'd see himself as he saw her, twenty years younger.

What had she done, he wondered? Did she have the baby? Did she get rid of it? Did she hate him? Love him?

Ever think about him at all? How could they have been so much in love and yet wound up with other people?

At the office, in the middle of preparing a brief, he'd think of Sandy—so young, so innocent, so sweet and loving. In bed with Buffie it was the same. Even years before, when they'd made love regularly, there had been times when it was all he could do to keep from calling out her name as he climaxed inside Buffie. Then, later, there were the dreams, wonderful dreams in which he wasn't trapped and confined in a life he had thought he wanted until it was his—

"Daddy?"

Dennis walked to the heavy oak door and opened it.

Melissa threw her arms around him as he bent down to kiss her.

"What's wrong, honey?" he asked, looking at his watch. "It's after eleven—can't you sleep? Don't you feel good?"

"I'm okay, but I think I heard Mom crying. Carrie's door was closed and her light was off..."

"I was just going upstairs, honey," he said. "Don't worry, it's just your mother's headache. We'll go up together and I'll tuck you in, okay?"

"Okay," she answered, her face breaking into a smile.

"Want to walk or want to ride?" Dennis asked, bending down.

"Daddy, thirteen is too old for that! But if you promise not to tell Carrie—"

"I promise," he swore.

Dennis carried her upstairs, kissed his daughter goodnight and closed her bedroom door, then went to the master bedroom. As he suspected, Buffie wasn't sleeping. The lights were off, but she was unmistakably awake and crying softly.

"Promise me," she demanded, as he walked through the bedroom, toward his twin dressing room and the lavish bath with its oversize sunken tub. He filled one

Bacarat tumbler with ice and Perrier from the small refrigerator next to the sink, and poured four fingers of Scotch into another. Without a word, he brought the Perrier to his wife's side of the bed with a tranquilizer.

"Swear to me that you won't have anything to do with that program," she said, swallowing the pill and a sip of mineral water. "Think of the girls!"

"The girls are fine. They're normal, healthy kids—all things considered."

"Think of me! And what about Mummie and Daddy? You owe Daddy a great deal—"

"I've paid your father back every cent I borrowed from him, and I've paid the added interest of your constant reminders. What more do you want?"

"They would die—" she began.

"I don't think so. Retirement and Palm Beach seem to agree with them. As a matter of fact, your father's in better shape than I am."

"Dennis, please! Promise me!" she begged as he undressed.

He drained his Scotch and got into bed.

"Buff, I'm tired. I had a hell of a day today, and I have to be in court at nine in the morning. So please, let's not talk about it more. Some other time, okay?"

2.

"ALMOST, BUT NOT QUITE. SEE, WITH DISCO, the whole thing is you have to keep the beat going. It's one-two, turn-two, three—then you start the turn. Let's try it again."

The husband stepped back, watching with the other four couples as Bobby O'Brian led his wife through a few of the steps they'd already mastered, then into the new one again. It still didn't work.

"I just can't seem to get it," the woman said, as Bobby's wife quietly moved through the studio toward the office. There was a folder in her hand, and she was still wearing the light blue leotards she'd put on for her Dance Yourself Thin class.

"Sandy, come here a sec, will you?" Bobby asked.

Sandy put on her best professional smile as she joined the group. Bobby's arm went around her waist almost automatically. "We're having a little problem. Want to help me out?"

"Sure," she said, putting the folder down on the floor.

She didn't know what step Bobby was trying to demonstrate, but it didn't matter. They'd been dancing together so long that she could follow him without even thinking.

He counted out loud as he walked her through the step once slowly, then again more quickly. "Now to the beat," Bobby said. His assistant had stopped the tape, and started it again. Bobby waited for a moment—as he told his students what to do when they danced—until he caught the rhythm of the music. The rhythm was as familiar to him as his own name, but it was important to set an example.

Sandy followed him expertly through the basic steps of the Hustle, grateful that it had caught on. Business had boomed with the popularity of disco dancing. Everyone in Houston—from the singles who went to Elan and the other clubs, to the older couples in posh River Oaks who gave the parties the papers wrote up—wanted to learn the new steps. The *Chronicle* had given the studio a big writeup, and she and Bobby had appeared frequently on the local talk shows, demonstrating the latest steps much as they'd done years before in front of the TBS cameras when they'd both been Regulars...

Before she realized what was happening, Sandy felt her foot catch on Bobby's leg. Suddenly she wasn't dancing with him, but looking up at him from the floor where she'd fallen. Flashing a quick smile at Bobby to let him know she wasn't hurt, noticing the relief in his face as he reached down to help her to her feet, Sandy smiled at the students.

"*That* step is easy," she said, so they'd know it was all right to laugh. "I do it all the time."

"Want to try it again?" he asked.

"Well, I don't want them to think that's the way we *really* dance," she said. It was familiar, practiced banter.

They went through it again, Sandy giving it her full attention this time, and did it perfectly, once to the left and again to the right. There was polite applause.

"Just remember, if your mind wanders, that your feet are sure to follow," Sandy told the four couples. She picked up her folder. "I'm gonna get while the getting is good!"

"That's the way," she heard Bobby saying, as she entered the office. "Good, that's very good—"

Sandy closed the door, leaning her face against the cool glass, savoring the soundproof darkness for a moment before she sighed and turned on the light.

Tripping in front of the students was no big thing; she'd done it before, and she'd do it again, like everyone else. But things had gone wrong all day long, ever since the phone call from New York.

Normally, she wouldn't even have been home on a Wednesday morning. But Bobby's car was in the shop, and she'd let him take her Impala, arranging with him to pick her up during lunch and take her to the studio. When the phone rang at 10:30, she assumed it was her husband, who'd gone in early to work on the new sound system they were putting in. All their friends knew that she usually spent Wednesday mornings as a volunteer at the Ben Taub Hospital, working with the therapists and patients. She had already called in and explained the situation.

Instead of the salesman or wrong number she expected, it had been Sheila Granger calling from TBS. She had outlined the upcoming Lee Dean special, including the plans to reunite The Regulars. Sandy had listened, excited and afraid, elated and depressed. She and Bobby would be the hit of the show, Sheila promised Sandy. Maybe they'd work out a disco number.

It had taken all the control Sandy had, and some she didn't realize she possessed, to ask the question in her mind.

"Are the others definitely coming?" she heard herself say, trying to disguise the quiver in her voice.

"I'm not sure as yet," Sheila answered. "You're a

difficult bunch to track down, and you're only my second call."

"Who was first? Connie?"

"Connie Donati?"

"It's Connie Schmidt now. She lives in Queens. I got a Christmas card from her a year or two ago. I'm terrible about writing, but I might have her address someplace if you need it—"

"Let me see what I can come up with," Sheila offered. "You wouldn't remember her husband's first name by any chance, would you?"

Sandy tried to think. "It's Charles—no, Carl. Carl Schmidt."

"Great—thanks a lot. I'll call her next. I spoke with Dennis yesterday," Sheila told her.

"Dennis," Sandy whispered.

"His wife, actually. Do you know her?"

"No. No, I don't."

"Well, he's going to get back to me. I'm going to try to get everybody. We'd love to have you and Bobby. Can we count on you?"

"I'll have to check with him, but I'm sure he'll be interested."

She'd taken Sheila's number and promised to be in touch.

She managed to get through the tasks of the morning. Making up the bed, doing the laundry, taking a chicken casserole out of the freezer to defrost for dinner—she'd done everything by rote, not even thinking. The call had unlocked a carefully protected part of Sandy's memory, like a secret key. Once the lock was turned, waves of emotion swept over her.

So real and sharp—it had been twenty years ago, but time had dimmed nothing. Sandy could remember hurrying home from school on the Friday afternoon the network announced the final decision. From the corner of First Avenue, she'd run down 68th Street toward York, stopping breathless in front of her apartment building, almost afraid to go in. There were just the two of them, Mom and herself, and Mom would be still at her job, saleswoman at Best's—a department store.

With trembling hands, Sandy looked in the mailbox—and there it was. The stationery was formal and heavy: the note short and to the point.

> *Dear Miss Atkins,*
> *The Trans-American Broadcasting System is pleased to inform you that you have been selected as one of the regular dancers to appear daily on the forthcoming Dancetime, USA!.*
> *Please accept our sincere congratulations.*
> *Kindly have your parents sign the enclosed consent form, and please contact me as soon as possible...*

It was a cold, snowy day. Sandy had run down the street, waving the letter like a triumphant banner. "I made it! Pam, I made it! Eddie, I'm gonna be on a TV show! Hey, Mr. Grabowski, I'm gonna be on television!" Friends, neighbors, and acquaintances told her that was nice, very nice, indeed.

She knew that her mother would be thrilled, but Celia Atkins took the news without emotion when she got home.

"What's wrong, Mom? Aren't you happy for me?"

"If it's what you want, Sandy," her mother answered with a sigh. "I know what it's like to want to grow up as fast as you can." She made the familiar trek to the kitchen for a first shot of vodka, then another. "I was once in a hurry, too. And look what it got me. A man who ran off and left me with a baby. A child to raise all by myself as both mother and father..."

Sandy had heard it all so many times that she'd learned how to tune it out. Her mother had always been bitter about the father who'd left before Sandy was old enough to remember him. But this time, Sandy felt she had to answer.

"I'm not in a hurry to grow up. I'm sixteen, Mom. I'm not a little kid. And I made it. I won! All those other kids, and I won!"

Her mother slowly shook her head. For a moment, Sandy was afraid she wouldn't give her permission.

"You'll see, Sandy," she said. "Oh, it looks like fun now. Dancing and boys and good times. But mark my words, they'll break your heart. They'll use you. They'll give you their sweet talk and sweep you right off your feet so they can get what they want. Then they'll use you and leave you—"

"Mom, it's just a TV show, that's all," Sandy protested, but the joy of her achievement was dampened.

Still, her mother had signed the paper, and she'd called the network on Monday. Her picture had been in the papers, along with the other kids who'd been selected.

When she reported to TBS, they were all there. The ten of them had gone into a room that looked like a miniature movie theater, and a man and a woman had talked to them. They'd been told that magazines and newspapers would be writing about them, and that the network publicity people would handle all the arrangements. They would be photographed, separately and together, both for magazines and glossies to send to viewers who wrote in. The network would screen all mail.

Dancetime USA! was going to be live and spontaneous, but they'd have a number of practice sessions in the studio in order to get familiar with the cameras. They would also be paired off with each other—The Regulars would have regular partners, which would make it easier for everybody and more exciting and romantic for the people watching at home.

Sandy had floated through those first weeks. The TV

studio was exciting. She'd only been in one before, when a bunch of kids from school had gone to see *Beat the Clock*. But it was so much more thrilling to be in front of the cameras. The other kids were friendly—the competition was over, and they were all winners.

The day that partners were paired, Sandy found herself hoping that she'd be dancing with the tall, handsome boy with the broad shoulders and brown hair. But she was teamed instead with Bobby O'Brien, a cute, pug-nosed boy from the Bronx. They made a better couple, Sandy realized, because they were better suited to each other in height. Bobby, it turned out, was a terrific dancer, and she told herself she was lucky.

But time after time, first in the practice sessions and later, doing the show itself, she found herself looking over Bobby's shoulder when they did a slow dance, her eyes fixed on the tall boy she'd noticed that very first day. Lorraine was his partner, but he began to return her looks, smiling in a way that made her blush.

"Are you busy Friday night?" he asked her one day out of the blue. It was a Tuesday, and the show was over.

"I—I don't think so," she'd heard herself answer.

"I'd ask you to dance," he said, "but maybe we'll be danced out by then. Want to go to a movie?"

"Sure."

All week long she'd been nervous, going through her closet and trying on and rejecting almost everything she owned. Her mother was pleased with the attention Sandy's being on the show had brought her from her friends at the store, and she'd actually cut down her drinking and the diatribes against the husband who'd deserted her.

But Friday night was a nightmare.

"Please don't, Mom," Sandy had begged, unable to keep her mother from refilling the glass in her hand, watching the clock and now dreading the moment Dennis would arrive.

"Not a one of them!" Celia Atkins told her daughter and herself. "There's none of 'em any good. They all want one thing, then they're gone. They take the best years of your life and use 'em up. There oughta be a law..."

"Please, don't drink any more," Sandy pleaded. "Dennis will be here any minute, Mom—"

"So what? They're all the same. The whole stinkin' lot of 'em—"

"He's—he's a nice boy," Sandy said, determined not to cry. "Don't ruin it for me, Mom."

"Me? I'm not gonna ruin you. He is! That's what they all want to do... Hey, where are you going?"

Sandy ran out the door and downstairs. Waiting for Dennis on the stoop, in the January cold, she asked herself, *Why?*

Why had her father left home? Was it because her mother was always whining and complaining, or did that start after he left? Why did Mom have to hit the bottle so hard when she finally had a date with a boy, *the* boy, who was more handsome than anyone she'd ever seen? Why did she feel so nervous just thinking about him? Why was he ten minutes late already, and why was she starting to cry, and why...

"Sandy?" She looked up, saw Dennis, and felt her color rise. "What are you doing out here? You'll freeze."

"I—I like the cold," she answered, smiling.

"Are you okay? Is something wrong?"

She knew he'd noticed her eyes, and she laughed it off. "It's just the wind. What are we going to see?"

"There's a new picture at the Roxy—"

"Oh, and the stage show, too. That sounds good."

He put his arm around her as they walked to the subway. His touch, even through her coat, excited her. In the theater, she couldn't concentrate on the story. She was too busy memorizing the feel of his arm, half on the back of her seat and half, casually, around her shoulder. She'd always loved stage shows (the Roxy and Radio City

Music Hall were her two favorite theaters), but that night she'd been eager for it to end, anxious to concentrate on him, to look at him instead of the performers.

They walked around Times Square for a while, and as often as she'd been there before it was like the first time. The man in the Camel cigarette sign seemed to be blowing bigger smoke rings. The flashing lights looked brighter; the city itself more exciting. Finally, they went into a coffee shop. Dennis ordered a cheeseburger, French fries, and a vanilla shake. Sandy had to force herself to sip the Coke and nibble at the grilled cheese sandwich he'd insisted she have.

She couldn't tell him that she was hungry in a way she'd never known before, or that she didn't fully understand the nature of her new hunger.

Dennis was seventeen and a half, but he acted so much older than that, so much more mature than any of the boys she'd known or dated. Most of the others were awkward around girls—everybody knew that boys developed slower. But Dennis was different, so sure of himself and so serious. So full of plans as he talked about college, then going on to to study law. She found herself caught up in his dreams, caught up in his hazel eyes.

It had been her idea to walk home, because she hadn't wanted the night to end. When it did, when he took her to her door and, without asking, turned her toward him and kissed her lips, her hands gripped the shoulders of his coat.

"I've probably bored you to death, talking about myself all night," he apologized.

"Oh no, not at all," she answered, wanting to tell him that she could spend the rest of her life just listening to his voice.

Her mother was passed out on the couch. Sandy covered her with an afghan, grateful to have the bedroom they shared to herself. Instead of sleeping, she lay awake for hours, trying to sort out her emotions. What else could it be but love? When she closed her eyes, all she could see was Dennis. She remembered every word he had said, reliving the past few hours. It was just like the songs all promised, and it had finally happened to her.

She was in love.

If Sandy had any doubts, they disappeared over the next few weeks. She and Dennis saw more and more of each other, talking before and after the show, walking through Central Park before he caught the train that took him to the ferry to Staten Island. On camera, dancing with Bobby, she felt as if she had a secret, a precious secret she was keeping from all the kids watching at home and even from the other Regulars.

The magazines continued to write about them, and since she and Bobby made a cute couple and picked up new steps faster than anyone else, it was only natural for the writers and the fans to think that they were going together off camera. "Let them think so... It's good publicity for the show and for you," the TBS people told her. Obediently, Sandy posed with Bobby, practicing their dancing for photographs, watching the Shirelles make a record on a photographed date. They were a popular couple at dances around the city, too, appearing with Lee Dean to promote the show. They'd do a spotlight dance together and sign autographs, each of them writing "Bobby and Sandy" as though it was a single name they both shared.

All the time, it was Dennis she wanted to be with. The funny thing was that Bobby had acted as if the story of their "romance" wasn't something that was made up, but something real between them. He asked her for dates, called her, and invited her home to meet his parents and brothers and sisters in Brooklyn.

She wanted to tell him the truth he was unable to see for himself—Dennis was the one she loved, the only one she'd ever love. How to say it was the problem. After all, they danced together every day on the show. They had to get along together, and she didn't want to hurt his feelings. Eventually she decided to continue to see him, since it served the purpose of protecting his feelings and because that way, her mother couldn't complain about her getting "too serious" with one boy. Besides, maybe Dennis would get jealous.

Bobby never spoke about his rival. On the set, he and Dennis were friendly. Sandy found herself liking Bobby as a friend, a brother almost, and friends were something she needed. Her old crowd at school had started to treat her differently after she was picked for *Dancetime, USA!*. Maybe it was because she couldn't hang around after school anymore, but hurried down to the studio every day. Or because her name and picture, along with those of the other kids and Lee Dean, were in the magazines they'd once all read together. Whatever the reason, she'd grown apart from the old crowd, and Bobby was a replacement for the friendships she missed.

Then there was Connie, the most popular of The Regulars. She was the kind of girl who managed to have time for everyone, always ready to listen to a problem or crack a joke. Sandy had liked her from the start, and one day, when they were alone in the dressing room the girls shared, Connie asked her how things were going.

"Which things?" Sandy answered.

"Boy things," Connie said. "You're pretty busy between Bobby and Dennis."

"Oh, *that's* what you mean," Sandy said, smiling as she brushed her hair. The peroxide streak just to the right of her natural part had begun as a mistake—she'd been trying to get a "highlight" one of the magazines had described, but Dennis had called and she'd completely forgotten about the bleach. Oddly enough, hundreds of kids had written about the streak, TBS told her, and *Dig* magazine said she'd started a whole new fad.

"Who has the inside track?" Connie asked.

"Dennis," she answered without hesitation. "I like

Bobby. I like him a whole lot. And his family, too. Did you know that his parents are great dancers? They won third place in the Harvest Moon contest at Roseland a few years back. They have all kind of trophies."

"That must be where Bobby gets it. You two dance great together."

"Thanks," she said, pleased. "We have a lot of fun together, too. But it's different from the way it is with Dennis. It's like—like..."

"Like what, Sandy?"

"I don't know, really. I can't figure it out."

Then, without planning to, she'd told Connie everything: how she felt about Dennis and how sure she was that she loved him, how much she liked Bobby as a person and didn't want to hurt his feelings, how puzzled she was that he didn't seem to notice or be jealous of Dennis.

"It's a real problem," she said.

"Sounds like you have the best of both worlds, Sandy," the other girl suggested.

"Huh?"

"Well, you're crazy about Dennis, and he feels the same. There's no problem there. And Bobby would have to be blind not to know it. So, either he's made up his mind to wait around until Dennis is out of the picture, or else he's glad just to be friends with you. What have you got to worry about?"

Sandy laughed. "Nothing, I guess. Not the way you put it."

And for a time, she hadn't worried at all.

It was as if fate had silently but certainly conspired with her. The viewers thought she and Bobby were a couple—and so did the kids at school who read the fan magazines. Her mother believed that she was dating both Dennis and Bobby. Connie and the other girls on the show thought it was "romantic."

She and Dennis were the only ones who knew that it was more, so *much* more.

The boys she'd dated before him (she'd always been considered cute and a good dancer; popularity had never been a problem) hadn't known the first thing about how girls felt, much less about how to make a girl feel good. On dates and at parties, they fumbled awkwardly, pretending not to be doing a thing as they grabbed your hand in their sweaty palms. Their kisses were sloppy—too wet or too quick as they closed their eyes, and often as not off-center as well.

Sometimes the more adventuresome and daring of them tried to go further, grabbing a quick feel of your bra. A hand at their sides could—without warning—slide to a knee and up over a thigh. Dancing, they'd hold you a little too tight, then tighter still as they pressed themselves against you.

When the boys weren't around, Sandy and her friends had giggled at their gawkiness and uncertainty. Boys, they agreed, liked to talk as if they knew it all. The funny thing was that few, if any, of them saw sex as anything but a game girls went along with in return for a movie ticket or being escorted to a dance.

There were some girls who went farther, of course— presumably with boys who did the same. They were in a clique of their own at school, and wore sheer, tight blouses and pegged skirts. They were the "bad" girls, the ones who wore ballerina slippers to class and who spit on their black eyebrow pencils, then painted beauty marks on their cheeks. For dances, they wore strapless gowns in harsh colors (where were their mothers!) instead of soft pastels over crinolin.

And they'd all done *it*—everyone knew. They dated seniors or boys from other schools, and sometimes older men who looked like hoods. They kept to themselves.

Occasionally one of Sandy's friends would confide that she had let a boy touch her "down there," or that she'd taken her bra off and let him feel her breasts. It was dangerous, they said, because it could lead to Other

Things—which led, in turn, to the Moment When You Can't Hold Back. Still, if you had a steady and he promised he wouldn't lose his respect for you, it was permissible so long as you were on guard against going Too Far.

Sandy herself had gone *steadily*, but never steady. Though she dated Bobby while seeing Dennis, Sandy knew that she loved one man in a way that defied labels or description. And while she'd never confided it to anyone, neither Connie nor her friends at school, she'd let Dennis make love to her less than a month after they started seeing each other. It didn't seem like "going all the way," as the girls she knew spoke of it. Like them, she had planned to save herself for her husband, and when they whispered and giggled at slumber parties about what a bride had to go through, she made faces and laughed with the rest of them.

When it happened, however, it was different from anything she'd heard or thought. It was a Saturday afternoon, and they were going bowling. She'd been ready when he came to pick her up, happy to ask him into the apartment since her mother was at the store.

"You look beautiful," he told her, as she opened the door.

"Oh, you!" she said, knowing that her pink pedal-pushers and her white cotton blouse showed her figure off to the best advantage. "You're always teasing me!"

"I'm not teasing," he insisted, reaching out to touch her cheek as though she were a statue. "You're the most beautiful girl I've ever seen in my life."

She didn't know why her eyes filled with tears. Reaching behind him, Dennis closed the door. He held her face in both hands, kissed first her tears, then her lips. Instead of merely enduring his embrace, she felt herself responding to it and knew that she wouldn't be able to stop herself, even if she tried. But she didn't even want to try. Instead, she wanted to open herself to him—her arms and her mouth and the rest of her. Her neck and her lips twisted and turned to meet his movements; her arms drew him closer and tighter.

If he was aware of the beads of perspiration at the back of her neck, he didn't show it. He led her through the room, their mouths locked together and the taste of his tongue filling her, as if he'd been there a hundred times before. As he knelt with one knee on the sofa, Sandy let herself go weightless. She felt as if she was floating down to the pillow of his arms.

Then he was gently lowering himself on top of her, his body slowly rocking back and forth, like music. He didn't ask, but slowly undid the buttons of her blouse. The skin beneath her breasts felt flushed and tingly.

"I love you," he whispered, reaching beneath her to unhook her bra. "It's all right."

She nodded silent agreement, trying hard not to shiver.

Even when, alone in bed, she had caressed her breasts, lightly pinching her nipples and imagining that her hand was a man or a baby, they'd never felt the way they did when he kissed them. His tongue was light at first, then his mouth was hungry and demanding. She arched her back to meet his desire with her own, and heard herself saying his name, over and over again.

Instinct and embarrassment (she felt wet: she hadn't been prepared to) made her force her legs closed when he unfastened the button and zipper at the side of her slacks. "It's okay. It's you and me," he said, as he slid her panties down. The tentative touch of his finger was like a shock. She began to whimper as he probed deeper, faster.

Dennis' left hand went to his own buckle and zipper. She'd never seen a man before, except in a dark photograph a schoolmate had found in her brother's room and brought for them all to giggle at. The smooth softness of Dennis, so soft and so hard at once, was a strange yet wonderful mystery as he guided her hand.

As much as she wanted him, she knew that the moment

to come would change her forever. She began to tremble.

"With me," he said, stroking her and parting her thighs. "You know you want it with me..."

He was right. And it didn't hurt at all, the way everyone said it did. After the initial shock of something—someone, Dennis, *her Dennis!*—inside her, it felt good. Never before had she known so surely what it was to want or to be satisfied. Afterwards, nestled against him, she discovered that the sudden change of feeling the girls had spoken of, the loss, was another myth. She hadn't lost anything—she'd gained access to a new world of sensation and passion. What it meant and how to control it didn't matter, only that she was part of it, with Dennis.

When he left, just before her mother came home, she had to make herself take a bath, reluctant to wash any part of him away. Her mother was pouring her second drink when Sandy got out of the tub.

"Did you go bowling?" Celia Atkins asked her daughter.

"Yes. It was fun."

"That's nice. Me, I worked so hard my feet are killing me..."

I don't look any different, Sandy realized. Not even my mother can tell.

The months that followed (though she didn't perceive them as months: time was divided into the hours she spent with Dennis, and the hours spent merely thinking about him) amazed her. Their deception was as easy as it was useful. Their friends, their families—nobody knew they were lovers, seizing every opportunity to make love. The urgency of their passion rocked her. To her relief and her dismay, Sandy learned that repetition didn't dull their senses, but only replenished them.

In their most intimate moments, she was able to block out the dark fear that was the sole blot on her happiness. *He's going away*... To help herself forget, she clung to him tighter and held him closer, filling the minutes when they weren't touching with talk of plans for the future, their future together, as if talking about it was some kind of guarantee.

Then there'd been the spring, and Dennis' graduation. He was her date for her junior prom, and she went to his senior prom as well as Bobby's. Graduation meant the end of high school. She'd known that Dennis was going away to school, but it hadn't mattered. She'd still love him, and she told him so. They'd have the summer, then in the fall he'd go away. But he would come back on vacations, and she'd visit him, and they'd write. Maybe she'd even move to Michigan when she graduated—

Bobby's voice brought her back to reality.

"It's noon, hon," he said, dangling the car keys. "Almost ready? You have a class at one—hey, what's wrong? You look like you've just seen a ghost."

Maybe she had, Sandy thought, looking at the man she'd married. Maybe she'd seen ghosts of them all...

"There's a letter here from our pride and joy," Bobby said, tossing the mail he'd brought in onto the counter. He bent down and kissed her. "You know, you don't look like a lady who has a nineteen-year-old son."

Sandy tried to smile, but couldn't.

"I—we had a phone call this morning," she began.

Later, Bobby tried to shake off the apprehension the prospect of seeing The Regulars again brought on.

It was the same old feeling and the same old fear.

"Crazy," he said, to himself in an effort to make himself believe that it was.

There was nothing to be afraid of any more—Sandy was his wife, and had been for almost twenty years. From the first time he'd held her in his arms, the first time they'd danced together, he'd known it. Even before. As far back as he could remember, Bobby had watched his parents dance together, their movement both precise and poetic, like some beautiful machine. It was more than steps on a dance floor or trophies on a mantel—it was a perfect partnership, physically expressed.

He hadn't even had a chance at first. Before he could ask Sandy for a date during those first hectic weeks of the show, she was seeing Dennis. He held her and danced with her in front of the cameras, but when the show was over, it was Dennis who walked her home, Dennis who took her out on weekends. Dennis, whose every word she hung on, whom her eyes always searched for when Bobby spun her around on the dance floor.

As good as she felt was how much his heart ached.

But they weren't going steady—at least neither Sandy nor Dennis told anyone they were. One day Bobby asked her if he could walk her home, when he knew that Dennis was going straight back to Staten Island after the show to study for a test. To Bobby's pleasure and surprise, Sandy said yes.

After that, she let him take her to the movies, went home with him to meet his family, and let his parents teach them old dance steps like the Charleston and the Continental and the Tango. Bobby felt wonderful...as long as Dennis wasn't around.

Not that she talked much about Dennis when they were alone together. Still, the perimeters of their relationship had been established. They were buddies, pals, the best of friends. But the kind of romance the magazines wrote about existed only in his own mind—and in the fantasies he confessed to in church each week.

And in church, he prayed, seeking relief from the pain of first love so intense and sharp that like everyone else in the world, he was convinced it was a special pain that had been visited solely on him. If only he didn't love her so much! If only she didn't have those eyes, and that laugh, and that streak in her hair. If only some miracle would make her forget Dennis long enough to really see him and his love for her.

Being with her was both joy and torment. A thousand

times he wanted to kiss her, but he didn't try even once: she might take it the wrong way, and that would mean risking whatever it was they had. His only comfort and his only hope were the knowledge that Dennis was going off to school in the fall. Then maybe, just maybe, he'd have his chance...

The show went on all summer long, since more kids were home to watch TV. The Regulars found parttime jobs, those of them who needed work: TBS even put a few on its payroll as messengers and file clerks, arranging their schedules around *Dancetime*.

As the summer ended, Bobby noticed the change in Sandy, the mounting nervousness, the way her eyes focused on Dennis. Maybe, he began to think, he didn't have the right to even try for her. Not if she really loved someone else so much.

Dennis left on the Friday before the show's new season officially started. On Monday, in the studio, Bobby's heart ached for Sandy. There were circles under her eyes as if she had cried all weekend. Her movements were stiff and slow, almost like a robot. Even if it was love, Bobby thought, maybe it was the wrong kind of love, to cause such pain and torment.

He knew what was wrong, but he couldn't bring himself to speak of it, not even to comfort her, for fear that doing so would forever cast him as only a friend.

"Let's go out tonight?" he asked with artificial ease on Friday night "One of the guys from school is having a party—"

"All right," Sandy said without enthusiasm, making his heart pound with joy.

He picked her up at seven o'clock. On the ride to Brooklyn, she was silent and preoccupied, speaking only when he asked her a direct question. Bobby's spirits were sagging when they got to the party, planned when the parents suddenly decided to visit relatives out of town. The lights were down too low too early, and too much liquor was mixed in a large bowl with orange soda.

"I'm sorry," he told Sandy, soon after they arrived.

"For what?"

"For bringing you here. It's—it's not good enough for you."

"Oh, Bobby, you're sweet. Would you get me a drink?"

He looked at the punchbowl. "It might make you sick."

"I feel sick already," she said. "Go on, Bobby. My mother lives on the stuff."

One drink turned into another, and another after that. Hard as Bobby tried to sip slowly and stay sober, it was difficult. Sandy seemed to be drinking as fast as she could. Within an hour, couples began to disappear, moving to the upper rooms of the house.

"Maybe we should leave," he suggested, not wanting her to think he'd brought her to the party to try anything.

"What's the rush?" she said, her voice slurred and her eyes slightly glazed. She was smiling as she watched a couple sneak away, their arms around each other. She held her Dixie Cup out for a refill.

"Where're they all going?" she asked, as two more couples went upstairs.

"They're...you know."

"No I don't know. Show me."

He knew he was blushing. "Sandy—"

"Come *on*!" she insisted, standing and pulling him to his feet.

"Okay. We'll go."

She didn't speak, but let him put his arm around her waist to guide her up the stairs.

"Let's explore," Sandy urged, taking Bobby's hand upstairs and pulling him through the darkness before he could protest. She led him toward another staircase, then up to a hallway.

"Oops!" she said, laughing as she opened a door, startling a boy and girl on a bed. She shut the door quickly.

"Sandy—" Bobby began, wanting to take her out of the house.

She moved closer to him in the darkness, her walk unsteady but her intention certain. "Kiss me," she whispered, as her arms encircled him. He had dreamed of this moment and waited for it since the first time he'd seen her, knowing how it would feel to gently press his lips against hers. But when it finally happened, it was different. Instead of being gentle, her mouth was urgent and demanding, her tongue pushing against his teeth. Her body strained against his in the darkened hallway.

Then she was leading him down the hall, opening doors and closing them when the people inside protested. There was nobody in the last room on the left. Sandy closed the door behind them and locked it.

She fell on the bed, pulling him down on top of her. When she began to unzip her dress, he forced himself to move back.

"Sandy—"

"Don't you want me?" she asked. The moonlight coming through the window made her skin look like marble. He ached with desire, and with the conflicting wish to do the right thing. "Don't you?" she repeated, her left hand caressing her bare right shoulder, gliding down to cup her breast.

"Yes," he moaned, no longer caring if it was a sin. "Oh, yes..."

Lots of guys he knew carried a Trojan in their wallets, and it occurred to Bobby that he had no "protection," but that was only a fleeting thought. Sandy's movements more than made up for his own inexperience, and he began to think that perhaps, in her own way, she'd longed for him, too. She began to murmur and make noises that seemed a mixture of pleasure and torment.

"What did you say?" he asked suddenly, breaking the rhythm of his body. He was certain he'd heard her call someone's name.

"It's nothing," she said, her hands on his shoulders pulling him back to her. "Nothing at all."

When it was over, he collapsed on the pillow beside her. He was so relaxed he was almost asleep when Sandy began to gag. He hurried with her from the bed and the room, finding the bathroom at the end of the hall just in time. He held her as her stomach heaved, then took a cloth from the towel rack, wetting it and wiping her face as if she were a child.

"I'm sorry," she apologized. "I think I had too much to drink."

He smiled and brushed her hair off her face with his fingers. "Come on, I'll take you home."

He waited outside as she dressed, then they hurried down the hall and the stairs, through the front door and onto the street, warm in the early September night. On the subway back to Manhattan, she fell asleep against his shoulder, and when he woke her and walked her to the door, they said good night awkwardly, without a kiss.

Everything had changed, he thought, riding home. *It was different between them now!* But Bobby's elation was tempered by a sense of guilt. He didn't just love Sandy—he adored her. As much as he'd enjoyed the feeling of sex with her (and the feeling of real sex with anyone for the first time) he was ashamed that he hadn't been able to wait. *I'll tell her I love her*, he promised himself. *We'll talk about it...*

He wasn't sure what he'd say, but he knew that the very next day, first thing, he'd go to confession.

It was two months before they spoke of that night, two months that bewildered him. Making love, he was sure, had bound them. But Sandy acted as though it had never happened. He called her the day after the party to make sure she was all right. "Of course I am," she said, acting surprised. "Why shouldn't I be?"

Monday on the show, she was no different than on any other day. When she let him take her out the following weekend, an unspoken signal kept him at the old distance—and set the pattern for the weekends that followed. Maybe, Bobby told himself, she'd been so drunk she didn't remember. But she *had* to remember. In spite of the sin, he'd thought and dreamed of it constantly, willing to undergo any penance to do it again.

Toward the end of October, Sandy seemed more preoccupied than ever. He wondered if it was Dennis, or maybe someone else, but he was afraid to ask her.

Then, on a night when he least expected it, he found out. He'd told his parents that Sandy wasn't feeling well, but his mother had insisted that he ask her to a dance at the church hall. Sandy had been so involved in her own thoughts when he asked her that he half expected her to forget the date. Dutifully, he'd picked her up, borrowing his father's car for the occasion, and she had been ready, waiting for him on the stoop the way she always did, not that he could blame her with a mother drunk all the time.

After a few attempts that went nowhere, he gave up trying to make conversation. *If only she'd open up*, he thought. *If only she'd let me help her...*

At the dance, she was polite to his parents and friendly to the people they introduced her to. She was a nice girl, the O'Brians agreed; of course it was a shame she was a Protestant...

Anyone who didn't know Sandy would have thought there was nothing wrong, but Bobby knew better. Beneath the controlled amenities, there was a desperate panic in her. Several times during the evening, it seemed on the verge of exploding. But she danced with him, with his father, and with other people who asked her.

Then the five-piece band played a polka. Halfway through it, she broke away from Bobby and ran outside. He followed to find her retching, sick to her stomach, as sick as she'd been the night of the party.

"What is it?" he asked, frightened. She mattered more

to him than anyone else in the world. "Do you want a doctor?"

She shook her head. He rushed inside to get her a cup of water, and she sipped it gratefully. When she turned to him, the streetlight made her tears look like liquid diamonds.

"I've been to the doctor," she said brokenly. "I don't know how else to say it, Bobby. I'm—in trouble." Sandy cried against his chest as he held her. He knew that he wasn't a boy any longer.

"It'll be all right," Bobby said. "We'll get married. You'll have our baby. We'll be a family. I love you, Sandy."

The look on her face was strange and confused, then she buried her head in his shoulder.

"I'm sorry," she wailed, breaking away, opening her handbag and taking out a hankie. She dabbed at her eyes, then put it back, pretending to look for something else. Bobby slowly snapped the bag shut and lifted her chin. The streetlight made her blonde streak look golden.

"I'll be a good husband to you," he promised. "And a good father. I'll learn how. I promise. You'll marry me Sandy, won't you?"

"Thank you," she sobbed, falling into his arms. And he'd known that what she was really saying was "yes."

Sandy realized that moving to Houston was a good idea. They'd done it carefully, so carefully that nobody on either side of the family had found out to this day. She'd been two and a half months gone when they were married in Saint John's, and though his family had been disappointed, they'd had to agree that moving to Texas and cashing in on whatever fame the show had brought them wasn't a bad idea, even though they'd have preferred for Bobby at least to finish high school.

Five weeks after the wedding, when he was working as

an instructor at a Fred Astaire studio where she was a receptionist (she could've taught, but he wouldn't let her, even if she wasn't showing yet), he'd called his parents with the "news" that she was expecting. That deception, coupled with her "premature" delivery, had worked.

In the hospital, as she went into labor, the fears that had haunted her since the wedding attacked like demons. Bobby's eyes were blue, Dennis' hazel. Bobby's hair was light and Dennis' dark. What would happen if God punished her by giving her a child who didn't look like Bobby's baby at all, but was the exact image of his real father? Her secret would be out. She'd be left alone...

"Here's your son," the doctor said as a nurse placed the infant in her arms.

"An adorable baby, Mrs. O'Brian," the woman in the white uniform said. "He sure takes after you."

"Thank you," Sandy said weakly, grateful to them and to God. She and her child were safe. Bobby would always believe the baby was his. His family would never know she'd been pregnant when they married.

If anyone had any doubts, they never said a word. By the time Bobby, Jr. was two months old and strong enough to make the trip back to New York, they'd been welcomed with open arms.

In the midst of Bobby's family's attention, Sandy had been shocked to find herself wondering if Dennis had come home for the summer. A dozen times, she had to stop herself from reaching for the phone and dialing the familiar number. But what was there for her to say? That he'd lied to her? That he had used her and left her pregnant?

That she couldn't even consider an abortion? She had to have the baby, had to hold on to the only link to him she had left. That she'd deceived Bobby, making love to him one drunken night when she'd called out Dennis' name in his arms and then let Bobby believe, because he always thought the best of her, that the baby was his?

That she still loved Dennis...

She'd tried to deny it, even asking God to help her find the strength.

She didn't want to ever think of Dennis again. Dennis wasn't half the man Bobby was, for all his dreams and plans. He didn't have the kindness or the goodness.

She was lucky. She was grateful. Bobby was as devoted a father as he was a husband.

He'd worked and saved. And she had kept busy, trying to erase Dennis from her mind. But it was hard to look at Bobby Jr. and not see his real father's eyes, or a glimmer of that smile. And it was harder still to exorcize the thoughts and images that came, uninvited, into her mind at the most unpredictable times. The months could go by with hardly a thought of Dennis.

When Bobby Jr. was old enough to go to school, they had saved enough money to open their own dance studio. She'd kept in shape, and Bobby had kept her up to date on the latest dances. Dancing, for her, represented a kind of freedom, a release for the pressure she felt at times but couldn't explain.

I should be grateful, Sandy thought countless times over the years. *I shouldn't even think of him.*

"I won't," she told herself aloud sometimes, for all the good it did. The studio was doing very well, Bobby Jr. was in his second year at Texas A & M. *I have a wonderful husband,* she thought, *a wonderful life. Should I risk seeing Dennis again?*

That night, thinking about the phone call from Sheila Granger, remembering The Regulars, remembering Dennis with an ache that seemed to tear her body apart, Sandy looked at her husband, asleep already beside her.

"Dear God," she whispered, pulling the bedclothes closer around her, "please don't let me talk in my sleep."

3.

TBS ANNOUNCES FALL SCHEDULE

The prime-time schedule for the Fall 1978 season, revealed in New York yesterday at a press conference at the offices of the Trans-American Broadcasting System, held a few real surprises.

In a lineup announced by Peter Townbridge, Prime-time programming VP, the network will attempt to bolster standbys such as *Newsroom*, the one-hour drama with an erratic performance record, and *Girls Night Out*, a second-season sitcom that began to build late in its first season, by scheduling them on "powerhouse" Monday, Tuesday, and Thursday nights dominated by proven winners.

The Unteachables, Show Biz, The Three of Us, and *Sugar*, along with *Girls*, are among the web's scheduled sitcoms. They'll be joined by two new arrivals, *Sister Act*, described as "a comedy about three beautiful sisters, with very different points of view and lifestyles, who share an apartment" and *Far Out West*, "a laugh-filled burlesque of TV westerns."

New dramatic series include *The Team*, "a one-hour continuing drama about the private as well as public lives of a major-league baseball team, concentrating on the players and their families." Also set are *The Marriage Doctors*, "an adult drama about a husband and wife medical team helping patients solve the intimate problems of marriage," and *Sports-Med*, in which "two doctors, a seasoned and experienced veteran and a newcomer who turned to medicine when a college accident cut short his football career, open a Manhattan practice concentrating on the problems of professional and amateur athletes."

Now!, an hour-long news-magazine format concentrating on "very timely stories," is an obvious attempt to cash in on the competition's success with *60 Minutes*, etc.

Wednesday and Saturday nights will continue to be dominated by TBS' reliable (the degree depending on the specific offering) movie nights, with theatrical and made-for-TV products mixed.

Townbridge announced "a very healthy number of specials" and several mini-series.

When asked to comment on recent statements from FCC officials and Congressional supporters who have accused the networks of "pandering to the lowest common denominator," Townbridge made obligatory mention of TBS' community service and public affairs programs, as well as "prestige" specials.

"We are an entertainment organization," he said, "with an admitted purpose of entertaining as many viewers as possible. We respond to their tastes and interests. To accuse us—or any network—of 'pandering' is a direct insult to our viewers, whom certain government officials seem to forget are also their constituents."

Several of the programming possibilities mentioned several months ago as being "under consideration" for a fall bow are still in various stages of development as possible replacements, he added.

The intercom buzzed, and Sheila was told that Kay Duvane was on the line.

"Isn't it silly?" Kay asked, her voice thick. "The dentist

says he has to yank that molar, or whatever it is, and he absolutely refused to do it unless I have someone here to take me home after the anesthetic wears off. I hate to ask, Sheila, but—"

"It's no problem, Kay. What's the address," Sheila reached for a pen. "An hour? Fine. I'll see you then."

She picked up the copy of *Variety* she'd been reading, skimming box office figures, production news, and contract negotiations. It wasn't really hard news, Sheila knew—most of it was planted by press agents and PR people. It was all promotion, not really much different from the full-page ads the networks and studios and independent producers took out to make sure everyone else in the industry was aware of their most recent accomplishments and products.

The fall schedule's official announcement was no surprise to anyone at TBS. Along with Kay, Sheila had attended screenings of the new shows (and those that hadn't made it) weeks—months, in some cases—earlier. There'd be no surprises for the viewers at home, either. The new TBS shows, like the new programs announced by other networks, were either "response" shows— variations on a successful series that someone else was running—or new adaptations of time-proven formulas.

Back in college, there had been lots of talk about the responsibilities of broadcasting. Television, Sheila's professors had said (and she'd believed wholeheartedly) had not only an awesome power, but a matching responsibility. It was the duty, the moral obligation of programmers, to upgrade the lives of those people the medium reached by informing and educating them, widening their horizons and, in turn, their aspirations.

Back in the classroom, it had all sounded so right, so idealistic.

In reality, it was just another impractical, if noble, concept.

Most people didn't want to be educated, even informed. The news was one thing, but any in-depth exploration of current events meant a surefire kiss of death in the ratings. The first moonwalk had been witnessed by millions of spellbound viewers. But coverage of subsequent lunar landings hadn't drawn nearly as wide an audience: the novelty had worn off. When a Presidential news conference preempted the soap operas that were the mainstay of TBS' afternoon schedule, the network switchboard (and the switchboards of affiliates) lit up with complaints. Enraged housewives wanted to know why their favorite soap wasn't on the air...Couldn't someone speak to the President about scheduling his press conferences at a more convenient hour?

To be sure, there were some who preferred the type of programs offered on Public Television—the documentaries, concerts, the English imports such as *Masterpiece Theatre*. The critics devoted a lot of column space to praising the quality of these programs and contrasting them to the offerings of commercial TV. Oil companies, fast-food chains, and various foundations provided the additional funding that enabled PBS stations to carry such prestigious programs. In return they were given a visual credit and often a voiceover announcing, "Additional funding to make this program possible was provided by..."

This was really another way of adding class to the corporate image...a toney commercial of sorts.

Once, Sheila had believed that public television was somehow "better" than commercial TV.

In time, her feeling had changed. Many of the supposed truths she'd accepted had turned out to be myths. At the top of the list was the inaccurate view of America that many people had, including some within the industry. They acted as if New York City was the only place that mattered—the rest of the country was, in their opinion, *terribly* unchic and unsophisticated.

The only paper that mattered was *The New York Times*, and its pronouncements were given an inordinate value. While Sheila believed that the *Times* was entitled to its opinions, its power frightened her. Broadway shows could open and close in one night if the *Times*' critic wasn't entertained, which hardly seemed fair. Obscure movies that were praised could play to trend-conscious Manhattan audiences for weeks or even months. In their effort to be on top of things, the status-seekers would even line up and wait in rain or snow to buy a ticket to some murky, subtitled import with "important social undertones" or the like.

In her neighborhood, a tiny Italian restaurant had changed completely after a *Times* food critic "discovered" it. Sheila had found it much earlier. Like other people who lived nearby, she'd eaten there regularly. After the *Times* praised the pasta, the once quiet, friendly atmosphere changed. Everyone in town, it seemed, was clamoring to get a table there—not so much for the food, but because the restaurant was "in." And "in" meant having a chance to let everyone admire your latest outfit from the latest status shop.

With television, it was the same. The paper gave PBS an inordinate amount of attention at the expense of the major networks. While many of public television's achievements were indeed praiseworthy, the paper regularly ran features about obscure documentaries and British imports.

Sheila found the *Times* necessary but burdensome: she preferred the less staid, more exciting *Post* and *Daily News*. And she loathed the cultural snobbery of people who thought they had a copyright on taste, particularly when they not only parroted opinions and preferences that were supposed to make them appear trendy, but also made fun of the rest of the country.

Most Americans, she knew, had little interest in multi-part imported dramas. It was one thing to take an English comedy series and Americanize it—that had been proven with *All in the Family* and *Sanford and Son*. Wonderful as the productions and performances might be, a lot of what was offered on PBS' *Masterpiece Theatre* had nothing to do with the lives and interests of American audiences. They worked hard at home and at their jobs, and when they finally sat down in front of their TV sets at night, they wanted to relax. The ratings clearly proved that they preferred American programs that entertained them.

Cable TV was a reality, bringing a wide choice of channels into nearly every home that subscribed to a cable company's service. Yet Americans in overwhelming numbers still went with the major networks.

Why then, Sheila wondered, were certain congressmen always ready to leap to their soap boxes at the first opportunity, decrying television as former FCC Chairman Newton Minow had done when he'd called it a "vast wasteland?" They deplored the programs the networks offered, and insisted that "something" had to be done.

Couldn't the viewer who wasn't satisfied with what he saw on his home screen already "do" something?, Sheila wondered. He had the choice of changing the station or turning off his set. And just what kind of "something" did those who claimed to be interested in improving the state of TV propose to do? Legislate for more money to support public television? Spend American tax dollars on foreign programs or esoteric shows that only a few people, proportionately speaking, would watch? Enact some sort of even tighter control over commercial TV, by which the networks would have to clear their programming with some governmental TV czar? It didn't agree with her vision of America. Not only did this infringe on the basic freedoms of the press and choice on which the nation was founded, but it implied that the American public was a bunch of boobs who didn't have the intelligence to turn a dial...

"I'm going to pick Kay up at the dentist," Sheila told her secretary. "I'll take her back to her apartment, then go home for the day."

"Will she be in tomorrow?"

"I don't know. Good night," Sheila said, though it was only four o'clock.

Ever since she'd been put in charge of the Lee Dean special, not only her secretary but everyone else at the network had been treating her with a new respect. She was no longer just "Sheila" or "Kay Duvane's assistant." Instead, she was looked at as a woman on her way up the ladder. Executives who'd never given her more than a polite smile—and not even that when they hadn't felt like it—had begun to say hello when she passed them in the halls or saw them at meetings or screenings.

It was as if she were about to be voted into some exclusive club. The final ballots hadn't been passed out yet, but the membership committee had given her the stamp of approval.

She felt pleased with herself as she entered the dentist's office. That feeling turned to genuine shock when she saw Kay, her face swollen and her mouth packed with cotton.

"How—how do you feel?" she asked.

"Worse than I look—if that's possible," Kay managed to say.

"She'll be swollen for a day or two," the nurse informed Sheila, "and for a couple of hours she may be a little woozy from the anesthetic. That will wear off. But see that she gets these prescriptions filled. One's an antibiotic and the other is for pain. No solid food for a full forty-eight hours."

"Jesus," Kay said weakly.

"You can have soup," the nurse informed her. "Call us tomorrow, Miss Duvane, and don't hesitate to call sooner if you're in pain."

"Don't worry," Kay said, steadying herself on the arm of her chair, then taking Sheila's arm. She leaned forward as if to share a great secret with the younger woman. "I *hate* soup," she announced.

One hour later, Kay was settled in bed. There was a pile of magazines on the table beside her. Mimi, her cat, was snuggled at her feet, not even looking up as her mistress clicked the remote control of the TV set.

"Try this," Sheila said, bringing a tray into the room. "And take your pills, Kay."

"What *is* that?" she asked, looking at a glass of reddish liquid. Salt, pepper, and a straw were also on the small rattan tray, along with a dish of ice cream. "It isn't soup, is it?"

"It's not *soup* soup. It's gazpacho, and it's fresh."

"Fresh?" Kay repeated, taking a tentative sip. "You know, this isn't bad at all. You actually made it?"

"In the blender," Sheila explained. "You throw in tomatoes, peppers, scallions, a can of consommé—"

"Please! I'm eating... sort of," Kay protested. "God, I loathe being sick."

"You're not sick. You're recovering."

"Well, it's the same thing. And you are an absolute love to bring me home and everything. Thanks, Sheila."

"I'm glad to do it. Anything else?"

Kay mulled it over. "I'd like to be twenty-five again. Can you arrange it?"

"Sorry. The best I can do is arrange for you to see the forthcoming TBS special that reunites The Regulars and the original host of America's best-remembered show from the rocking, rolling, fabulous fifties—"

"Let me guess," Kay said. "That inspired copy must have come from promotion, right? Best-remembered, my ass! Although it does have a certain unavoidable ring...Oh, the hell with it. How's the show coming along?"

"You don't want to talk about work, Kay. Take it easy. Give yourself a break."

"I am. Darling, my mouth feels like hell and that pain pill won't take hold for another twenty minutes. Tell me what's happening. It'll give me something to concentrate on besides this damn jaw."

Because of last-minute shuffles in the fall lineup, the never-ending meetings, and the general pace of their work, it had been nearly a week since she'd actually talked with Kay about the special, Sheila realized. She wasn't sure where to begin.

She decided to tell Kay the good news first. Dennis Bradshaw, in spite of his wife's adamant insistence that he wouldn't be interested, had called and said he'd like to appear on the show. Sandy and Bobby O'Brian were also lined up—as two regulars who'd married and were professional dance instructors, they'd be definite assets.

"They sound perfect," Kay agreed. "Don't forget to tape special promos for the affiliate in, where was it again, Phoenix?"

"Houston," Sheila corrected her.

"I was close, anyway. While you're at it, remember to order promos for as many of the local markets as you can—wherever the other Regulars are from. By the way, whatever happened to that heartbreaker with the long hair—dark—and those almond eyes? You should have seen the mail she got from men back in the Stone Age when I was doing publicity."

"She was popular with the boys, huh, Kay?"

"Boys, my ass! If those were high school boys who wrote to her, they were certainly majoring in sex. We used to pass the best letters around the department. They weren't just hot, Sheila—they sizzled!"

Sheila paused, puzzled. "It's funny, isn't it? Even in the fan magazines, Lorraine said she liked the attention. But I haven't been able to locate a trace of her."

"Let me think," Kay said, searching her memory. "I think she did some modeling... yes, I'm sure of it. One of the big agencies—big back then, I mean—offered her a contract. I remember she did some work for *Seventeen*, that sort of thing."

"I'll check it out. Thanks for the lead."

Sheila told her about the other Regulars she'd located, and those still to be found. All in all, she assured Kay, it was moving right along. Working on the show and keeping up with her work as Kay's assistant (the additional assistant hadn't been hired: Kay hadn't been taken with anyone she'd interviewed) meant a double work load, but she was thriving on it.

"We're trying to get Tommy Del," she said. He'd been a teen idol with three chart-busting hits in a row before vanishing into obscurity.

"Tommy Del," Kay repeated, shaking her head. "I haven't heard of him in years. Did you find his agent?"

"His *former* agent. He used to be with William Morris. But his agent said that Tommy Del got out of the business eight years ago. He was working small clubs and lounges in Vegas before he retired."

"Watch him come out of retirement when you dangle a network spot in front of him," Kay said with a wink. "Once they have a taste of the spotlight, it's like an addiction."

"Then there's Alice Lane—" Sheila began.

Kay's face changed. "Don't tell me. Not that bitch!"

"I know. I hate her too, and everything she stands for. But she did have a big hit twenty years ago this coming November, and that's when we air."

Kay shook her head slowly. "Once when she opened her mouth, something like music used to come out. Now it's more like bile. But if she had one of the top hits, that month, I suppose we're obligated to have the monster on..."

"After all, we created the monster, didn't we?" Sheila said. "Television, I mean."

"I'm not sure I understand, Sheila. Tell me what you mean."

Sheila felt unexpectedly nervous. Kay, after all, wasn't feeling her best. This wasn't the time to say something that might grate on her nerves. Still, she'd asked for an explanation.

"What I'm talking about is the coverage all the networks have given her," she explained, sitting on the edge of the bed. "When you get down to it, who *is* Alice Lane, anyway? Okay, back in the late fifties, she was a sort-of hot singer with a few hits. She was pretty, in a girl-next-door sort of way *if* you like the girl next door. But she was so phoney and so, well, so sweet that I'm surprised she didn't give people diabetes."

"Ouch!" Kay protested, holding her jaw. "Don't make me laugh. It hurts!"

"I promise," Sheila vowed. "Look, Kay, in our business, we respect trends. In music, trends are even more important. By the time the Beatles and the other English groups started to make it big in the early sixties, people like Alice Lane were out of date. Most of them either tried to change with the times or bowed out gracefully."

"But not Alice," Kay said.

"Not by a long shot. I spent a couple of hours looking at the clip files and the film we have on her. She was the first star to denounce the changing taste in music as 'indecent,' remember?"

Kay thought for a moment. "That's right. It was something about drugs..."

Drugs, Sheila explained, had only been part of Alice Lane's tirade. Just as there had been some who attributed juvenile delinquency and every other problem affecting American society in the fifties to rock and roll, Alice Lane had insisted that the music made by "long-haired, disheveled performers" was undermining the very fabric of American society.

She'd hinted that it was part of an international conspiracy to make teenagers from Good American Homes take drugs, drop out of school, run away from home, and live "in sin."

"She actually said that? *All* that?"

"All that and more, Kay," Sheila confirmed. "Once she got started, she kept going. It was like you said before. She was one of those people who got hooked on being in the public eye."

With her recording career only a memory, Alice Lane had become a self-styled spokeswoman for a number of causes. It was hard to tell exactly what she was in favor of, since an attack posture kept her on the offensive. But her list of anti-causes was virtually endless. Over the years, she'd spoken out against the "immorality" of women's liberation, the ERA, and busing. She was against recognizing China, pardoning draft dodgers, welfare, homosexuality and gay rights. She didn't approve of couples living together without benefit of marriage; the SALT treaties; tax exemptions for religions she didn't personally recognize; the Panama Canal treaty; fluoridation; and using cats and dogs in medical experiments.

"Don't forget sex and violence on television," Kay added.

"Alice has never criticized television, Kay."

"Hmm. Must be an oversight."

"No," Sheila said. "It's good business. Why bite the hand that feeds you?"

"Come again?"

"That first time she criticized music, where do you think she did it, Kay? Right on TBS, on the network news. Over the years, it's been the same way. Every time she has one of her pronouncements to make, we're right there at her press conferences and speeches with the news cameras and the microphones. Don't get me wrong—we're not the only ones. The other networks are there, too."

"She may be a lunatic," Kay replied, defending the network and its policies out of habit, "but she *is* news. She's controversial—"

"What she is, actually, is dangerous," Sheila insisted, interrupting. "The *issues* she talks about are controversial. They're all things that people feel highly emotional about. The scary thing is that I've found myself agreeing with some of the things Alice Lane says. I didn't think we should have given up the Panama Canal, and I don't think that forced busing is the way to integrate schools. But she's—*inflammatory*, that's the word. She has a way of tying it all together.

"And television has given her the perfect forum for her views. We've *made* her news. We've given her the power she has. Her newspaper column is syndicated all over the country—she'd never have the column if she hadn't gotten so much exposure on television. She's held several local offices in California, thanks to TV coverage, and now she's even talking about running for the United States Senate."

"She doesn't have a prayer," Kay said, dismissing it.

"That's not the point. The fact that an Alice Lane can even come close—even run—frightens me. We—television, that is—brought her into millions of homes. We've made her a national figure, and the more outrageous she gets, the more attention we give her. There are a lot of people who are unhappy with their lives, or the things going on in this country. They're frustrated, and they want changes."

"That's democracy, Sheila—"

"Of course it is. But instead of looking for answers, ways of making positive changes and improvements, they rally around a rabble-rouser like Alice Lane."

"If you feel that strongly, Sheila, don't book her for the special."

"Don't think I want to."

"You don't *have* to. There are lots of singers around."

"But she had her biggest hit during the week we're researching for the actual anniversary. It's a fact—not one I like, but it's true. If I don't book Alice Lane this once, when she really belongs on television, I'm doing the same thing she does—letting my personal prejudices influence the truth, and affect other people."

Kay looked at Sheila for a long time. "I admire your values. God knows it's hard to hang on to any of them in our work. Personally, I'd forget her. If you're set on signing her, make sure the contract says 'no politics' in plain language. She comes on, does a medley of a couple of songs—you work it out. When Lee interviews her, she sticks to the good old days, with no preaching."

Sheila smiled. "I've already thought of that. How are you feeling, Kay? Want to sleep for a while?"

"I wish I could. That pain pill is working, thank heaven, but I'm wide awake. Codeine always does that to me."

"How do you know it's codeine?"

"Darling, I know *all* about pills. Haven't you seen my medicine cabinet? It's an arsenal. Now don't worry—I'm not about to take that long walk into the Valley of the Dolls. After a while, as you'll find yourself, enthusiasm isn't always enough to keep you running. And youth has a way of sneaking off... which reminds me. Don't you have a date or something to do? I don't want to keep you, grateful as I am for the company."

"I don't have time for dates, Kay."

The older woman looked at her with a mixture of self-recognition and fear, as if seeing Sheila for the first time. "None at all. You don't see anybody?"

"Not really."

"What about Ed Goldman?" Kay asked, sounding like

she didn't want to believe it. "You dated him, didn't you?"

Sheila nodded. Ed Goldman had been an up-and-comer, one of the bright young men of the network. He'd been on his way to the top with a promotion that put him in line for a vice presidency in a couple of years. Sheila had liked him and enjoyed being with him, but the relationship had come to a sudden end when he left the network to work for one of the hottest independent production companies specializing in situation comedies.

"He's in California now," she told Kay.

"I know! We'll send you out there on official network business. Then you can see him." Kay was delighted with her idea.

"You don't understand," Sheila said. "Ed and I liked each other, but it wasn't love. Besides, he's living with that Sherry something or other, the one we saw in that pilot about the woman mechanic."

"What about Marc Wallace? I didn't mean to peek, but I did see several messages from him on your desk a while back..."

"That's another story. Marc talks shop all the time. I know he's a dynamo, and I really respect his work. But I never feel relaxed with him."

"So much for the boy whiz of Madison Avenue. Those advertising people are all the same. Anything happening with Lee Dean?"

"Lee Dean? You mean with the special?" Sheila asked, confused.

"I mean with you—*personally*."

Sheila didn't know whether Kay was kidding, serious, or a bit high on her pain pill.

There hadn't been a moment when she'd even thought of Lee Dean in anything but a professional way. He was easy to work with, all things considered. But at times he struck her as being a little confused or disoriented, as if he couldn't really believe he was back at TBS.

Sometimes when they discussed the special, Sheila noticed Lee's attention wandering. She hadn't expected him to be exactly the way the old press clippings painted him, but she'd thought he'd be a little more outgoing. Instead, she told Kay, it was almost like something was wrong—only Lee wasn't saying what it was.

"It could be a case of once burnt, twice shy," the older woman offered. "The network was horrid to Lee about that payola mess. One day he had a flourishing career and a national TV show. The next day it was as if he and the show had never existed. There are easier things to handle in life—"

"But he did take bribes, didn't he? I'm not saying that TBS couldn't have been less brutal, but it wasn't altogether a case of Lee Dean being a victim of the big bad network—"

"A victim of circumstance is more like it. I know how it looks to you, reading about it in the clippings and the history books. But they don't always convey the human side of things. Lee Dean was in the right place at the wrong time."

"But he *did* take money, Kay."

"Gifts, maybe. *Not* money. And they were gifts to him, not bribes. I was there, Sheila. I *know* how it happened. It wasn't as if Lee did *Dancetime* just so he could go on the take. We picked him, groomed him, and promoted him as the greatest thing since the wheel. When the show clicked, it was bigger than anybody had expected—Lee included. The record companies and promotion men and managers were on him like dogs on a bone. They all told him it was perfectly all right to accept favors and freebies. And it was. Payola wasn't even a word until those hearings started: it didn't become a crime, legally speaking, until they were over and a bill was passed.

"Maybe Lee should have known better. But maybe success was so sudden and so new to him that he didn't even have time to think. Maybe the network should have looked out for him, taught him the ropes." She knew she was getting worked up.

"I—I never thought of it quite that way," Sheila said, eager to change the subject. "Anyway, there's nothing going on personally between Lee and me."

"And there's nobody else?"

"It's like I told you, Kay. Right now, I'm concentrating on my career. These are the years that really count. I'm learning a lot, thanks to you. Later on there'll be plenty of time for other things."

"I hope so, Sheila," Kay said, taking her hand. "You watch out. Concentrating on your career can get to be a habit. And that ends the lecture. Now it's time for me to freshen my powder, as we used to put it."

She swung her legs out of bed and rose to her feet. After a few steps, she nearly lost her balance, saved from a fall only by Sheila's rescue.

"Lean on me, Kay," she said, helping her friend to the bathroom.

"I do," Kay answered.

Sheila helped Kay back to bed when she came out of the bathroom. "Would you like me to stay over tonight? Just in case you need something?"

"I couldn't ask you to do that—"

"You're not asking. I'm offering. I'd feel better knowing you weren't alone. I can go back to my place in the morning and change."

"If you're sure..."

"Positive," Sheila insisted.

"Hey," said Kay, "why don't we *both* relax? Look in my closet and pick yourself out a nightgown and robe. I've got tons of them. Get comfortable, then we can—"

"Watch some television?" Sheila said.

"You took the words right out of my mouth," Kay Duvane said, laughing though it hurt.

4.

"LOOK AT THIS ONE," AL HARTLEY SAID, turning a page. "There she is, see her? She hasn't changed a bit. Not my Cathy."

He glanced across the coffee table, and gave his wife an adoring smile, leaving Sam and Bertha Applebaum, the new neighbors who'd bought the condominium next to theirs, to admire the clippings carefully preserved beneath plastic overlays.

"How lovely," Mrs. Applebaum said. "And how exciting to think that all of you are going to be on television again after all these years. Why, it'll be just like old times, won't it?"

"It's going to be great!" Al agreed. "Cathy can hardly wait, right, honey?"

"I'm looking forward to it," she answered.

"Of course, my little girl was always the most beautiful of the bunch," Al told his guests. "Turn the page, Bertha. Go on. See for yourself."

"Al, stop it," Cathy said. "They're probably bored to death!"

"Not at all," Mrs. Applebaum assured her. "And not my Sam. He always had an eye for a pretty girl."

"No harm in looking," Mr. Applebaum added.

"Well, I'm going to put some more coffee on," Cathy told them, refusing Bertha's offer to help her.

"They're doing the special in November..." Al's voice followed her into the kitchen.

She put the last of the dinner dishes into the dishwasher and turned it on, the noise drowning out the conversation from the living room. It had only been two days since the call from New York had come, but already Al had seen to it that everyone they knew had heard the news. Not only had he told all their neighbors in the upstate New York town of Elmira, he'd called their friends and relatives as well. He even wanted to call the local papers and the TV stations, and he would have, too, if she hadn't told him that the network would take care of that kind of thing when the time came.

He was proud of her, Cathy knew, but then he'd always been proud of her: the special just deepened his pride. It was hard to realize that they'd been married for almost twelve years, hard to think about how much time had passed. He still looked at her as if he was seeing her for the first time. As if what he saw overwhelmed him.

Though she protested when he insisted that everyone who came through their door look at the scrapbook of her *Dancetime, USA!* days, she never moved the book from its place on the coffee table. It was the special thing about her, her biggest achievement and accomplishment in life, one of the things Al loved most.

Getting the coffee out and starting the electric coffee maker, Cathy Hartley thought of how far she'd come. It wasn't so much a matter of distance as time. Yet Al acted as if nothing had changed at all, as if no time had passed.

She was still "cute," She was his "little girl," the girl in the pictures in the scrapbook.

Those had been the golden years of her life, the time when it felt as if the best of everything was her due. There'd been nothing to worry about except clothes and dates and dancing. The worst thing that could happen was a pimple.

She'd inherited her mother's Danish coloring—the perfect ivory skin, the golden blonde hair, and the china-blue eyes. Her father's love of athletics (he'd had a season with a Yankee farm team before giving in to his own parents' pressure and completing his training as an accountant, giving up on a pro career) had been passed along to Cathy in the form of natural grace and agility. How she looked, she'd always believed, mattered a great deal. As a young child, she'd seen the pride in her mother's eyes when strangers stopped to comment on "that beautiful child." Within ten minutes' traveling time of their house in the Bronx, there were eight aunts and uncles as well as her father's parents. There were many cousins in the family, but Cathy had known from the start that she was the favorite.

She had felt like a doll everyone wanted to dress up. The flurry of knitting, crocheting, and sewing (not to mention shopping) had started when she was a baby. "Cathy looks so adorable, doesn't she?" the relatives would ask each other as she dutifully modeled their latest creation or discovery... not that anyone had any real doubts.

In school, it was the same way.

Looking good and being pretty, she discovered, were assets she'd been favored with. The teachers were patient, even indulgent, with a child who was so lovely—even if she did have a problem with arithmetic. The other girls all wanted to be her friends, and later all the best-looking boys wanted to date her.

Popularity was something that came easily. Cathy Kiley, as she'd been then, had been born to be the girl who played the Virgin Mary in the Christmas pageants, and Snow White. It was a foregone conclusion that she'd be invited to the best parties and asked to join the best clubs and sororities.

Like an actress cast in a movie, Cathy had played her part. The role had been laid out for her, along with a supporting cast of admirers and friends who told her, again and again, how lucky she was. There was little time to think about her real feelings, for which she was grateful: when she did think about them, there was a lot of confusion in her mind—and nobody to care about the part of her that had nothing to do with how she looked or whom she dated.

It wasn't that she didn't like the attention and the compliments. They were a part of her life, a measure of her worth and value. She liked having a whole rainbow of sweaters. Felt circle skirts in aqua, pink, white, and baby blue were necessities, part of what other people expected. The time she spent washing her hair, setting it (even sleeping on big, uncomfortable rollers) and brushing it out was important. Taking care of her skin, being on constant guard against the appearance of blemishes, was an investment in herself.

People, after all, responded to what they saw.

But none of them, not even the girls she shared her secrets with after school, were aware of the part of her that didn't show. Only her parents had even a glimmer of it—and they didn't understand.

It started the summer she was fourteen, a few days after the end of school. She'd been voted Most Beautiful Girl in the freshman high school class, an honor that pleased her very much. With school over and a whole summer ahead of her, there'd been a sense of release—this, her mother had assured her, was the happiest time of her life.

Unexpectedly, the dreams had begun.

They were never exactly the same, though similar things happened in them. Sometimes total strangers threw acid in her face and disfigured her. Or cars she was riding in had terrible accidents in which she was thrown through the windshield, her face slashed by shards of glass. Or she was trapped in fires that burned her face and hair, and attacked by witches and monsters who cast spells on her, changing her from a pretty girl into an ugly crone.

The nightmares were terrifying. She'd wake up, screaming and covered with sweat. It was only when her father rushed into her bedroom, snapping on the light and holding her in his arms, that she'd calm down.

"You're my little princess," he'd say, embracing her. "You're my beautiful little girl." The words always made her feel better, and by the end of that summer, the dreams stopped.

Cathy had thought about telling Mary Ellen Tagliafero, her best friend. Time and time again, she'd started to confide in her about the nightmares.

Mary Ellen's friendship, though, bordered on downright worship. Unlike Cathy, she hadn't been blessed with perfect features. In spite of exercising and following all the diet advice in the magazines, her body was basically squat: her legs would always be thick. "You're so lucky," she told Cathy over and over again, "you have the kind of looks that everyone wants." So even with her closest friend, Cathy had been hesitant to reveal the crack in the veneer of the all-American girl.

A year and a half later, Gamma Phi, her high school sorority, convinced her that it was her duty to try out for *Dancetime, USA!*. The idea struck Cathy as silly—there'd be so many kids from so many different schools competing. What was the point? She'd been content to enjoy the popularity she already had, but her "sisters" had been adamant. More to please them than anything else, she wrote to TBS for an application, filled it out, and returned it with a photograph.

The letter telling her that she'd made it to the elminations came as a shock, and while her friends rejoiced, Cathy had panicked. They acted as if she'd been picked to be a Regular on the show already, when in reality all she'd gotten was an invitation to continue in the competition. How would they feel if and when she lost? What would happen to her popularity? The girls who admired her and the boys who flirted with her would discover that she wasn't "perfect" after all. She would lose everything...

The subway ride from the Bronx to midtown Manhattan had been torturous. She had insisted on going by herself in case she was eliminated. That way, she thought, she'd have time to cry and get it out of her system, then go home looking like a good loser and a good sport.

But at the studio, everyone else seemed as nervous as she was, even if some of them seemed better at hiding it.

That first audition had been a madhouse. There weren't nearly enough seats in the studio, and everyone had wanted to sit up front, in view of the panel making the selection. A man who identified himself as the producer of the show had calmed them down, introduced himself, and explained that *Dancetime* was going to be *the* show for teens to watch. The Regulars, he'd said, would dance on it every day. They'd be talked about, written about, and admired by other kids all over the country. He reviewed the criteria to be used by the panel: a combination of looks, dancing ability, and "most important," acting naturally.

Cathy watched and waited as the other eager teenagers were called to the stage. They gave their name, age and school, then boys and girls were paired by height and asked to dance on the stage while a record played. The contestants had never danced together before, and it showed. Some of them had tried fancy steps in the hope of attracting the judges' eyes, but usually all they managed to do was confuse their partners. Most of the dancers were then thanked and told to leave.

Please give me somebody good to try out with, Cathy had prayed, waiting to be called.

She made herself act as casual as possible when she stepped before the judges. She wasn't Cathy Kiley... not the *real* Cathy Kiley. She wasn't worried about losing her looks and the popularity they had brought her, or about not being chosen for the show. Instead she was the lucky Cathy everyone thought they knew—the girl who had it all.

Ritchie, a dark-haired boy from Queens, was teamed with her. He was a good dancer, not a showoff, but the kind of guy who led in a way that made his partner look good. Cathy was aware of the way her skirt spun and her hair flew out, falling back into perfect place, as he spun her around.

She was asked to stay. At the end of the day she was one of less than a hundred teenagers who would go on to the finals. A few of those who'd been selected, it turned out, weren't even high school students but professional performers who'd applied for the show in the hope of getting a break that would further their careers. They were eliminated in the course of interviews, as were applicants who had poor academic records, or whose families were planning to move.

Cathy had no trouble getting the principal himself to write one of the two required letters of recommendation: her minister had supplied the second, describing her as "a fine example of decent, Christian American young womanhood." Her grade average was B-. Two auditions later, Cathy was a Regular.

Her picture in the paper, the big press party the network had thrown (the first time she'd met Lee Dean), the layouts for the teen magazines—it had been a whirlwind time of such heady pleasure that it didn't seem real. TBS staff members explained that they hoped to create an "image" for each of the girls. Sandy was the "pert and perky" girl, a little on the short side, but with a big dose of personality. Lorraine was the girl the boys noticed first.

"With that hair and skin," one of the publicists informed Cathy, "you could do commercials for our sponsors. You have the looks every girl in the country would like. You're going to be the girl with the answers to beauty problems, okay?"

Of course she agreed, just as she accepted Hank, a studious-looking boy with glasses, as her partner. He wasn't the handsomest of the boys, but Cathy didn't mind: his average looks made her looks all the more special.

Once she got used to the cameras, doing the show was a dream. She thrived on the attention, the fan mail, the sheer fun of it. Her pictures were sent all over the country to viewers who wrote in for it, along with a booklet, "My Own Beauty Secrets." The magazines ran stories month after month, in which she and the other girls on the show were depicted as the best of friends—which wasn't exactly the truth.

For one thing, they came from all parts of New York City: friends usually came from your own school or neighborhood. Too, they were all members of an exclusive group—The Regulars. And the competition didn't end with the elimination. Who was the most popular with the kids watching at home?, who got the most fan mail each week?—none of them admitted it to the others, but each of them was aware that there was still a contest of sorts.

Her parents, Cathy knew, were proud. Her mother was basically a quiet woman, but Dad had made sure everyone knew that his "cute little girl" was on TV every day.

Time had flown by... then suddenly it seemed to stop.

Toward the end of her senior year, everything changed. The constants in her life were turned around so quickly, and in such rapid succession, that she was dazed. The stories about payola hadn't meant much to her. Even when Lee Dean's name came up. The Regulars thought he would just go to Washington tell the truth, and that would be that.

He'd told the truth—and the show, with no warning, had been yanked off the air. Cathy had felt as if her identity, her whole *raison d'être*, had gone up in smoke. Then, just when she needed him most, an accident on the Pelham Parkway killed her father. Knowing that he hadn't suffered was some consolation. Time, everyone told her, would help... But it hadn't.

She found it impossible to concentrate in class. Her teachers were understanding, giving her grades she hadn't earned, and she graduated with honors. But there was no joy in her graduation, and while her father's family was in the auditorium as she made the obligatory walk to the podium to receive her diploma, then the Good Citizenship pin the faculty had awarded her, her mother, still sick with grief, was home in bed.

Since her father's death, her mother never seemed to stop crying. The doctor gave her pills for her nerves, but she never left her bedroom. When Cathy got home graduation night, her mother was a pale, motionless figure on the bed, an empty bottle of pills in one hand, a picture of her dead husband in the other.

The following summer and fall passed without any awareness on Cathy's part of the changing seasons. She went through the motions of life, guided by her aunt and uncle, whom she went to live with, and other relatives who acted as if things were somehow going to be all right.

She didn't bother with friends any longer. Each week Uncle Frank drove her to a doctor for a fifty-minute talk. Nobody would admit it, but she knew the truth. The old Cathy was gone. The girl who'd been so pretty and so popular had disappeared. She didn't even look the same. She was plain, ugly...

"Sure I can't help?" Bertha Applebaum entered the kitchen. "That coffee is done."

"I—I was just about to put some cookies out on a tray and bring it in," Cathy said, realizing she'd stayed too long in the kitchen and in the past.

"You certainly have a devoted husband," the other woman said.

Cathy forced a smile. "Al is wonderful, but he goes on and on about that silly scrapbook—"

"I don't blame him," Bertha told her, helping her take the cookies from a jar, setting them on a plate. "You should be very proud yourself, especially with that TV show coming up. Tell me, how did you and Al meet?"

Cathy was aware of the outspoken question: what was she doing married to a man so much older?

How could she explain what she didn't understand herself?

Someone, the psychiatrist, probably, had suggested that Cathy get a job. Aunt Paula had come up with the idea of approaching the cosmetic company which had been one of *Dancetime, USA!*'s sponsors. Like the other advertisers, they fumed when their best entree to the teen market had disappeared after the payola scandal. Thanks to the publicity she'd received, Cathy was a means of cashing in.

They had trained her, and Cathy found herself making special appearances at department stores, standing in front of a portable display of blowups of herself, urging teenage girls to buy the company's cleanser, astringent, and makeup. She usually drew a good crowd, and did a lot of business. After two years, however, the crowds began to thin. The requests for autographs from people who remembered her grew less frequent.

Because the company was expanding, Cathy was sent to set up new department-store outlets in Omaha, San Antonio, Phoenix, and Bangor. She spent several months in each city, training salesgirls, working with buyers, and supervising the counter. At night, she'd go back to the hotel room that was her home and sooner or later, it would happen.

She would begin to feel closed in, not only by walls but by memories. Nobody was with her when the past and present began to blend, when she stared into the mirror and saw the changes that time and tragedy had wrought in the face her father had once called so "beautiful."

Nobody was there when she needed someone... anyone... but Cathy eventually found that there were places where it was easy to find an admirer. The dark, downtown bars offered not only the numbing escape of alcohol, but the company of men who were willing, even eager, to tell her what she wanted to hear. If they were lying, if it was only an excuse, a means of getting her to their beds... well, it didn't matter.

Between cities, back home with her aunt and uncle, Cathy would feel disgust for what she'd done. There was consolation in knowing that she'd never have to go back to Phoenix, or Wilkes-Barre or wherever, again. There were promises to herself that it would be different next time, that wherever she traveled next, things would be better.

Somehow, though, it was always the same. Year after year, in city after city, she'd found men, more men than she wanted to think of, let alone count, who'd been willing to give her enough attention to make her feel pretty, if only for a little while.

Then she'd been sent to launch the line in Elmira, New York.

The store was no different from the dozens of other

department stores where Cathy had done her job. She worked with the salesgirls she hired until they were thoroughly familiar with every item in the line, and understood how to lead a customer who came in for one product to a sale that included several. She worked with the store's fashion coordinators, setting up a fashion and beauty clinic to promote the line. She saw to it that the beauty editors of the local and neighboring newspapers were supplied with publicity material, so that they could make their readers aware of the new products.

There was only one difference: Al Hartley.

At first, when she saw him in the cocktail lounge, Cathy barely noticed him. It was only when the bartender placed a daiquiri in front of her on the bar "courtesy of that gentleman over there," that she'd seen him. Another lonely salesman, she thought, or a married man out for quick action. She smiled and Al came over.

"I'm—I've never introduced myself to a young lady in a bar, miss," he said, shyly. "Not that this isn't a fine place..."

There were lots of lines, and she'd heard them all. But the way Al almost fell over his words made Cathy think that perhaps what he said was true. When he asked if she'd like to move to a table, she agreed.

If he wasn't able to look her in the eye, once they sat down together, he couldn't stop staring at other parts of her body. He apologized, explaining that he simply didn't know how to act.

"You're the most beautiful girl I've ever seen," Al said, in obvious awe.

His honest humility took Cathy by surprise, touching her in an unexpected way. As she listened, Al told her about himself.

He wasn't married; he was a widower. Barbara, his wife, had died two years before after a long struggle with cancer. He spoke of the twenty-nine years they'd had together—happy years until she became ill, marred only by their inability to have children. He spoke of the confusion, loss, and resentment he'd felt after Barbara's death, of the terrible feeling of being alone in a house in which he'd once had a partner.

Friends, Al explained, anxious to help him, were continually fixing him up with widows and divorcees.

"And you haven't met anyone you like?" Cathy asked.

"They're nice women," he said. "Lovely people. I don't know, maybe because Barbara and I had so much time together, I didn't notice it in her case. I'm not making comparisons, mind you, but these women...they're so—well, so old-looking. They seem like veterans. They have old ideas. They make me feel old..."

Al and Cathy began to see each other regularly. He made her feel young: his honesty was contagious, and she found herself talking about her own emotions. Her father's death and her mother's suicide were subjects she had never discussed with anyone but the doctor. Letting the truth and the pain out made her feel the way she remembered feeling as a girl, before everything went wrong.

Never once did Al try for anything more than a quick good-night kiss, when he took her back to her hotel. He was content just with her company, proud to be able to sit across from her at a restaurant, or next to her at a movie or concert at the Municipal Auditorium. When Cathy told him about having been a Regular, he was impressed and excited. He was delighted to pour over the clippings, publicity pictures, and snapshots of the show.

"You're my little girl," he said, embracing her.

A month later, when she was about to return to New York, he asked her to marry him. Cathy accepted. Their announcement came after the fact—they flew to Las Vegas for a quick ceremony and a week-long honeymoon, and sent telegrams back to Elmira and the Bronx.

Relatives and friends were polite about the surprise.

Cathy had wondered what her aunt and uncle would say, but when she and Al drove to the Bronx to meet them, the first evening went beautifully, almost as if Al and her two closest relatives had known each other all their lives. Only when she went into the kitchen to help with the dishes had there been any question.

"Do you like him, Aunt Paula?"

"Why yes, of course I do, Cathy. But isn't he just a little old for you?"

"I never thought about it," she admitted. "Do you think he is?"

"Not if he makes you happy, Cathy. Paul and I want you to be happy."

Al Hartley was twenty-one years older than his wife.

Back in Elmira Cathy realized quickly that the age difference so unimportant to her was a subject of gossip. Many people considered her a gold-digger, out to separate Al from his money (he owned a brokerage house). They said that old Al Hartley was making a fool out of himself by marrying a girl young enough to be his daughter. Only the kinder gossips added that he deserved whatever happiness he found.

The truth, Cathy knew, was that if he'd married her in an effort to feel younger, it was another thing they had in common. What she loved most about him was the way he saw her—young, beautiful, untarnished by the past she insisted on sharing with him. He'd look at her pictures in the scrapbook, and he'd look at her now, twenty years later, and he saw no difference at all. He made her feel that time hadn't just stopped: it had somehow been turned back.

"I guess we're ready," Bertha Applebaum said, as the last cookie was placed on the plate.

"Yes, I'm ready," Cathy answered, following with the coffee tray.

"There she is!" Al said, as if she'd been gone for hours. "There's my little girl."

Cathy smiled, the perfect hostess to her new neighbors. With them, and with Al, she felt safe. She was her husband's little girl, so young and so beautiful. She was the most active of all their friends, the one who could play three sets of tennis at the club or wear the new, revealing gowns. They looked at her with envy, admiration... just the way it had been when she was one of the Regulars.

She was thirty-eight years old. Could she somehow manage to be a Regular again? Could she face the cameras again—and survive?

5.

"BUT *WHY*, MOM. I COULD DO IT THERE—"

"You're not going to do it there," Connie Schmidt told Jimmy, her nine-year-old. "You're going to do that homework right here in your room and I'm going to see it before you go anywhere. And do it carefully, Jimmy. I want to see a much better report card than the last one."

"Oh, Mom," he said, going back to his books. "Tell your sister to turn that stereo down, too!" Connie called after him. She stirred the tomato sauce and tasted it, then added more sugar: Carl loved her sauce, but anything acid made his stomach act up, and sugar was the best way of cutting the acidity of the tomatoes.

"... According to the latest statistics, released today in Washington, the government estimates that a typical American family will spend an average of sixty-six thousand dollars during the first twenty-one years of each child's life," the TV announcer informed her. "Details at five o'clock."

"Blessed Madonna," Connie said. "Enough TV, Ralphie. Turn it off like a good boy, okay?"

Her six-year-old had come home complaining of a sore throat, and she'd let him watch TV in the kitchen since he'd been unable to go to his Cub Scout meeting.

"Mommy, do we have sixty-six thousand dollars?" he asked.

"No," she answered.

"Does that mean we're poor? Are we gonna have to eat food like they bring to church when they collect the cans for the poor people?"

It was hard not to laugh, but Ralphie's face showed real concern.

"Of course not, honey," Connie told him, stroking his forehead. "We'll be just fine. Go lay down till Daddy comes home like a good boy. You can read or color in your bed." She kissed him quickly.

Before he was out of the room, Angie entered the kitchen, her fourteen-year-old features set in a pout.

"Jimmy says I have to turn the stereo off—"

"Not off. Just down."

"But it's Patti Smith, Mom—"

"Angie, I don't care if it's Pattie Page—"

"Who?"

"Never mind. Just turn it down."

"Oh, you're so—so old-fashioned!" her daughter said. With her usual sense of the theatrical, she made a dramatic exit.

"Hi, Mom!" Carl, Jr. said, coming in the back door. "What's for supper."

"Chicken," she answered.

"Ya? Funny, it smells like sauce."

"That's for tomorrow. I'm making lasagna. Are you working tonight?"

He told her he was, and she reminded him again about not throwing his dirty, gas-station overalls into the laundry basket, where the grease got all over everything.

"I promise," he assured her. She told him that Jimmy had a sore throat and that it would be nice if he spent a few minutes with his brother after he set the table.

She checked the potatoes, baking with the chicken in the oven, and the carrots cooking on top of the stove. Only when the clatter of dishes had ceased in the dining room, and her son had gone to his room, did she allow herself the luxury of a break. Duke, the twelve-year-old German shephard, was curled up under the table. As Connie sat down, the animal looked up and half-heartedly flicked his tail.

"And what do you want, as if I didn't know?" she asked. With a sigh, she got up and opened the cabinet under the sink to get him a dog biscuit.

She'd come to relish the last half-hour before Carl came home, when she was sometimes lucky enough to have the kitchen to herself. Not that she'd accomplished everything she'd planned to do during the course of the day, but that was something she was used to, too.

It had been three months since Louise, eighteen, had gone to the Sisters of Mt. Carmel upstate, and Connie still wasn't sure how she felt about it. Louise was the first of their children to leave home, and there was that to deal with. Ever since she'd had Louise, Connie had been thinking and dreaming about the wedding her daughter would have—bigger than even her own. She'd been saving for it since Louise's birth, just as her mother had saved for her wedding. Instead, Louise, always serious and so good in school, had chosen to become a Bride of Christ. She was certain that she had a true and real vocation. Connie found herself feeling proud of having been able to give her child a good, religious upbringing at a time when so many people were drifting away from the church, but she felt a sadness as well.

The firstborn child is always special, she thought—even if a good mother tries not to show it. If her first year at the convent proved that her call was true, they would never have those special mother/daughter moments. Connie told herself that she was being selfish, and made a mental note to bring it up at confession. After all, if God had called Louise to serve Him, it was a blessing. Who was she to wish otherwise? She and Carl had other children, all of them healthy, thank God.

Carl, Jr., and Louise were just a year apart in age, but they were a world apart in interests and personality. Where Louise had always been quiet, Carl Jr. was noisy, even boisterous. Louise had always loved to read—Carl, Jr. only picked up books or magazines about cars.

"Looks like he'll be a heck of a mechanic," her husband said, when the boy announced his plans to go to a manual training high school. "And he'll also be happy. That's what counts."

Connie had had to agree, even if it meant that her dream of watching Carl, Jr. graduate from college would never come true. You couldn't plan your kids' lives for them, no matter how good your intentions were. Angie had demonstrated a definite talent for mathematics, and Jimmy was interested—at the moment—in science. Ralphie, in less than a month, had "decided" he wanted to be a rock star, then a pilot, then a racing driver. Connie had learned to sit back and wait for nature to take its course.

Sitting at the kitchen table, she thought of everything she'd planned to do that day—and of all the tasks that had gone undone. First, when the breakfast dishes were done, she had taken the new robe she'd bought for her mother back to Macy's: ever since the stroke, Mama found it hard to get things on and off unless the sleeves were wide and loose. It had taken her nearly an hour, searching in every department, to find something that was the right size, weight, and cut.

Then she'd gone to the nursing home where her mother

was recovering, putting in her usual two hours, staying a little bit longer to visit with Regina, her sister, who arrived at noon from Mineola.

From the nursing home, she'd gone to the market, shopping not only for herself, but also for Dora Hershel, her next-door neighbor who'd just come back from having a cyst removed in the hospital.

Marcie Abruzio, her best friend and head of their church group's Sunshine Committee, was going to Denver to spend a month with her daughter: Connie had been unable to turn down Marcie's request to take over the job of sending out the club's social correspondence (the birthday and "get well" cards), and they'd spent nearly an hour making a list of who had an anniversary coming up.

When Marcie left, Connie had started cooking and tried to go over the bills, but it was impossible. Between her friends and her sisters (and her sisters-in-law), the phone hadn't stopped ringing. She'd finally given up even trying to work on her budget. The kids had begun coming in from school.

Kids... There were times when having five of them gave you no special advantage in understanding them, Connie thought. And, too, there were times when she found it difficult to believe she'd ever been as young as her children—any of them—were. Being "young" was so different nowadays.

If she (or any of her six brothers and sisters) had ever dared to talk to Mama and Papa the way her brood routinely spoke to her and Carl, they'd have been unable to sit down for a week. Though her mother was a first-generation American and her father had only been a baby when his family emigrated from Milan, there'd been an Old World atmosphere about the house in Brooklyn, and a definite Old World value system instilled in her from her earliest memories.

Home, church, and school had been the focus of their lives. The course and boundaries of their existence were staked out by Mama and enforced by Papa. "Disrespect," whether for the authority of a parent, a teacher, or (heaven forbid) the teachings they learned in Catechism, was the unpardonable sin. Looking back, Connie realized that it had really been no different for any of their Flatbush neighbors. Whether the "old" country in question was Italy, Germany, or Ireland, the tradition of ironclad parental rule and right was the same. The mother tongue might be Yiddish, Polish, or Russian instead of Italian; it was still used when parents wanted to discuss something without the children understanding—as, of course, they inevitably did.

In her own family, as in every other, there were occasional acts of defiance and rebellion. Anthony, her oldest brother, had been fated for some kind of collision course with their parents. He'd been an altar boy, going along with Mama's plans to a point, but even their priest had gently explained that he wasn't the sort of young man cut out for the priesthood. Compounding matters, he then insisted on quitting school and taking a job on the docks. Mama had told him that he must get his diploma, and Papa had warned of what would happen if he continued to "disrespect" his mother.

As long as she lived, Connie would never forget the scene that had taken place on the Friday night when Anthony announced that he'd officially quit high school and would be starting work the next Monday. The dinner table went dead silent. Papa's face flushed and his eyes burned with fury. Mama sobbed. Then Papa had struck his son. Anthony raised his hand, threatening for a moment to return the blow, but instead he turned and left the room. Minutes later, without a word of good-bye, he left the house, suitcase in hand. It took three years, until he married, before his parents spoke to or forgave their oldest son. Connie was ten years old.

When she was fifteen, it was her sister Rosa who was causing problems.

Mama and Frieda Goldman had known each other for years—not surprising since the two families' backyards adjoined. Morning after morning, hanging the wash or beating rugs, they exchanged the neighborhood news. Once Rosa Donati and Joe Goldman began walking to and from school together every day, though, the two women had huddled for secret talks. As different as their faiths and backgrounds were, they shared a common belief that while America was the Great Melting Pot, and while It Took All Kinds, it was important that their children recognize that Sticking to Your Own Kind was a basic rule of life when it came to romance.

For a full year, Mama had waited, worried, and prayed at mass each day that the Blessed Virgin would intercede and bring Rosa to her senses. Her hopes had risen briefly in December, when Joe, who was half a year ahead in school, had graduated. He was going to work for his uncle, who had a wholesale button business on Canal Street on Manhattan's Lower East Side. There'd be plenty of girls—nice girls, and his own kind, too—for Joe to meet. Rosa would find a nice boy, one of *her* kind...

But if anything, Rosa's feelings grew more intense as Joe acquired maturity, sophistication, and a third-hand Dodge. When Mama and Papa refused to let her go out of the house to meet Joe at night, Rosa either stayed in or involved her sisters in plans and schemes of deception. Just as the Goldmans' rabbi had been unable to dissuade Joe from his romantic pursuits, the priest sadly reported that while Rosa had indeed listened to him, and seemed well aware of the problems mixed marriages inevitably brought, she'd been unwilling to give the boy up.

The help of relatives was sought. Through aunts and uncles, a succession of Nice Italian Boys from Good Catholic Homes came to call on Rosa. Rosa was polite, but she firmly refused to see any of them a second time. Over the clothesline, Frieda Goldman sadly commiserated: it was the same with her Joe and the Nice Jewish Girls they tried in vain to interest him in.

The September after graduation, Rosa and Joe eloped. Neither the Donatis nor the Goldmans would recognize the ceremony performed by a New Jersey justice of the peace, and both families spoke of having "lost" a child.

Connie hadn't even bothered to tell her parents about the *Dancetime, USA!* competition when she entered it. It was one thing to be able to do the latest steps at a church-supervised record hop, but it was quite another to be chosen to do them—from hundreds of kids—on a television program. She'd never expected to get as far as the first elimination, but to her surprise, she made it. Other girls were prettier, she knew, but everyone always told her that she was "loaded with personality." Maybe the judges thought so, too, Connie decided, and considered personality more important than height or a pretty face.

When she became a finalist she had no choice but to tell Mama and Papa the truth. *How* to tell them was another matter. Then Celia, her older sister, had come through. Ever since Celia had married (a Nice Italian Boy her parents approved of) and had her first child, she'd been on a different footing with Mama. The shared experience of marriage and childbirth entitled her to greater respect than the kids at home. If Mama wouldn't come around to Celia's way of thinking, she'd at least listen.

While Connie babysat, Celia had discussed *Dancetime, USA!* with her parents. It would be a guarantee of Connie's whereabouts, she pointed out—they wouldn't have to wonder where she was every day after school. Somehow Celia managed to convince them to permit their daughter to become a Regular. After that, being chosen was almost an anti-climax.

From the start, she made friends quickly. The other

girls had been stand-offish with each other, continually competing. Connie knew she didn't have Cathy's perfect, doll-like coloring and features, or Lorraine's figure and stature. Mama would have killed her if she'd tried to put a streak in her hair like Sandy. Since she wasn't in the race for Resident Beauty of the show, the other girls were friendlier to her. Coming from a big family made her a natural listener (not that there'd been much choice at home), and she'd inherited her mother's practicality. Within weeks of *Dancetime*'s debut, the other girls were telling her their problems and asking for advice.

With the exception of Sandy, who was crazy about Dennis and adored by Bobby, and Donna, who sometimes dated Don, no real romances sprang up between The Regulars, though the magazines made up endless stories for the fans. Connie had promised to light a candle when she was paired with Tony, by far the slickest boy in the group, but she never considered bringing him home. He was the program's resident greaser, with the longest hair, slicked back and kept in place with the frequent use of the comb that was a fixture in the back pocket of his tight black pants.

His coat and tie were things he endured for the sake of being on television, just as he trimmed his sideburns to conform with the network's regulations. Connie knew there was no chance of dating Tony, in spite of the fact that he was Italian and handsome. But they'd been friends; Tony treated her almost like a sister, and the other guys adopted the attitude. She was easily the most popular member of the group, always ready to lend a shoulder or crack a joke.

It was a comfortable image, and the show itself was so exciting that Connie had been more than happy to accept her role. Once the initial novelty of celebrity wore off, she found herself enthralled by show business, amazed by the differences between the way things looked and the way they were. The teen idols who appeared on the program as guest stars were an education—male heart-throbs and girl singers as well.

Until she was selected by TBS, she had always believed that everything she read in the papers was gospel: she didn't know what publicity was. Like everyone else she knew, Connie had taken it for granted that when a performer appeared on TV singing a song, he was actually singing. It was what the kids watching at home thought, too, she realized, except for the couple of times that a record got stuck, or skipped while a performer was lip-synching his or her number.

Still more surprising was the awareness that many of the overnight sensations who had top-charted songs weren't even comfortable with their success. The viewers at home never saw the way some of them paced or bit their nails as they waited off-camera. Once on camera, they turned on a casual style that was studied and practiced. The fans saw only the performance, and the fancy clothes.

There was big money in show business, Connie began to think. And there was the possibility of a big, bright future for her. The magazines said that Fox was considering making a movie starring Lee Dean and The Regulars. True or not, this news gave Connie a sense of her own position.

People already knew who she was. Those who *really* knew her told her over and over that she had a terrific personality and a natural sense of humor. If Annette could be a star, if Patty Duke could be a star, why couldn't Connie Donati be one, too, she asked herself?

For the first time in her life, she began to make concrete plans for her future. She'd never given the subject much thought, resigning herself to marrying the way Celia had, to raising a family. Much as she loved Mama, though, Connie felt things Mama didn't fully understand.

Mama liked the endless scrubbing and polishing, the familiar routine of the cooking and washing and ironing.

Connie longed for something else, something *more*, but since she had no idea of what the something was, she tried to suppress her feelings.

Once she discovered show business, her hidden dreams rushed to the surface.

I don't have to spend my life in a kitchen, she decided. *I can spend it in the spotlight!*

When she was asked to appear in her class show, as a result of being a Regular, Connie was convinced she was on her way. She decided to do a comedy skit rather than a serious number. With the help of a few friends, Connie staged a burlesque of *Dancetime, USA!* in which she played a singer whose record got stuck. It was the hit of the show, and everyone congratulated her on not only being funny, but being good-natured enough to laugh at the show and therefore herself.

Being at the studio every day gave Connie an opportunity to meet and observe agents and managers. Once she decided to make show business a career, she made it a point to remember their names—and to make certain they remembered hers. A book had informed her that contacts were an "important part of the business."

Watching the real performers in front of the cameras, she gave her fantasies full reign. She knew just how she wanted to look when her turn came—not too artificially glamorous, since most of her fan mail said that she looked so "real." No, she wouldn't straighten her hair (she *might* have it done at a fancy salon), and she wouldn't wear gobs of makeup—only enough to make the most of her brown eyes and full lips, which she decided were her two best features. She'd smile and be very sincere when she thanked an audience for its applause, and why not? It would be fun...

"You're crazy," Celia told her, when Connie confided her plan during the program's second season. "What can you do that people would pay to see?"

Connie was taken aback.

"I can do lots of things," she said, trying to "project" confidence. Mrs. Trahorn, who taught the dramatics course at school, had told the class that it was essential to *project* an emotion one wanted to convey.

"You'll break your heart," said Celia. "New York is full of kids your age who think that show business is waiting for them. They end up going home to their folks without a cent left... unless something worse happens. What you should really be thinking about is finding yourself a nice man like I did..."

Thanks but no thanks! Connie thought, biting her tongue. Celia was twenty-two, and already expecting her third child. Her hair always seemed to be in rollers, as if she never removed them or brushed her set out. She'd once had a nice figure, but it was gone. Her days revolved around diapers and formula and taking care of her husband Frank. If it made Celia happy, Connie decided, that was fine... but *she* was going to have *more*!

Movie rumors continued to crop up from time to time, but there was never anything concrete. In the meantime, there were the record hops where she and Tony and other Regulars would make guest appearances with Lee Dean. There was no pay—not that it mattered: the recognition and response she got from the crowds were enough, and besides, it would count later as professional experience.

Connie expected the show to launch her career. The last thing in the world she'd ever imagined was that *Dancetime, USA!* could be cancelled, even after the scandal. But one day Connie arrived at the studio to find the doors locked. The Regulars were permitted to use the stage door: maybe, she reasoned, there had been a mixup. She'd go around to the front...

Two hundred and fifty angry teenagers, many of whom had waited months for tickets, were refusing to listen to the voice of Carl Knight, the show's producer. Again and again he raised his hands, trying to quiet them.

"... Give me a break, will you, kids?" he asked. "I'm

sorry. I know some of you have come a long way. But until further notice, the show has been cancelled. We have tickets here for some of the other TBS programs—"

"We don't want 'em!"

"We want *Dancetime, USA!*"

"Where's Lee?"

Connie had stared in disbelief at the familiar faces of Tony, Cathy, and the others. It wasn't happening! It couldn't happen!

The Regulars had pushed themselves through the crowd, toward the producer.

"It's like I said," he told them. "We've been cancelled."

"Until further notice," someone said.

Earl Knight sighed. "That's right. That's what it says in the official release. We've got your numbers. Go on home. We'll call you."

On the way back to Flatbush, Connie wondered when Earl would call. Celia told her later that the show was gone for good.

That June, Connie Donati graduated from high school. Mama and Papa told her to get a job. Celia suggested that Connie give her a hand for the summer, then go job-hunting in the fall when student help wasn't available and the opportunities would be better.

What Celia was really doing, Connie understood, was giving her a chance to "get it out of her system." Mama was never told about the afternoons spent in New York, auditioning for bored producers at cattle calls and trying to see agents who weren't the least bit impressed with her clippings from the fan magazines.

Dramas, comedies, musicals—*what* the show was didn't matter. The important thing was getting a part, her *first* part. By August, without a big break in sight, she'd begun to panic. A girl she'd met at one of her auditions had told Connie about a Greenwich Village nightclub that held talent nights every Thursday. You signed up, waited for your turn, then sang or did a comedy routine. The girl wasn't sure just which one, but a very big star had been discovered there by one of the big agents (she wasn't exactly sure *which* big agent, but assured Connie that she'd recognize the name) who was scouting for new talent.

Outside of family get-togethers, when she was allowed a glass of wine, and graduation night, when she'd gotten sick from drinking beer, Connie had never had a real drink... much less been in a real nightclub. Determined to succeed, *and* prove her talent and independence, she told her parents she was going bowling "with the girls."

Instead, she took a subway to Washington Square.

The Champagne Room was not the glamorous night club she'd imagined, nor did anyone sitting at the tables covered with red-and-white checkered tablecloths look like an important agent. But the manager dutifully wrote her name down and asked if she had any music.

"I'm going to do comedy," Connie answered, praying that she wouldn't forget any of the monologue that had earned her an "A" from Mrs. Trahorn. The manager looked at her for a long moment, then nodded and directed her to a table.

She was pleased when a waitress asked her what kind of cocktail she wanted without even asking to see her ID. She ordered a Manhattan because it sounded sophisticated—she hoped. When the waitress demanded seventy-five cents, Connie was certain it was a mistake.

"I'm in the show tonight," she explained.

"Sure, honey. So's everyone else," the woman told her, holding her hand out. Connie handed her a dollar bill from her plastic clutch bag, hoping that the quarter tip wasn't too big or too small. The drink tasted awful.

The show began. The MC was the manager, who introduced the various acts, using the time between them to urge customers to "drink up," and to remind everyone that in addition to the possibility of being "discovered," the winner—the act that received the most applause at the end of the evening—would receive a bottle of imported champagne, courtesy of the Champagne Room.

The first three acts were atrocious. A nervous bleached blonde, trying hard (but not too successfully) to look this side of forty, sang "Blues in the Night" so fast it sounded as if she were in a race with the piano player. An ancient-looking man told jokes that were even older than he was. A pockmarked, hook-nosed man sang "Out of This World"—and looked it.

The "talent" ranged from nonexistent to semi-passable. Sitting alone at the small table, Connie tried to tell herself that it wasn't so bad. She was bound to come off well if only in comparison with the other contestants. But she knew it *was* that bad, and worse: any hopes she'd had, any sense of finally having arrived in The Big Time were dashed. The small club was stifling. She downed her cocktail in spite of the taste and ordered another, hoping it would make her feel more relaxed.

"And now, Miss Connie Donati," the MC said suddenly. "Let's give her a big welcome, ladies and gentlemen. Connie Donati!"

The repetition of her own name startled her. Connie glanced up, wondering how four glasses, all of them empty, had somehow gotten on the table before her. She vaguely remembered pulling dollar bills from her purse and handing them to the waitress.

As she tried to hurry from her table to the spotlight, the polite applause died. She forced herself to smile, and went right into the monologue that had been such a hit in her dramatics class. One joke died, then another, then another. Connie tried to remember the words and tried not to sweat as she stumbled over the awkward pauses where the laughs were supposed to be. The lights in her eyes were bright, but she could still see the faces of the customers: they were turned away, avoiding eye contact with her just as she'd avoided it with the dismal performers who preceded her.

A lump formed in her throat, forcing her to push the words out. She heard her voice break once, then again. *It couldn't be happening! It wasn't true!* Yet it was: she was a dud, a bomb, a washout. All this time Celia had been right, and she'd only been fooling herself. She wanted to be home—anywhere but in the spotlight, making a fool out of herself. Crying would only make it worse, and she wouldn't let herself do it. She'd force herself to finish, even if she did have to go to the bathroom, and she felt faint and nauseous at the same time.

But suddenly she was unable to continue. The facade cracked. In mid-sentence, Connie Donati bolted, tears of embarrassment blinding her. She bumped into tables as she propelled herself toward the door. Only when she was on the sidewalk did she realize that she'd left her purse at her table: it was a long walk home to Flatbush.

"I think you forgot something, miss," a deep voice said as she stood there, crying on the sidewalk. He handed her the bag, and his handkerchief, and told her that his name was Carl Schmidt. He'd decided to stop in for a drink because one of his friends was in St. Vincent's Hospital recovering from a fall he'd had on the job—and he insisted that she hadn't been that bad.

"I was awful," Connie wailed, sitting beside him in his battered Nash. She wasn't even thinking of what Mama would have to say about having let a strange man drive her home.

"I don't know," he answered lightly. "I think you're pretty cute."

Three months later, they were married. Carl's father was German, but his mother (to the Donati's delight) was Italian. Instead of reading *Variety* and *Backstage* in search of professional opportunities, Connie found herself scanning the *Times* classified section for apartments, and searching *Ladies Home Journal* for easy-to-fix, easy-on-the-budget casserole recipes.

Thinking about it, she laughed aloud. She'd ended up a carbon copy of Mama after all.

"Gonna let me in on the joke?" a familiar voice asked.

"Hi, honey," she said, smiling and standing to enter the circle of her husband's open arms. As they kissed, she clung to him tightly.

"What'sa matter?" Carl asked, stepping back to study her face. "Nothin's wrong, is it?"

"No, everything's fine. Wonderful, in fact," Connie assured him.

In a fraction of a second, Duke was nuzzling his way in between them, Ralphie came in complaining that his throat felt worse, Jimmy announced he was "starving," Angie's stereo was back at full blast, and the phone was ringing.

"I guess I spoke too soon," Connie told her husband, taking command with a veteran's precision. "Jimmy, go and wash your hands—you're not coming to my table with hands like that. Tell your sister to answer the phone, since it's probably for her, and tell her to turn that thing *down*!" Duke sat patiently as she dished out his dinner of leftovers and dog chow, and Ralphie promised to be a good boy and go back to bed, provided she'd read him a story when she brought him his tray.

It was business as usual, she thought. *Home hectic home...*

That was when her daughter came in to tell her that a lady from TBS-TV was on the phone, asking for her.

6.

THERE WAS ONLY A 60-WATT BULB IN THE small lamp beside the bed, and that was obscured by the dirty shade. *What a stinkin' hellhole*, Tony Merino thought, turning toward the light. The springs of the bed creaked with the movement, punctuating the ceaseless sound of traffic from the street below and the grinding motor of the fan that stirred the air instead of cooling it.

The envelope explained the delay between the time the letter had been sent and the time it had reached him—rerouted to two different addresses before it turned up in his mother's mailbox. She had forwarded it to Miami with the usual threatening letters from lawyers and bill collectors. He'd read it so many times in the past two days he knew it by heart. Still, he carefully removed and unfolded it again, his lips moving slightly as he went over the familiar words typed beneath the embossed network logo.

Dear Mr. Merino:
After trying unsuccessfully to contact you by tele-

phone, I'm writing in the hope that this letter will reach you.

I hope, too, that you'll accept this invitation to participate in what promises to be one of the most exciting events of the coming television season. This fall, the Trans-American Broadcasting System will present a Dancetime, USA! special themed around the twentieth year reunion of this landmark program's Regulars. Lee Dean will once again host, and he guests will include several of the top stars of the 1950's recreating their hits of two decades ago.

As a part of television history, I'm sure you'll enjoy this chance to catch up with a number of old friends, including your former partner, Connie (Donati) Schmidt, as much as the many viewers who remember you will enjoy seeing you again.

Naturally, TBS will take care of all travel arrangements and expenses while you are in New York, where the special will be done as the show itself was—live.

Your presence would contribute greatly to what promises to be a memorable television special, and what we hope will be a pleasant experience for you. Won't you call me, collect, at your earliest convenience? I look forward to speaking with you.

Cordially,
Sheila Granger,
Staff Producer

He stared at the heavy piece of stationery for a long time, then let it fall to the frayed chenille bedspread. Propping a sagging pillow behind his neck, he leaned against the iron headboard and lit a cigarette. Just for the hell of it, he French-inhaled the way that was so cool in the old days. As he released the smoke, it rose in a leisurely spiral before the fan dispersed it.

Jesus, he told himself, shaking his head, wouldn't you know it? Of all times, the letter had to come now. Not a few years ago, when he'd been raking the bucks in back in

Vegas. Or even a few months back, when he'd been in Palm Beach with Joan. No, it had to come now, when he was alone and broke, with everything good in the past and nothing but crap in the foreseeable future.

Once, the future was a thing he'd taken for granted—when he bothered to think about it at all. Time in general hadn't been divided into what had gone before and what was to come: it was all *good* time, and he'd been certain that it would last forever.

If only someone had told him! If only somebody had taken the time—just a few minutes—to take him aside and explain that it wasn't going to *always* be that way... that you had to make the most of the good times when you had them, because bad times were sure to come.

Where had the twenty years, his whole life as an adult, gone? How had he used up so much time? He could recall moments, episodes, but where was the space between them? Months and whole years, even, were blank. The realization made his head ache, and Tony closed his eyes, trying to shut his senses off. There was no point in making himself feel bad. Okay, so he was down on his luck. So what? That was the way the cookie crumbled, but it didn't mean there weren't other cookies in the box.

His luck would change. A break would come along. Something would happen, something that would put him back on Easy Street...

Easy Street? Who was he kidding? It had been a hell of a long time since he'd been able to fool himself. He'd been able to turn away from the truth, or a part of it, but it had still always been there, under the surface of his thoughts. His life had been comfortable at times, luxurious even. But nothing had come cheap, and certainly not for free. It had been livable, but it had never been as good as he'd expected it would and should be. He'd had a set idea in his mind of how it would feel when all the pieces of the puzzle came together. Over and over he tried to find the situation that felt perfect.

There'd been a lot of near misses, times when he'd tried to make himself believe that he'd found it. Even if he didn't acknowledge the tension and the sense of being off-target, they'd been there. Sooner or later, they always managed to catch up with him.

The funny part was, he'd always been the guy everyone thought was on top of things... Jesus, what a goof! That was what he wanted them to think, of course—putting on an act, making them all believe that it was for real, had been part of his private survival formula ever since he could remember, starting when he was a kid, growing up in Hell's Kitchen.

He often wondered if any of those buildings had ever been new. The neighborhood was poor and tough: school taught you how to read and write and count, but the street gave you another education. If you had anything, there was always somebody looking to take it away. You had to fight for what was yours, both to get it and to hold it.

For a long time, he'd been afraid of confrontation to the point of terror. All the other boys had been filling out, putting on weight and muscles, but the only way he'd grown was up. Tall and skinny, he was sure he'd get creamed in a fight, going out of his way to avoid trouble. Then, one day, the sweet knowledge had come to him. Without knowing how, he'd found out; he understood that if you acted tough, if you had the balls to carry it off, you didn't have to prove it. It was a combination of how you looked and moved, what you said and what you wore... an *attitude*.

By the time he hit high school he had it down to a science. Pointed black shoes (there was a rule against wearing motorcycle boots to classes), white socks, tight black pants low on his hips with a garrison belt, a tight white T-shirt with the pack of Luckies stashed in the rolled-up sleeve, and the motorcycle jacket he'd purposly scuffed up to make it look like a veteran of a dozen street fights. There were plenty of them, too; once in a while he had to fight in spite of himself.

Most of the time, though, there were other guys to do the fighting, guys who had muscle power but nothing more. They envied his style, the way he smoked a cigarette (copied from James Dean movies) and continually combed his dark hair, slicked back at the sides and falling forward in curls over his forehead. He had an easy way of talking to the girls, who spent hours writing his initials and his name on their notebooks, and who giggled and sighed about his long sideburns.

He'd been brighter than he'd let on, ignoring even the subjects that interested him because it wasn't cool to be a grind. Instead, he used his mind to come up with the wisecracks that sent him to detention room or the principal's office—but not until everyone had laughed and agreed with their looks that Tony Merino wasn't afraid of anybody.

There were other kids—most of them, in fact—who tried to look and act older and more sure of themselves than they were. At dances, the facade was readily apparent. Overly made-up girls trying to look sophisticated stayed on one side of the room; boys, uncomfortable in the required ties and jackets they hardly ever wore (and had usually outgrown) were on the other. Only a few couples regularly danced, but Tony was always among them.

Whom he danced with didn't really matter, as long as she didn't have two left feet or try to lead. Most girls were more than content to go limp in his arms, to let him pull them so close that their necks were locked against his shoulder, his pelvis, pushed forward, a temporary part of their bodies. When a song was over, they'd try to walk calmly back to their friends—as if their cheeks weren't flushed—to answer the questions about What It Felt Like. If he could mouth off in class, or perpetuate the myth of his own invulnerability when he hung out with his friends, it was on the dance floor that he shone. Spinning a partner away from him, drawing her back with a snap of his wrist, he knew that there were dozens of envious eyes on him. He was smooth, sharp, and cool... *real tough*.

When one of the guys awkwardly asked him where and how he learned to dance that way, Tony replied that he didn't know. It was the truth—the movement and ease came naturally to him, as if his lanky body had been created for that purpose. The mother who'd died before he was old enough to remember her, and the father who made only an occasional drunken appearance at the apartment where he lived with his grandmother, had met at a dance, Tony had always been told. Sometimes he wondered what they had looked like, moving together to the music. He was aware of the admiration and envy for his natural talent, though he pretended to take it for granted. It was another tool in the arsenal of his self-defense.

He enjoyed it, but that was about as far as it went. The thought of entering the TBS competition to become a Regular on *Dancetime, USA!* hadn't occurred to him. Diane Curran, the girl he was dating at the time, was the one who wanted to enter. She talked him into going to the first tryout with her. She wasn't picked, but Tony, who filled out a form because he was handed one, was selected. Diane had cried, and when he told her to forget the whole thing (which was just what he was planning to do) she became even more upset: he *had* to go back, she insisted! He *couldn't* pass up this chance...

The whole crowd had picked up on it. Once he realized that the show carried status that could enhance his image, Tony decided to try out in earnest.

The other finalists, he noticed, were more in the image of clean-cut, all-American high school kids. Even with his sideburns trimmed a fraction of an inch, and his leather jacket temporarily exchanged for sharkskin, he stood out, a little rougher, a little wilder, and a little more dangerous than the rest of them. He hadn't really expected to be chosen (and he wasn't about to change his style just to get on some TV show), and he hadn't much cared. Just by making it to the last round of the selection, by getting his picture and name in the paper, he'd added to his own legend.

When he was picked as one of The Regulars, the whole school had gone crazy. The principal had overruled his homeroom teacher, Mrs. Streen, who refused to give him the required recommendation: having one of his students on the program would reflect well on the school, and who knew? It was possible that the opportunity would make Tony more responsible.

From the start, Tony Merino had been popular with the millions of viewers who watched *Dancetime, USA!* every day. Connie had been a perfect partner. Not only did she pick up steps quickly but, like Tony, she was a little different from Bobby and Sandy, Lorraine and Don and the others. They were both dark-haired and olive-skinned—as "exotic" as TBS dared to get without risking the wrath of southern affiliates. The magazines, fed by the network publicity department, called them "Dance Party's Perfect Couple," with Tony playing "Mr. Cool" to Connie's image as "The Girl Who Makes The Regulars Giggle." Layouts proclaimed him "*Dancetime*'s Resident Dreamboat," and his mail reflected thousands of teenage crushes.

Unlike the others, Tony had been streetwise enough to figure out the angles. Lee Dean and TBS had a good thing, he'd thought—it was an "honor" to be one of The Regulars, which meant you didn't get paid. But there were ways of promoting clothes, ID bracelets, records, and even a new record player... As long as the magazines wanted to take pictures and ask questions, why not pose with albums you got for free, in clothes that were supplied by stores and manufacturers eager to have their merchandise seen and quick to pass out free samples.

Just as he'd once made the kids at school think he was sure of himself when he wasn't, Tony made The Regulars and the home viewers believe that he was as sharp as a tack. In time, he'd even begun to convince himself. After all, hundreds of letters poured in each week from girls who told him he was the handsomest guy on the show. Looks and style were what life was all about: Tony Merino decided that he was a natural-born winner.

The good times, he'd been convinced, were going to last forever. And they could have—if Lee Dean hadn't been such a jerk.

None of the other Regulars had even acted as if the payola scandal mattered, not that any of them cared much about news in general. New songs, new styles, what the magazines wrote about them and how much fan mail they got were more important considerations than the Cold War and the space race. Still, when the papers had begun writing about payola and the Congressmen in Washington started demanding investigations, instinct had told Tony that the party just might be over. Sure enough, it was.

Tony had sized things up. Dick Clark had issued a sworn notarized statement and ABC had backed him fully. That, as Tony saw it, meant that hot as the investigators might be for a chance to come down on Clark, they wouldn't find anything to "uncover." Lee Dean was another matter. Everyone knew that the promotion men for the record companies were tight with him, and he was always hanging around with them. The weekend vacations, the gifts he received for doing them the favor of pushing their new artists—it may have been standard operating procedure in the business, but once the media got through with it, things were going to look bad.

The thing to do was to plan ahead. Along with Connie and another couple, he'd appeared at a big party one of the record companies threw for an announcers' convention held in New York. All they had to do was dance to a few of the records the company was pushing to the deejays, then spend an hour and a half giving tape interviews the announcers could take home and play for their listeners. In return, the record company gave each of them an expensive radio, a camera, and a load of albums.

What impressed Tony most of all wasn't the gifts, but a brief exchange he had with Dorothy "Dolly" Michaels, widow of the man who'd founded the CJ label. Her husband, Tony learned, was one of the entrepreneurs who'd made a fortune by getting in on rock and roll when it was wide open and new. The traditionally conservative major labels had insisted that the "new" music was just a trend, a fad that would pass. But innovators like Herman Michaels had seen the magnitude of the new trend, and they'd signed up street-corner groups, turning unknowns into stars and establishing themselves and their labels in the process. From rented studio time, a couple thousand dollars' worth of borrowed capital, and a knack for guessing which songs would click in the new and burgeoning market, Herman Michaels had turned CJ Records into an established label with an unusually high percentage of gold records.

A heart attack had killed him in 1957, but Dolly, his wife, had come into the business, taking up the slack and refusing the offers from competitors to buy her out. Her acumen surprised many... the many who didn't know that from the very beginning, she'd been a combination bookkeeper, talent scout, and sounding board for her husband's business ideas. She planned out the promotion CJ would do for the deejay convention, and it had been her idea to bring in the *Dancetime* Regulars. Tony had been a little surprised to find her standing beside him as he drank a Coke at the cocktail party, where CJ artists and The Regulars were mingling with the announcers, but she'd quickly put him at ease.

"You're Tony, aren't you?" she asked, introducing herself. "I've enjoyed you so much on television."

He wondered if she was teasing him: *Dancetime, USA!* was for kids, and she was somewhere on the other side of thirty-five.

"I know what you're thinking," Dolly said, laughing. "And yes, I am a little...more mature, should I say?...than most of your viewers. It's part of my job, Tony. I try to keep up with the trends and interests of the market."

They spoke for a few minutes, the conversation light and pleasant on the surface. Beneath it, Tony sensed something he couldn't quite define. Dolly seemed to be studying him, as if sizing him up. Without knowing why, he felt a kind of nervous excitement.

"What are you planning to do when you're through with the show?" she asked him.

He shrugged. "I'm not sure."

"Really?" Dolly asked. "You strike me as the kind of man who has his future all planned out. Well, if you should decide to try the record business, you be *sure* to come see me first. We just might be able to make an arrangement of some sort." She'd stroked his cheek with her fingers, letting her hand linger a moment longer than the gesture required, then she'd gone off to mingle with the crowd.

Time and time again, lying in bed at night, Tony found himself thinking of Dolly Michaels. He tried to convince himself that she'd just been trying to make conversation. That was all—she was just being pleasant. But the look in her eyes and the memory of her hand, cool and smooth against his cheek, were impossible to shake off. It was almost as though she was...well, if it wasn't for the difference in their ages, like she were coming on to him, for Christ's sake! The thought excited him.

As the payola mess grew stickier, his sexual fantasies about Dolly changed into something else. He'd been wrong to think that she was physically interested in him, Tony decided: she was a businesswoman, and she figured that because of his experience on *Dancetime* he could be useful, maybe in promotion or something like that. It could be the start of a career, and a damn good one at that—the promotion men who hung around the show always had cars and girls and plenty of cash. A general diploma wasn't exactly a passport to opportunity, and that was all he'd graduate with. Maybe he'd be better off using the education he'd gotten from being on *Dancetime* on the fringes of the music business. After all, he knew what kids liked and what they listened to.

"Well, this *is* a pleasure," Dolly Michaels said; when her secretary led him into her office. "Care for a drink?"

Tony was about to ask for a Coke when she came around the desk, passing close enough so that he could smell her perfume, and opened a cabinet to reveal a built-in bar.

"Sure," he said, trying to sound casual. "Whatever you're having."

"Scotch," she answered, pouring them each a hefty shot over ice, then adding a splash of water. "To the future?" she asked, handing him a glass, taking a sip of her own. "Your future, I mean. Poor Lee's really in trouble. When does he testify?"

She was testing him, Tony realized, to see if he was aware of what was going on. "Next week. Tuesday, I think."

Dolly sighed, sitting on the sofa. "It's a shame. Everyone says that it's going to be heavy. You were wise to come and see me before it happens."

"I—I was thinking about what you said, remember? About working in the record business?"

"Oh, yes," she answered. "You graduate this year?"

"In June."

She studied him carefully. "I think there ought to be something for a boy—sorry, a *man*—like you, Tony.

Come here and tell me about yourself." She patted the seat beside her. Nervously, he sat next to her, giving Dolly a capsule version of his life story. She listened attentively, but her eyes flashed with a kind of amusement he couldn't understand.

"I pick things up fast," he said, campaigning for a job.

"I'm sure," Dolly replied, softly and coolly. "Let's give it a try."

He'd expected to start in a routine job at the record company—something that would familiarize him with day-to-day operations. Dolly, however, had other plans. The office, she explained, ran itself: her husband had hired the best people he could find to keep things operating on a daily basis, in order to have more time to devote to creative decisions and expansion plans. She followed the same guidelines, she explained, and often worked at home, making only a token appearance at the office. Home, an apartment on West End Avenue, would be a much better place for him to learn the business: they wouldn't be bothered by calls and interruptions, and he'd have a chance to observe her at her really important work. He could start in a day or two, if he liked, coming after school.

"But what will I do?" he asked awkwardly. "What'll my job be?"

Dolly laughed. "Don't worry. We'll find something. You'll be my personal assistant for now. How does that sound?"

It sounded great, Tony thought, congratulating himself as he left her office. If she took an interest in him and taught him the ropes herself, there was no telling how far he could go. Maybe he'd even become a producer in time. The hell with *Dancetime*—he was headed for the *big* time...

A few days later, in the privacy of her spacious bedroom, Tony Merino, nearly eighteen, became Dolly Michaels' paid lover. She had no intention of teaching him the record business—instead she concentrated on his sexual education.

"I'm thirty-six years old, I have more money than I can spend, and I'm bored to death," Dolly told him matter-of-factly. Tony listened, both to her words and to the silent language of her body. There was no comparison between Dolly and the girls he'd known before: they were girls, and she was a woman. Where they were just discovering their sexuality, she was devoted to pursuing the pleasures of sensation. Naturally, she explained, one had to be discreet—there was no sense in their going to the office and letting nasty rumors start. Of course, she'd find something for Tony to do officially, since the record company was paying his salary... He could have a nice little office and listen to tapes and records that artists sent in in the hopes of getting a contract, perhaps. But his real job would be keeping Dolly Michaels happy and satisfied, making her feel not so thirty-sixish and not so bored. In return, he'd draw a weekly salary of a hundred and fifty dollars, as well as fringe benefits in the form of clothes, jewelry, and assorted gifts.

Part of him felt proud and slick—the other guys he knew were all working at half-assed jobs for a minimum wage, getting dirty all week and getting drunk weekends. They envied his clothes and his cool, his way of getting over. Tony never told them the truth, of course, at least not the center of it. They knew only that he worked for CJ Records, and when they began asking questions, he began staying away from the neighborhood and the old crowd to avoid them.

Avoiding the truth in his mind was something else. It *was* pretty slick, he tried to convince himself, and Dolly was a hell of a broad. His technique as a lover had improved vastly, along with his versatility. Tony felt no guilt or shame when he was with her, but away from her, thinking about it, a feeling of disappointment gnawed at him. Just as she'd taught him about sex, Dolly had instructed him in the ways of escaping uncomfortable realities. There was liquor, of course. And pot—he picked up her supply from a musician she knew in the Village. And there were pills that could key you up or calm you down: Dolly had a collection of them in her medicine chest—and a group of cooperative physicians all over the city when the supply ran down.

What's going to happen to me? Tony Merino found himself thinking for the first time in his life. *What will happen when this is over? Where do I go from here?* For the moment, the "job" was fine. An inner sense told him that it wouldn't last, and drugs helped him avoid thinking about the future.

If he could have relaxed, if he'd had a sense of security, Tony came to think in time, perhaps his life would have been different. Dolly could be charming, loving even, when she was in a good mood, but her moods were quick to change with the drugs she took. She could be—and was—impatient, even demeaning at times, as if testing the boundaries of his patience, or dependence, or both. Just when he was convinced that it was all over, there'd be a trip to Las Vegas, or Palm Beach, or an expensive gift.

While she was careful to hide him from her professional contacts (a former competitor of her husband's, who'd sold his record company to one of the more progressive major labels, was her official escort for industry functions), she made no effort to hide him from her friends. If anything, she flaunted Tony, taking pleasure in the way other rich widows, divorcees, and bored society matrons looked at him with desire, and at her with envy.

The relationship lasted five years, until Dolly decided to marry Max Elkins, a man who started in the business with her husband. The record company, she explained to Tony, was getting to be a drain—Max would be able to run it, or sell it as he'd sold his own, or something. Besides, she was getting older (even if she didn't feel it). It was time for both of them to think about long-range plans. CJ Records would, of course, continue to pay Tony a salary ($250 per week by then) until he "got settled."

Ruth Osborne was a friend of Dolly's whom they'd visited at her Bucks County house several times each summer. From the beginning, Ruth had been involved with "Marco," whom she referred to as her "protégé" and whom Dolly privately called, "an imported Spanish omelette." Marco had departed for the greener pastures of a Philadelphia society woman who promised to finance his decorating career. Tony spent three years with Ruth, leaving to marry the daughter of one of her best friends, Beth Collins.

With Ruth's money behind him, and the expensive Pennsylvania country setting as a backdrop, Tony had found his affair with Beth thrilling. On their own, however, trying to scrape up a living in Pittsburgh, the marriage ended in less than a year. Beth's parents had finally paid him ten thousand dollars to grant their daughter a divorce (and hopefully an annulment). He went to Vegas, intending to parlay his stake into some *real* capital, and within two months he was broke.

But Vegas had offered Carol, a blonde with a forty-two-inch silicone bustline. For a year and a half, Tony had lived with and off her, accepting the cut she insisted on giving him from the money she earned turning tricks at downtown hotels. When he held her in bed, he tried hard to forget that she was a whore and that he was—in fact, if not in deed—her pimp. One day, they told each other, they'd leave "the life" and Vegas behind them—when they saved enough money. But while they waited for the future, they not only smoked a lot of grass and popped a lot of pills, they shot dope as well. The savings account they started never had a chance to build, and eventually Carol told him that she'd fallen in love with a stripper named Donna from Phoenix.

San Francisco, Los Angeles, Chicago, Detroit ... he'd

traveled across the country and through his youth as if compelled, continually searching for something he couldn't find. There were good days, good months, good *years*, even—times when Tony almost managed to convince himself that he was on top of it, that he had made it. But each affair ended; each of his rich (or at least comfortable) keepers became infatuated with somebody else (or bored with him). Need, with each successive move, slowly became an ache: momentary panic turned to a barely sublimated, almost constant sense of desperation. His need for drugs—any kind of drug that would help him escape, if only temporarily—increased.

Fifteen years after he'd appeared for the last time on *Dancetime, USA!*, when he was thirty-two years old, it occurred to Tony Merino that perhaps he was never going to find anything permanent to hold on to. The promises his youth had made him (or those beliefs he'd chosen to read as promises) might never be realized. In a last-ditch attempt to build up the bankroll he believed would be essential to any thought, any form, of security, he got a job as a blackjack dealer in Vegas. This time, he told himself, he was going to cut down the drugs, or cut them out entirely. There wouldn't be any broads to complicate his life: he'd concentrate on money and building up a bankroll. That was the year he was beat up and kicked out of town when one of the pit bosses accused him of playing partners against the house with a smalltime hood.

Telling himself he was lucky they hadn't killed him, Tony drifted to Florida.

He'd been to Palm Springs several times since Dolly Michaels first took him, enough to understand the character of the place. For all its pretensions and its contingent of real social names, it wasn't blue blood that counted in Palm Springs as much as green cash. The bored, the pleasure-seeking, and the decadent were indulged in their quest for self-satisfaction, so long as they kept up a facade of decorum and gave big enough parties.

If Amanda Sanderson was close to sixty and had a gratingly loud voice, she also had an address book full of the right numbers and a bottomless bank account. Under her patronage, Tony Merino was accorded instant acceptance as her latest "find."

Telling people what they wanted to hear had become more than a habit for him—it had become a way of life, a means of existence. At night, when she cuddled against him in one of her designer peignoirs, he heard himself whisper that she was the most beautiful and exciting woman he'd every known. Closing his eyes, trying to focus on a half-remembered face he could never really identify, he'd say the words that made her believe it was she who'd aroused him.

He learned tennis and backgammon, and tried very hard not to think of the future.

The past was more hospitable, particularly if he went back far enough. Connie, Don, Sandy, Dennis, Bobby...from time to time he found *Dancetime* in his thoughts. He wondered what they, the other Regulars, were doing at the very moment he sat at a table at Amanda's country club, or lay by her pool in the desert sun. Sometimes, when he escorted her to a party or dinner dance, he'd find the figure of Amanda melting as he guided her across the dance floor. In spite of her marked tendency to try to lead, he'd look at her and see someone else, a much younger woman—a *girl*. And in her eyes, he'd see a shadow, a ghost of himself as he had once been.

The affair with Amanda lasted three years, till the time she had a stroke. A cluster of long-lost relatives from Nebraska appeared to take over her "affairs." She had generously provided for Tony in her will, but the dead Amanda was declared incompetent. With only the money in his checking account and a few pieces of jewelry he'd been able to pilfer, Tony decided to try Palm Beach.

This time, he vowed, it would be different. He wouldn't depend on anyone—he'd make his own life and future.

He'd get a job as a waiter, or a captain at one of the better restaurants... maybe one of the better clubs. In the meantime, he'd "invest" in a room at The Breakers, just to check out the action...

Joan Carpenter was the veteran of three progressively more successful marriages that had taken her from hopeful actress to the pages of *Palm Beach Life*. Besides an eighteen-room house, she had a yacht that slept ten and a condo at the Jockey Club in Miami, where she frequently went to watch her horses race. She was expert at going through the motions of being the gracious hostess and socialite, but her nocturnal habits (indulged when friends and guests were safely out of sight) included experimentation with a wide variety of drugs, exceeded only by the range of her sexual partners. In Tony, she'd sensed if not a kindred spirit at least a man who'd been around... a conspirator who would not only allow her to indulge to excess (not that he had much choice) but actually help her.

They made their way through the drug and orgy circuit, going to London, Paris, Rome, and Marbella—wherever the action was. Slowly, though, Tony had felt a change begin to take place. In the beginning, other men and other women had been exceptions rather than the rule. Most nights, Joan had been content with her Black Russians, her drugs, and Tony. After a while, the pattern changed. Her demands grew. She began to argue when Tony refused to make it with a thin, white-haired German baron they met in Marbella, and for a year afterward it was a steadily downhill course.

"There's no point going on with this, is there?" Joan finally asked him wearily. They were back in Palm Beach, where he was accepted as a fixture in her life. He didn't answer because he couldn't. Clearly, their relationship had long since run its course. Now, it was only familiarity that made her keep him around, and only his total lack of pride—and the insecurity and fear that bubbled just below the surface of the emotions he allowed himself—that made him stay.

"I think it's time we went on to other things, don't you, darling?" she asked pleasantly, sipping a Black Russian and reaching for her checkbook. "Naturally I'm prepared to be reasonable, but for your sake, Tony, I hope you *do* something with this money. You're getting ... well, you're a tiny bit old to be kept, don't you think?"

The check for twenty-five thousand dollars made him thank her, not remind her that she was getting older.

He'd gone to Miami convinced that the opportunity he'd been waiting for had finally arrived. It was his chance, his time, his long-awaited opportunity to make his own future. If Joan had discarded him, her friends (out of curiosity more than manners) were still civil and even pleasant. A group of her cronies from the track were forming a syndicate to purchase a colt with spectacular lineage, a sure winner. There were five equal shares making up the hundred-thousand-dollar purchase price, and one was available ...

It was a shame, everyone agreed. A shame, but of course those things *did* happen. Who could have known that four months after being shipped to Florida, the horse would fall and break his leg during training? Naturally the only thing to do was to destroy the poor animal. If the fortune she'd been capable of winning hadn't materialized ... well, it could be worse. There was always the tax loss to be taken.

For Tony Merino, the loss was complete. He worked his way down a clearly delineated stratum of hotels. Each night he told himself that he was going to reverse things, get a job, set his life straight. Each day he found out he couldn't. It was less painful to forget over drinks in a cheap bar, to hang around until somebody came in with some smoke, or some pills, or a hit of second-rate cocaine.

Sometimes he'd get high enough to really remember the old days, that time when it had all seemed so easy and so damn certain, *guaranteed*.

From the street below the window, he heard the shriek of brakes, the skidding tires and a crash. He started to walk to the window but stopped at the mirror instead. He stood there, transfixed, studying his reflection. The once jet-black hair was streaked with gray now. There were dark circles under his eyes, lines deeply etched into his skin. He decided not even to bother looking down at the accident outside the window.

What the hell? He was a wreck himself.

7.

"JUST A MINUTE AND I'LL SEE IF HE'S IN, MISS Granger," Anne said, putting the call on hold. "It's that woman from TBS again, Don," she told her boss. He shook his head, and she went back to the phone. "I'm sorry, Miss Granger, but Mr. Simpson is out of the office. I don't think he'll be coming back today. Yes, I did give him that message, but he's been very busy lately... Of course I will... you're welcome. Good-bye."

She hung up and called to her boss in the inner office: "She asked me to be *sure* to remind you to call her back, Don. That's three times in the last two weeks. What's it all about, anyway? Are you giving up architecture to be a TV star?"

"Now how did you know that, Patty?" he said, with a look of feigned surprise. "Promise me you won't tell Rona."

"Rona?"

"Barrett."

"Word of honor," Anne vowed. "Not that it couldn't happen. You're handsome enough to be discovered."

"I've got to work on the plans for that shopping center in Encino. Close the door, will you—and take messages. I don't want to be disturbed."

"Sure thing," Anne said.

The moment the door was shut, the smile left Don Simpson's face. For a while, he tried to work at his drawing board, but he found that he couldn't. The new shopping center, planned as the most lavish in the San Fernando Valley, was a crucial project—several of the top firms in Los Angeles had gone after it, and landing it for Simpson Associates had been a major coup.

For the past week, though, Don hadn't been able to get very far past his initial concept. Maybe, he thought, he'd been working too hard. Or maybe he had a mild case of the flu. But he knew that wasn't it. The fact was, he was in perfect health and he thrived on his work. The problem with the shopping center had started the first time the woman called to explain about the *Dancetime* reunion special. Ever since, he'd been unable to think of anything else.

He had tried to stay calm, to sound casual as he spoke to her. She was full of enthusiasm—not surprisingly, since she worked for the network—and she told him what a "wonderful experience" it would be, a chance to see his old friends again. When she pressed him for a commitment he was evasive, in spite of her determined efforts to pin him down. Finally he agreed to call her back in a few days. But more than a few days had passed, and his feelings were still in a state of confusion.

His initial reaction was surprise: *Dancetime, USA!* was so far in the past that it seemed to be ancient history. The whole idea of TBS commemorating the program, even as a special, seemed totally bizarre. Of course, the whole country had gone nostalgia crazy. From TV shows to fashion, the fifties were back in style. The trend hadn't yet affected architecture, but it had certainly influenced interior design. The West Hollywood and Beverly Hills shops that specialized in expensive, trendy accessories were all featuring gray and pink china leopards—exactly like those that had once graced the tops of so many family television sets.

If he understood the network's interest in the *Dancetime* special, his own reaction was harder to fathom.

He knew that youth, the teenage years in particular, was supposed to be the "best time of your life." For the other Regulars—and for most of the kids he knew in high school—this had probably been true. Their parents, like his own, had handed out allowances and paid all the bills. Politics and world affairs had been things that only parents, teachers, and a few "eggheads" gave much thought to.

Don smiled ruefully. A superficial glance at his features still reflected the image of the all-American boy, exactly the role he'd had on *Dancetime, USA!* Just as Tony had been the show's resident Mr. Cool, he'd been the resident Clean-cut Kid. By the time he was sixteen, he'd reached his full six-foot height. Football, basketball, baseball—he played them all in school, but swimming (he was the captain of the team) was where he really excelled.

His look and style had been "collegiate," from the letter he wore on his sweater over an Oxford shirt (allowed as a substitute for the required jacket) to his light tan chinos and Weejuns.

Don got up from his drawing board, went to the desk, and opened the bottom drawer. Reaching under the stack of old plans and sketches, he took out the folder he'd brought from home last week. It had taken two days of rummaging through a lifelong accumulation of memorabilia to find it, but there it was—the sheaf of pictures and press clippings from his days as a Regular. Don slowly shook his head as he studied the almost forgotten faces.

The somewhat stocky broad-shouldered boy with the crewcut blond hair was obviously himself. Don could vaguely remember looking as square as that, it was the attendant *feelings* that had him puzzled. To all appearances, he'd been one of the gang, an attractive kid without a care in the world. He had friends and popularity, and he'd done well enough in school to graduate—from high school and college—with highest honors.

Studying had never been a problem, the way it was for so many the kids. If anything he looked forward to the problems in algebra, and be liked to memorize historical dates and Latin conjugations. Like *Dancetime* itself, they were things he could fix his mind on, things that filled up the time and gave him a welcome escape from the fears he couldn't make himself confront...

His parents often told their friends that they considered themselves "lucky." Other families were fleeing from Manhattan, complaining that the city was going to hell. Both Don's parents were native New Yorkers and both were "theater people." Douglas Simpson was a stage manager; Lynne, his wife, a theatrical designer. If none of their interest in the stage had filtered down to their only son, they didn't seem to mind, though they were delighted when Don was picked as a Regular.

It wasn't so much the carrying on of a family show-business tradition as simply another affirmation that they were Good Parents. In spite of a growing rate of crime, gang violence, and juvenile delinquency in general, they had managed to raise a son who, everyone agreed, was a fine young man. What's more, they'd done it without moving to Long Island, Westchester, or some other place that would mean a long daily commute for both of them when they were working.

Making his parents proud was important to Don. He couldn't hope to compete with the glittering friends his mother and father traveled with, but at an early age he learned that he'd be rewarded if he simply did what they liked. They wanted him to do well in school, to excel in sports, to have friends and go out on dates. He did all of these things, and when the three of them sat down for one of the "talks" that Lynne Simpson considered important to have with your children (particularly with an only child), he repeatedly assured them that everything in his life was fine.

Being good parents mattered to the Simpsons. At their frequent cocktail parties, they argued that there was no reason why show people couldn't be ideal mothers and fathers—wasn't their son Don proof? It might be different, perhaps, for *actors*, who traveled all the time, but anybody who thought that a career in "the business" (two careers in this case) and a disturbed offspring went together had obviously not met their Donald. They pointed with pride to his friends, his swimming medals, his report cards.

Giving his parents what they wanted had been relatively easy for a time. Then, in high school, it suddenly became more difficult. The locker room and lunch-break talk about girls that began in junior high reached epidemic proportions. As his friends boasted about their sexual conquests, exchanging the names of girls who "put out," Don listened, wishing he could really share the excitement he pretended to feel. He laughed at the jokes, and later, alone, he told himself that making out was just a matter of time—like shaving, it was something he'd grow into. He was just a little slow, that was all. His body had grown fast. His sexual desires were certain to catch up.

Don had desires. The trouble was they weren't the same desires all his friends shared. Without knowing why, Don found himself flushed during gym class, terrified that his body might betray him. He couldn't be *that way*, he told himself. Everybody knew that *queers* and *homos* were easily identifiable. They had high voices. They lisped. They broke their wrists when they gestured, wiggled when they walked, and wore green and yellow on Thursdays. They had nothing to do with *him* . . .

From as far back as he could remember, Don's parents

had warned him against the dangers of talking to strange men. In Central Park, in the library, and on the street, strange men were to be avoided at all costs: if one of them tried anything "funny," he was to tell the closest policeman; the police knew how to deal with "that sort of thing." Later, his parents had liberalized their viewpoint and his, at least slightly. There were some people who were "different," Lynne Gibson explained to her son. It was wrong to make fun of them or pass judgment on them—they could be perfectly charming, were often talented, and did no real harm as long as they stuck to "their own kind."

Who was and who wasn't provided a frequent topic of conversation among the Simpsons and their friends. Though they changed the conversation when Don entered the room, he overheard many rumors concerning actors, designers, and playwrights. When it first occurred to him that perhaps he might be similar, he panicked. True, his parents prided themselves on having a "mixed bunch" at their parties, and on being tolerant of the "shortcomings" of certain co-workers. But how, Don wondered, could they ever accept a son who found himself drawn to those magazines, displayed in the windows of little book stores around Times Square, that featured nearly naked bodybuilders in provocative poses "for the art student?" What would they say if they knew that it was only fear of being caught—by them, or the police, or someone he knew—that kept him from accepting the invitations, spoken and unspoken, of certain men who haunted the New York Public Library, and the parks, and the subways, looking at him with a certain interest that marked him immediately (he feared) as one of their own?

The Simpsons were agnostics, as they proudly informed their friends, but in school and in the Boy Scouts, there was ample enough warning against the "sin" of immorality (let alone "perversion") as expressed through such behavior. In sports, Don pushed himself to the limit, driven by the fear that somebody observing could read his dark and shameful thoughts. If he performed well enough, if he pushed hard enough to make people notice his grades and his skill at athletics, then maybe—just *maybe*—his secret would be safe a while longer.

Dancetime, USA! had been a very convenient disguise. A friend of his father's had told the Simpsons about the show, about to go into production, and they in turn told their son. Don liked to dance, didn't he? He was always going to dances...

In truth, he went to dances not because he wanted to, but because it was another *normal* thing to do. Unlike his friends, he wasn't too interested in copping feels, or pressing close against the girls' bodies (though if he did it enough, he thought, maybe he'd become normal). If he went out with the most desirable girls in his class (and as a letterman, he more or less had his pick), if he held their hands and put his arm around them at the movies and kissed them good night, maybe in time he'd *want* to do those things.

Girls didn't repel him... in fact, he liked them. But his feelings toward them, he suspected, were as platonic as the friendships boys felt for one another. The right girl, he convinced himself, would make a difference, maybe that was what he'd needed all along. In search of her, he went out with cheerleaders and with studious long-haired girls; with girls who wrote poems for the literary magazine, and with girls who read movie magazines, sighing over Ricky Nelson, Tab Hunter and Robert Wagner. He found himself liking some of these girls more than others, having more to talk about with the intelligent ones than the dumb ones, but the spark, the magical moment the songs all promised, never happened.

If there was a right girl, a girl who could make him feel the way a boy was supposed to feel, he'd have a good chance of finding her on *Dancetime*, Don told himself when he was selected as a Regular. And from the start, he was popular with the girls on the show and the girls at home. Lorraine, his partner, told him they made a perfect couple.... They carried the illusion into the pages of the fan magazines and onto the set, a convenient arrangement in view of Lorraine's romance with a junior at NYU (not even her parents knew) and Don's own secret.

Tony was sharper and smoother, Bobby was a better dancer, but Don drew his fair share of fan letters, not only from girls who thought he was cute and "keen," but also from their parents.

He held one of those letters in his hand, the stationery turning brown around the edges and the ink somewhat faded.

> *Dear Don,*
> *When this rock and roll music first caught on, I hated it something fierce. So did my husband. We didn't want our Peter and Francine listening to it or watching your show. Then, just last week, I was home with a backache (my back acts up something terrible sometimes) and the kids turned on Dancetime after school.*
> *I can't say I like the music, but I saw Lee Dean congratulate you for being chosen captain of the swimming team and being on the honor roll as well. You impressed me as a fine young man with good manners and a head on his shoulders. I bet your folks are real proud. I just wanted to tell you that you set a fine example, as far as I'm concerned, and to wish you the best of luck. If you're ever in Cedar Rapids, you're welcome to visit.*
> *Best wishes,*
> Celia Clooney
> *P.S. Just between the two of us, our Francine has a crush on you. Any chance of getting an autographed picture? Her birthday is next month, and I'd love to surprise her.*

He never took Mrs. Clooney up on her invitation, but two eight-by-ten photographs, one of him alone, signed, and another of Lee and all The Regulars, with their signatures imprinted, had gone to Cedar Rapids, courtesy of *Dancetime, USA!* and the Trans-American Broadcasting System.

He wondered what Mrs. Clooney would have said if he'd shown up on her doorstep and told her the truth? That instead of Francine, he might have liked Peter?

As the months passed, the pressure of deception began to weigh on him. If nobody knew his secret (and nobody seemed to guess), if it was no more apparent on the TV camera than it was in real life, maybe it wasn't true after all. Maybe he'd imagined the whole thing. Or, he sometimes feared, perhaps something *else* was wrong with him, something even worse. Whatever it was, he felt he had to know once and for all.

Don found himself increasingly drawn to 42nd Street. The book stores with their displays of lurid covers and titles were the libraries he searched for valid information. At first, he only bought a few books with homosexuals in them, hiding the books in his bedroom and reading them, with a sense of dread, only when his parents were safely out of the house. The cover copy promised "a stark and startling look at the netherworld of the Third sex," or a "peek into the lavender world of twisted love." The homosexual characters were either tortured, or effeminate, or both: their greatest pleasure seemed to be dressing up in women's clothes. Don felt no bond of identification with these men, which was reassuring.

But there were other books, marriage manuals and lurid stories about "loose women dedicated to pleasure and sensation," which aroused him. With these books, he'd give his imagination—triggered by the more explicitly descriptive passages—full reign. The images of lush, full breasts and silky-smooth skin didn't excite him nearly as much as the bulging muscles and hairy chests of the women's lovers. Afterwards, when he'd satisfied himself, he felt shame and embarrassment—and worse, total alienation.

Homos—*queers*—must be like the men in the stories, weak and effeminate. If he liked men—if he *had* to be homosexual—why couldn't he at least like men who were that way? It was bad enough to be a *fairy*, but it was worse to be attracted to the kind of men who weren't fairies and who wanted women.

Once or twice, Don thought of finding a doctor somewhere and talking about it. But a doctor would want to know his name and address, and he'd be certain to call his parents with the news. Don had no friends close enough to confide in. If he even hinted at his problem, it would be all over school in a matter of hours. It was easier, though it wasn't "easy" at all, to go on pretending, to be the model son, the model student, the model all-American boy for the nationwide *Dancetime* audience.

When the show went off the air, Don felt a secret, strange relief. At least he could stop some of the pretense. He made no effort to keep in touch with the other Regulars. They were part of the past, he told himself: his eyes were on the future, on the hope of making some kind of sense out of what went on in his body.

His parents had encouraged Don to pursue a career in the theater. He had always shown talent in art—he could design both sets and costumes. More to please them than anything else, he studied *Theatre Arts* for possible schools. Inwardly, though, he was set against it from the start. The theater, he knew, was full of *them*, and they were a part of the problem, not the solution.

When Don announced his interest in architecture, his mother and father approved. It was a good field; his mother pointed out that architecture offered plenty of room for "artistic expression." They were a bit disappointed when he decided to go to the University of Virginia, rather than a Manhattan college that would have allowed him to live at home, but they were pleased when he was accepted.

He viewed college as a fresh start, a second chance at making a normal life for himself. The combination of his looks, athletic ability, and his *Dancetime* fame (a few of the girls recognized him first, and it was all over school by the end of his first week) won him a popularity he'd never sought or wanted. The fraternities competed for him, and though he hadn't planned to, he found himself joining the one with the highest percentage of jocks and the biggest reputation for rowdiness. Surrounding himself with "normal" friends, he told himself, would normalize him.

Don dutifully invited girls to parties and dances, necking, petting, and feigning an interest he didn't feel. Hard as he tried, however, Don couldn't bring himself to make love to any of the women he dated. It wasn't that the idea repelled him (a realization he found reassuring). In fact, he was curious to test his own reactions, to measure his experience against those that were continually the main topic of conversation at the frat house.

The fear that he might not be able to carry the act through to completion, that the woman might somehow be able to sense his inexperience—and worse, his *difference*—held him back. Ironically, this only increased his popularity: unlike many of his fraternity brothers, he didn't try to force his dates into sex; so the girls told each other that Don was not only handsome and popular, but a "gentleman" as well. He acquired a reputation as a good, fun date—the kind of man a girl could feel comfortable calling when she didn't have a date for the sorority dance.

Because it was important to the house, he tried out for the swim team. He made junior varsity easily, and was chosen co-captain. Sometimes in the locker room, as at the fraternity, Don would feel strange, unwelcome stirrings at the sight of a naked or nearly naked body. He forced himself to look away, to think away. Even when alone, he no longer sought frequent self-release, because of the mental complexities involved in the elementary sexual act.

By the time he graduated, he had a new secret. Though he was twenty-two, supposedly still at an age when his sexual desires were at their peak, he was virtually asexual. He had the body and build of a jock, a stud, the kind of guy who scored with one woman after another. But his actual life was sexless.

An army recruiter had painted an attractive picture of life in the service. It wasn't the increased pay rates or the benefits that made Don enlist, however, but rather the hope that the experience (preferable in any case to that of being drafted, which was a possibility once his student deferment was up) might toughen him, hone him, sharpen the edge of his masculinity. First in Fort Benning, then in Berlin, then in Vietnam, he acquired a reputation as a "good soldier," friendly to a point but something of a loner even in a crowd. He considered reenlisting and a career in the service: instead, he left after his third tour and moved to Atlanta, where he worked for an architectural firm specializing in shopping developments.

The wives of his bosses and co-workers went about the task of finding him the "right" girl as if Don were a rare species in a zoo that had to mate to perpetuate its own kind. At one dinner party after another, he was introduced to a succession of visiting relatives, eligible girls from "fine old families," and divorcées. Patiently, his hostesses waited for a spark to ignite. Don made polite, dutiful conversation, escorting the most interesting of the women (and those whom duty obliged him to take out) to dinner, or a movie, or a dance. But the relatives went home, the unmarried socialites looked elsewhere, and the divorcées—attractive as they found Don—were introduced to other men.

It was a shame, the would-be matchmakers agreed, for a man to be so handsome, so charming, so well-mannered, so single—and so *alone*.

In reality, loneliness, had been a part of Don's life for so long that he rarely felt it as such. A few of his office friendships extended beyond work to an occasional game of tennis or evening of cards. Most of the time though, he read, or watched TV, or tackled the work he brought home from the job—easy and solitary ways of filling the time and avoiding painful self-confrontation.

There was no denying the truth, as he perceived it, but there was no point in dwelling on it, either. He was a freak—a man without a sex life. His basic urges, he suspected, were somewhere under the surface. But over the years, sublimating them, directing them into work or physical activity, had become a habit. At times—those times when he couldn't help it—he found a bitter, painful irony in what he thought of as his fate. As long as he'd been marked, doomed to a monastic existence through no discernible fault of his own (except the inability to control feelings he had never understood), why couldn't he have been blessed with a firm and zealous religious faith? At least, Don thought, alone in bed and unable to sleep, aching in spite of himself for the presence of someone, male or female, beside him, at least he could have found fulfillment that way. Self-denial in a monastery would have a purpose.

Mostly, though, he tried not to think of such things at all. He read everything he could on architecture, and as a hobby, he simulated plans for buildings already built—some well-known and some obscure—that he admired. He gave them to friends on anniversaries and birthdays. The total commitment to his career, coupled with his talent, won him the respect of his colleagues. When an offer from a large Minneapolis firm came, Don's boss, knowing he couldn't meet the money, encouraged him to take it.

"We hate to lose you," he told Don, "but it's a big step. You should take it. Minneapolis is a very nice city. Maybe you'll find that perfect woman my wife is so sure you need."

Don smiled.

What he found in Minneapolis wasn't the perfect woman (or man) but a new awareness of change. During the years in Atlanta his life had taken on a regular, lulling rhythm. The new Twin Cities setting broadened his horizons. One of the people he worked with was an exceptionally talented and dynamic woman named Bernice Flannery. In addition to her family and her work at the office, she was involved in the women's movement. She told him about her consciousness-raising group and the committees she was involved in. Discrimination, equality, and liberation, Don realized for the first time, weren't limited to members of certain races or religions. Bernice introduced him to the work of Betty Freidan and Gloria Steinem. Don assimilated the thoughtfully articulated points of view, the bitterly angry tirades against men, the complaints and comments from career women and housewives, women who were married, single, and lesbians.

The vocality of the lesbian feminists, and their acceptance by Bernice and a surprisingly large proportion of the heterosexual faction of the feminist groups she talked about, had a profound effect on Don. The other men at the firm tended to kid Bernice about her beliefs: Don asked questions, frequently had lunch with her, and accepted her invitations to lectures and discussion groups. At first, he'd been self-conscious, worried about being the only man present. But there were other men, he discovered—friends, husbands, and relatives committed to the broad principles involved.

Some of the men, Don soon realized, were gay: the alliance between gay-lib groups and those seeking equality for women seemed natural. A couple of the men were effeminate—but only a couple. The others were noticeable only by the points they raised, not the mannerisms he'd felt threatened by since childhood. Don envied their easy acceptance of themselves and wished that he knew and liked himself better. *If only I were younger,* he thought. *If only I could be young at a time like this...*

He began to pick up copies of *The Advocate*, as well as *Ms.*, at the newsstand. The proprietor didn't appear to be shocked or even take notice of his purchase. For the first time in many years, he entered an adult book store. He found there weren't merely one or two gay titles now but entire shelves of porno novels that celebrated physical sensation. Instead of a few semi-nude portraits in "art" and physique magazines, there were rows upon rows of full-color magazines with no pretense to art at all.

Times had changed.

Don wanted to change with them. The trouble was, he didn't know how. As ideas, Don had no trouble accepting gay pride and sexual freedom of any kind. As realities, it was a different matter. He'd punished himself for so many years for a sin he hadn't committed—a "sin" which now appeared to be not a sin at all—that he didn't know the first thing about how to do the thing he'd always longed for and feared.

He began driving down Hennepin Avenue, past the city's best-known gay bar. Once or twice, he actually parked the car. But he couldn't make himself go in. The old ghosts, almost a lifetime of fears, held him back. Walking downtown, or sometimes alone at a movie, he'd find himself looking at strangers in a new way. Often, men his own age (or older, or younger) would return his look with a lingering, unmistakable gaze of interest. It was the thing he wanted, and the thing he had always dreaded, and when it happened, Don looked away hurriedly, feeling his skin flush and his body go tight. Later, at home, his fantasies would build as freely as his anger at himself for what he would never let happen.

He lived two and a half years in Minneapolis, winning praise, awards and, for the first time in his life, beginning to feel comfortable with himself. When an offer came from a major Los Angeles firm, Don accepted it gladly: he felt ready for another change of locale, and more important, he knew it was long past time for a major change in himself. California, he knew, was at the forefront of the gay lib movement.

His adjustment to LA was so natural that for a few weeks he began to worry, once again, that something must be wrong. Easterners had always joked about the "laid back" attitude of Californians: Don felt as if the more casual life-style had been created to make him feel comfortable. The formalities he associated with work were missing—everyone from the receptionist to the head of the firm spoke on a first-name basis. His neighbors at the apartment in Westwood were a cross-section of actors, UCLA students, and transplants from every part of the country. The swimming pool was like a club that united them in a surrogate family.

His co-workers, accustomed to making newcomers feel at home, welcomed him into their lives. In Minneapolis, friendly as the people had been, it had taken time for real friendships to develop. In LA, Don found himself invited right away to cocktail parties and barbecues, where he was introduced as if he were an old friend.

At one of these parties, a wine and cheese tasting given by two young actresses in his building, Don found himself describing his excitement at living in LA to an interested, dark-haired young man named Gary.

"In other parts of the country, people are afraid to find out who they really are," he said. "But here, it's practically the number-one hobby."

Gary smiled. "For some people that's all it is. You know what I mean—they may talk about the pursuit of higher consciousness and getting in touch with their feelings, but that's all it is. Talk. It's a new way of keeping up with the Joneses."

"Don't you think the consciousness-raising groups have their merits?" Don asked.

"Sure. For some people. I have a few friends who've really been helped, and I'm for anything that makes a person feel better. It's just that I think you can't expect someone else's value system to work for you. It can help you form your own, but ultimately you have to decide what you believe in and what you don't. You have to come to terms with yourself—and you do that on your *own* terms."

"You sound almost like one of those people who starts a movement," Don answered, smiling. "You're very convincing."

Gary laughed. "I'm afraid my approach is pretty traditional. I'm a psychologist."

For the next two hours, they talked about their work. Gary told Don about the agency in Hollywood where he put in several volunteer hours each week in addition to his regular practice.

"Runaways, people who come here expecting to be 'discovered' and find themselves broke and lost, suicide attempts, drug abusers—it's a pretty wide range," he said.

"Doesn't it get depressing?" Don asked.

"Not really. That used to worry me when I was in school. I love the work, the idea of it, but I used to have my doubts about whether or not I'd be able to keep my objectivity and my sanity."

"You don't look any the worse for wear," Don said.

"Thanks. What's happened, actually, is that my work helps me as much as them. Problems are different in details and circumstances, but dealing with them is a basic kind of process. It's easier with some and harder with others, of course, but helping other people helps me deal with my own stuff."

The crowd had thinned out, they realized; there were only a few people left.

"I'd better get going," Gary said, shaking Don's hand. "It's been nice talking with you. Let's get together again."

They exchanged phone numbers, and Gary said good-bye. Later, as Don was helping the girls clean up, Gary returned.

"My damn car won't start," he said. "Can I use your phone to call the auto club?"

"I'll drive you home if you like," Don heard himself say.

Driving up into the Hollywood Hills with Gary beside him, Don felt a peculiar excitement. Soon they were at Gary's small house with its wide expanse of glass windows and its view of the lights of the city below. Gary asked him in for a drink.

Over brandy, Gary produced a joint and offered it first to Don.

"Does Dr. Freud recommend it?" Don asked, hesitating. He'd only smoked pot a few times; it gave him a headache instead of a high.

Gary laughed. "Freud was too busy totting his coke to tangle with grass. But I guarantee you a good buzz—it's some stuff a friend brought back from Maui."

An hour, two joints, and a couple of drinks later, Don felt better than he'd felt in months. The years that had gone before no longer seemed to matter. When Gary leaned toward him, grasped his shoulders and kissed him, Don let himself go instead of pulling away. The fears and inhibitions he'd lived with as long as he could remember tried to surface, but the grass and the brandy came to Don's aid and helped him overcome the conditioning of all the past years.

It was only hours later, that he even remembered them. When he did, talking about them felt as natural as making love for the first time had. Gary listened patiently, asking only an occasional question. When he finished Don felt somewhat embarrassed.

"I didn't mean to bore you with all that," he apologized. "It must be exactly what you hear at work."

"Not at all," Gary said. "The people who come to me for help can't do it alone. You did. I admire that."

They began to see each other regularly. Gary, Don learned, had had a lover for five years before they broke up. For the past seven months, he'd picked up men in bars for casual sex, reluctant to get involved in another relationship. Since sex was new for Don, as was the acceptance of his homosexuality, Gary encouraged him to play the field as well—to experiment with a lot of partners and discover the parameters of his own sexuality in the process. Don tried to follow the suggestion, pleased at his ability to attract attention and to respond physically. At least the machinery worked, he told himself: it hadn't rusted from lack of use.

But sex, pleasant as it could be, was only part of what he wanted. The men he met, for the most part, were interesting. Still, none of them offered the natural ease and friendship he'd felt almost instantly with Gary. Through the first months of their relationship, these grew and intensified. After four months, the two men became lovers.

Three years later, Don was a happy man. His work was going well—he'd started his own firm, and was attracting more clients than he could handle. He and Gary had bought a house together. Don had torn out walls and altered rooms, turning a small, boxy 1930's house into a contemporary home with an open, spacious feeling. For the first time in his life he was comfortable and content.

Each month, each year, the old fears had become more remote. Still, he had never publicly "come out." What his parents thought, Don didn't know. They rarely met; he tried to keep his personal life private. He didn't feel brave enough to go public, to announce his new sexual orientation to the world at large.

And now, the *present* had come back to haunt him. A woman named Sheila Granger wanted Don to help her recreate "the old days," days Don would be happy to forget forever. He didn't want to be remembered. The old Don Simpson was dead.

What would they say—the millions of people who knew him from television, his classmates, his old friends from Atlanta and Minneapolis, his parents, The Regulars themselves—what would they say when they saw him reappear, a bachelor at almost forty, still unmarried?

Did he have the courage to risk it?, he asked himself over and over. Did he have the guts...?

Book Three

1.

"I'VE BEEN HOPING WE'D HAVE A CHANCE TO get better acquainted, Miss Duvane," Mike Palmer said. "Of course these past few weeks have been a little hectic—"

"I'm sure," Kay agreed. "It must be quite a change from the West Coast—and from movies to television, of course."

He smiled, offered her a cigarette, and lit one himself, settling back in the armchair while Kay sat on the sofa. "Being vice president of network operations isn't that different from running a movie studio," he told her. "It's all trying to please the public, isn't it? Turning out product people will want to see, examining mistakes to see what went wrong..."

His voice trailed off, and Kay felt her nerves tense. She fought to keep the polite smile on her face.

"You're referring to *Emerald Shores*, I take it?"

"That was a point I wanted to discuss. I'm sure you share our disappointment."

Anger welled up inside her, but experience helped Kay retain a veneer of composure. "I'm probably more disappointed than anyone else at TBS, Mr. Palmer—"

"Mike, please. We're going to be working together closely, I hope."

"I'm sure we will—*Mike*."

"You were saying?"

"I was saying that I was very disappointed in the numbers. I'm always disappointed when a TBS project doesn't deliver what we expect it to—particularly when it's one of my own projects."

He nodded and inhaled. "Then tell me. What do you think went wrong?"

The question was hardly a surprise—ever since the first overnights had come in on the three-part miniseries, Kay had pondered it. *Emerald Shores* had been a strong concept: a mixture of sex, murder, and scandal set against the glamorous background of a Florida condominium. It was a variant on the time-proven *Peyton Place* formula, and from the initial phases of production to the final editing, every aspect of the production had been first-rate. She'd argued for—and won—another round in the battle of the budget, pointing out that the program had the potential of becoming a regular prime-time series such as *Dallas* or *Vegas*. Two million dollars and a day after the final segment of the miniseries had aired, however, *Emerald Shores* was an unmitigated disaster. The ratings weren't just bad—they were dismal.

"Actually," Kay said, carefully choosing her words, "I don't think anything went wrong with the program itself."

Mike Palmer raised his eyebrows. "Really? I understand that Ken Montgomery was replaced in the middle of production. I thought that might have been a factor."

"I'm not going to blame Ken," Kay said. "His doctor found some sort of growth—benign, as it turned out—and wanted to operate right away. Ken's a marvelous director, of course, but frankly Peter Logan did a superb job. He reshot a few scenes and improved the final product."

Mike Palmer tilted his head, considering her response. "But surely you'd agree that an expensive miniseries—well directed—should perform better?"

"Of course. But any miniseries depends on its initial audience. Monday night, when *Emerald Shores* premiered, NBC ran a Bob Hope special. ABC had a football game, and CBS had a Barbra Streisand movie with two strong sit-coms leading in. The fault, Mr. Palmer—sorry, *Mike*—wasn't with what we were offering, but with the strength of the competition."

"Do go on," he urged her.

"What I'm saying," she explained, "was that it was just one of those nights. Hope always pulls—we all know that. Streisand is the number-one box-office star, and even her worst pictures have a built-in audience. Football is football. It's that simple."

"I don't think we can call it simple—may I call you Kay? We'd all be remiss if we were too casual about our failures—"

"I'm sorry," Kay interrupted icily, "but I can't consider *Emerald Shores* a failure of mine, or of anyone involved in the production. As a matter of fact, I'm quite proud of it. I worked very hard on that project. I know what it cost the network, and I know how much of my time I devoted to it. If you think that I'm pleased, or 'casual,' as you put it, about the Nielsen's—"

"Wait, wait!" the man said, putting his hands up. "Perhaps I made an unfortunate choice of words. I'm well aware of your track record and your dedication to your work. I didn't mean to suggest that you took this particular program lightly. And I certainly didn't mean to offend you. It's just that in my new capacity here, I'm interested in learning from mistakes as well as successes. I know I don't have to tell a woman of your experience how fast this medium changes. Keeping up with those changes, trying to anticipate public taste—it's hard work."

"I'm very well aware of that, Mr. Palmer," Kay answered. This time she didn't even try to be informal. "I've been doing it for more than twenty years. I've made my share of wrong decisions, just like everyone else in the business, and when I'm wrong, I admit it. But if I had the decision to make again, I'd still recommend *Emerald Shores* without reservation."

"Then why did it bomb?" he asked, pointblank.

"For one thing, I wanted a couple of bigger names for the leads—actors who aren't usually seen on TV. In my opinion, this would have been insurance against just the kind of counter-programming situation we ended up with. Instead, I had to use talent that we could go with in case we spun off a regular series. It was a gamble, and one I wouldn't have taken if I'd made the choice."

"But you didn't."

"No," Kay said, "I didn't. And I didn't make the programming choice, either."

"Then you wouldn't have run *Emerald Shores* this week?"

"Not in a million years," she replied, looking him straight in the eye. "I'd have stuck with the regular lineup, or gone with a movie. If we had to lose the night, I'd have lost it with a bad show, a dog. That would have given us one bad night instead of three. I believe I made that point in a memo to programming."

"I see," Palmer said, almost formally. Then his manner softened. "You have confidence in your judgment. I like that."

"Thank you."

He cleared his throat. "I've been going over some of the projects you're working on. I understand that it wasn't all smooth sailing with *The Cardboard Kingdom*."

Kay laughed drily. "Ellie Loring is a prize bitch, and the director is a bastard. But it's going to be one hell of a show."

"Good. And the Lee Dean thing?"

"Coming along. I've put my assistant, Sheila Granger, on it. She's a very capable young woman."

"I'm glad to hear it," Mike Palmer told her. "After all, we live in a youth-oriented society. It's good to have young blood at top levels. Well, I know we'll be speaking again soon. I appreciate your coming up on such short notice." He extended his hand.

"Anytime," Kay answered, giving it what she hoped was a painfully firm handshake.

She walked to the elevator slowly and calmly. Only when she reached her private office, where Sheila was waiting, did she vent her fury.

"Goddamn that little pisspot!" Kay said, slamming her fist down on her desk.

"Calm down, Kay—"

"Calm down! How the hell can I calm down? Some little jerk has the nerve to call me on the carpet! Our resident boy wonder. Well, he may have been hot news over at NBC, but he still has plenty to learn!"

"What did he say?" Sheila asked. Trying to soothe Kay, experience had taught her, was a wasted effort—she did much better to let Kay get it out of her system.

"Oh, he was just flexing his muscles. Breaking in his office, you might say."

"How about a cup of coffee?" Sheila suggested.

"I'd rather have a gun!" Kay answered. Then, as if weary of the whole thing, she sank into her chair. "You know, the part I can't get used to is that he's so damn young. Vice president of network operations, and he's barely thirty."

"Thirty-one," Sheila corrected her gently. Ever since Mike Palmer had made a surprise move to TBS, the papers and magazines had given him a lot of coverage. They called him "young and dynamic," and hinted that it would be only a matter of time until he became the youngest network president in television history. Even before he actually moved into his office, Kay had shown an unusual and uncharacteristic animosity toward him. Sheila tried to understand it, but her occasional questions brought forth no information. Kay had never had any direct dealings with Mike Palmer—at least not until this morning, when he called and summoned her upstairs.

"You know," Kay said, as if reading Sheila's thoughts, "I've been called on the carpet before. It's part of the game. In this business, when you have a hit everyone wants to take credit. When you come up with a bomb, all of a sudden it's a do-it-yourself project."

"Is—is that why you're upset, Kay? Was he blaming you for *Emerald Shores*?"

"Not directly—he's too smart for that. But he's so damn *young*, Sheila. Oh, I know that doesn't mean anything to you. But just wait a few years. Here I am, with more than twenty years at this network, and some, some *kid*, who's been here a week, is telling me how important young blood is. He made me feel about a hundred and twenty."

The time and closeness the two women shared gave them an insight into each other's private emotions. What Kay was really feeling, Sheila understood, wasn't just simple anger. Deep down, she was scared.

"Don't let it get to you," she urged softly. "It's not as though your job is on the line—"

"That's what *you* think! In this business, your job is *always* on the line. Look at Harry Refferty. He was VP of network operations for nearly five years. Dinner with the chairman of the board, golf dates—everyone thought he'd die in that office of his. Then the Springfield affiliate switches over to ABC, the financial people start to get nervous, and good-bye Harry, hello Whiz Kid." She sighed. "Sometimes it makes me wonder what the hell I'm hanging on for. But the hell with that. What's up with you?"

"It can wait, Kay. Maybe you'd like to be alone, relax for a while—"

"No, go on. As long as I'm in this jungle, I might as well have a banana. Shoot."

Sheila opened the folder she'd brought with her, and for the next twenty-five minutes they discussed the *Dancetime, USA!* special.

Finding a sponsor had been no problem—the target audience was perfect for a soft drink company, and one of the cola companies had jumped at the chance to take the full ninety minutes. A group of nostalgia-themed commercials was being shot, and the company was arranging a sweepstakes contest to go along with the theme. Full-page ads in *Cosmopolitan, TV Guide, Time, The Journal, McCalls* and other magazines would feature the "Rockin' Fifties Are Back Again!" theme, as would displays in supermarkets. By filling out an entry blank, contestants would have a chance to win a variety of prizes, from golden-oldie record albums to a '58 Thunderbird. Five grand prize-winners would get an all-expense-paid trip to New York the week of the special. They'd be in the bleachers when the reunion special was broadcast, and they'd also receive fifty hundred-dollar bills.

Every magazine ad and display would specify the show's air date and time, and would remind the public to "watch the fabulous *Dancetime, USA!* Reunion on TBS."

"That should help," Kay agreed, pleased with the copy of the rough layout the advertising agency had sent. "What about the record deal?"

Just as the sponsor had seen the wisdom of cashing in on the program in a big way, the film and camera manufacturer who'd bought the commercial time on the music special preceding the reunion had put together a collection of 1950's hits. The album was a premium, available for two dollars plus proof of purchase of three rolls of film. The network's business-affairs department had convinced the camera manufacturer to call the album "*Dancetime, USA!*'s Fabulous Fifties Favorites." It hadn't been easy, since the camera people didn't even have a fifteen-second spot on the reunion show, but finally the deal had been worked out with the inducement of five minutes of commercial at a cut rate later in the season.

Increasingly, book publishers were tying in with TV. Just as major motion pictures from original screenplays were novelized as paperbacks, successful TV series and the biggest movies of the week were transformed into fiction. Hot stars, especially those who appealed to young audiences, were the subject of trade paperback "scrapbooks," among them Shaun Cassidy and John Travolta. Now that television had been around long enough to have a past, there was an increased market for nostalgia books as well. Some of them were generalized reviews of *Television's Golden Age* or *The Complete History of Soap Operas*. Others dealt with specific programs, such as the original *I Love Lucy, The Honeymooners, The Star Trek Catalog*, and *The Today Show*. Two weeks before the reunion special aired, every book store in the country would display Tower Books' large-format paperback entitled *Dancetime, USA!—The Fabulous Fifties in Pictures*.

"You may not believe it," Kay said, glancing over the book jacket copy Sheila handed her, "but there actually was a time when all the network worried about was putting on TV shows. Now everything's merchandising. But it helps. How are things going with the publicity people?"

How to exploit the maximum PR potential of the special had been a subject of several meetings, though the show was months away. The department had been enthusiastic, which was a decided plus—some specials, though they had quality productions and artistic merit, were hard to publicize: a few stories could be placed in newspapers, or a photograph, but that was it. The *Dancetime, USA!* reunion, on the other hand, was a publicist's dream. Nostalgia, human interest—all the elements that the entertainment editors went for were there.

As the air date approached, a massive campaign would begin. In addition to photographs and releases mailed to all the major papers in the country, there would be magazine features, interviews, and press conferences—all geared for maximum coverage.

The technical end of the production was coming along—the set, the staff, the details of the budget. The show would be done live on a reproduction of the original *Dancetime* set, rather than in a variety of locations.

"How are we doing with talent?" Kay asked.

"Well, there's one definite commitment—Alice Lane," Sheila answered.

Kay rolled her eyes. "Of course. She'd go to the opening of a grave if she thought there was some PR to be gotten. Did you happen to catch her on *Dinah* the other day? Maybe it was Merv or Mike, but one of them."

"What did she do?"

"Oh, her usual routine. She sang a couple of songs and launched into an attack on busing. I want to make sure that she doesn't get a chance to do any politiking with us—not just on the special, Sheila, but in interviews related to the show. What Alice Lane wants to crusade for on her own time is her business. But on TBS time, she's going to stick to the fifties—period!"

"I'm with you."

"How about Tommy Del? How are we coming?"

Sheila paused. Tommy Del's reaction had surprised her. From what she knew of performers, she'd expected that the former teen idol would welcome the chance to appear on a major network special. Instead, though, he'd given the network a polite refusal. Lee Dean had called him with a personal plea, but Tommy had been noncommittal. That part of his life, he said, was over. He had no desire to rehash it.

"We're not going to give up," Sheila vowed. "Tommy

was glad to hear from Lee. He invited him to visit his place in Massachusetts for a weekend."

"Good idea," Kay approved. "Once Lee has a chance to turn on the charm, Tommy will come around."

Sheila paused. "Lee suggested that I go, too," she said softly.

"Why not? You've been working hard—the worst you'll get out of it is a couple of days out of town. The network will pick up the expenses. What's happening with the Fantastiks? By the way, Nat was *furious* when he heard that Sylvia had agreed to do the show. He really hit the ceiling. I shut him up, though—we just have to give a couple of his new acts guest shots on one of the variety things."

"I've pretty much left getting the other Fantastiks up to Lee. He knows them, and I gather there's a lot of tension between them. He seems to think he can work it out."

"He'd better. I promised we'd deliver Sylvia on his say-so, and we don't get her without those other two."

"We could always go with some other group, couldn't we, Kay?"

"If we had to. But Sylvia is a guaranteed grabber. And the Fantastiks together again—it would be a real coup. Let Lee try his best. I'd hate to have to stick in some also-ran group the public's seen a million times. While we're on the subject of old faces, how many of The Regulars are firm?"

There were six firm commitments, Sheila explained. Dennis, Sandy and Bobby, Cathy, Connie, and Don—finally—had agreed to appear on the show. Tony, after three weeks, had called to say that he'd "try" to make it.

"I've written to him again," Sheila said. "Maybe he'll give us a definite yes. It's funny, isn't it?"

"What?" Kay asked.

"Well, a couple of The Regulars—Don, Tony—they're kind of on the fence about doing the show. I'd have thought they'd be glad to get together again."

"For old times' sake?" Kay asked, mildly amused.

"Something like that."

"Sweetie," the older woman said gently, "you're too young to know what old times really feel like. Everybody gets older, and everybody changes. It's the same kind of thing that happens with school reunions. You see the people who were your best friends—the boys you were crazy about, and the girls you shared every secret with. You think about the old days, and you realize how much you've changed and grown apart. It's sad in a way."

"I never thought of it like that."

"And don't forget, we're not asking these people to just get together for an intimate little party—we're talking network TV. Anyway, it sounds as if everythings going fine. You're doing a terrific job, and I'm very proud of you."

"Thanks, Kay," Sheila said, meaning it. "And I want to thank you for giving me this chance—"

"Chance, hell! You earned it. Now tell me—how does it feel?"

Even before she spoke, the joy on Sheila's face answered the question. "It's—it's wonderful. Better than wonderful, if there is such a thing. Even the headaches and the hassles are worth it. It was that way from the start—working with you, I mean. But this way, doing it myself, watching it happen and come together... it's thrilling, corny as that sounds."

Kay's manner softened. "It doesn't sound corny at all, Sheila. I remember the feeling myself. And I'll give you one bit of advice, if you don't mind—"

"Please."

"Hold on to the memory of how it feels now. Hold on to it as tight as you can while it's exciting and new. Because the thrill wears off."

"Not for me," Sheila said. "It could never wear off."

Kay got up, walked around the office, and took a seat on a corner of her desk. "You don't think so?"

279

"Maybe it sounds naive to you, but I can't imagine that happening. Television is just like I always hoped it would be, just like I wanted it to be! I love it—watching the way things all come together, knowing that the million and one little details are going to add up to a program that millions of people are going to watch. It must be... well, the way a painter feels when he's working on a picture. One brush stroke follows another, and eventually you have a finished painting that everyone can see—"

"There's just one difference," Kay reminded her. "A painting gets many viewings, over a long period of time. Even if an artist isn't recognized till after his death, the work endures. Let's say that he isn't recognized at all. Maybe his style isn't the kind of thing that most people go for. There's still a chance that somebody will see a painting—whether it's in a museum, or a junk shop, or Aunt Bea's attic—and appreciate what he was trying to do.

"In this business, except for a few shows like *Lucy*, it's one chance only... with maybe a rerun or two. The real tragedy is that quality, even commercially speaking, doesn't always make the difference. I've had my share of flops and turkeys, but there was nothing wrong with *Emerald Shores*. Everyone involved with that project gave it the best they had, and the end result was damn good. But something like that gets programmed at the wrong time, and bingo—the party's over. All that work, all that time, all that effort down the drain. If we'd had the numbers, there would have been full-page ads in *Variety* and *The Hollywood Reporter* and TBS would be congratulating itself. Instead, I get called on the carpet by some child prodigy who needs a scapegoat.

"I'm not trying to throw a wet blanket on your enthusiasm, Sheila. I'm happy for you—really I am. But realizing the truth is important. It's good to care, but you have to learn not to care too much."

"How do you do that?" Sheila asked.

Kay laughed. "That one, tootsie, is the sixty-four-thousand-dollar question. If you find the answer, do me a favor, will you? Let me know."

2.

"I THINK YOU'LL REALLY GET A KICK OUT OF seeing this footage," Lee Dean said, leading Dee Phillips and Virgie Kendrick into the screening room. "Miss Granger—Sheila, here—has done a great job of putting the clips together."

"Actually it's been more of a pleasure than a job," Sheila said warmly. "I love your music."

They took their seats, signaling for the lights to be cut and the film to be rolled.

A black-and-white image of a young Lee Dean filled the small movie screen. Teenagers crowded around the bandstand as the camera moved in for a closeup.

"Okay, guys and gals," Lee said, "today we have another *Dancetime, USA!* exclusive—and this one is special. It's the very first TV appearance of one of the hottest new groups in the country, and they're headed straight for the top. So let's give a rockin' welcome to Dee, Sylvia, and Virgie—otherwise known as The Fantastiks!"

The soundtrack was filled with applause. The camera

moved to a shot of three young black girls. Their hair was teased, and they wore full felt skirts and white blouses. As their record played, they mouthed the words and went through a few steps of a dance routine. Their lip-synching was far from perfect—even the self-consciousness of being in the front of the TV cameras showed.

Sheila found herself glancing at the two women, twenty years older now than the images on the screen, as they watched themselves. Dee looked amused—Virgie, on the other hand, stared at the screen with something Sheila couldn't quite define.

The number was followed by an ovation from the audience, then the three girls were sitting in the midst of the teen audience, in front row of the bleachers, as Lee Dean interviewed them.

"Okay," he said, "we've heard the hit—and it's the first of many hits you're going to have, if you ask me. Now let's get to know you. Let's start with you, Virgie. How does it feel to have your first record climbing all the way up the charts?"

"It's sure a thrill," she answered, the enthusiasm making her speak hurriedly. "It's like a dream come true for us."

"I'll bet," Lee told her. He turned to Dee. "Tell me, when the three of you got together to sing for the first time, did you have any idea you were going to become recording artists with a hit?"

"Well," Dee answered, looking at the other two girls and giggling, "*we* had the idea—but we weren't sure anyone else did."

"I think we can say you were on the right track," Lee said, turning to Sylvia. "Tell me something else. Lots of kids want to sing, but you three have done it. Any secrets of success you'd like to share, or any plans for the future you can tell us about?"

Sylvia, even then, seemed more at ease than the other two girls. She smiled broadly. "We've been singing together forever, it seems like. We've been friends ever since way back when. I think that enjoying our work and enjoying each other have helped, and I hope we can go on doing it forever."

"Well, all of us at *Dancetime, USA!* wish you the very best. Good luck to all three of you Fantastiks—and come back and see us again soon."

The film clip ended, and the lights came on.

Dee laughed. "We were green as the grass, and we looked it, didn't we? You know, I can remember waiting back in that dressing room for our cue. We must have checked our hair a hundred times at least, right, Virgie?"

"I guess," Virgie answered sullenly. She was still looking at the screen, as if reluctant to accept the fact that the film clip had ended.

"Those days were sure something," Dee said. "The shows, and all that traveling! It was crazy."

"It was a crazy time, all right," Lee agreed. "But it was crazy in a special way. It meant a lot to so many people. That's why TBS is doing a special on those days."

"You told me on the phone," Dee said. "You're bringing The Regulars back, huh? And some of the old acts?"

"That's right," Sheila said. "And we're going to do the special live—just the way it was done in the old days."

Lee picked up the cue. "We want to have the best acts—the ones who had the big hits twenty years ago. And to make the show really special, we'd love to have The Fantastiks make an appearance."

There was a long silence. Finally Virgie broke it, making no attempt to hide the anger in her voice. "Haven't you heard? There are no more Fantastiks, Lee. Haven't been for a long time—ever since that bitch left us high and dry to go out on her own—"

"Virgie, you don't have to curse," Dee began, but she got no further.

"I'll say anything I damn please. You don't care—you

got that husband of yours, and you got your kids, and you got religion. And Sylvia's got herself a career. Big-star Sylvia, doin' clubs, and concerts, and movies. Did she ever give a damn about us? Did she ever care what the hell happened to us, long as she got her own way? The hell she did!" She turned to Lee and Sheila. "You two must be out of your minds. Miss Sylvia is a single—she's not part of a trio that isn't even working any more."

The tension in the room was electric. As calmly as possible, Lee explained about seeing Sylvia's show in Las Vegas. The tribute to The Fantastiks, he told them, would be a standout of the show—everyone remembered the trio and their hits. He told the girls that Sylvia had agreed to do the special as one-third of The Fantastiks, then waited for their reaction.

"I don't know if I could even do it," Dee said. "It's been so long. I do most of my singing in the shower these days, except for church."

"You could rehearse," Sheila suggested. "It would be a real treat for your fans—"

Virgie cut her off, standing up suddenly.

"Yeah? Well, the hell with the goddamn fans!"

"Virgie—"

"You let me talk, Dee, you hear? Where were our damn fans when Sylvia up and left the act? We went out on the road working twice as hard. We broke the new girl in and had the old songs down pat, and the new ones, too. We'd be up there working our asses off, and they'd be yelling out, 'We want Sylvia!' Remember that?"

Dee sighed. "Virgie, that was so long ago—"

"Oh, sure!" the other woman said. "You don't have to tell me. It was a hell of a long time ago! We were big-time. The number-one girl group. Then that selfish bitch decided it wasn't enough for her. It wasn't enough for her to be the lead singer, and the one they always made the fuss over. She was the one who got her picture in the fashion magazines and all that. And then she was the one who took a walk! She didn't give a good goddamn about me *or* you! And now you're taking her part—"

"I'm not taking anybody's part," Dee insisted, forgetting that Lee and Sheila were in the room. "Look what she's got—"

"I'm looking, all right! I can't help but look! She's had one damn hit album after another! Her face is plastered all over the movie magazines and everywhere else. Every time I read a gossip column about some fancy party, there's Miss Sylvia on the guest list. She's got everything, *that's* what she's got!"

Dee's voice was as calm as Virgie's was excited. "She's paid for it. You know that. Look at her life. She's had divorces—"

"So what? She can afford 'em! You know, you always were Miss Goody Two-Shoes about her. Poor Sylvia. Her marriages didn't work out. Well, my heart is just breaking. Let's take a collection up for her, poor thing!"

"Virgie, you could show some Christian charity—"

"A lot of charity she showed me! *And* you. She went off on her own without so much as a by-your-leave, and we could have gone to hell for all she cared. She's a mean, selfish bitch who used us—*both* of us—to get just what she wanted!"

Lee Dean cleared his throat. "Look, I didn't mean to upset you, Virgie. I thought it might be nice for the three of you to get together again, just for one night. It would be good for the show, but it could do a lot for you, too."

"Like what?" Virgie demanded.

"Like your record royalties, for one thing. National exposure would move a lot of your old albums. You know that. And the network would pay you, of course—"

Virgie grabbed her coat and bag. "Well, big damn deal! No way, no time, and nohow! That's what I think about it!"

"Virgie!" Dee called, but Virgie was already storming down the hall.

"Should I go after her?" Sheila asked.

"Don't bother," Dee answered. "When she gets her temper up, there's no point in even trying to talk sense to her. She's had a hate on for Sylvia for years—ever since the act broke up."

Lee began to pace. "I never figured she'd react that way. Sylvia told me Virgie was bitter, but she's still doing what she can in the business. I was sure she'd go for it—"

"You have to understand her, Lee," Dee began. "You see, it didn't just start when Sylvia left the trio... But you don't want to hear all this—"

"I do," Lee insisted.

"I'd like to know," said Sheila, "if you don't mind my listening."

Dee smiled. "Well, a cup of coffee sounds like a mighty tempting inducement."

Minutes later, they were in the TBS cafeteria, and Dee was going back in time, to the earliest months of the trio's success.

They'd been equals, Dee explained. Even though Sylvia sang lead, they'd each had the same share of the money the act earned from records and personal appearances. But even then, when they were just getting started, Sylvia had been sure of herself, more comfortable with the initial phases of success.

"Maybe part of it was because she was singing lead," Dee explained. "You know how it is—when you have three girls on stage, you need somebody to do the talking, introducing the songs and handle the patter between numbers. Sylvia just took to it, so she did it."

At the time, Dee hadn't been jealous—and if Virgie was, she kept her emotions to herself. The realization of their common dream, the success and recognition and celebrity they wanted and fantasized about, had seemed almost unreal. If the timing had been different, if they'd clicked a few years earlier, they might have had a different career—one limited to black audiences. But in the late

1950's, the racial boundary lines (at least the ones in the minds of young record buyers) had been shaken by the rise of rock and roll.

Jet, Ebony, and the other black publications wrote stories about the three girls who'd gone from Harlem to the top of the charts: the white press followed. The trio was young and attractive—their story had human interest value.

"Whenever they wanted to do an interview," Dee recalled, "Sylvia was ready. We could be exhausted—they used to work us pretty hard, between recording and doing shows and learning new routines—but she never passed up a chance to talk to a reporter. And she had that same knack for talking with them that she had onstage with the audiences."

Without anyone's planning or even discussing it, Sylvia became the spokeswoman for the trio. It went with her position as lead singer, and with her ability to tell the story of the group's rise to fame over and over again with an enthusiasm that made it sound like she was relating it for the first time. It wasn't that she schemed or planned it, Dee explained, but suddenly it was as if the group was "Sylvia and The Fantastiks."

"But didn't you know this was happening?" Sheila asked, wanting to understand. "Didn't you talk about it?"

"Honey," Dee answered, "we didn't know *anything*. We hadn't been around the business. If the record company or our manager told us to do something, we just did it, that's all. I remember one time we were on the road for two months, nonstop. We didn't even have the sense to figure out that we could tell somebody we were tired. We wanted to rest."

When the girls did complain, it was only to each other—and even then, Sylvia never protested the traveling and the crazy hours.

"She thrived on it," Dee said. "She actually wanted us to work like that. It was all going along, you know, one hit and then another. I guess Sylvia figured that if we stopped, broke the rhythm of it, we might lose our momentum."

If the demands were great, the rewards were, too. Besides the satisfaction that came with having made it, there were financial rewards. The pleasure of being able to go into a store and buy a dress or a bag without checking the price, the luxury of having more shoes than you could wear—for three girls who'd spent their lives scrimping to pay off overpriced, shoddy merchandise on layaway plans, it was intoxicating.

The novelty of having money and having beaten the odds brought the three girls closer together. As their fame grew, they found themselves invited to parties—both press functions where they were guests, and private affairs where the wealthy trend-setters gathered together the celebrities who were "hot" at the moment.

"I never felt comfortable at those things," Dee said. "Virgie didn't either. It was like we didn't belong and we knew it. Everyone was nice as could be, telling us how much they liked us and all, but I felt... well, like we were something in a zoo. Sylvia was different. She took to that part of it like a duck to water. The fashion designers and the hairdressers fussed over her. You have to remember that back then, it wasn't like it is today. You didn't have black models in the magazines and on the TV commercials. But the NAACP and CORE and all those groups were bringing it up, and I guess Sylvia was smart enough to see that she could get something out of it."

Her natural beauty and her slim figure made Sylvia an ideal candidate for the fashion magazines: in return, the editors could counter protests about discrimination with layouts that featured "the lead singer of the fabulous Fantastiks" in the latest Seventh Avenue creations. Management had advised that it would be a good idea to capitalize on the media coverage Sylvia was getting, and to translate her publicity image to the act. Instead of deciding on costumes and hairstyles together, as they'd done before, the three of them began wearing clothes that looked good on Sylvia—and often didn't flatter Dee or Virgie.

"At first, we were like sisters. Closer than most sisters, even," Dee told Lee and Sheila. "But Sylvia started running with that social crowd, and Virgie and I began to stay away. We didn't hang around together the way we once did—it got so we usually just saw each other backstage and during the shows."

Sylvia began to date actors, artists, and assorted "Beautiful People." She was photographed for the papers and gossip columns, and the movie magazines began to transform her casual dates with actors into major romances, and suggest that she was planning to go into pictures herself.

"I don't know if she had the idea, or if all that publicity gave it to her," Dee recalled, "but she began to see things differently. It wasn't the three of us together any more—it was just Sylvia. She had people telling her that she didn't need us. We were holding her back. She could make more money on her own. Virgie was getting jealous of all the attention Sylvia was getting, and our contract was coming up for renewal with the record company. A lawyer got hold of Sylvia, and that was it—she just announced one day that she wanted to go out alone."

"That must have been awful for you," Sheila said.

Dee shrugged. "It was a shock. But I didn't take it as bad as Virgie. I don't know... it's like lots of things. When we were kids in Harlem, the idea of being stars was the most glamorous thing in the world. But after five years, all that traveling was getting to me. You know how it is, Lee—the hotel rooms start looking the same, even if you're in a suite. I had some money saved up, and I'd done a lot for my family. I was hurt, but Virgie was in a rage.

"She started right in about how she and I would get

another girl and be bigger than ever. It just didn't work out that way, that's all. The girl we got was a mess—drugs, the whole bit. We still had the name, but we didn't have the hits. When you've played the top spots, it's not easy to get used to the second-rate clubs. When people used to fight to get in to see, and then suddenly you look out on empty tables . . . well, I gave it a couple of years and I said to myself, enough is enough.

"Why beat a dead horse? I met Sam—you'll have to meet him, Lee, he's a wonderful man—and I got married. I figured I'd done what I set out to do, and it was time for something else."

Lee looked at her with something warmer and deeper than a smile at an old acquaintance.

"I have to tell you, Dee—I really respect you," he said. "You were able to walk away from it and leave the whole thing. Some people can't do that."

Dee laughed. "Don't go pinning medals on me so fast! I'm not going to say it was easy. You get used to first-class service, and fans, and all that attention. It takes a while to be just another lady in the check-out line at the market. But the party was over, and like I said, I was lucky. I had a chance at something even better than a career. I started a family.

"Lee, you have to understand something. Virgie never gave herself a chance for anything else. She's too full of hate. Sure, I get a twinge once in a while when I see a magazine cover and there's Sylvia, looking like a million dollars and making a million to boot. But I think about the problems she has. Married how many times? Three or four, anyway.

"Put everyone's troubles in a bag and you'll end up picking your own, my mama used to tell me."

"Well, I'm not exactly pleased with mine at the moment," Lee told her. "I told the network that I could deliver The Fantastiks. It was stupid of me, but I was just sure that if I got Sylvia to agree, there'd be no problem with you and Virgie, Dee. I never thought you wouldn't want to—"

"Hold on, now," she answered. "Who said I didn't want to?"

"But you told me it's all behind you. And Virgie won't—"

"Who says?" she asked, interrupting him. "Lee, I said I got out—but I didn't say I wouldn't go back for a night. And Virgie? Don't you worry. She's mad because she knows the whole thing hinges on Sylvia. But she'll come around. I'll talk to her." She looked at her watch. "I've got to get going."

Lee Dean took her hands in his as she stood. "Do—do you really think you can talk Virgie into it, Dee? I'd be more grateful than I can tell you—"

"Then you say a prayer, okay? And then you'll be able to thank the Lord instead of me. Well, I'll be talking to you, Lee. Nice meeting you, Miss Granger—"

"Sheila."

"Sheila," Dee repeated warmly. "And you pray, too. Maybe we'll all get what we want."

3.

"MISS LANE IS HERE, MR. MORGAN," THE secretary announced over the intercom.

"Give me a minute to put that tape on," he answered, knowing that Alice, in the reception room, wouldn't overhear his voice, "then send her in."

Matt Morgan picked up the cassette he'd pulled out in preparation for the meeting with his client, and put it into the tape deck built into the shelves below the window. Seconds later, the sound of her new single filled the office. He pretended to listen, comforting himself with the view of Los Angeles through the window.

> *Sometimes it's hard to know,*
> *Just who I am.*
> *So many people tell me who to be.*
> *They say to join the march,*
> *And be a liberated woman,*
> *With sexual equality.*
> *They say, "Leave that pot of soup,*

*Join our women's group
Like they talk about on TV."
But to tell it like it is,
I wasn't born to be a Ms.
It took a man to make
A woman out of me...
You make me glad to be a woman
Lovin' a man like you.
Maybe I'll never be liberated
But I'll always tell you the truth.
Yes I'm glad to be a woman,
And I'm happy in our little world,
And if I sound kinda old-fashioned,
I guess I'm just an old-fashioned girl...
Now some girls call
Their husbands "pigs"
And talk about their women's rights,
But I'm just glad
You bring home the bacon,
And you come home to me at night...*

"Alice!" he exclaimed, as his secretary led her through the door. He flipped off the cassette player. "I was just listening—"

"I know," she said, smiling sweetly. "You must have put it on as soon as your girl told you I was here."

"How can my favorite client accuse me of something like that?" he asked, playing the scene for all it was worth.

Alice sank into the red leather chair across from his desk and sighed wearily. "You're such a pathetic liar, Matt. It's a good thing you're a manager instead of a performer—you really can't act. Tell me, since you can't stop listening to it, what do you think of the record?"

"What do I think? Like I told you on the phone, it's great. It'll move you right into the country market—"

"Don't sentence me to the sticks, Matt. Urban-country is the hottest thing in radio, after all."

He got up from his chair, coming around to sit on the edge of the desk. "Did I say that? I'm just saying it's going to do very well in the traditional country market. Facts are facts, Alice—career girls in New York and Chicago who like Waylon Jennings and Willie Nelson aren't exactly going to relate to that number as much as housewives. That's all I'm saying."

Her blue eyes focused on her manager with determination. "I'd better get promotion from the record company, Matt—"

"Relax. I spoke with them again this morning. They're going ahead with the press conference. And the tie-in with the anti-ERA group, too. Just like you wanted."

Alice was pleased. "Good. The publicity will be terrific."

"By the way, I'm drawing up the papers... You know, the ones for your donating the ten percent of the record to that group—"

"Ten percent of the *profits*—my performing profits only, not the writing royalty—and after expenses," she reminded him.

Matt Morgan nodded, amazed as always by her ability to load the percentages in her favor. Not only had she found a writer with a corny country song that conveyed an anti-women's-lib message, she'd also managed to talk the young songwriter into giving her credit (and half his royalty) as co-writer. One of the anti-ERA groups she'd been involved with was putting up money to promote the record, and Alice had "generously" donated ten percent of her income from the song to further the group's work. She'd come up with the idea of a press conference, making sure the pro-ERA groups knew all about it so that the maximum amount of controversy would be generated.

When it came to public relations, Matt told himself, Alice Lane was an unqualified pro: for a so-so singer with no real hits since the 1950's, she'd managed to perpetuate a career that should, by all the rules, have died a natural death a decade before. There were dozens of singers more talented, and when you came down to it, she'd had a grand total of three top-ten hits (and ten also-rans) in the heyday of her success.

Even then, Alice Lane's image was almost out of date, an anachronism. While other singers in the same mold, singers such as Connie Francis, sang songs asking where the boys were, Alice had clicked with numbers that preached the apple-pie ideals of waiting for "pure, special love" and "one man to love forever." Back in the late 1950's, a lot of people had dismissed her as being a goody-goody, with more image appeal to parents than musical appeal to their teenage sons and daughters. A *Rolling Stone* article on 1950's singers had described her as "being so cloyingly wholesome that she made Annette Funicello seem downright wicked."

When the English Invasion knocked many performers in her league out of the business and out of the public eye, Alice Lane had found a unique way of staying in the spotlight. Instead of bowing out gracefully, settling for an occasional booking in a second-rate club or hotel, she'd decided to fight the tide. She'd denounced the new sounds as "decadent"—and suddenly become more popular than ever. The only thing that changed was her audience: rather than going for the teenage record buyers, she was speaking and singing to women's clubs, church groups, and meetings of various organizations committed to one of her causes or another.

Exactly what the cause was didn't seem to bother Alice—as long as it was basically conservative enough to fit in with her wholesome flag-waving image, and controversial enough to afford her a chance for more coverage by the news media. She had parlayed her position into a new career that made her a popular commentator at parades, a guest soloist performing "The Star-Spangled Banner" at sports events, and an occasional guest at the White House. There were also regular guest shots on TV, some of them featuring her as a performer, others giving her air time as an outspoken and newsworthy "personality."

By no means, Matt knew, was Alice Lane everyone's

cup of tea. A lot of people—most, in fact—didn't care about her one way or the other. But outside the mainstream there was a periphery of cause-involved citizens. Some were committed on principle; either pro or con. Others didn't care what the issue was as long as there was a cause to rally around, an issue to help fill the loneliness or provide an outlet for the frustration in their lives.

Often, over the years, other managers and agents he knew had teased Matt about his client. When pressed to explain why he kept her on his list, he answered honestly. Besides the lucrative commission from her public appearances (Alice believed in being paid to appear on behalf of the causes she believed in), she was a fascinating woman, obsessed with her own career to a point far beyond the egocentric self-involvement characteristic of many performers. Staying in the public eye was more than a job—it was her lover, her only interest, her whole life's focus, a crusade.

From time to time, she went too far in her desire to get attention, so far that Matt was afraid she'd finish herself off. It was one thing when she spoke out against drugs (even if she continually hinted that they, like "immorality," were part of a Communist conspiracy). It was one thing to have been a definite hawk on the Vietnam issue—after all, Alice, to her credit, had gone overseas to entertain the troups for the USO. But advocating harsh penalties for marijuana use, and vehemently opposing amnesty for draft resisters long into the 1970's, were something else. Alice had a way of going too far at times—of embracing emotional causes and issues that might win her press coverage, but were sure to lose her fans. He'd spoken to her about it repeatedly, worried that she might not be able to see the inherent dangers of her publicity-at-any-price philosophy.

But for every attack against her from the liberal press, she was able to produce a favorable clipping from a conservative outlet. She was honored as "Woman of the Year" several times by prestigious groups—and through his client, Matt Morgan had understood fully for the first time the extent and power of American conservatism. It had been a long time since Alice Lane had a hit single, but her albums of patriotic songs sold regularly—if unspectacularly. And maybe her new move toward a more country sound would pay off.

"With all the attention people are going to be paying to the single, Matt," she said, as if reading his mind, "I want to make sure that every release mentions the album. Make sure the record company pushes that angle, will you?"

"Right," he said, going back to his chair to make a note. "Now let's talk about this TBS thing, the Lee Dean special—"

"What's to talk about? I want to do it!"

Matt shifted nervously. From the moment the network had contacted Alice's agent, there'd been no doubt that the appearance would be an important break. It wasn't just a matter of national exposure—she'd had plenty of that. But the whole format of the show, with its nostalgia angle, gave Alice the chance to present herself in a context that was sure to help her image... provided someone could make her cooperate. By singing the old songs that had established her in the first place and refraining from making political announcements, she'd broaden her base of appeal. The network had offered good money, twenty grand for Alice, but they'd stipulated that she was to sing and not to sermonize. The two, over the years, had become inseparable parts of her "act," and getting her to see it TBS' way wasn't going to be easy. Her agent hadn't even tried. Instead he'd called Matt, reminding him that he was her personal manager, and therefore the responsibility was his.

"I know you want to do it—and you should," he said, choosing his words carefully. "You're booked for a couple of dates in Florida around that time, but we can change them around without any trouble—"

"Okay. So?"

"So... Look, Alice, I'll level with you. I've never tried to stop you from doing it your way, have I? From saying what you want—"

"What I *believe* in," she corrected him.

"Right. What you believe in. I may not always agree with your point of view, but you have every right to express it. And I've always admired your dedication."

A little flattery, he knew, couldn't hurt.

"But this time," he continued quickly, "I'm asking you to listen to me. The show is about the good old days. The songs, the dances, the kids who used to be on *Dancetime*. The network is selling nostalgia, Alice. Memories. Then—back in the 1950's—and not now. They want you as an entertainer, but they don't want comments on politics or anything like that. No controversy, just the sweet Alice Lane as she was in 1958."

He could see her bristle before she spoke. "If I'd stayed the way I was in 1958," she told him, "I'd be out of work. Let me ask you something, Matt: do you think it's pleasant to be picketed when you make a personal appearance?"

"Alice, sweetie—"

"Let me finish!" she insisted, standing up to pace around the office. "Do you think I like reading that I'm a kook or a nut? And how about what happened in San Francisco, where they threw the eggs? I don't kid myself. I know the whole world isn't crazy about me. But some people are. They like the way I sing, but what they really like is that I'm in a position to express the things they feel and believe, the things that don't get said by other people. And if you think I'm going to turn my back on them just to do a TV special, you have another think coming!"

"Hold it, hold it!" he implored her. "Cool off, Alice.

Let's put this thing in perspective, huh? I'm not asking you to turn your back on anything—"

"You're telling me to shut up, aren't you?"

"Not at all!" he insisted. "Alice, I *know* you. I respect you. Not just as a talent, but because you're smart enough and shrewd enough to see all the angles. All I'm saying is that this one time—*one* time—do it their way. Go along with the network and just sing the old tunes. The next day, you'll be in a perfect position to get coverage on whatever you want. You can cooperate with them and still use the situation to your advantage. That's all I'm saying."

"How?" she asked, suddenly more interested than angry.

"Like this," he explained. "You said it yourself—you have your fans, but not everyone is among them. A lot of people don't agree with the things you say. Maybe they didn't like something you said a long time ago and haven't really listened since. By doing this special TBS' way, you'll make them say, 'Hey, Alice Lane sings a great song. She's not so bad.' Then, the next time you talk, they'll listen. They'll be more receptive."

"Who else is doing the show?" she asked.

"Lee Dean is hosting it, remember him?"

"I thought the network fired him."

Matt laughed. "Alice, you know this business—'I'll never work with you again until I need you.' He's lined up The Fantastiks—with Sylvia—and I think they're getting Tommy Del, or they're working on it. You three will be the pro talent, then they have The Regulars—those kids who used to dance on the show—set. The special is going to get a lot of attention in the industry because they're doing it live, like the old days. It'll have prestige. It'll be good for you."

"All right," she said with a sigh of resignation. "You have my word. I'll just sing."

"Fine! That's it. And you won't be sorry. You'll see—it's going to be to your advantage."

"You can tell the network then," she said.

Matt cleared his throat. "I will. I'll give them your personal assurance. And of course when you sign the contract... You know how they are, honey. Everything in writing. There's a clause in it about..."

For a moment, he thought Alice was about to explode, but she contained herself. They took a few more minutes to chitchat about the record, then he walked her to the door, wiping his forehead in relief when she was finally gone. Another problem solved, he told himself, another crisis averted.

Another try at shutting me up! Alice Lane told herself, heading for the freeway that would take her back to Orange County. She'd managed to control her anger in the meeting with Matt, but that didn't mean she didn't feel it. And rightly so, she believed—from the very start, the whole business had been against her.

Even in the beginning they hadn't liked her. She'd been too "white," too "waspy" in the 1950's—a time when you had to come from some slum to be an overnight sensation. But she'd come from one of the best neighborhoods in Trenton, and she'd had singing lessons since she was ten years old, and when her father's bank had bailed out a troubled record company, her career had been launched.

Daddy and his friends had hated pop music—the country, they said, was going to hell in a handbasket, with kids dancing to "jungle" beats and listening to records that encouraged promiscuity and immorality. The success she'd had in the old days, success in spite of the people in the business who thought she was too square, proved that her father knew what he was talking about and that he wasn't alone.

At first, she'd actually doubted him. The black groups and the Italian singers she met and worked with were nice kids—or so she'd thought for a time. Granted, they came from underprivileged backgrounds and had no breeding, but what could you expect? They'd been friendly if somewhat distant—at least while she had her hits.

Then things had changed. All of a sudden she was finished, washed up, through. Her father's death had only made it worse—there'd been nobody to turn to for advice...certainly not her mother, who spent her afternoons at the club and never got involved in business. But Alice had inherited her father's will to succeed, and miraculously his friends had taken an interest in the career she'd all but decided to give up.

The ironic part was that they weren't at all the type of people who cared about popular music. Politics and finance were their fields, along with big business. But they'd helped her see that she had a duty to help keep America from "going under," and what's more, they'd showed her how to do it.

She gloated, thinking of that first press conference when she'd denounced The Beatles and the other groups. If she'd had the idea on her own, she wouldn't have known how to go about getting coverage. But a few of her father's friends had made a few calls, and the press had turned out in droves.

Ever since, it had been easy. She'd had no problem espousing the causes that were important to the people who had given her a chance to reestablish herself. After all, decency, patriotism, and conservatism were the backbone of the country, as Daddy had taught her. Because she was young and because she was a singer, she had the chance to influence a group of people who might not have responded to politicians or senior statesmen of the anti-liberal movement.

Speaking out, articulating a point of view that would guarantee her coverage in certain influential newspapers and on certain radio and TV stations, came easily. All you needed was a few of them—the liberal media outlets, while they didn't like her, couldn't ignore her...especially when there were people to write her speeches and guide her thinking on The Issues.

For a time, she hadn't been able to understand the necessity of the secrecy of it all. Why, she'd wondered, couldn't she come out and say that the ideas she expressed came from some of the most powerful people in the nation? But that had been explained—*they*, the other side, used all kinds of subversive and nefarious methods to infiltrate American life at every level. If Alice's backers and promoters came to light, she'd lose her credibility. What she was doing, she'd been told, was turning the tables on the very people who wanted to subvert the country by using their own tricks against them.

It had worked better than anyone had hoped. Instead of phasing itself out, her career had bloomed and grown. Of course a lot of stations didn't play her records, and a lot of television shows didn't invite her on as a guest, and a few comedians delighted in incorporating jokes about her into their routines, but what could you expect? Show business, everyone knew, was dominated by *them*—and she'd made it very clear that she was on the other side.

Like a crusader—she often thought of her career as a mission—she'd fought it out. She'd endured the jokes and the snubs and the insults, and it had been worth it. Joan Baez hadn't been invited to entertain in the Nixon White House: Alice Lane had. Jane Fonda wasn't asked to sing and speak at veterans' conventions—Alice Lane was the star entertainer at many such events.

Much of the country, she thought as she drove, didn't even know how grave the crisis was. They thought that politics were a thing that happened only in Washington, or at that *awful* United Nations. They didn't realize that the basic values of the country were in danger of being undermined and even overthrown from within.

Well, if they didn't know, she did—and so did some other people. The media, dominated by leftwingers, tended to paint everything she got involved in as "extremist." She took satisfaction in the fact that, like her or not, they had to pay attention to her. They were smart enough to know that she had too many fans, too big a following, to be ignored.

She didn't for a minute fool herself into thinking that Matt Morgan was on her side. He was interested in her success only to to the extent of his commission. It didn't really matter—if he used her, she certainly used him, too. And smart as she was, Matt didn't fully understand that a song like "Glad to Be a Woman" could and would influence more people against the ERA than any ten speeches.

As for the Lee Dean special, that was something else again. How dare the network stipulate that she couldn't express an opinion, that she promise to just stick to the old days if she appeared on the show! The answer, when she thought about it, was obvious—it was all part of the plot, all part of the same conspiracy that she'd battled against for years.

They wanted to shut her up... not only to silence Alice Lane personally, but to silence the expression of everything she represented. And they were naive enough to think that a chance to do a TV special was going to make her give up her convictions...

The anger left her as her Chrysler merged with the freeway traffic. *How silly!* She'd gladly sign any contract they wanted. When her agent told her about the special he explained that in addition to singing, Lee would interview her and the other guests about their memories of the 1950's. What's more, the show was going to be done live.

Which, Alice Lane thought with a smile, meant that she could say whatever she pleased when she got in front of the microphone—and there wasn't a damn thing TBS or any of the rest of *them* would be able to do about it.

4.

SHE SAW IT AGAIN—THE PERFECTLY FEAtured face with its porcelain skin and high cheekbones, the almond-shaped eyes accented by the graceful, natural line of the brows. Like pages of a book, different views of the girl filled her mind. Candid shots taken on a TV set, photographs posed for the fan magazines, head shots and composites and fashion poses from the pages of *Seventeen* and *Glamour* and *Mademoiselle*. They changed, one after another, the sequences gaining momentum until she had only a fraction of a second to glimpse them.

A single photograph froze in place, but this time the girl wasn't smiling or posing. Her eyes were glassy, her dark hair—usually immaculate—wild and unkempt. The image was neither black nor white nor color, but tinged with a sepia-like tone. The still photograph suddenly came to life, the mouth opening in a final, silent plea for help—

"Help!" Sheila Granger cried, twisting and turning to free herself from the sheets and blankets. She could hear her own ragged breath and feel the pounding of her heart as she sat up in bed. She forced herself to return to the present, to reality, hurriedly turning the lamp beside her bed on to reaffirm what she already knew: it had only been a dream. Another dream—the same dream again, in fact—but she was in no danger.

Mimi, in her temporary care while Kay was in California for a few days of meetings at TBS' West Coast headquarters, had opened her eyes from her adopted place atop the dresser and meowed, surprised by the light. Sheila shook her head, ran her fingers through her hair, and checked the clock: it was 3:20. She reached for a cigarette from the pack on the table beside her, lit it, and settled back against the pillows, telling herself that in a couple of minutes she'd be ready to fall asleep again. But bed reminded her of the nightmare, and as soon as she'd gotten herself comfortable, she swung her legs to the carpet.

"Want some milk?" she asked the cat, grateful for any kind of company. Mimi waited until she'd left the bedroom to leap from the dresser, racing to the kitchen and wrapping herself around Sheila's legs as she opened the refrigerator. "We'll both have something," Sheila said, pouring some low-fat milk into Mimi's dish. Staring into the refrigerator, she ruled out yogurt, cheese, and a glass of diet soda before deciding that she didn't really want anything at all and closing the door.

"Nice kitty, nice Mimi," she said, as the cat lapped the milk up. Once Mimi finished, she picked the cat up in her arms, feeling the vibrations of purring against her breasts as she made her way to the living room. On the sofa, with Mimi in her lap, she smoked her cigarette and tried to come to terms with what was happening.

There was no sense pretending that everything was all right, because it wasn't: she hadn't kept actual count, but over the past few weeks, her usually steady sleep had been broken by nightmares several times. Almost always it was next to impossible for her to get back to sleep again, and she'd find herself dragging through a day that began with several extra minutes before her makeup mirror, camouflaging the circles under her eyes.

Maybe it was the lack of sleep, but she'd found herself nervous and irritable on the job as well, snapping at secretaries, being less patient with people than she'd ever been before. She always felt bad afterward and tried to apologize if possible, but it was as if her malaise was out of her control, as if her emotions were no longer responding to her will.

It didn't take an analyst to figure out what the dream meant—the face belonged to Lorraine, one of The Regulars she'd tried to track down. The pictures, she realized, were all photographs she'd seen, either in the research files or in the portfolio that Dana Brent, the retired modeling agent Kay had suggested as a lead, had shown her.

The memory of that encounter made Sheila shudder in spite of the warmth of the night. Dana had been somewhat strange from the start, and it had taken several phone calls before she finally agreed to allow Sheila to come to her apartment in the East Eighties. Sheila had done her best to break through the icy manner of her hostess, commenting on the collection of Chinese pottery and admiring the Oriental rug.

"You want to know what happened to Lorraine?" the older woman had asked, canceling out the amenities. "I'll tell you. Maybe that's why I've kept this portfolio for so many years, hoping that someday somebody would ask."

She motioned to the black leather case on the small table between her chair and the sofa where Sheila sat. As if she were a child in school, Sheila obediently opened it, studying the familiar image in the 11″ x 14″ photographs and the tearsheets from magazines.

"*You* happened to her! Or rather the ones like you!" Dana said bitterly.

"I don't understand," Sheila protested.

"Of course you don't! You don't have time in that ugly

business of yours. You people took a nice girl who should have gotten married and had a family—and probably would have if she'd been left alone—"

"Miss Brent," Sheila replied, "I don't know what you mean. I'm not familiar with Lorraine—"

Dana glared at her. "And you're too young to have been involved with that program, aren't you? You people!"

"I think I'd better leave," Sheila began. "I didn't mean to upset you. I was simply trying to track Lorraine down for a special we're doing, as I told you on the phone—"

"Track her down?" The older woman's hand fixed itself on Sheila's wrist. "That's easy. She's buried in that cemetery you must pass when you go to the airport. She killed herself eight months after the program went off the air. She was buried a week before she turned nineteen—and that network of yours didn't send as much as a card! Not as much as a condolence for what amounts to murder!"

The silence had hung heavy between them, and Sheila was torn between a desire to understand and an urge to run. Dana's hand relaxed its grip, as if to let her make her own decision.

"I don't understand what you mean."

"What I mean is using people. Television isn't unique by any means—modeling does it, too, but in its way it's more merciful. You don't make it to a cover overnight. It takes time to build a career, time to establish yourself, time to see if you're strong enough to survive. Lorraine never had that chance. One day she was an attractive but average girl. Then along came *Dancetime*, and suddenly she was somebody, a personality. Nobody prepared her for it, Miss Granger. Nobody ever told her it might stop. And when it did—when she was no longer useful to your network—nobody even called her as much as once to help her deal with it.

"I know what you think—I'm old and crazy. Senile, if

you prefer. But I'll tell you what *I* think. I think your business is ugly. You take people and make them famous overnight. You chew them up and spit them out and you don't even watch where you're spitting! You're like drug pushers—as long as there's something in it for you, as long as you can sell your commercial time, you're happy to keep the supply coming. But what happens to people like Lorraine when the supply is cut off?

"I'll tell you what!" the woman continued, her voice shaking with emotion. "They become addicts without a supply. They don't even understand the nature of their addiction. For people like Lorraine, staying in the limelight becomes more important than anything else in life. She came to me as desperate as a junkie, Miss Granger. Desperate and begging! There was no way in the world that she was strong enough to survive the rejection that goes with a career, but thanks to you people, she needed it to make her life valid. I tried my best. My best! And so did she.

"But she was another pretty young girl—and she didn't have the strength and confidence. Every time she got passed up for a job she came to my office and cried! She sobbed! I told her—pleaded with her—to give it up, forget about it, but she couldn't. And let me tell you, I didn't want to get involved. I didn't feel it was my job to straighten out your network's mess!"

"Excuse me, but I don't see how Lorraine's personal problems were my—that is, *the* network's—mess, as you put it."

"I'm not surprised that you don't. Neither did anyone else—even when it might have done some good. As the head of a modeling agency, I worked with all the networks. I had a call from TBS looking for girls to act as hostesses on a new game show...pointing to prizes, modeling coats, that sort of thing. It seemed to be the perfect answer for Lorraine, and I was sure that when I explained the circumstances, she'd get the job.

"I got her an interview—and they picked someone else. They told me they wanted a 'new face.' Lorraine was eighteen years old, and she'd been on *Dancetime* from the beginning. But that didn't matter! Not one goddamn bit. A few days after, Lorraine was turned down, she slit her wrists in a tub of hot water. And she was buried without so much as a flower from TBS!"

Sheila was disturbed by the story, but felt obligated to come to the network's defense.

"Maybe they didn't know," she began.

"I made damn sure they knew!" Dana Brent said, banging her fist against the arm of her chair.

"Look, I'm sorry. I mean that, Miss Brent. I'm sorry for Lorraine and I'm sorry for you. I didn't mean to upset you. But you should know, I think, that Lorraine is an exception. The other Regulars didn't get 'addicted,' as you put it. They went on to lead relatively normal lives. It's a matter of facts and numbers—"

"Exactly!" the older woman said triumphantly. "That's what it always comes down to with you people. Ratings. Percentages. Demographics. *Numbers*! Well let me tell *you* something—when you're talking about people, the exceptions count, too. The lives count! And don't be so sure that being on that program didn't affect other people, Miss Granger. Just don't you be so sure..."

Sheila had beat a hurried retreat. Back at the office, she told Lee and Kay about the meeting. They calmed her, and Sheila had thought the experience was behind her, chalking it up to an old woman's eccentricity and bitterness.

Now, sitting with Mimi on her lap, she wasn't so sure. At the beginning, the whole project had been an up—a personal triumph and a professional chance to forge ahead. It was what she had worked toward from the start. Granted, there'd been a few problems, but then there always were. TBS hadn't been fair to Lorraine, perhaps, or to Lee Dean either, but then what big business was predicated on fairness? As Kay said so often, it was a constant fight for survival, an endless foray through a jungle.

So Lorraine was dead—it was too bad, but that was in the past. Andy, the "shrimp" of the old days, was dead, too, killed in Vietnam. Hank, who'd seemed so mild-mannered, was in prison, doing a seven-to-ten-year sentence for armed robbery. Donna, the "overdeveloped" blonde, had parlayed her moment of fame into a nude centerfold, then vanished from sight after a series of engagements in second-rate strip joints... Was TBS to blame for all those problems?

What about Dennis and Sandy, Connie and Bobby and the rest of them whom she'd tracked down? None of them had expressed any opinions about television being some devouring monster that callously used people, then rejected them. Lee Dean had more right than anyone to feel bitter, but he was able to put the past behind him. And what about Kay? Everytime one of her specials made it big, people raced to claim credit. But let a show get bad numbers and everyone from the writer to the programming department laid the blame on her.

It's not like I thought it would be, Sheila allowed herself to admit as she paced aimlessly through the living room.

But what *had* she expected? Show business was ugly—that was nothing new. Every business in the world was the same at the core, but in show business the heights and depths were more public and apparent. Television was a cutthroat industry, but then any highly competitive industry was. The novelty of working at TBS had finally worn off, and with it her naiveté.

Back in college, she viewed her career as a kind of race, a struggle to get from one point to the next. With time, and with a chance to observe her mentor, Kay, Sheila's conception had changed. Getting from one point to the next was only part of it: staying in place was just as hard... sometimes harder.

She went to the window, looking down on the street

and across it. There were lights on in several windows and as always, they made her wonder if other people were awake, struggling with questions they didn't really want to think about. Maybe in the darkened apartments as well there were people like herself, unable to sleep, staring out the window, thinking about their jobs and their lives...

My job is my life, Sheila realized. It was ironic, but the more she moved forward in her career, the more it consumed her. It had been weeks since she'd had a real date. She'd lost touch with the few friends she had outside the office. Kay Duvane was her closest friend. Much as she cared for and admired Kay, Sheila wasn't at all certain that she wanted a life like hers.

Is it worth it? she found herself thinking. Then, abruptly, she turned from the window, not wanting to have to decide, not knowing how to answer her own question.

She turned the TV on, switching from one station to another. The networks were off the air (twenty-four-hour programming, everyone agreed, would be standard in another few years), but the local stations were on as usual, running old movies and rerunning their morning and afternoon talk shows to fulfill the FCC's community-service requirements. She winced as she watched a public service spot for a day-care center: on the record, the station would be able to record an official good deed, but what woman in need of a day-care center would be watching TV at this time of night?

The spot ended, and Sheila found herself in the middle of *The Women*. She'd seen the picture several times, but decided to watch it again. It was a lot better than worrying...

5.

FOR A TIME—A TIME SO LONG AND SO PAINful that he'd almost accepted it as a kind of sentence for the rest of his life—he'd been on the edge of a decision, longing, aching, for someone or something to push him one way or the other. Which, he'd asked himself, was worse—quitting, giving it up, or admitting that there wasn't much left to walk away from? Then Janis had come into his life, and the task of deciding had been as easy as the choice was apparent. Then, without reason or warning, she was gone, and he was alone again.

A familiar lump welled up in Tommy Del's throat as he showed Kay and Lee the snapshot he always carried with him—Janis and little Jessica, just a year old then, in front of the house in Agawam.

"It must have been very hard for you," Kay said awkwardly.

Tommy nodded. "I felt...cheated. All those years I'd been looking for something—the kind of life we were just starting to make, and then I lost it. I was angry, confused... the whole bit. But Janis' family was terrific. And we'd built a pretty strong foundation. Jessica is four now. She's like her mother, more so every day. I'm grateful for the time we had. I just wish it had been sooner."

Lee Dean nodded. "And you like Agawan?"

"Hey, it's Aga*wam*," Tommy corrected him. "It's an Indian name. It's a great little town, right across the Connecticut River from Springfield. Lots of trees. Peace and quiet—"

"Take me!" Kay implored him, in mock desperation. "After a week on the Coast, it sounds like heaven."

"I'll tell you one thing," Tommy said, smiling, "it sure as hell beats singing a bunch of oldies but goodies for a half-crocked audience in a Vegas lounge—and those were the gigs I got when I was lucky. Janis and I met there, you know..."

It was where they'd met, but it wasn't where the story began. That was in his home town of Central Islip, on Long Island. He'd been in a vocal group, just four guys fooling around because it was something to do: he'd never deluded himself about having an exceptional voice. But somebody knew somebody whose father was in the music business, and one day the four of them had gone into Manhattan with a song a couple of the guys had written, more for the hell of it than anything else.

The song didn't fool the music publisher they auditioned for. After a few bars, his bored look let them know that he recognized it as an amateur effort, a ripoff of a dozen songs like it. He'd let them finish more out of politeness than interest. Then, when they were about to leave, he called, "Hey, kid—you with the hair," and they'd all turned around. He singled out Tommy Delessio, gave the other boys a couple of dollars, and told them to go to the coffee shop downstairs for a soda "or something."

"Can you sight read?" he asked Tommy.

"What?"

"Forget it. Let's hear you sing something."

Tommy looked at his shoes.

"Come on, sing something. Anything you like," the man urged. After a half-minute of silence, he became impatient. "Come on, come on, for Christ's sake. Sing anything—"

A hundred songs were racing through Tommy's head, but for some reason the only one he could think of getting all the way through was "Happy Birthday to You!"

The publisher laughed. "You're no Sinatra, kid, but you've got a sense of humor. I'll give you that. I got a friend who might be interested. Give me your phone number and I'll have him call you."

He'd gone downstairs, taken a little teasing from his friends, and returned to Central Islip. Two weeks later, the phone rang: a Mr. Silver wanted to talk to Tommy. He was a manager, he explained to Tommy, and his specialty was new, young talent. Would it be possible for Tommy to come into Manhattan to see him?

The next Saturday, Tommy took the train alone.

That night, still in a state of shock, he sat in the living room as the man who'd driven him back to Islip in a Lincoln explained it all to his parents.

Music was changing, and changing fast. A big voice and training weren't everything—certainly not as important as they'd once been. It was the age of Made and Discovered Stars—Fabians, Frankie Avalons...and who said they all had to come from Philadelphia? With the right material and the right production, Tommy Delessio (the last name would have to be shortened, Mr. Silver advised) could be one of them. It would mean hard work, he said, looking at Tommy. But it was hard work that paid. Granted, Tommy would have to quit school, but a career was an education in itself. A hit record could make a fortune...

Tommy quit school.

He lost five pounds and had his long black hair cut by a barber Mr. Silver insisted was "the best."

He went to a dentist Mr. Silver knew to have a chipped front tooth capped (he'd pay back the money when he made it), and to a skin doctor who cleared up a few persistent pimples.

He posed for publicity shots, learned to sign his name as "Tommy Del" (Mr. Silver picked it), and went into a recording studio on West 56th Street on a Wednesday afternoon in July 1958. By the end of August, Tommy Del's version of "A Teenage Tragedy," a formula love song, was the number-six hit in the country. He appeared on *American Bandstand* with Dick Clark, and on *Dancetime, USA!* with Lee Dean, lip-synching to his record. He toured the country making personal appearances at record hops and in stores, where girls screamed as they thrust their autograph books toward him.

His next record, another run-of-the-mill tune with a sentimental lyric, did even better: "I Just Can't Believe You're Gone" made it all the way to the top of the charts. There were interviews and photo sessions with the fan magazines, contests in which readers could win a five-minute phone call from Tommy Del, or a chance to get his "personal" ID bracelet. Those who didn't win weren't left out: they could order their own "personal" Tommy Del ID bracelet for just $1.95, in their choice of "genuine simulated" gold or silver finish, direct from Silver Enterprises.

Tommy's third single was another smash, and whatever fears he had about not being able to reproduce the sound on the record were, as Mr. Silver promised, groundless. When he played the rock and roll stage shows that were touring the country, the girls screamed so loud that how he sounded didn't even matter. There were more singles in the next few years, and albums as well. Love songs, Christmas songs (one side pop seasonal numbers, the other side carols)... *Tommy Del by Request, Tommy Del—Just for You, Tommy Del—All Alone*... One followed the other for four hectic, dizzying years.

Only later, when he looked back, did he realize that the first two years were his biggest. The bookings and TV shows had continued into '60 and '61, but his later singles were never quite as popular as his first hits. He had an "official" Tommy Del fan club (presided over by Mr. Silver's organization) and several unofficial ones as well. The ads in the back of *Hit Parade, Dig* and *Teen Romances* offered photographs "suitable for framing" of Tommy Del, along with Elvis, Sal, Fabian, and Ed "Kookie" Byrnes. He crossed the country time and time again with Mr. Silver at his side, just to Hollywood for a guest spot in a beach party exploitation picture (and a less successful western), then back to New York to do the *Ed Sullivan Show*.

Each week the checks arrived at his parents' new home in Babylon—with deductions for travel, food, lodging, clothing, coaching, and the related expenses Mr. Silver deemed "necessities."

By the time he was twenty-one, in March of 1962, Tommy Del was a has-been. It wasn't his fault, Mr. Silver assured him. His singing had improved, and he'd learned through the experience of hundreds of theater dates how to work an audience. But times and tastes changed—what could a person do? For his part, Mr. Silver was going to London, where the new groups were waiting to be discovered, packaged, and promoted. He gave Tommy the name of an agent and wished him the best of luck. It wasn't a case of leaving a sinking ship, Mr. Silver assured him: he was simply exercising a clause in their contract that allowed him to terminate his responsibilities as personal manager. They'd be in touch, and of course they'd still be involved in record royalties...

In a way, Tommy had felt ready to quit there and then. He was tired of the traveling and the hotels, but he realized that, outside of singing, there wasn't anything he knew how to do. The agent he'd been referred to assured him that he was still a draw, a name, and could get work. It wasn't until he was out on the road again that Tommy realized how fast and how far he'd slipped.

Teenagers no longer screamed so loud that they drowned his singing out. The audiences at the small clubs in the small and medium-sized towns he played were more interested in their drinks than in his music—and as likely to heckle him as to applaud. A living was a living and a job was a job, he kept telling himself, even when the reviewers who'd never known about the mixing and amplification that gave him his sound on records wrote that he'd lost his touch.

The towns kept passing by and with them the years. Often he thought of quitting, of going into something different, but a voice inside him told him to hold on, to stick it out, to wait for the break that would put him back on top.

Toward the end of the 1960's, he began to think it might really happen. Enough time had passed to make the kids who'd been teenagers when he arrived on the music scene parents themselves, and for the fifties to be considered "nostalgia." Promoters began packaging rock and roll "revival" shows, touring the country with them. Tommy found himself working with the acts who'd been big in his peak period, and if the money wasn't anything like it once had been, at least the paying customers were responsive.

He signed with a show being packaged for Vegas, and it played the lounge at the Diplomat for six months. When the run ended, he decided that he liked staying in one place for a while, got himself some new arrangements, and began to work the lounges as a single again. Occasionally he'd take a booking out of town—Miami in the winter, Puerto Rico, a cruise ship, whatever. But Vegas became his home base.

It wasn't the Vegas of Sinatra and Sammy and the other superstars, but it beat a blank—until Janis came along. He spotted her at a front table during his midnight show at the Flamingo. *Just another fan looking for a musical trip back to the good old days*, he thought, but at least she was polite enough not to talk or rattle her glass as if he wasn't even there. He sang "A Teenage Tragedy" to her, winking when his set was over. At the 2:00 A.M. show, she was back again at the same table. This time, he checked her out as he worked the audience, pegging her as a horny broad who wanted to screw a name as part of her trip to Vegas. She was built, and her auburn hair caught his eye. Once he finished his show, he hurried back to the near-empty room just in time to catch her, inviting her to have a drink.

If he expected some awkward fawner who would flatter his ego, make a little small talk, and take a quick trip to her room, he was in for a surprise. She was candid—even to the point of admitting that she was thirty-one—and he found himself being candid in return. They both laughed about the pictures that she, like a million other girls, had sent away for from the magazine ads: the "assortment" of 8" x 10", 5" x 7", and "wallet-size" photos of the stars, all 1,000 of them for a buck, turned out to be a folio containing just a couple of the larger sizes, and microscopic postage-stamp-size pictures of "stars" so small and poorly printed, a few dozen to a page, that just trying to count them could give you a headache . . . let alone trying to figure out who they were.

She'd seen him once before in person, Janis told him, on *Connecticut Bandstand* out of New Haven. He nodded, recalling the show he'd guested on several times and the numerous local variants on the same theme in every part of the country. They'd both come a long way, they agreed—and the trip, they admitted to one another, hadn't been that easy. Janis told him about a long, drawn-out affair that had ended badly: Tommy, seeing her as a person rather than a fan, heard himself telling her what it felt like to be imprisoned in a career that was going nowhere but downhill.

"Why don't you get out?" she asked him, that night and often during the rest of the week she was in Vegas. They saw each other virtually all the time when he wasn't working: Janis had come for a vacation with a girlfriend from Springfield, who'd become so hooked on the slot machines she didn't miss Janis at all.

The sense of loss he felt as he drove her to the airport tore him up. Casual affairs and casual sex had been a life-style in his world. He'd made love with Janis, but there had been a difference... It was really *making love* and not merely sex.

They began to write and call each other, and Tommy began asking himself the same questions she'd asked him. Why not get out, chuck it all, forget it? The golden days were gone and they'd never return. His work wasn't making him happy, and it had already made him more money (even after Mr. Silver's dubious accounting; his parents' illnesses and deaths; his own expenses) than it ever would again. The desperation, the feeling of not being able to do anything else *but* sing, began to leave him under Janis' gentle guidance. He had money enough to buy any kind of business he liked, she pointed out; he was in a much better position than he let himself realize.

He had contractual obligations, and she had a secretarial job at Milton Bradley in Springfield. On weekends, they sometimes met (the hotel was nice about giving her a seat on the junket flights, if they weren't full). He had two weeks off and spent them in Springfield, staying at a hotel but spending most of the time with Janis and her family at their house, realizing how much he was missing.

Neither of them wanted to make a mistake, but in less than a year they were sure. Janis, her parents, and her sister flew to Vegas, where they were married. She stayed with Tommy for the final three months of his last engagement, then they moved back to Massachusetts, staying with her parents while they looked around for a house and a business. They both liked to watch things grow: when a nursery was put up for sale in Agawam, across the river from Springfield, they bought it. The old farmhouse that was part of the property had been an inducement. Together, they began to fix it up. Between the house and the business, their lives were full. When Janis became pregnant, Tommy felt more happy and complete than he ever had.

Little Jessica had made them more than a happy couple. They'd been a family, a unit, with a bright and full future ahead of them.

Then, when Jessica was eighteen months old, it happened. That day in April started out like any other day, with Janis making breakfast and straightening the house before working on the books. Late in the afternoon she asked Tommy to watch the baby while she went to the market. She'd be back in a few minutes—she just had a few things to pick up. Half an hour after she left, he got the call. The Massachusetts state troopers had been polite, but there was no way that consideration could temper the impact of their message. He heard only scattered words that his mind struggled not to accept... "accident... Route 91... no survivors..."

She hadn't suffered, people kept reminding him—that was at least some kind of blessing. But if Janis' death had been instantaneous, it still didn't change the fact. She was dead and gone. The happy time—the only happy time of his adult life—had come to an abrupt and unfair end. Standing at his wife's grave with the baby in his arms, on the many visits he made to the cemetery during the following months, Tommy Del seethed with a silent rage. *Why?* There had to be some reason, some explanation.

"God's will," comforted Janis' family, who tried their best to help Tommy, but he was unable to reconcile his image of the Creator with his wife's death.

He became bitter and withdrawn. At times he heard himself being rude to Janis' parents in spite of (maybe because of) their determined efforts to claim him as one of their own. He was short-tempered with customers, almost as if he were deliberately trying to destroy the business. But people were patient. He had suffered and they knew it, and even if he refused to believe it, in time he'd feel better.

"I guess they were right," Tommy told Kay and Lee, as he came to the end of the story. "I miss her. I'll always miss her. Having the baby makes it even more painful, in a way. I love Jessica. I'm grateful to have her—she's a living part of Janis and me, and what we had. But I see so much of Janis in her, and there are so many times she'll say or do something and I wish that Janis was there to see it.

"We're doing okay, though," he told them, smiling now. "A four-year-old is a real handful. Between the business and the baby, my days are pretty full. Would you believe it, this is the first time I've been in New York in years? And we're only three and a half hours away."

Lee Dean cleared his throat. "You—you never thought of leaving Massachusetts. After it happened, I mean? You never thought of getting back into the business?"

Tommy shook his head. "Not seriously. I'd only be hurting myself and ... well, negating everything I learned from Janis in the little time we had. She showed me that there was so much more to life, Lee. That I could be happy, be content doing something else. I like the work—and moving plants around and gardening are a lot more strenuous than swinging a mike cord and singing the same old songs. Sure, the idea crossed my mind a couple of times. But those times passed."

Lee and Kay exchanged glances.

"Would you consider going back for one night?" Lee

asked point-blank. "I'm talking about the TV special, Tommy. Just one night and out..."

Tommy listened as Lee told him about the *Dancetime, USA!* project. It was impossible to read the singer's reaction from his expression.

"I don't know, Lee," he said at last. "I really appreciate being asked, I can tell you that."

"Hey, you're part of what they call 'those golden years,'" Lee said.

Tommy laughed. "Who'd ever have thought those would be our good old days, huh? Look, I'll think about it. I kind of hung all that up, but it is only one night, as you say. And it's special—"

"Of course it's your decision," Kay inserted, "but you might want to keep in mind that even though you retired from the business, Tommy, you were really saying good-bye to working a lounge in Vegas. The special would give you a chance to say your professional good-bye to a lot more people—and a lot more of the fans who remember you from the old days."

He considered the point. "I don't know. Maybe they're better off remembering the skinny kid who used to mouth his records—" He stopped as a figure appeared in the doorway of Kay's office. She was a young and attractive woman, and their eyes locked for several seconds.

"Tommy Del, this is Sheila Granger. She's handling the special..."

Sheila apologized for being late. Her meeting had run longer than she'd expected.

"Why don't you two get acquainted over lunch?" Kay suggested boldly. "Maybe you can talk him into doing the special, Sheila."

"I'll try," she answered. "That is if you're free—"

"I don't have a thing to do," Tommy confessed. "When I told my family—my late wife's family, I mean—about Lee's call, they insisted I come down for a couple of days. So here I am."

"Tell you what," Kay interjected. "I have a couple of things to go over with Sheila. Lee, why don't you take Tommy to your office, and Sheila can pick you up when we're through."

Only when the good-byes had been said and the two men had gone did Sheila turn to Kay. "What are you up to? Trying to play matchmaker?"

Kay waved the idea away. "Me? Don't be silly! Not that it's such a bad idea. He strikes me as a man with a real head on his shoulders. He was smart enough to get out of the business, and he's raising a child by himself. I really admire him."

"He looks so much different from what I expected," Sheila said.

"What were you expecting?"

"I'm not sure. I saw the film clips and the stills from the fifties. I knew he wouldn't look the same, but he's... well, the passing years have treated him well."

Kay smirked as she studied Sheila's face. "A minute ago you asked me if I was matchmaking, so let me ask you this one. Do I detect something beyond professional interest?"

"Don't be ridiculous," Sheila said, wondering why the question made her bristle. "I just met him."

"You could do a lot worse than that man, Sheila—"

"Come on, Kay," she moaned. "I just met him!" Why, Sheila wondered, was Kay's teasing, which normally she'd have enjoyed, getting to her? Was it because she was still having the sleeping problem and feeling even more tension today than usual? Or was it because in spite of her feigned indifference, she'd definitely found Tommy Del more exciting than she'd expected him to be. Not wanting to hurt Kay's feelings, she forced a smile. "Look—if we decide to run away together, I promise you'll be the very first to know."

"Promise?" Kay asked.

"Brownie's honor," Sheila said, holding her fingers up

and laughing. "Now let's get to that review of the publicity meeting. It was really something—they're going all-out. I'll give you the capsule version quickly, though—after all, Mr. Right may be waiting."

6.

THE CAB PITCHED AND JERKED ITS WAY downtown, and Kay Duvane rolled her eyes in a mixture of mock fear for her life and very real exasperation. A *bumpy ride*, she thought—*it goes with the rest of the day*. To distract herself from the cab ride, she tried to search her mind for a recent day that hadn't been full of havoc and confusion, but the search was futile. The personnel department had organized a special seminar on "Executive Health Maintenance," and along with the other vice presidents and key TBS people, she'd attended the three-day "miniclinic."

There'd been a time when the caché of being included in the category of "important network officials" would have made her spirits soar. That time, Kay realized as she listened to the seminar doctors talk about preventive medicine and anti-stress regimens, had passed: instead of being pleased with herself, she was actually scared. The physician who examined her as part of the clinic reviewed her entire medical history, glancing over the material she authorized her own doctor to send him.

Most of the lectures on heart disease and other topics, he'd told Kay, were directed at men—but she wasn't to make the mistake of thinking that, as a woman, she had a natural immunity. The very fact that she was a woman in a male-dominated work "setting," as he put it, was an additional stress factor, whether she knew it or not. She had to be on guard against overworking her body and her nerves—menopause, or the "middle-year crisis," as the doctor phrased it, was just around the corner, and her body would be undergoing hormonal change. It was a critical time...

"What time isn't?" she said out loud to herself.

"What did you say?" Lee Dean sat down beside her.

"Just talking to myself," she told him wearily. "It's probably a sign of the mid-life crisis. Honestly, the health seminar put the fear of God into me. They told us all the horrible things that stress can do and said we should relax. They just forgot to tell us how."

Lee patted her arm reassuringly. "We'll have a nice relaxing evening—"

"That's what *you* think!" Kay corrected him. "I'm horrid to drag you all the way downtown for this art thing, Lee—and you're an angel to put up with me."

"I wanted to take you out anyway, Kay, to a quiet restaurant. This... what's the name of it again?"

"Institute for Alternative Television," she told him.

"Well, maybe the Institute for Alternative Television will be more fun."

She grimaced. "'Fun' isn't exactly the word I'd pick. But our beloved network president is a big supporter of this whole video art thing—and everyone in the business is going to be there. You know how furious publicity was when that Liz Smith item ran. This way, they can at least create the illusion that they're controlling what information gets out and what doesn't."

Only the previous day, Liz' column had run the first item about the upcoming special. Over the past few years, secrecy had become a matter of increasing importance at all the networks: once the competition got wind of a project and an air date, they had a decided advantage and could counterprogram to maximum advantage. Everyone involved with the *Dancetime, USA!* reunion had vowed secrecy, and Lee Dean had been keeping the "low profile" the public relations department suggested in the hope of obtaining maximum press coverage at the time the special aired. Now, almost two months ahead of time, Liz had the story—and the publicity people were fuming. The opening of the exhibit at the Institute for Alternative Television would attract a guest list of those who made and wrote about TV. They'd all have read that Lee Dean and TBS were back in business, and by taking him as her escort, Kay would convey the importance of the project's stature.

"Things down here have changed so much," Lee Dean said, looking out the cab window once they were south of Houston Street. "I didn't think people lived down here."

"They didn't much in the old days," Kay said, grateful that they'd finally made it to SoHo. "Living in a loft is 'in' these days. The Village is old-hat. To tell you the truth, it may be chic as all hell, but I still get the bends when I go below Fourteenth Street."

Lee shook his head. "You still have that sense of humor. I remember your doing that, Kay—always coming back with a quick answer."

"A lot of good it does me. You really remember that, Lee?"

"Sure I do. I remember a lot of things from the old days."

"We're here," the driver announced. Over Lee's protests, Kay paid—she'd get the money back on her expense account, she explained.

There were a few people on the sidewalk, but the street itself was dark. Kay took Lee's arm, leading him through the unremodeled doorway of what appeared to be a commercial building.

"Trust me," she teased, as they waited for the elevator. One moment they were standing in a narrow, harshly lit hallway covered with peeling green paint. The next, they were inside a small but streamlined elevator of polished aluminum. Thin tubes of neon ran across the walls and ceiling, flashing in a programmed pattern. "Enjoy the ride," Kay told him. "Our taxes are paying for it—the artist got some kind of government grant, they tell me."

"Artist?"

"The one who stuck the neon on the walls," she explained, as the door opened silently. The sound of a punk rock band drowned out the possibility of conversation.

The crowd was both elegant and electric; attire ran the gamut from jeans and T-shirts to gowns and tuxedos. There were artists and network executives, men and women from the worlds of fashion, publishing, and the music business.

Kay, her best professional smile fixed on her face, spoke under her breath: "The same old crap—new crap, in this case. Everyone out to freeload and be seen, and telling each other how chic they all are."

She led Lee into the huge loft, nodding to acknowledge an occasional greeting. Many people were clustered around a number of color TV sets mounted at eye level. One set displayed a tape collage of footage shot at natural disasters, intercut with still photographs of people Kay didn't recognize. She pointed at a passing waiter, and Lee grabbed two glasses of champagne. They sipped them, watching the screen and looking at the floods, fires, hurricanes, and parched landscapes.

"... Awfully *jejeune*, don't you think?" a bearded man in a white silk suit asked his companion, a woman with a mane of blonde hair that fell past the bare shoulders of her Halston gown.

"You must try to interpret it in the context of his other work," she answered. "Phillipe has an extraordinarily fatalistic sensibility..."

"Jesus!" Kay said, speaking softly into Lee's ear, noting the name of the artist on the small placard in front of the set.

"Stunning!" a birdlike women with silver hair exclaimed, clasping her hands in admiration. She looked at Kay and Lee. "Stunning, don't you think?"

"Decidedly," Kay answered, "in every sense of the word."

She led Lee away. The punk band was blaring out a three-chord song, and occasionally a decipherable word of lyric cut through the deafening cacophony of noise. It was either "blood," or "kill" or "shoot." Photographers were taking pictures of the crowd.

They moved to another TV set, watching an art work entitled "Kinetic Rhapsody #5." A series of minute dots, row after row of them, went through subtle changes of color, displaying a startling variety of shades and tones of blue and green. A single magenta dot darted through them, never stopping or changing its color as the other dots continued their delicate variations.

The work had an almost mesmerizing effect. To her surprise, Kay found herself captivated by it. Impressed, she began to rethink the whole idea of video art. At first, it had struck her as an absurdity: television was about programs, she'd always believed; the closest it came to being a real art form was when it produced programming that was good.

There had been technical changes and advances in the medium—new cameras, new methods, and new equipment as well as improved sets for the consumer. She had duly noted the changes and incorporated them into her thinking, but she'd been far too concerned with getting programs on the air to really involve herself with hardware and technology, except as it affected her work.

Video art, as a concept, had riled her at first: the networks, the electronics manufacturers, and even the big foundations were handing out equipment and grants left and right, and instead of getting jobs and working for a living, a bunch of scruffy-looking kids were getting a free ride, fooling around with videotape cameras and telling each other it was "art."

They made "meaningful" short films, or they parodied commercial television. Sometimes the results were touching or funny (though not the sort of "funny" that the folks at home would ever see over one of the major networks), and they could demonstrate the talents of newcomers who would eventually make their way into the mainstream of commercial TV.

Abstract video art was something else again. The first of it she'd seen had made Kay wince: it was nothing more, she told herself, than a cross between test patterns and color bars and the psychedelic hippie art that was all over the place. Watching a bunch of colors explode on a TV screen wasn't her idea of a good time, thank you very much! The critics, to a large extent, shared her opinion, but a few of them had written excited, enthusiastic pieces about a "new medium of artistic expression in its infancy." Kay had dismissed the view as "filler"; something to write about ... another new idea (or variant on an old one, in this case) the media would exploit in order to perpetuate itself.

Spotting trends had always been a long suit in her professional hand: when the whole video scene mushroomed, she'd been dismayed. It was no longer a matter of "underground" art. Video works were represented in some of the best collections of modern art. Major museums were buying pieces and mounting exhibits.

Solid-state technology had cut down on the amount of repair and maintenance work the family set (or sets) required. Besides envisioning a day when the set would be simply one part of a home video center complete with cassette deck and videodisc player, the marketing people at the major manufacturing firms were already talking about a future in which people would buy units that displayed programmed works of video art, much as they now bought paintings. If they were right—and they usually were—that meant that one of the artists whose work was included in the show they were now seeing might one day be as popular as Norman Rockwell or Andrew Wyeth.

"What do you think?" Kay asked Lee, watching the red dot's ceaseless movement against the subtly changing background of "Kinetic Rhapsody #5" before them.

"To tell you the truth," he answered, "it kind of reminds me of a woman looking for her car in a parking lot."

Kay laughed loud and heartily. Lee slipped his arm around her, and she settled against him. They made their way through the exhibit.

Some of the works were abstract and some literal, some good and some atrocious. Kay felt a relief in being able to make a judgment (albeit her own) between them, in being open enough to adapt to the times, if not change with them. An hour and several more glasses of champagne later, after she and Lee had chatted with the more important TBS officials as well as the competition, Kay suggested they leave.

On the street, she looked relieved. "That goddamn band! Don't they ever take a break?"

"That's the sound of New Wave music," Lee told her. "It's catching on."

"Not with me, it's not! I loathe it. It's... disgusting, to put it mildly."

"Don't forget 'degenerate,'" Lee suggested.

"That, too."

"—and detrimental to our young people—"

"Decidedly."

"Then maybe we should take all the punk records and burn them," he suggested. Moments later they were both doubled over with laughter, remembering one of the

Dancetime publicity stunts from two decades before. A southern preacher, who'd been outspoken against the menace of rock since its inception, had conducted annual burnings of rock records at an open-air revival. Young people were encouraged to come from all over the country with albums and singles for the fire. Photographs of the minister, standing pompously in front of the massive flames, always received good coverage in the press. TBS' publicity department had decided that a shot of Lee Dean putting out a similar-looking fire might receive equal attention. Naturally, there was no thought of an actual confrontation with the minister (which might offend Bible-belt viewers). Instead, they got the record companies to give them cartons of dud product from their warehouses, and they went out to an empty lot in Queens to stage the shot, with Lee dressed as a fireman putting out the flames.

The accompanying press release had quoted Lee in an articulate defense of both the music itself and the importance of using reason and common sense to understand the issue.

"Did you think up that stunt?" he asked Kay, when they finally got a cab.

"Guilty," she admitted. She gave the driver her address before realizing it. "It's early—why don't you come up for a drink? Or we could pick up something from the deli if you're hungry..."

An hour later, they were eating ham sandwiches and drinking wine in her living room. Mimi, who usually didn't take to strangers, was purring at Lee's feet.

"The things we used to do to get coverage for that show!" Kay said, clearing the plates away.

"What do you mean 'we?'" Lee asked. "I only did what I was told. You were the one who set them up."

Rinsing the dishes, Kay smiled to herself. It was true. She'd worked her behind off as a publicist for *Dancetime,*

USA! From the time she'd been assigned to the show, she recognized it as her chance to make a name for herself, to show her ability.

"I'm glad it's all worked out so well for you, Kay," Lee said when she returned. "You always knew what you wanted."

"I was pretty determined, wasn't I?" She poured some wine and sat beside him. "Not that I had much choice—you don't get anywhere in this business by sitting back and waiting for things to happen. Speaking of which, how do you like what's happening with Sheila and Tommy?"

Lee shrugged. "I think it won't come to much of anything."

"Lee, darling, she's gone up there for two weekends, or is it three? And he's been here in town. That's *something*..."

"A little fling for Sheila, maybe, but that's all," he insisted.

"Why do say that?"

"I know the type. She's a great person—don't misunderstand me. She's a real go-getter. But she's going after big game, Kay. She's dedicated to her job, and there's no room in her life for any man. I think she's a lot like you."

"Ouch!" Kay said, wincing.

"Sorry," Lee apologized, taking her hand. "That came out all wrong. I don't mean it as a criticism. I'm glad for you, and I'm grateful you're the way you are. Otherwise I wouldn't be working on the special."

She looked into his eyes. "Are you enjoying it, Lee?"

He paused, considering the question. "It's...it's different than I thought it would be, to tell you the truth. I don't know what I expected. But being away so long, thinking about it—you know how it is. You remember things and people the way they were. You don't think of them as having changed." He squeezed her hand, and she returned the quick, gentle pressure.

"I don't suppose you ever thought of me in all that time," Kay said hesitantly. "Not that you should have—"

"Sure I did. You're one of the few things that turned out the way I expected."

"Really? What do you mean?"

He stood up. Kay tucked her knees beneath her, leaning back on the sofa to watch him as he walked.

"I always thought you'd get it, Kay—the title, the salary, the big office. If it had been a race, I'd have put my money on you."

"Thanks—I think."

"You knew what you wanted, and you went after it. Remember when we used to talk about the future? You used to tell me about your plans..."

As his voice trailed off, Kay felt her face flush. She had to look away.

She hadn't wanted to think of those moments of intimacy and, until tonight, she'd been able to avoid them. Putting Sheila on the project had helped: with Sheila in charge, there was little opportunity for her to be alone with Lee for long periods. Whether he had picked up on her emotions, or felt the same way she did, Kay hadn't been sure, but Lee had been equally businesslike, occasionally referring to having worked with her two decades before but always stopping there.

Now, for the first time, the unspoken agreement had been broken. The memory of those days filled the room, and with it the memory of the nights they'd spent together. They'd both been filled with the elation of their first success, and they shared it as they shared their work. There had been no reason, really, to keep their romance secret, and in fact Lee always invited her to parties and PR appearances, pointing out that she could make valuable contacts. Kay had been the one who'd insisted on keeping things quiet—she didn't want anybody to think that her job working on *Dancetime*'s publicity was a plum she got as the star's girlfriend. Besides, the secrecy of meeting at his apartment or her place—a small studio on West 48th Street back then—made the affair more exciting.

It started suddenly a few weeks after *Dancetime* went on the air. Word was in that it had clicked with the viewers; everyone involved with the show had been in high spirits. When Lee invited her to dinner one evening, Kay assumed that he wanted to discuss publicity. She'd never thought of him in anything but a professional context. He was the product—or part of it, as the program's host—and her job, the stepping stone to the career she was fixed on having, was seeing that the product got pushed. Lee had always been pleasant and willing to cooperate with her, but that night over dinner, she saw other sides of him.

He told her what it had really been like for him, all the struggling and loneliness and doubt that was left out of the official bios. He told her how much the chance to host the show meant to him, and how grateful he was for all the work she'd done in his behalf. To her surprise, Kay found herself strongly attracted to Lee as a man, and when he drove her back to her apartment, she invited him up.

That had been the first time... the first of many that followed. She told herself that it wasn't an affair. It was simply a convenience, an arrangement, *fun*. She fought against letting herself care because caring would only complicate her life and divert her from her avowed purpose. As the months passed, though, she discovered that she was feeling the emotions she'd sworn to resist. In meetings, she silently bristled when Lee was discussed as if he were a piece of meat, a thing instead of a person. When *Dancetime*'s unit publicist left to do a new variety show at CBS, Kay was promoted. She tried to "trade up" Lee's image, to broaden the very appeal that she'd helped to create.

They'd tried to keep it casual (again at her insistence), but Lee had actually proposed, then gone even further, pressing her when she stalled for time or told him that marriage wasn't in her plans for herself. Still, the idea had been more than mildly tempting: being the wife of one of the hottest personalities on television would have its rewards. The show's popularity showed no signs of slipping, and even if it should, TBS would be able to utilize Lee Dean in another capacity. The network had a major investment in him, and regardless of what eventually happened with *Dancetime* (assuming anything happened at all), they'd want to capitalize on their investment.

At first, the payola scandal hadn't seemed serious.

True, the music industry was on trial, and a few radio deejays were on the carpet, but Lee wasn't involved in actually booking talent or picking the records that were played on the air. Kay kept close watch on ABC's press releases. When the network stood firmly behind Dick Clark, she'd been relieved. Nobody was going to let a mere accusation cause problems.

Then, unexpectedly, it happened. The vice president of daytime television called her into his office. The news was quick and brutal: TBS was dropping *Dancetime, USA!* and washing its hands of Lee Dean. She argued, reminding them of ABC's policy regarding Dick Clark and *Bandstand*. That, the executive explained, was a different situation. Dick Clark hadn't done anything. He'd go to Washington, but no matter how they tried to rake him over the coals, they wouldn't find any skeletons in his closet. Just as ABC had investigated Clark, TBS had looked into Lee Dean's finances.

Maybe he hadn't taken graft, but it looked as if he had—and how it looked was how the American public would see it as shown by the House committee. The folks at home didn't know that it was standard procedure for the record companies to give people like Lee Dean gifts and vacations to win or keep their good will. It was dirty laundry, and when it was aired in public, it would look as if Lee had been on the take. In order to protect its own image, the network had no choice but to drop him like the hot potato he'd be after he testified in Washington.

The choice, Kay knew, was her own... to go with Lee, who'd be finished in broadcasting, or to stay with the network. The daytime VP told her that Lee's firing wouldn't reflect on anyone involved with the show. Her work in particular, he said, had been excellent, and her future at TBS was "extremely promising." The network was relying on her expertise in handling the "delicate matter" of Lee's firing.

She hadn't liked herself for doing it, but she made her decision. With all her heart, she wished she were different... *better*. She didn't want power and success to be as important to her as they were. She wished she could feel that love was enough. But she didn't, and that was that, and she hadn't given Lee any warning about what was going to happen. Kay tried telling herself that she was being considerate—as it was, he'd been nervous enough about Washington, and there was no harm in letting him think it would work out well. Inside, though, she knew that one (and perhaps the main) reason for her silence was her desire to get ahead. If Lee knew or thought the network was going to dump him, he might say something in his testimony that would be detrimental to TBS' interests. It was better, as the network had decided, to let him think the network was behind him.

The ink on the mimeographed press releases was dry before he even came back from the hearings in the Capitol. He'd been crushed and lost and broken... and she had been in Southampton, taking a week off at a house the network rented for use as a summer vacation home for executives. It wasn't summer, and she hadn't been an executive, but the message, the tantalizing hint of it, had been clear.

He made no effort to contact her when she got back, and she didn't try to get in touch with him. Instead, she went out to California, supervising a press junket for a couple of TBS' summer shows.

On her return, she'd been promoted to a supervisory job in the publicity department, with a raise to complement her new status as part of the management "team." She bought some clothes, moved to a new apartment, changed her phone number...and tried not to think about Lee.

In time, it was easier.

Everyone, Kay discovered, stepped on someone to climb to the top. Nobody said it was pretty—and it wasn't. Assistants who were too overtly ambitious, secretaries who spread gossip, co-workers who were jealous or threatening—you got rid of them if and when you could. You had to compete fiercely to get ahead, and you sometimes had to be ruthless to survive.

There were times, though—sleepless nights and moments of daydreaming at her desk—when she thought of Lee, and of her part in his downfall. She couldn't have done anything to save him, Kay told herself; she'd tried her best and failed. After all, she'd only been one person and the network was... well, the *network*. But she could have been fairer, more decent, and kinder, and seeing him in her living room tonight, she felt the old shame.

"I was horrible," she said softly. "I know what I did. It doesn't do a damn bit of good to apologize now, but for what it's worth I'm sorry." She felt the tears in her eyes—and looked at her lap so he wouldn't see them.

He lifted her chin, making her look at him.

"That was a long time ago, Kay," Lee Dean said. "And it doesn't matter."

"If—if there was something I could have done," she

told him, the words rushing out. "But there wasn't. Not a thing. I—I felt terrible, Lee. I felt dirty. But I wanted the damn job—"

She was standing now. He put his finger to her lips and pulled her close to him. She cried for Lee, and for herself, for the nights they'd shared and the years they could have had together, for his holding her now, and for all the nights she cried alone with nobody to comfort her except a stray cat she picked up one cold, lonely night.

"That's why you really went to bat for the special, isn't it?" he asked her gently.

Kay nodded, her body still shaking. "I—I wanted to make it up to you, for what I did. What *we* did at the network. As much as I could, anyway. And in a way, I wanted to make it up to myself. Oh, Lee—"

His lips covered hers, and his hands slid over her body as they had so many years before. She felt him tug at the zipper of her dress, then the garment fell to the floor. She kicked free of it as he lifted her in his arms, carrying her toward her bedroom as if it were an old, half-forgotten place he knew from the past...carrying her with the strength and assurance of a man twenty years younger...

7.

THE PUBLICITY DEPARTMENT HAD TRIED TO hold out for a cover story, and in a roundabout way they almost got it—but *People* decided finally to go with a cover shot of Sylvia—and two pages about her new movie. The publicity department had, however, gotten a four-page story inside the magazine: *People* worked with the TBS researchers who'd interviewed The Regulars at their homes, and there were "then and now" shots of them, as well as a page on Lee Dean himself.

Look was doing a layout on the changes in television technology, and the fact that the special was being done live.

Press kits had gone out to all the editors on the network's "Fabulous Fifties Night," complete with releases, bios, and a selection of photographs. Since *The Rockin' Fifties* and *Dancetime, USA!* would run back to back on a Sunday night, the publicists were counting heavily on the entertainment editors of the Sunday papers for a last-minute PR blitz, and canned features had been shipped to secondary markets, with Lee Dean doing phone interviews with editors in the bigger cities.

The tabloid papers had joined the bandwagon, though some of the stories they were going to run—particularly those concentrating on the tragedies of *Regulars* who'd died, were ghoulish and grizzly. *Cosmopolitan* had sent a writer to interview Sheila for an article on women in television, and it would reach the stands early the following week.

Promo spots had been done. Lee Dean would be one of the guest celebrities on *Guess Again*, TBS' most successful game show, all week long. *TV Guide* had interviewed him on the subject of the "good old days," and they'd done an accompanying photo feature on the reconstruction of the old *Dancetime* set.

A group of feminists had vowed to picket the studio to protest Alice Lane, whose recording of "Glad to Be a Woman" had hit the top of the country charts. Sylvia wouldn't be able to join the other two Fantastiks until the day of the special itself because of her movie, but a special rehearsal had been scheduled.

The artist-relations people had made all the arrangements for The Regulars. Because they'd only be making one network appearance, they weren't required to join AFTRA. TBS was picking up all their expenses, from plane tickets (limousines would meet their flights) to suites at the Plaza. A full schedule had been mapped out for their week in New York. They'd have time to work with the director, and to run through the show several times. In the old days, *Dancetime* had been live and unrehearsed. The network wanted to maintain the *feel* of the show, as it had been, (that was the whole point of doing it live), but nobody was about to do ninety minutes of primetime TV off the cuff. The script had been written and rewritten, and each segment of the show would be timed and checked.

Producing a special, Sheila had learned working for

Kay, meant a lot of responsibility. But a good producer was smart enough to know how to delegate authority. The associate producer she'd hired, Paul Kaufman, had worked on *Good Day*, the network's ill-fated attempt at a national daytime talk show, and understood the special problems of live television. Harvey Craig, the director Kay had recommended, had a number of awards shows and comedy specials to his credit: the choice had been a good one, and Sheila had been able to leave most of the technical decisions and below-the-line matters to them.

The staff was assembled, the week scheduled, and the promotional machinery was already rolling. On paper, at least, everything was going along just as it should—but for the life of her, Sheila Granger couldn't help feeling that something was wrong.

Maybe, she thought, it was Kay. For some reason neither of them could understand, Mike Palmer seemed to be gunning for her. Their private meetings always rattled Kay, and a couple of times in meetings he made pointed remarks about the importance of a "young" outlook in such important areas as special programming. While Kay fumed, Sheila felt her own anger mount as the executive twisted the knife.

"Why is he such a bastard?" she asked Tommy. "Kay's done a terrific job for the network. She's dedicated her whole life to her work. Now, instead of respect, she's getting aggravation. I don't believe it!"

"It's the nature of the beast," Tommy answered, matter-of-factly.

Sheila didn't reply, but she knew he was right.

At one time, she had dismissed Kay's occasional pronouncements about the uglier aspects of the business as simple frustration. But working on the special, Sheila saw things she wasn't expecting. What's more, she'd had to accept them, unpleasant as they were. Working with Lee Dean, she'd come to like and respect him. As the airdate approached, she watched network executives make it a point to take him to lunch or stop by the office to chat with him.

They acted as if he were a long-lost friend they'd just run into, when in fact they'd have cut him dead only a few months before. Both those staff members who'd known him in the old days, and those so young they could barely remember seeing him, shared a common desire to be on a first-name basis with Lee, in case his special was a big success, but if it wasn't, Lee would be lucky to get a hello out of them.

It was the old guilt-by-association paranoia. The press, Sheila knew, was certain to bring up the matter of the payola scandal and Lee's dismissal by TBS. Lee, she'd been relieved to discover, was equally aware of the problem. She talked it over with the head of publicity, and they came up with a special release on the subject that cited the 1950's as a time of "fear and frenzy"; they capsulized the background of the payola mess, so that it read like a battle for the survival of rock and roll. Lee, according to the impression the release gave, had been a valiant soldier in defending freedom of choice. He was quoted as saying that he'd been "young and inexperienced, and unaware of the broad implications of what were then standard promotional practices in the industry." He had "no resentment" toward TBS, and it seemed natural to bring the *Dancetime, USA!* reunion idea back to the network that originated it.

TBS, for its part, was "glad to welcome back a man who holds a special place in our history; in the history of television itself; and in the history of American popular music."

It was a whitewash, a careful rewriting of history, and as such it upset Sheila very much. But, Kay pointed out, the rewriting was practical and it served the purpose as gracefully as possible under the circumstances. What could Lee do? Come out and say he hated the network for throwing him out in the cold? Of course Lee Dean would have executive-producer credit, but did a credit flashed on a TV screen for a fraction of a second make up for the twenty years he'd been away?

"If I were Lee, I don't think I'd have bothered to come back," Sheila heard herself telling Tommy. Reporting on what happened during the week had become a habit during the weekends they spent together at his place in Massachusetts. On Fridays, when she arrived, he'd have drinks waiting, and he'd encourage her to get it all out of her system.

Once she did, she discovered to her delight, she was actually able to put television, TBS, and Lee Dean out of her mind for two whole days. Jessica, Tommy's daughter, had taken to her at once. They spent Saturdays taking the little girl to the zoo in Forest Park, or to ride the merry-go-round at Riverside. They'd go for rides in the Berkshires, too, stopping for a picnic lunch, or discovering quiet old inns and restaurants.

On Sundays, Tommy took Jessica to Sunday school, then came home with her to eat the dinner that Sheila always insisted on cooking. He'd argued at first, telling her that he wanted her to relax and not to work, but she'd explained that, living alone in New York, she never cooked: she needed the practice to keep her hand in.

The first time she made a roast, she did it because she thought she should. Then, to her own surprise, Sheila found she really *did* enjoy it. Preparing a meal and watching Tommy and Jessica enjoy it were simple activities with immediate satisfactions, absorbing but unpressured—too much trouble to go through if you were alone... but then she wasn't alone when she was with Tommy. Lately, she'd come to feel that she had two lives. In one of them, she was alone—Sheila Granger versus the world of network television. It was a life that centered around her work. She had a home, of course, but increasingly, the pleasure she took in her apartment lessened. When you came right down to it, she told herself, it was just a place to recuperate in, to rest up from one day's exhaustive combat and prepare yourself for the day to come.

These feelings had started when Tommy and Jessica came to New York for a weekend, and she stocked the refrigerator with real food instead of the few convenient junk things she usually bought. Dishes in the sink, clothes thrown casually around, and the sounds of a man and a child had given the place a special quality she didn't fully appreciate until her guests had gone.

On weekends, all through the summer and through the fall, she lived another life. Titles, the size of an office, and ratings—none of these things seemed to matter. If she wanted to spend the whole weekend in a pair of jeans and a comfortable old shirt with her hair tied back, that was fine. There was no need to worry about making an impression either on Jessica, who was so lovable it was impossible to resist her, or on Tommy, who'd fallen in love with her in spite of herself.

It had been so long since she'd been strongly attracted to a man that the initial chemistry between them had been dismaying. After their first few dates in Manhattan, during the week he came to talk with Lee, Sheila made a mental list of everything that was wrong with him. It wasn't professional, she tried to tell herself. At best, this was a half-hearted defense, since there was no law that said you couldn't get involved with somebody you met through work. He was a landscape gardener, she told herself—they came from two different worlds, even if he had been in her world once, and left it willingly.

He had a child. That, more than anything else perhaps, had worried her. When she spent her first weekend in Massachusetts, her fears disappeared. Jessica was a bright, good-natured little girl. The rest of "the family," his late wife's family, was equally pleasant. Instead of resenting her, or being cool with Tommy because he was expressing interest in another woman, they seemed to be actually delighted.

For a time, Sheila gracefully walked the boundary line between the two different worlds—one in which she felt like a professional and the other in which she was a woman. Carefully, she tried to restrain her emotions, enjoying the weekends for what they were, but reluctant to let herself feel too much.

The only times she really lost control were the nights and mornings when she and Tommy made love. The intensity and urgency of their lovemaking amazed both of them. It was as if their bodies were two halves of some single whole, each needing the other to be complete.

Then, gradually, all her defenses had fallen.

Instead of changing the subject, or being "sensible" when Tommy talked about his feelings for her, Sheila listened. "I love you," he told her.

"I love you," she repeated, almost afraid of the words but knowing they were true...

"What are you doing? An audition for *Lost in Space?*"

"I'm sorry?" Sheila said, looking up to see Kay Duvane in the doorway.

"That faraway look, my dear... Hey—are you all right?"

"I think so, Kay—"

"But you're not sure, huh?"

"Maybe not," Sheila admitted. "Nothing big. It's just... I don't know. That's part of it, too."

"Well, *I* know," Kay informed her, shutting the door. "They call it nerves, Sheila. Opening-night jitters."

"What?"

"Come on, darling, you've seen it in the movies. Opening night on Broadway? The star gets a little shaky—"

"But—"

"No buts about it. You have our version of stage

fright—screen fright." Before Sheila could argue the point, Kay gave her a hug. "I felt the same way, Sheila. The first time I was really in the driver's seat was way back in . . . well, let's not go into that! I was just like you, getting the whole thing together, working my ass off, worrying about a million details and sure that I'd forgotten something."

"You know, I was thinking about that a while ago."

"See? And listen, that show I did was a silly little afternoon mystery thing—not a major special. I know it hasn't been easy, and I know you've worked hard. Probably I should have been a little bit more helpful, but I've wanted you to do the work just to see what it felt like. And to see how you'd handle it. I'm proud of you, Sheila. You're a real pro."

An unexpected wave of emotion poured over Sheila. She swallowed back the lump in her throat. "Thank you, Kay. You don't know how much I appreciate that, especially coming from you. There isn't anyone I respect more in the business."

"You earned it. And if you're wondering why you feel so shaky in spite of knowing what a good job you've done, I have the answer to that one, too."

"Really?"

"A pro is always nervous, Sheila. It never stops. The minute you sit back satisfied with yourself, you've had it. You have to keep your edges sharp. It's an instinct."

Sheila laughed nervously. "You make it sound like a predatory instinct. Like an eagle sharpening his talons, or claws—"

"Or whatever it is that eagles have? I get the idea. Well, that too. But it's worth it, Sheila. Wait and see. Today is Friday. On Sunday the Regulars will begin coming in, and we'll be exactly one week away from countdown. It's going to be a bitch of a week, in case you didn't know it, but when it's all over—when you see that special and know that ten million other people are seeing it, too—it'll all be worth it. Look, since it *is* Friday, what do you say we get out of this place. Where's Tommy?"

Sheila smiled. It had been just like him to insist on leaving Jessica with her grandparents a few days early and to come to New York to help her over the weekend.

"He had an appointment with a vocal coach," she explained. "He's afraid his voice is out of shape."

"With a face like his, who cares? Is he going to meet us?"

"Yes. At the studio."

"Good. So is Lee. I made a reservation for dinner at Tavern on the Green. Ready to take a look at the set?"

Sheila grabbed her coat, bag and production book, crammed with notes about the special.

The November air was cool and sharp as they left the building, but instead of hailing a cab Kay guided Sheila toward a waiting limousine.

"The way I figured it," she explained, "if the show is a hit it won't matter. And if that prick Palmer has his way, I won't be working here much longer anyway. Might as well go in style."

The city was already dark, and although they were only going across town, the traffic was heavy. Though part of her mind was on the set, completed only that afternoon, Sheila found herself more absorbed by thoughts of Tommy. She wanted to confide in Kay, both as a friend and as a woman. But Kay, she decided, wouldn't understand, it was unfair to expect her to. Television and work were the only things that mattered to her... Not only wasn't she in love, she didn't even have a man in her life. Of course Lee had been taking her out, but that didn't count. It was only a business friendship...

"We'll be a little while," Kay told the driver, when they finally reached the theater.

"Yes, Miss Duvane," he said, helping them from the car.

"My God, if this old place could talk!" Kay said.

"Funny, isn't it, Sheila? It's still here after all these years. They've done specials here, game shows, and heaven only knows what else. And now, after all these years, they're doing *Dancetime* again." She shivered, though it wasn't that cold. "If I close my eyes, I can almost see them—the kids lined up to get in, the Regulars and the guest acts coming in through the stage door... well, let's go, shall we?"

"Are Mr. Del and Mr. Dean here yet?" Kay asked the guard at the stage door. "Yes, ma'm. Mr. Del just arrived."

Kay turned to Sheila and winked. "Good. We're fashionably late."

The lights were dim as the two women wrote their names on the sign-in sheet, then made their way through the dark hallway.

"Got your dressing rooms assigned?" Kay asked.

"The best I could. Of course there aren't enough of them to go around—"

"Don't worry about it, dear. Nobody's ever satisfied. And if they bitch to you, you can blame it all on the production assistant."

The sound of their footsteps echoed as they walked toward the wings of the stage.

"*Oo-wah!*"

The sound took them by surprise. Kay's hand grabbed Sheila's arm, and her feet froze in place. Seconds later the sound was repeated, followed by laughter. It was Tommy, they realized, fooling around with Lee.

"I think he went to that vocal coach in the nick of time," Kay said. They were nearing the stage, but she hung back deliberately. "God, it's all coming back to me. Those kids—not the ones dancing, Sheila, but the performers. Some of them were wet behind the ears. *Dancetime* was their first TV show. Sometimes they'd freeze so bad we'd have to pour them out there."

"... Remember that one?" they heard Tommy asking

Lee. "And how about 'Teen Angel'? All those songs about death—it was sick."

"Of course I remember that one," Lee answered. "I remember all of them."

Kay first glanced at the set, then stared in amazement, spellbound. She forced her lids halfway closed, purposely blurring her vision. As if by magic, the years seemed to melt away.

The set was just as it had been. The bleachers were the same, and the podium, and the gigantic bulletin board with the pictures and autographs of the stars. Lee was already there talking to someone—the way she'd seen him so many times before or after the show . . . so many times and so many yesterdays ago.

Someone—was it her?—was running toward him. He turned, smiling as the girl came closer. But she, Kay, wasn't running to Lee . . . or even running at all. Instead it was Sheila, as young as Kay had remembered herself, rushing toward the arms of Tommy, the man beside him.

"Kay? Where are you?"

"Coming!" she called, refusing to cry. With a great effort, she made her legs work. "Tommy, Lee—well, they did a hell of a job, don't you think?" She made herself look the set over carefully. "Yes, a hell of a job."

"Are you feeling all right?" Lee asked.

"What do you mean?" she asked, a little too quickly.

"You're pale. You look like you've just seen a ghost."

Their eyes locked. Kay had to blink the tears back. *Maybe I did*, she thought.

"Tell you what I could use," she said instead.

"What's that?"

"A drink. A nice big drink. A *bunch* of drinks, now that I think of it. Come on—let's go out and get plastered."

Book Four

1.

THE KNOCK AT THE DOOR OF THE SUITE WAS firm and persistent.

They looked at each other, puzzled.

"Don't do that," Sandy said, as her husband automatically started to open it. "Ask first. Robbers are always breaking into hotel rooms in New York—"

"Who is it?" Bobby asked obligingly.

"Delivery from TBS."

They couldn't tell if the voice was male or female. Sandy stepped back as Bobby opened the door.

"Surprise!" a dark-haired woman called out.

"Connie?"

"You got it!" Connie said, rushing into the room and into his arms.

Bobby laughed and hugged her, then lifted her off her feet, spinning her around.

"Sandy! Make him stop!" she protested. Then the two women were laughing and crying and hugging each other all at once.

"You look wonderful!" Sandy said.

"And you lie like a rug—but I love it. Wow! Isn't this exciting?"

"The plane trip, and the limousine..."

Connie sighed. "Unfortunately, there weren't any flights available from Queens, and any fantasies I had about a glamorous, romantic limousine ride went out the window. The only way I could get the kids to promise they'd be good was to let the youngest ones come along and have a taste of luxury."

"Oh, Connie—"

"It's okay. In by limousine, back by subway. There's a moral in there somewhere, I think, but the hell with it."

"Where's your husband?" Bobby asked.

"Carl? Not all of us married dashing dance instructors, you know. He's in construction—the dirty part. He had to finish something at the building site—"

"What a shame," Sandy commiserated.

Connie snorted. "Are you kidding? This is the first time in years I've had a day to myself. Besides, I'll have the distinction of being the only woman at the Plaza whose husband comes back to his suite in dirty work clothes. Terribly chic, you know. Is that a pot of coffee? Carl ordered some from room service this morning and said it was almost as bad as mine, but I don't believe him."

Moments later they were seated in the living room.

"So what did you think when they called you about doing the show?" Connie asked. "A real bolt from the blue, huh?"

"I couldn't believe it—" Sandy began.

"It's already been great for business. We got a story in the paper, and we were on the TV news," Bobby informed her.

"Such celebrities, you two! I'm very impressed. *I* went on a diet," she informed them. She stood up, parodying a model as she posed in her blue polyester pantsuit. "You are now seeing the new, streamlined me. As streamlined as you can hope to get after half a dozen kids—"

"That many?" Sandy asked, wide-eyed.

"More or less, but who's counting?"

"Hey—have you seen anybody else?" Bobby asked.

"You know, it's funny," Connie told him, taking a sip of her coffee. "I thought I saw Cathy downstairs in the drug store. Actually I was prowling around, and she was coming out of the drug store. It looked like her. Anyway, I was *sure* she saw me, but before I could get to her she popped into an elevator. Weird, huh?"

"Maybe it wasn't her," Sandy suggested.

Connie shrugged. "Tell me—I didn't do something awful to her way back when, did I? Like borrow a lipstick and forget to return it?"

"You always could make me laugh," Sandy said.

"And the way you two danced could always make me jealous. I hear you're doing a number on the special."

"How did you hear that?" Bobby asked.

"Just snooping around. Actually, it was so easy it wasn't even fun. Since I live the closest, I'm the one the research department called when they wanted to know something. You give and you get, I told them..." For the first time, the smile left her face. "Do you know about Hank?"

"And Andy and Donna—"

"I still get the chills when I think about Lorraine," Sandy said, interrupting Bobby. "After all these years. Isn't that strange?"

"It was the first time anything happened to one of us," Connie suggested gently. "I think that was one reason why we didn't stay in touch. It was frightening."

"I *meant* to write to you," Sandy said, grateful for a chance to change the subject. "I don't even have a good excuse. Not all these years' worth, anyway."

"I know how it is. A million times I started letters, but one of the kids wanted something, or I was late for an errand...Twenty years! I still can't believe it."

"Me either," Bobby agreed. "We'll have a chance to catch up—"

"That's what you think!" Connie corrected him. "I take it you haven't seen the schedule they've set up for us."

"Not really," Sandy told her. "The young man who met our plane gave us a copy. Get it, Bobby, will you? It's in my bag."

"For starters, today we go over to TBS for lunch, then we go over the special. We come back here and change, then we go to the studio for a screening of something or other—"

"Right," Bobby said, checking the schedule he brought from the bedroom. "*The Rockin' Fifties*. That's the one they're going to show before our special on Sunday."

"And there's a cocktail party—'

"'An opportunity to meet the *Dancetime* special staff and crew informally, along with its sponsors and TBS personnel,'" he read.

"Tomorrow morning, we meet the press," Connie informed him. "That's the morning. We have a press conference, then some interviews. And posing for pictures. Then we have a run-through or a rehearsal, or whatever they call it—"

"It sounds like you're right. We'll be busy," Sandy agreed.

"That's just two days' worth of it. It's like that all week long. By Sunday, we'll be dead! What do they think we are? Teenagers?"

"Oh, Connie—"

"I know. I could always make you laugh. Too bad the laugh lines don't show." She looked at the watch on her wrist. "We ought to get started if we're going to be on time. Want to share a cab?"

"I just need to fix my hair," Sandy told her. She looked at Connie's pantsuit, then at her own dress, wondering if the pink, lime, and bronze diagonal-striped pattern that had seemed so perfect in Houston was wrong for New York.

"It's perfect," Connie assured her, reading her mind. "You never had to worry—everything looks good on you. I bet you haven't gained a pound."

"It's the dancing. Working with Bobby keeps me in shape. When our boy is home, he never stops eating—"

"I'm going to get my jacket," Bobby announced.

"—and I eat right along with him. But I manage to lose it."

"How is he?" Connie asked. "I've been so busy talking—as usual—that I haven't let you get a word in."

"Oh, he's fine," Sandy answered, beaming. "He's on the dean's list in school. I have a picture in my wallet."

As Bobby returned, she excused herself, checking her hair and makeup and toying with the idea of changing her dress. She'd waited twenty years for this day, and she wanted everything to be perfect. *Pink*, she thought, *he always liked me in pink. But maybe I should have worn a softer pink, a solid pink instead of a pattern...*

"Hey, come on!" Connie called. As Sandy returned, bag in hand, she had to smile.

"Just like the old days, Bobby. She always was rushing me—"

"And you were always late! You were always doing your makeup—"

"That was Cathy!"

"Was it?" Connie asked, puzzled. How much did they really remember, she wondered, and how much had they forgotten? How much had they wanted to forget?

"I think so," Sandy said, taking her wallet out. "Anyway, here's a picture of our son. Bobby took it just a couple of weeks ago."

"Wow, he must be a real heartbreaker," Connie told her. "He's how old now? Nineteen?"

"Twenty," Bobby said.

"He looks just like his father," Connie said.

Sandy's hand shook as she took the wallet back. "The coloring is the same, but he has my eyes. I guess you're right, though. Most people say he's the spitting image of Bobby." *Does she know?* Sandy wondered. *Do they all know?*

"Time to get a move on, as we say in Texas," Bobby said.

"I'll run up to the room—pardon me, the *suite*—and get my coat. Let's meet outside in front."

From the beginning, Dennis Bradshaw thought, as the cab made its way uptown, his having been a Regular on *Dancetime, USA!* had been a point of contention between them. Buffie had been horrified, as if she'd discovered that he'd served time in prison—or something worse. He'd never bragged about it, but he hadn't tried to hide it, either. And while he hadn't understood her reaction, he'd gone along with her ... for a time, at least.

Considering the invitation to rejoin the Regulars for the special, he'd refused to try, as Buffie had, to line the girls up on one side or the other. He'd been unmoved by Buffie's tears and her tantrums. For weeks, the battle had raged. After he made his decision, when she refused to allow the TBS researcher into "my home," he told her that it was his home, too, and scheduled the appointment at his office. He was careful to tell Sheila Granger that his wife wouldn't be participating in the program or the publicity.

"How will *that* look?" Buffie asked him. "What will people think?"

"I haven't the vaguest idea," he answered, "but if they ask me why you're not there, I'll say that it's because you're afraid your crowd at the country club might leave you out of one of their earthshaking bridge games—"

"Don't you dare laugh at me!"

"Who's laughing?"

"Then go! Go to your ridiculous TV show. You can be a dancing fool! You don't need me for that. But if you go, don't come back!"

"I have to do it, Buff. It's important to me..."

"Then go! Go right now! And don't come back."

To her surprise and his own, he'd taken her at her word. It was only a separation, he told the girls as calmly as possible. He and their mother needed time to think things out. Then he packed a bag and went to the Gotham, where he sometimes stayed when he had a late night or early appointment in the city.

The first night, he'd felt elated, flushed with a sense of freedom he hadn't known in years. He fully expected to lose the feeling, but it stayed with him. When he'd imagined what leaving Buffie would be like, his fantasies always ended with guilt and remorse. But now he felt relatively free of them: the girls were old enough to understand, certainly, and it had been Buffie who insisted on the showdown.

His recent dreams of Sandy had amazed him with the intensity of their eroticism, a quality his dreams hadn't had since he was a young man. And it was as a young man that he appeared in them—a young man who hadn't made the wrong choice. In sleep, he relived what he now saw as the golden time of his life, the time when all his options had been open. He was a teenager again, dancing each day on the show, spending as many hours as he could with the girl he loved.

"Sandy..." Dennis whispered.

"What'dja say, bud?" the cab driver asked, looking at his passenger in the rear-view mirror.

"Nothing. Just talking to myself," Dennis told him.

Sandy...Closing his eyes, he remembered her youth and innocence. Her skin was soft, her cheeks tinged with a flush of excitement. She always seemed to be waiting for him with a streak in her hair and love in her eyes. Waiting...and this time he wouldn't disappoint her.

He was thirty-eight—it wasn't eighteen, but it wasn't old. Twenty years had gone by, but measured against a lifetime that wasn't so long. He was still a young man, even if his hair was graying. He could still make the right choice, still atone for having made the wrong one...

"Okay, bud. That'll be three eighty-five," the cab driver said.

Dennis Bradshaw fumbled in his wallet, then handed the man a ten-dollar bill.

"Nothin' smaller?"

"Keep it," Dennis said, opening the door, staring up at the TBS Building. This time, he told himself, it had to be better...

"Connie!"

"Don! You look sensational."

"Tony, my God!"

"Lee! How good to see you!"

"I'm so excited..."

"Hello, I'm Sheila Granger. We spoke on the phone..."

"Bobby!"

"Hey, pal, how've you been?

"I can't believe this whole thing!"

"Was it really twenty years ago? *Twenty* years?"

"I'm Kay Duvane. It's a pleasure to meet you—"

"Sandy!"

"...those full skirts we wore! Remember?"

"The dances! And those wonderful old songs! I can still remember..."

"Did we look like *that*? My God!"

"Dennis!"

"I'd like to introduce—"

"Can you imagine it? We're all together again!"

"Remember?"

"Of course I remember!"

Remember...?

There were kisses and hugs, handshakes and slaps on the back. There was laughter, and there were tears. It had been too long, they all agreed, and yet it was as if no time had passed at all. They all looked wonderful, they told one another. They all looked the same—they'd know each other anywhere.

Wasn't it exciting? Wasn't it wonderful? They couldn't wait, and they wanted the week to last forever.

The air was thick with emotion. Hardly anyone touched the buffet. Kay told Sheila that *The Waltons* had nothing on this scene, and wasn't it a shame there wasn't a writer around: maybe they should commission somebody to write about the *real* reunion, the drama the public wouldn't see. That might have the makings of a different kind of special...

It was a shame that Cathy was sick in bed at the hotel, but the doctor said it was just an upset stomach, that she'd be fine after a little rest...

Sandy smiled and tried to control herself, but it was a losing battle. She'd waited and dreamed, but this was *real*! There he was, just across the room! The gray in his hair made him even more handsome. Bobby was shaking his hand—it made her tremble to remember his touch. Then Bobby was being called over by Tony and Connie, and it was as if the room and everyone else disappeared, and she and Dennis were alone...

"Is—isn't this silly? I planned out what I'd say to you, and now it's flown right out of my mind."

He took her hand in his. "You don't have to say a thing. Just let me look at you."

"Don't stare like that, Dennis. I look terrible—"

"You're beautiful," he said. "You always were the most beautiful girl in the world."

"You're teasing me!"

"No," he said with certainty. "No, I'm not."

"I—you... Maybe we shouldn't have come..."

"You don't know how many times I've dreamed of you,

Sandy. So many nights I've held you and kissed you—"

"I saw your home in a magazine a few years ago. It's lovely—"

"We moved."

"Well, I saved the pictures anyway. Our house is a split-level. Bobby had the kitchen redone for our anniversary. He put in an island—you know—and a new microwave. And let's see,—oh, an ice-maker, and one of those grills that lets us barbecue inside. We love to barbecue, but it gets so hot in Houston. There was a picture of your wife in the magazine. She's very pretty—"

"We're separated, Sandy."

She was trying for restraint, but his eyes held her, drawing her closer. "Our life is probably so dull compared to yours," she babbled, her voice betraying her increasing desperation. "Of course the studio keeps me busy—"

"Sandy—"

"I teach exercise classes, too. Besides the regular dancing, that is. And I do volunteer work at the hospital—"

"Sandy—"

"And can you imagine it, I ride, of all things. Me, from New York. But you know what they say, 'when in Texas—'"

"I didn't plan it," he said. "Back then, I never meant to hurt you. You know that, don't you—"

"And . . . oh, Mexican food. I'm crazy about it. I took a course and learned to cook it. People say it's just like the real thing, but I don't know. We've been to Mexico several times—"

"Do you ever think about me, Sandy?" he asked. "Ever at all?"

She bit her lip, determined not to cry. "I—yes. I try not to, but I do. Sometimes it's in dreams, but mostly it's in the mornings, when I'm alone."

"You do?"

She nodded. "But I have so much to keep busy with.

Bobby wants me to have more help in the house, but I *like* to clean. It fills the time. It keeps me... busy."

"Are you happy? Does he make you happy?"

"He's a wonderful man. He has loads of energy—of course he works too hard, but he thrives on it. We both keep busy. It's better that way, Dennis. That way, I don't have time to ask myself questions—"

"I've always loved you, Sandy."

"Don't say that. Please don't—"

"It's true. You know it. And I know you still love me. Sandy, it's not too late. We'll make it the way it used to be. They way it should be..."

Across the room, Connie was busily talking with Tony, while Don and Bobby discussed the merits of the Sunbelt. Bobby tried to concentrate, but it was hard.

"Well, what do you guys think?" Lee Dean asked. "It's like old times, isn't it?"

In spite of himself, Bobby glanced at his wife. She was looking into Dennis' eyes with an expression he hadn't seen in years, but one he remembered. It was happening again, he told himself. It had never really stopped happening at all.

"Like old times," Bobby said, doing his damnedest to keep his voice steady. "*Just* like old times."

2.

AFTER LUNCH, THEY TOURED THE TBS BUILDing, then went to the screening room, where Shelia Granger outlined plans for the coming week and a publicist filled them in on the next morning's press conference.

There was time for a shower before the screening and the cocktail party, and Don Simpson took advantage of the opportunity. Maybe, he told himself, that was just what he needed. He undressed, leaving a trail of clothes marking his path through the suite.

The needle spray of the hot water was relaxing, but it was his nerves and not his muscles that were tense.

Seeing everyone again had been a more emotional experience than he'd expected—although being in New York again was part of it, too, perhaps. Agreeing to do the special, he told himself when he finally made his decision, was a test of his own maturity.

He was proud of himself for being able to handle it—so far—and grateful to Gary. The last thing he'd wanted to do was to carry his anxiety about the decision home. He tried not to, and to an extent he succeeded. But besides knowing him and loving him as a person, Gary, as a psychologist, knew human behavior. He hadn't pressed the point—instead he'd been patient and tolerant of the moods Don hadn't always succeeded in camouflaging, and he waited for Don to bring up the subject.

His life with Gary was an accomplishment Don took pride in. Introducing Gary as the man he lived with, both to gay and straight people, was much easier than he'd ever imagined it could be. Instead of hiding their bond, he found himself actually wanting people he knew to meet the person he so admired and cared for. And all of them were pleased for him.

Los Angeles, however, wasn't America; Don knew that much. Local friends who were interested in his happiness weren't necessarily representative of the entire country.

Among the people he'd met through Gary were a number of gay men and women who were militant about their rights. They weren't asking for all that much, they explained—they merely wanted, and intended to have, the freedom of choice they were entitled to as Americans. Don agreed with them in principle, and with most of the tenets of the gay rights movement. But, as with every cause, there were extremists. No bill or piece of legislation, Don felt, be it on the federal, state, or municipal level, was going to guarantee equal employment regardless of sexual preference. In theory, it sounded good. But in practice, well, that was another matter.

"Look," he told an activist friend of Gary's, "I admire your dedication. I know that in trying to secure gay rights, you're working for me. I appreciate it, maybe more than you know. But laws and marches are only part of what's needed to change social attitudes. Time and understanding count—and understanding takes time.

"I don't favor laws that require an employer to reject a

job applicant on the basis of his or her sex life. I'm an employer—and in all honesty, I don't think I'd like to have an effeminate man, a butch woman, or a drag queen working as a receptionist. If I owned an apartment building, I don't think I'd want to rent to a very promiscuous individual, gay or straight..."

The activist had argued, telling Don that he'd been "brainwashed" by a repressive society. The encounter gave Don plenty to think about. Happy as he was to finally come out of his personal closet (a closet marked "Very Screwed Up," not "Secret Homosexual," he told himself), he felt no sense of gay mission. Whatever their sexual orientation, people had to come to terms with themselves in their own time and way. He wasn't proselytizing a way of life. There would always be some individuals who would feel threatened by, and hostile to, the homosexual minority.

If he were committed to the gay movement, Don knew, he would have had no second thoughts about appearing on the show. It would be an ideal platform for reaching an audience of millions. If he admitted and spoke about his homosexuality, given the chance by the producer, it might even help.

The trouble was, he didn't want to. Perhaps, he thought, he was afraid—unprepared or unwilling to deal with the reactions he'd get. Maybe it was selfishness. Happiness, after all, was something that had eluded him for so long: now that he'd found it, his commitment was to himself and to Gary—and to the private pleasure and fulfillment they shared.

TBS had offered plane tickets and reservations for two: Don considered not telling Gary about the second ticket. Then he decided that the best thing to do would be to tell Gary the truth—he hadn't yet lied in their relationship, and he didn't intend to start at this point—but to go to New York alone.

"If that's the way you'll feel comfortable, good" Gary

said. "I know it's hard enough just to go on the show, to see people you haven't seen in so long, and to deal with all the memories and attitudes you'll confront—"

"But I don't want to do it alone," Don had heard himself saying, to his own astonishment. "I'd like you to be with me..."

He turned the water off and stepped out of the shower, drying himself off with a towel, then wrapping it around his waist out of habit. The sound of the television surprised him.

"Hi," Gary said.

"I was just thinking about you," Don said, kissing him.

"Wondering where I was, huh? I stopped by the Museum of Modern Art. I didn't realize how long I stayed. How was lunch? All the old faces still look the same?"

Don smiled. "Not really, but everybody lied to everyone else and said they did. We'd better get ready. It's almost time for the screening and cocktail party."

"Are you certain, Don?" Gary asked. "I want you to do what you feel—not what you think is right. They're not always the same thing, and my feelings for you won't change, no matter what you decide—"

"I know that," Don said. "But we've been through this before. I'm not trying to advertise my life. If I was straight, I think I'd still be the sort of man who relishes privacy. I'm not going to hold hands with you—hell, we don't even do that at home—or kiss you in front of a crowd. But I am going to say that you're my friend, and I'll be proud to say it to anyone. Because you are..."

"I'm proud of you," Gary said, hugging him.

"Then come on," Don told him. "If we don't make it fast, we'll have to wait till the thirty-year reunion..."

It went off without a hitch. By all rights, he should have been relaxed, relieved, and grateful for the cash in the envelope in his pocket. But hard as he tried to concentrate on the screen and the monitors—with their film clips of Elvis Presley, Fabian, The Supremes, and all the other groups who'd been part of the 1950's sound, Tony Merino was nervous.

Getting up, splashing his face with cold water, might help, he thought, but he decided against it. Getting up would mean "excuse me's" to Connie and her husband, who were sitting next to him, and to Don and the man beside him. Then he'd have to find his way to the exit, passing the other rows of people from the network and the guests they'd invited to the screening. It wasn't worth the effort, particularly since it would give so many of them a chance to see the sweat on his forehead and the shaking which he couldn't, for the life of him, control.

What the hell is it? he wondered. Okay, so he'd been worried about doing the job: the job was over. Phil, the buddy of his who'd set it up, had told him that it would go off "like a snap," and it had. He had the cash to prove it.

Anybody who had seen the man who'd visited him leaving his suite in the Plaza wouldn't have looked twice. He looked no different from thousands of other businessmen in Manhattan. Only a few people had known that there were four pounds of pure cocaine sewed into the lining of the attaché case Tony carried on the flight from Miami and exchanged with the stranger.

The thought of how much that coke would be worth on the street, when it was cut, made Tony sweat. All night he'd lain awake. Visions of the money he was making filled his mind, as scheme after scheme occurred to him. He could take the coke and vanish—but that would make some people very angry, and they were the kind of people who knew how to find a man who disappeared. He could say that somebody ripped him off, perhaps due to a leak at the top. He might pull off playing dumb, but then he'd have to unload the merchandise. There was nobody he could trust not to rat on him.

More than anything, he thought about the consequences if something went wrong. Possession of narcotics. Possession with intent to sell. Transporting illegal drugs across state lines...It was trouble, federal trouble if he got caught. No matter how much information, no matter how many names and addresses he gave up, he'd still be looking at a trip to the penitentiary, and to a nice long stay once he got there.

It's over, for Christ's sake...He glanced at Connie, wondering if he'd said the words or merely thought them. At least he'd been paid well...It was the easiest five grand he'd ever made. That is, if you didn't count the aggravation. God, he was too old for muling drugs. That was the kind of thing kids did.

And that was one thing he knew: he wasn't a kid any more.

He'd managed to convince himself that the trip would be fun. Courtesy of TBS, it would be a free chance to check out the action in Manhattan, to connect with a couple of pals he hadn't seen in a few years and see if they had any scams he could hook up with. He'd borrowed a few bills and gotten himself some new clothes, new luggage and a haircut. He'd even bought a hot diamond pinkie ring.

That afternoon when they saw each other again for the first time in twenty years, the looks on the faces of the other Regulars told him he'd managed to pull it off. He was still the same old Tony, slick and sharp. A silk suit, a shirt that looked like a custom job (he'd had a tailor he knew monogram it), a twenty-five-dollar tie, and a pair of lizard shoes fooled everyone else, but he knew the truth.

Without exception, the other Regulars had married or made some kind of normal life for themselves. And there he was, the dude who was supposed to be the big operator, the one out of the bunch everyone would have put money on to become a big winner. He was a flop, a failure, an also-ran...and to top it off, he was alone...

Just as in the old days, he had no choice but to play a

role. When they asked him what he did for a living, he said, "This and that," alluding to mysterious "investments" with a wink of his eye. Don gave him an inadvertent break when he alluded to real estate, and Tony hadn't denied it.

Real estate?... *Jesus, what a joke!*

Aside from the five G's—one third when he picked up the shipment, and the other two-thirds when he'd handed it over—he didn't have a pot to piss in or a window to throw it out of. He couldn't go back to Miami—not with the hot checks he'd written still bouncing.

He'd gone to see his grandmother. Stone deaf, she was on the far side of eighty, and not always certain who was who any more. He'd gone to see her after the package was picked up, stopping to pick up flowers and candy and a bottle of the brandy she used to like.

The old neighborhood didn't look the same. Half the block had been torn down and turned into a luxury highrise, and the stores had all changed hands. Most of the people who lived in the older buildings were blacks and Puerto Ricans. But his grandmother still lived in the old apartment, and the familiar furnishings had brought tears to his eyes.

"She's not too good," Rosa, the overweight cousin who cared for her, told him. "Don't be surprised."

Still, he wasn't prepared for the sight of the old woman being wheeled into the living room, or for the vacant look in her eyes.

"It's me! It's Tony!" he said, shouting in her ear when his cousin told him to speak up. "I brought you this..."

When he placed the flowers on her lap, she smiled, stroking them as she would a small animal.

"Pretty," she said.

"Ya. Ya, they're pretty. And this..."

She'd almost looked like her old self when he put the box of candy on her lap, but before she could open the box, his cousin yanked it away.

"What the hell—"

"She can't eat it. On account of her sugar."

"How about a drink?" he asked, pulling the bottle from its bag. "She can at least have one drink—"

"The doctor says no—"

"Well, I say she can, for Christ's sake! She's my grandmother, and I say she can!" he insisted, anger and frustration filling his head.

"Sure, you know everything! You come here once every ten years, bigshot, and you know more than the doctor. You don't know shit. You don't have to feed her, and clean her—"

"Okay! All right!" he shouted. The veins in his head were pounding. "I gotta go. You take care, hear me?" he said to the old woman, kissing her cheek.

"Tony, you be good boy," she said, her voice only a rattle.

The words, the ruined echo of the voice he remembered, made him want to shake her.

"Sometimes she's like that," his cousin explained. "The doctor says it happens that way. Sometimes they know what's going on and sometimes they don't. It's their veins—"

"I'll see you," he told her before hurrying down the stairs, then down the street to the nearest bar, where he had a double shot of bourbon. In the men's room, the door locked behind him, he took the vial from his jacket pocket and tapped the white powder into the miniature silver spoon. He inhaled it first up his right nostril, then his left. Within a few minutes, the cocaine hit him, giving him a surge of energy and raising his spirits.

A toot of coke, Tony thought. That was what he needed now. It would keep him from thinking that everyone else had *somebody* and *some place*, and that he was homeless and alone. It would help block out the memory of what he'd done to get the money in his pocket, and the memory of his grandmother... What would happen to him when he got old? There'd be no relatives to look after him. He'd end up in a public hospital or a nursing home, he thought, not sure which was worse.

Time—it was the only real perfect crime in the world...a thief who robbed you so expertly you didn't even notice what was being stolen until it was too late...

"Where are you going?" Connie whispered, as he started to leave. "This is almost over."

"I know," he answered, squeezing by her. "I'll be right back. I gotta see a man about a horse."

"Oh, Tony," she said, giggling. "You haven't changed a bit."

"Thank you," Kay Duvane said from the center of the stage, and the audience applauded. She waited for the reaction to subside. "I'm glad you agree with me that we've just seen a winning special. I think it's going to come in in a big way next Sunday night."

There was more applause. The screen behind her disappeared into the rafters to reveal a closed curtain.

"Now," she said, "I'd like you to meet the people who will be making another exciting ninety minutes of television back-to-back with what we've just seen. Lee Dean..."

Lee bounced onto the stage, waving to the audience and accepting an ovation.

"And the people who'll be making headlines at our press conference here tomorrow," Kay continued. "The *Dancetime, USA!* Regulars!" Some of them nervous, some more relaxed, The Regulars took the stage. The applause was loud and long.

"Now let's open the curtain," Kay said, "and have you join us up here to get to know them."

The heavy maroon curtain went up, revealing an unlighted set. Then, suddenly, the lights went on, and the audience gasped. Wide-eyed, the audience stared at the re-created set and the life-size photographic blowups of

The Regulars as they'd looked twenty years before.

"We weren't going to show them to you till tomorrow at the press conference," Kay told the group onstage. "But we thought they'd help get you in the mood." She led them toward the set and the two portable bars that had been set up. The audience joined them as taped music began to play in the background. Kay and Sheila began the introductions.

"Don't you want to see your friends, honey?" Al Hartley asked his wife. "I'm dying for a drink myself..."

They were standing at the edge of the crowd. They'd arrived just as the screening started, and taken seats in the back of the theater.

"Go on," Cathy urged him. "I'm going to make my way slowly. I just don't want to rush it—the doctor said to take things easy."

"I'll wait," Al offered.

"No, go on, please. I—I want to sneak up on the old gang. I'll find you later and you'll have a chance to meet everyone."

"If you're sure."

"Positive," she said, watching him head for the bars.

In truth, Cathy was terrified. Three months earlier, when her period was late, she attributed it to nerves over the reunion. A postcard reminded her that it was time for a medical checkup and she made an appointment with her gynecologist.

No, she told the doctor, this wasn't the first month her cycle had been off. She'd been a week or so late the previous month and two weeks off the month before that. Yes, her flow had been a bit lighter—and come to think of it, it had lasted a day or two longer than usual. Other changes? Well, she was tense, Cathy admitted, and more prone to depression recently...

When the blood test came back, Cathy faced her doctor again. The older woman was both calm and kind.

"What's happening, Mrs. Hartley, is that the natural

supply of estrogen in your bloodstream is decreasing. It's a matter of production slowing down. Of course, it's a normal change—one that we all go through at some time..."

Change? The change? No, it wasn't possible! She was too young! Menopause was something that happened later, something that made a woman look old and feel dried up—

"There's no reason why you should feel any discomfort or concern," the doctor said. "This time of life needn't be a problem for you—I'll do all I can to help. You can help yourself by reading this book, and having this perscription filled. *No Pause at All* will give you insight into what's going on inside your body. The Valium will help you when you feel nervous. I'd like to see you again in two weeks, when we'll discuss the benefits and risks of supplemental estrogen. Call me if you have any questions or problems before then and, above all, don't worry."

Don't worry? It was easy for the doctor to say, Cathy thought, but impossible to do. Her insides were drying up—she imagined them shriveling and withering away, convinced that everyone could see it. They knew, they *all* knew! And no one could halt the process, neither Al nor anybody else...

She found herself weeping, unable to stop, grieving for the youth and femininity she knew she was losing. At times she was convinced that Al now despised her, though he continued to hold her and pamper her and call her his little girl. She struggled to hide the emotions and fears she couldn't control, waiting for solitude to let herself go.

The pills were a godsend, the only crutch she had, but when she went through the initial prescription and two refills in a matter of weeks, the doctor cautioned her against excessive reliance on tranquilizers and a resultant dependency. The gynecologist wrote a new prescription, though, and as insurance, Cathy went to another doctor with a reputation as a liberal dispenser of pills and got some also from him. The pills didn't reverse the "changes," but they helped to numb her response. With the drugs, it was possible to think of the upcoming special without feeling morbid.

Almost in a daze, she watched the plane tickets arrive in the mail. Had she actually agreed to participate? She told herself that she must be going mad. Even doubling up on the Valium, Cathy wasn't able to keep a thing on her stomach the two days before they left Elmira. *If only I'd had a facelift*, she thought, remembering those she'd detected on other women. She considered changing her mind and canceling out, then decided that not getting through it somehow would brand her a coward for life.

In the limousine from LaGuardia, a young man from the TBS publicity department made pleasant conversation and filled them in on the week's schedule. Cathy felt weak. Sunday night and all day Monday, she stayed in bed. TBS insisted on sending the doctor who treated the actors on the TBS soap operas produced in New York.

Cathy manufactured symptoms (a vague ache in her stomach; fatigue) and the doctor gave her a shot and a vial of yellow capsules. "A little virus," he diagnosed. "Rest and relax. You'll be fine tomorrow." His tone implied that she had no choice.

And now it *was* "tomorrow."

"Cathy? Cathy Hartley?"

She turned, her eyes as wide as a frightened animal's. The surprise on her face threatened to turn to visible anger: who was this woman—this *young* woman?

"I'm Sheila Granger." The woman extended her hand.

"I—I thought you'd be older," Cathy heard herself say, wanting to bolt and run back to the hotel, back to Elmira.

Sheila laughed softly. "Well, you look exactly as I pictured you, although I did have the advantage of all the old publicity material."

Old... Cathy said to herself. That's how I look...

"I'm so glad you're feeling better. We were worried about you," Sheila was saying.

"I'm fine. Thank you for the flowers."

"Our pleasure. Of course you missed the luncheon today. Have you had a chance to talk to anyone?"

"No," Cathy lied. Last night while Al took a walk, she had pulled on her clothes and gone down to the hotel drug store, uncertain of her purpose. There she'd seen Connie. She knew that Connie had seen her, but Cathy escaped into the elevator, finding it impossible to face even the friendliest of the old Regulars.

"It's kind of hard to find anyone in this crowd," Sheila offered kindly. "Let me help you—"

Cathy pulled back quickly as Sheila touched her arm. "I'm—I'm still a little weak," she tried to explain.

"We'll fix that. Let me get you a canape."

"No—let me just go to the ladies' room. I want to put some lipstick on."

She was aware of Sheila's stare—which only served to unnerve her even more.

Instead of trying to explain further, Cathy bolted away, hurrying back down the steps, up the aisle toward the lobby and the ladies' room she'd lingered in until the screening had already started. She fumbled in her purse for the tranquilizer she felt she would die without.

3.

"SHE WAS ALWAYS ON THE HIGHSTRUNG side," Connie told Sheila the previous night when Cathy had disappeared into the ladies room and didn't return. Kay was deeply engrossed in conversation with the sponsor's reps, and Sheila had turned to Connie in desperation. Together, they'd gone to find Cathy and brought her back to the party. She was quiet and seemed almost dazed, Sheila thought, but Connie had said it must be an after-effect of the flu medication, and promised to keep an eye on Cathy.

As she went backstage, where the hairdressers and makeup people were putting the final touches on The Regulars for the photographers and reporters who'd be attending the press conference, Sheila noted that Connie had done as she'd promised: Cathy was sitting at her side, still looking slightly dazed. Connie smiled and gave Sheila the subtlest nod to let her know that all was well. Sheila nodded in return. Smiling, under the circumstances, was out of the question.

"Thank heaven you're here!" Maxine Aiken, the publicist, said. "I need all the help I can get. And the director was looking for you. Something about a dance number—"

"That will have to wait," Sheila said, barely concealing her fury. "Maxine, would you come with me? I want to talk to you."

"But the press! I was just briefing everyone on what to expect—"

"I'm sure you can spare a minute," Sheila said firmly. She turned on her heels, and the publicist, ten years older than she was, followed with a sigh.

"What is the meaning of this?" Sheila demanded thrusting a newspaper in front of her eyes. She pointed to a gossip item in the tabloid.

> OLD ACQUAINTANCE DEPT.: Big wheels at a certain network are spinning at the Big Production Romance between a young lady producer on the way up and a has-been singing idol of Greaser vintage who hit rock-bottom way back when!!!

"It's a blind item," the publicist offered. "No names are mentioned."

"Thank you for that invaluable piece of information!" Sheila snapped. "I'm not asking you to tell me what I already know. What I want to find out is how that item got planted."

"I didn't do it! Nobody in my department did it. That column is a hodgepodge thing the paper throws together—"

"I thought I made it very clear at our meeting last week that I didn't want my personal relationships discussed or exploited!" Sheila pressed.

"Yes, you did, but—"

"But what? Any idiot can see they're talking about Tommy Del and me. And I don't like it, Maxine. Not one bit!"

"I *told* you, Sheila, I didn't do it! Anybody could have done it—"

"Anybody? What anybody? Who?" Sheila snapped.

"It could be—"

"Who could it be? *Who*, damn it!" She heard herself ranting like a shrew, but Sheila couldn't stop herself. Tommy had spotted the item, and while he tried to laugh it off, she knew it had hurt him.

"*Anyone* could have called it in," the publicist reiterated. "Maybe an enemy of yours."

"Enemy! I don't make it a practice to turn people into enemies!'

Now Maxine's temper was rising. "No? Well you certainly don't make friends by attacking the people who are trying to help you turn your special into a success. I'm sorry about that silly item, Miss Granger, but it happens all the time. I didn't plant it, and I don't intend to take any more abuse from you because of it!"

She stormed away, Sheila, alone, pressed her hand against her forehead, realizing that her fist was clenched. *God, I'm turning into a monster!* she thought. Increasingly, she was finding it hard—impossible at times—to control her temper. Her mother nearly burst into tears the last time they spoke on the phone; Sheila had been short-tempered and impatient. She'd also been snapping at the assistant director and the wardrobe man. Even Tommy had noticed her tension and commented on it. *I'll apologize to Maxine*, Sheila vowed, *but this isn't the time*.

Press people were already beginning to file in, carrying cups of coffee and Danish from the table set up in the lobby. They brought their press kits as well, crammed with releases—bios of Lee and The Regulars, stories about the special, and photographs.

"Okay," Maxine was telling The Regulars, "remember—the reporters want a good story, and they're on our side. Don't be nervous, and don't worry about saying the wrong thing. Later on, once they've had a chance to talk to you as a group, we'll be doing the personal interviews, and you'll have a real chance to talk. For now, just concentrate on having a good time and being yourselves."

Myself, Cathy thought, *the way I was before I started turning into an old woman.*

Myself, Dennis thought, staring at Sandy, until she looked back at him, *the way I should be. With the girl I was meant to be with.*

Myself, Tony thought. *The way I am ... Jesus help me!*

Myself, thought the others, each in his or her own way...

They stood together in a semi-circle with their arms around one another. They posed clustered around Lee Dean, and with the life-size cutouts of themselves. In two facing lines (boys on one side, girls on the other), they pretended to do the stroll; in front of the podium, with Lee presiding as if the show was on the air, they froze in bop steps.

After the photographs, the questions began.

How did it feel to be back together again? How had they been chosen as Regulars originally? How had being on *Dancetime, USA!* changed their lives? What did they think was so appealing about nostalgia, and why was the whole country going 1950's-happy? What did their friends and families think about the special? Their children?

What did they remember most about the show, about the fifties? Were times better now, or worse? Had the "good old days" really been that good?

Unless they were specifically directed to her, Cathy didn't answer any of the questions. Don's answers were thoughtful, almost intellectual. Tony turned the charm on, and Dennis was surprisingly nostalgic. As usual, Connie was quick with a joke. Bobby and Sandy, as two of the old-timers who'd married, were easily the favorites of the press.

Sheila kept a close eye on Lee Dean: several of the reporters kept bringing up the payola scandal—as she'd known they would.

"Don't you feel that you were a scapegoat?" someone asked.

Lee didn't miss a beat. "I really don't think about it that much," he answered. "It was a long time ago, and at the time, it was painful. But after I left TBS, I realized that if I spent all my time looking back, I'd never have a future. I try to look ahead. Right now, I'm looking ahead to Sunday night."

"How about Dick Clark?" a woman from a music magazine asked. "What do you feel when you see how well he's doing—and when you consider that ABC stood by him during the investigation?"

"I admire and respect Dick Clark," Lee replied. "Actually, I'm grateful to him. If it hadn't been for Dick and *Bandstand*, I don't know if I'd ever have had a chance to do *Dancetime, USA!*. The only thing I envy him is whatever secret he has for staying young."

There was a smattering of laughter—it was a good, clever answer, Sheila thought.

"As for my feelings about TBS," Lee continued, "I admit that when the payola thing happened, I was disappointed. Maybe, as someone said a moment ago, I was a scapegoat in a sense. Things have a way of balancing out, though. The network might have been more supportive back then—but they also could have hired someone else to host the show in the first place."

The questions went on for another fifteen minutes, then it was over. Maxine thanked everyone for coming and reminded them that The Regulars and Lee would be available for interviews through the TBS publicity department. Most of the reporters left, but a few—those who had interviews scheduled—lingered on.

"Miss Granger?"

Sheila was taken by surprise. The girl in tight jeans and a work shirt had a pad and pencil in her hand. "Yes?"

"I'm Diane Carr. I'm doing a story on the special for *Rolling Stone*. I was going to ask Maxine to set up a time for us to talk, but if you have a minute..."

Sheila thought of directing her instead to Lee, or someone else who would actually be on the show. The *Stone* story wouldn't break till after the special had aired anyway.

"It's kind of hectic today," she finally said, "but I could take a few minutes now, if that would help."

"Super," Diane said, smiling. "You're producing the show, right? Was it your idea?"

"No, it was Lee's. He brought it to the network. We've been working together very closely on it."

"Isn't it a little unusual for someone as young as you are—too young to remember the fifties—to be doing a special about them?"

"Not really," Sheila replied. "We've done a lot of shows about the American Revolution, and nobody at the network is old enough to remember that. Sometimes not being personally familiar with the subject matter is an asset. You do a better, more objective job as a result."

"Was it hard getting The Regulars together?"

Sheila shook her head. "Not really. You heard what they said themselves—the special is giving them a chance to have a personal reunion—"

Isn't the whole thing rather contrived?"

Sheila was confused. "I'm sorry. I don't think I understand the question."

"What I'm saying is that if they were really such good friends, wouldn't they have kept in touch? None of them have seen each other since the show went off the air—"

"They live in different parts of the country," Sheila said quickly. "Don't forget, they were all still teenagers when *Dancetime* went off TV. They've gone in different directions."

"But not even a phone call?" the reporter asked.

"What are you getting at?"

Diane put down her pad. "What I'm saying is, I wonder if television doesn't sometimes get the boundaries between what's real and what looks real confused . . . or if television doesn't do it purposely to confuse the viewers.

"Your publicity department has put out reams of copy about this thing," she contunued, when Sheila didn't immediately answer. "They're building it up as a big sentimental reunion, heavy on 'warm personal drama,' to quote one release. Isn't that just so much hype? These people aren't friends. If it wasn't for you and your network, they would probably have gone the rest of their lives without seeing each other again—and they wouldn't have cared in the least. I get the feeling that TBS is... merchandising emotions. Manufacturing them and merchandising them."

"To a large extent, that's what television entertainment is all about," Sheila said, carefully choosing her words. "People like to see crime shows, because they enjoy the excitement. They watch *Little House on the Prairie* and the soap operas because they identify with the human dramas and emotions those programs portray—"

"But everyone knows that those are just stories and characters made up," the reporter argued. "But people on the *Dancetime* stage are real. Do you think it's—well, fair to them? Isn't it a case of television manipulating not only the viewers, but the men and women who are going to appear on that special as well?"

Sheila was getting annoyed. If this girl was going to do a hatchet piece on television, there was nothing to be gained from cooperating with her. "I'm afraid I don't see the point you're trying to make."

"My point is this: twenty years ago, your network took a bunch of average teenage kids and made them celebrities... 'famous for fifteen minutes,' as Andy Warhol put it. The show went off the air and that was that. Now, twenty years later, somebody figured it's time to trot them out again, to pretend that they were friends and to hoke up a sentimental reunion, to exploit The Regulars *and* the viewers—"

"I don't see the value of continuing this discussion,"

Sheila said, standing abruptly. "You have your opinions. You're entitled to them, but in my opinion they don't happen to be accurate. Not in the least."

She hurried away before the reporter could answer, feeling that she could have handled the situation better but not knowing at all why she'd let Diane Carr get her so upset.

"... Of course we can't wing it—we want a good, tight show. But we want the people watching at home to feel that everything is spontaneous. Does everyone understand?" the director asked.

They sat around him with copies of the script in their hands, and they looked at one another.

"You mean we're supposed to trick the people watching, right?" Tony Merino asked.

The director coughed and glanced quickly at Lee Dean and Sheila. "I wouldn't put it quite that way," he said. "It's more like ... acting. Think of it that way. It's *television*. Now, let's go over it again ..."

Over the months of pre-production, the special had evolved and taken shape. The original idea Lee had presented to the network—the reunion concept—was still the core of the show, but a format had been developed around it. Simply having The Regulars dance on a recreation of the old set was out of the question, even with the added human interest of interviews.

The Fantastiks and Tommy Del would provide a lot of entertainment, along with Alice Lane, but still that didn't add up to a workable way of filling ninety prime-time minutes.

Working with the writers and Lee, Sheila came up with an overall approach that everyone liked: a teenage view of what life had been like in the 1950's. There would be segments that utilized film clips to "salute" the major movies of the period, with scenes from *The Blackboard*

Jungle, Rebel Without a Cause, and the other films that teenagers had sighed over. Another segment concentrated on the old monster movies that had been the staples at the drive-ins.

Using kinescopes, a look at television in the good old days had been worked up, featuring the best-remembered programs and performers from not only TBS, but the other networks as well. Sid Caesar, Ernie Kovacs, and Milton Berle; Lucille Ball, Phil Silvers and George Gobel; Howdy Doody, *Dragnet*, and Ed Sullivan... these performers were certain to stir old memories.

Old news footage yielded another strong segment that covered fads and crazes from hula hoops to "Sputnik Fever." Lee would interview one of The Regulars, steering the conversation toward the segment coming up. The subject of movies would provide a natural lead-in to the film clips.

Another element had been needed, Sheila felt, and for weeks it eluded her. Then one day, she got it. NBC's *Saturday Night Live!* had proven itself to be a strong show, and the other networks had gone looking for young comedians in an effort to compete with the popularity of the Not-Ready-For-Prime-Time Players. Rather than create a unit of its own, TBS signed The Amateurs, a group of eight young performers who got their start in clubs specializing in improvisational comedy. They went on to do a well-received revue Off-Broadway, and TBS gave them a long-term deal that guaranteed them specials and guest shots. Once they became known to viewers, they'd be ready for a series—just in time for the return of variety shows, which everyone said were due for a comeback in a couple of years.

Sheila came up with the idea of having The Amateurs appear on the special, doing skits with a fifties theme. Kay and Lee had agreed that it would add a comic touch, and the troupe had prepared more material than would be actually needed as insurance; the worst thing that could happen with a live TV show was "dead air time," with no way of filling it.

As they fashioned the script, all the various elements came together. A good pace was set. The Regulars themselves seemed pleased, Sheila noted. Hard as it was for her to be objective, she felt a surge of pride and accomplishment.

"You'll be sitting in the bleachers just like the old days," the director told The Regulars. "You'll feel right at home."

Because the bleachers would look empty with just the handful of Regulars in them, it had been suggested that the promotion department work up some sort of contest with a local department store. A prize would be given for the most authentic fifties costumes, and the winners and runners-up would fill the empty seats. Sheila had been against this idea, arguing that it would give the show a circus-like feeling: in the same way, she'd rejected the idea of letting members of the studio audience (an important factor, since there'd be no chance to use canned laughter or applause) sit onstage. There was a certain poignance in having the bleachers almost empty, she felt—it would help create the nostaligic, sentimental mood.

"I don't think I have to tell you people about dancing behind the camera line," the director said. They laughed, remembering how couples would push, pull, and jockey for a position that would guarantee a closeup. "There'll be a lot of film clips. You'll see them on the monitor. You'll have a spotlight dance, each of you—we'll work out partners tomorrow, and the records we'll be playing for your number. What we're going to do during those numbers is cut back and forth to you and some old clips and stills of *Dancetime* in the old days. Sandy and Bobby, you two are going to be the exception. Everything's set with your routine, right?"

Bobby nodded. "We've got it all worked out—"

"As long as you don't change the song," Sandy added.

When the idea of having Sandy and Bobby do a contemporary number came up, the old *Dancetime* theme music had been rearranged, set to a disco beat. A copy of the recording, done by the network, had been sent to the couple in Texas to practice with; another copy would be played on the air. In the same way, Alice Lane, The Fantastiks, and Tommy Del would all sing live to prerecorded accompaniment.

"Don't worry about that," the director assured her. "TBS is putting the new version out as a single on its own label. The record is breaking this week on the disco stations.

"In the next few days, we'll run through everything on the set. There isn't much blocking to worry about, but we want you to know where the cameras will be. Let me reiterate that we don't want you to feel you have to memorize the scripts you're holding. I would, however, appreciate your going over them a few times, just so you know what Lee's going to be talking with you about, and at what point in the show we'll be focusing on you. Sheila? Anything else?"

"We've spoken about this before," she told the group, "but keep in mind that on Sunday we'll have people here to do your hair and makeup. I'd like you to bring the clothes you'll be wearing on the show with you tomorrow when you come for the run-through. Our wardrobe mistress will take care of them, I promise. She feels safer when she knows she has everything pressed and locked away. Okay?"

TBS had given each of the Regulars five hundred dollars to buy their clothes for the show. This wasn't strictly legal, but it was a means of compensating The Regulars for being on the show.

"Oh, yes," Sheila said, "there are a couple of surprises

we've planned that aren't in your scripts. I'm not going to say any more than that, except to tell you we think you're going to enjoy them a lot."

Lee said a few more words, and then they were finished. Maxine reminded everyone that interviews with individual reporters had been set up for later in the day. She'd be in touch with everyone as soon as they got back to the Plaza, and a TBS publicist would be on hand to make sure the sessions went smoothly. Of course, if they could remember to plug the special enthusiastically, it would be greatly appreciated...

"These must have cost a fortune, don't you think?" Dee Phillips asked, moving her body so that the hot pink sequins shimmered.

"Big damn deal!" Virgie snapped. The dresses were beautiful, but she had no intention of admitting it.

"Now what kind of thing is that to say? Sylvie didn't have to have them made for us—"

"She doesn't have to do a damn thing for me! I don't need her charity, and I'm not gonna kiss her ass on account of one damn dress, either."

Dee sighed and shook her head, There was no point in telling Virgie that she didn't have to use that kind of language—it would only provoke her further. "Nobody's saying anything like that. I just think it was nice of her to pay for our costumes, that's all."

"Oh, *sure* it was," Virgie said sarcastically. "Not that she even bothered to ask us what we wanted to wear! Miss Sylvie picked out the dresses, and Miss Sylvie picked out the songs. Of course, Miss Sylvie is too big a star to rehearse with us—"

"Lord, give me strength!" Dee said, exasperated. "You know as well as I do that she's making a movie in California. That's why she's coming in Saturday night. And that's why they did the tapes out there. Let's try it again, just to see how the clothes work."

The network had provided the rehearsal space and a technician to work the tape. At Dee's signal, he started the machine. The familiar musical introduction began, horns against a driving backbeat. It was funny, Dee thought, but after so many years she remembered every note of the music. Sylvia's voice, dubbed in for reference, began the verse: an exact duplicate of the tape, missing only the lead vocal line, would be played on the special.

> *Hard times, they ain't nothin'*
> *New to me.*
> *We had 'em back when I was raised.*
> *Mama used to say, "We don't have*
> *Nothin' now,*
> *But I know I'm gonna see*
> *Some better days..."*

"*Some better days,*" the two women sang, standing on either side of an imaginary microphone, watching themselves in the mirrored wall opposite.

> *Those better days, they sure*
> *Took their time.*
> *Mama had to scrimp and save,*
> *And now that I'm grown up and*
> *doin' the same,*
> *I'm grateful for the lesson*
> *Mama gave...you see*

"Here we go," Dee whispered.

> *Mama made do—*
> *I can, too.*
> *Mama taught me how to get by—*
> *Not nowdays.*
> *But I think about my Mama*
> *And I try...*

Sylvia's voice began the next verse.

*One of us kids was always
gettin' sick;
There was always new shoes
to buy.
When folks asked Mama how she
Kept on keepin' on.
She said, "I praise the Lord
and then I try..."*

"Hey!" Dee called, as Virgie suddenly walked away. "Where you going? We're not through—"

"Shut that damn thing off!" Virgie barked at the man running the tape. The room was strangely silent.

"Virgie? Girl, what is wrong?"

Virgie whirled around. Her eyes were burning with anger. "That song! She picked it on purpose! She wants us to come off like fools—all that crap about hard times and makin' do. We're gonna look like poor-ass niggers!"

"That was our biggest hit! You know that! Twenty-three weeks on the charts. Besides, we're doing the medley, too. You're just looking for something to find fault with—"

"Lookin'? I don't *have* to look! I know where the fault is, and it's Sylvie!" She grabbed the zipper of her dress, tearing at it. The garment fell in a heap around her feet, and she kicked it.

"Can't you try to put those thoughts out of your mind?" Dee pleaded. "We're doing the show. Millions of people are going to see us, Virgie—the same people who were so good to us, buying the records and all. For their sake—"

"The hell with them! They sure as hell didn't think about us when *she* left, did they? Why should I care about them?"

"For yourself, then. This hate is eating you up."

"You're damn straight!" the other woman snapped. Oblivious of the gaping technician, she grabbed the sweater and slacks she'd worn to the rehearsal and pulled them on. "I do hate! I don't know how you can't, but I know I do. I hate that Sylvia. I hate her with all my heart. And I can't wait for the chance to tell her so!"

Before Dee could stop her, Virgie rushed out the door.

"Excuse me, but is that all for today?" the technician asked.

"Ain't it enough?" Dee answered.

He left, and she was alone. Maybe, she thought, it had been wrong of her to talk Virgie into doing the show.

"Oh, Lord," she said, sighing as she picked up the gown Virgie had kicked across the room. She examined it carefully—there were no rips or tears, and the wrinkles would hang out. She held it in her arms, smoothing it, silently praying that everything would work out... *somehow.*

4.

"YOU'RE SURE YOU DON'T MIND, HONEY?" Bobby asked again. "We can go out if you'd rather—"

"I told you, it's fine," Sandy insisted, trying to sound casual. People moved around them in the bustling lobby of the Plaza as music from the violinist in the Palm Court drifted through the air.

He smiled at her. "The hockey game is on in another ten minutes. We could order from room service—"

"Why don't you go up, Bobby, and order whenever you're hungry? I think I'll check in with Connie. Maybe we'll drag Cathy along and have a bite."

"And some girl talk?"

"How did you guess?" she asked.

"Because," he said, kissing her lightly. "I know you. See you later on."

"Enjoy the game!" she called brightly, as he started for the elevator. He turned and waved, and then it hit her: the moment she'd waited for for so long was finally at hand.

She'd begun to wonder if perhaps it would never arrive.

All day Tuesday and Wednesday, she and Dennis hadn't had a chance to say more than a few words in private. She couldn't make it obvious and run the risk of Bobby catching on, Sandy knew. Instead, she had to make small talk during run-throughs and rehearsals, as if Dennis were just another old friend from the past.

In all the fantasies and daydreams she'd had about seeing him again, it never occurred to her that logistics would keep them from actually spending much time together. To be so close to him, so close to making the dream of her life come true, and yet unable to get away... it was too terrible to think about.

In bed with Bobby, she would close her eyes, pretending to be asleep. She imagined what it would be like to bolt from the room, to run to the arms of Dennis. He was handsome, as handsome as she'd known he would be... maybe even a little more. And as she'd hoped, he still longed for her. It wasn't just the things he'd said on Monday. Again and again during the past few days, their eyes met.

Come to me, his look told her. *Come to me and we'll start over. We'll make up for all the lost, lonely, wasted time that should have been ours.*

I will, Sandy had thought. *We will...*

And now, finally, it was going to happen. Bobby was upstairs by now, with the television already on. He'd never think of questioning her story about spending this time with Connie.

"May I help you?" the operator asked, when Sandy lifted the house phone.

"I'm sorry," Sandy said, hanging up quickly. Announcing it, calling him first, would spoil it somehow.

Her hands trembled as she got into the elevator. She tried to make herself feel like one of the other passengers, but she was aware of her uniqueness. *I'm going to my future*, the pounding of her heart seemed to say. *To my life—*

"Excuse me—this is my floor," she heard herself say, when the elevator stopped on seven. When the door closed behind her, Sandy stood in the quiet of the hallway. *My nerves*! she thought, trying to calm them. *I don't want him to see me all nervous* ...

Closing her eyes, she tried to picture what he'd be doing when she knocked on the door. Not watching a silly hockey game like Bobby, that was for sure. He'd be reading a book, an *important* book. Or maybe he'd be going over some legal papers from his office ...

"This is silly," she whispered. Why wonder and wait, when all she had to do was walk along the carpet, then take a right turn and another few steps. She did so, then knocked on the door—

"Surprise!" she said, a little too brightly. Was she imagining it, or were there tears in his eyes? He swept her into the room, holding her so tight she couldn't breathe, so tight she hoped he'd never let go.

"My God, I was beginning to think you wouldn't come at all," Dennis said, releasing her, then holding her again as if he didn't believe it was happening.

"I—I had to wait for the right time. Oh, Dennis ..."

Their lips met, then their mouths. Closing her eyes, Sandy felt herself hurtling back in time, remembering the taste of his tongue and the touch of his hands on her body. She was dizzy, floating, and yet at the same time she was aware of something that had been waiting inside her for a long, long time—so long she'd nearly forgotten it—coming alive again.

"I've dreamed this so many times," he was saying, letting her go at last. "I want it to be perfect."

She watched, catching her breath, as he took a bottle of champagne from the small refrigerator.

"I've been saving this for you," he told her. "For us."

He opened the bottle and brought it, bubbling, to the coffee table. Hurrying away, he returned with two glasses.

It's like a movie, Sandy thought. *The champagne, the*

glasses being there, his pouring it without spilling a drop—

"To us," Dennis said.

To which us? Sandy wondered, not wanting to think of anything but Dennis, puzzled by the intrusion of the thought. *Us now? Us back then? Us as we've been ... apart? As we could've been? Should have been—*

"What are you thinking?" she asked him, wanting him to have some answer that would make it right.

"I'm not thinking," he told her, smiling. "I'm feeling. That's all—and it's everything." Dennis took her hand, brought it to his lips, and caressed it. He never took his eyes from hers.

"Don't do that," Sandy told him, nervously giggling and bringing her free hand up to her hair, patting it.

"Don't what?"

"Look at me that way. Like I'm—I don't know. A painting... something like that."

"But you are. You are a painting. I've had a picture of you in my head all these years. So many times, Sandy. I looked at that picture and I ached for you."

When Dennis left her, when she married Bobby, she made herself forget the things she felt with him. The way his fingers both froze and burned her. The way the rest of the world melted away until there were only the two of them, alone together, frozen and suspended in a special place of their own.

She'd had to forget those old feelings in order to live with herself and with Bobby. But as Dennis held her, the feelings she'd almost forgotten came racing back over the lonely expanse of the years—so many years—she'd been without him. It was a sensation that both comforted and frightened her. She began to cry in his arms, and turned her head away from him.

"I wasn't going to cry," Sandy told him, her voice breaking. "Whatever happened, I promised myself I wasn't going to cry."

"It's all right," Dennis breathed against her cheek. His fingers stroked her hair. Cupping her chin, he gently turned her face to his, then tenderly kissed the tears from her cheeks and eyes. "Don't cry. I'll never make you cry again. I won't hurt you—"

"You said that last time," Sandy told him. The words were out of her mouth before she realized it, the combination of the champagne and her excitement making her mind move its own way, out of her control. She had wanted to be with him, in his arms, and she still did. For the life of her, she didn't know why she suddenly pulled away, walking to the window.

"Do you still hate me for that?" Dennis asked. "After all these years?"

Her hand brushed the curtain back, and Sandy gazed down at the fountain in the plaza below. In spite of the hour, the sidewalks were crowded with people on their way somewhere.

"I was hurt, Dennis. And so alone."

"I was confused," he said. "All mixed up. We both were. You understand that, don't you? We were a couple of kids. What we felt was more than kids felt—we just didn't know how to handle it."

She looked at him, slowly and sadly. "I would have done anything, Dennis. But there was nothing I could do."

He was determined to make it right. "Sandy, I've thought about it so many times. We felt *passion*. The hell with being kids! Do you have any idea of how many people go through life—their whole lives—without knowing what passion is?"

"Maybe they're better off," she answered quietly. "They can't miss what they've never had."

"But I've missed it. I've missed *you*!" he insisted. "We've both suffered enough, haven't we? And it's still there—everything I felt for you and you felt for me." He reached his hand out to her. "Come on. Let's start making up for all that lost time."

Part of her wanted to rush to him, but an image in her mind held her in place. Bobby was alone in their suite, his shoes off, a beer or a drink in his hand as he lay stretched out, watching the hockey game...

"What is it?" Dennis asked.

"I don't know," she told him, trying to force a laugh. "Isn't it crazy? I thought I'd come here, and it would be easy—"

"It will be," Dennis promised. "We'll pick up the pieces."

"Where you—where we left them, Dennis? That was twenty years ago. We both have different lives now."

"What kind of lives?" he challenged her. "The kind of lives we want?"

"The kind of lives we *have*," she answered. "Sometimes things happen that make you stop thinking about what you want. You concentrate on what you need to get along... to get through one day after another..."

"But that's just existing, Sandy. That's all we've both been doing. Don't you see? Now we have a second chance. A chance to really live!"

She wanted to believe him. Walking toward him, she remembered how her heart used to leap when she saw him. She wasn't sure if she was feeling it again or just recalling it.

"Believe me," he begged, taking her hand. She let him guide her around the sofa and settle her down beside him.

He refilled her glass. For a time, they sat together on the sofa, Sandy with her legs tucked beneath her, her head against Dennis' shoulder. Their arms were tight around each other, as if the space they shared was an island. His hands stroked her neck and back and arms, breaking contact only to refill their glasses.

"I don't want to let go of you," Dennis whispered at

last. "I couldn't stand losing you again."

He stood, taking the glass, empty now, from her hand.

"Come with me," he told her, holding his arms out. Then her hands were in his and he was helping her up. It was almost like dancing, Sandy thought—he was backing across the carpet, facing her, holding her hands. Her eyes never left his; her steps matched his own. Together they moved toward the bedroom.

"Let me," Dennis begged, stepping behind her. She felt his fingers at her neck. Her dress slid away and his lips glided over her neck and shoulders.

"Hold me," she said, turning to face him. "Just hold me for a while, okay?"

Like frozen dancers, they stood still. A wave, an ocean of emotion was raging inside her. She had to talk about it or she'd drown.

"You don't know how badly I wanted you to hold me back then," she confided, trembling. "I needed you so much I wanted to die—"

"Don't say that."

"Why not? It's true. Don't you want to hear it, Dennis?"

He kissed her forehead and brow. "Darling. Of course I do. But why dwell on the past and all that pain? Not when we have the future."

Something at the very core of her being was shaking.

"The light," she managed to say.

"All right. Whatever you want is all right." He hurriedly turned the lamp on the bedside table off. A glow from the living room framed him as he came back to her, tearing off his jacket and tie and shirt.

Sandy stroked his collarbone, rediscovering it tentatively. Then, with an urgency that totally overcame her, she buried her face in his chest, feeling the hair against her cheek, wanting to stay there forever.

He unhooked her bra, cupping her breasts, bending to kiss and lick them. His mouth moved lower, covering her stomach, then lower still as his fingers eased her pantyhose down. She felt her thighs quiver as his tongue slid over them, and she had to choke back tears for all the times it could have been—*should* have been—like this. Then his tongue was inside her, and the sensation blotted out all the other time there had ever been or would be.

Her hands held to his hair as he knelt before her: if she didn't hold on to something, she thought she would drown or float away.

She was twenty years older than she'd been the last time they made love, yet she felt like a young girl again, embarrassed and blushing. "It's going to be just the way it was, Sandy. You'll see."

He stepped out of his pants, folding them over the back of the chair. Sandy pulled the blanket and sheet back from the bed.

"I loved you so much," she told him, as he stood beside the bed.

Even in the darkness, his eyes pierced her as he looked down into her face. "You still do. And I still love you."

His hands on her breasts sent a current of desire and memory surging through her. It didn't seem possible, but it was happening... She remembered not only the way he'd looked and the things he'd said and done, but the way he'd made her feel. Now he was making her relive it all again.

It felt the same now as then, but it *had* to be different. *She* was different, Sandy knew. She'd nursed a baby, *his* baby, at her breasts—

"Sandy," he whispered, lying beside her, pulling her close. "My Sandy. You haven't changed. I knew you wouldn't. The way you feel..."

His lips and tongue caressed her nipples—one, then the other. Cradling his head, she looked down at his hair, her fingers touching the strands of silver gray. The muscles of her stomach jumped as his hand moved to her thighs.

"Remember the first time?" he whispered. "At your

apartment? On your mother's couch?"

"I remember," she answered, closing her eyes, seeing a girl in pink pedal pushers and a white blouse. As he'd done then, he took her hand and placed it on himself.

"I want you so much. There've been so many nights, Sandy. So many! I dreamed of you all these years. I knew that someday we'd be together like this again." He eased her thighs apart. "Your eyes, Sandy," he said, kissing them and sliding into her. "Your mouth..."

"Dennis," she cried, as the confusion faded and she surrendered to sensation. She held him like a young girl holding her first lover. Time slipped away as the intensity of her arousal and desire built. For a time, she was young again, not only in years but in experience. She was a girl who believed in the future, a girl who had faith in all possibilities, a girl who'd never been hurt...

Then, too soon, the time was over. She felt herself coming back as he collapsed on top of her, then rolled off to the side.

"Where are you going?" he asked, as she slid out of bed and began gathering her clothes.

"I have to get dressed, Dennis."

"But why?"

She wondered if he was teasing her again.

"I have to get back. Bobby's waiting—"

"Forget him," he said, as she began to dress.

The words had a surprising sting. *The way you forgot me?* she nearly said. But this time she was able to stop herself, to tell herself that the excitement had made her nerves shaky.

"I can't do that," she told him, straightening her dress in the full-length mirror on the bathroom door. She took a brush out of her bag and began to fix her hair.

"But you'll get away again, won't you?" he asked.

She paused, wondering why her answer made her feel strangely ashamed. "Yes. I will," she said at last.

"When? Tomorrow?"

"I can't promise, Dennis. We have to be... oh, what's the word they always say in the old movies? 'Discreet.' That's it—"

"We don't! You can leave him. Come to me. Stay with me now..."

She glanced at his reflection in the mirror. For an instant, she wanted to do as he said. Slowly Sandy shook her head. "It's not as easy as that."

"It can be," he insisted. "It used to be."

"Oh, Dennis," she sighed, wanting to stay, eager to leave. "Everything used to be so much easier."

"Twenty-one," the dealer announced, turning over a six of spades.

"Shit," Tony Merino muttered, as the stack of chips disappeared. The blonde beside him laughed tipsily.

"Never seen anything like it," she said. "But I'll get him this time. Hey—double up to catch up, isn't that right? Huh?"

"Yeah," Tony answered. "Double up to catch up." He placed five hundred-dollar chips in the rectangle. The dealer gave them their cards mechanically, offering insurance when he drew an ace.

"Sucker bet," the blonde said. Tony hesitated and passed. The dealer flipped his down card over. It was the king of diamonds.

"Goddamn it," Tony cursed.

"Never seen a thing like it," the blonde told him again.

It had to change soon, Tony thought. Either that, or he'd wake up and find he'd just been dreaming. He'd had his runs before, bad luck and good, but this wasn't luck at all—it was a curse.

The idea had seemed like a natural: arranging for the limo to drive him down to Atlantic City in style, he'd had the confidence of a winner—and forty-three hundred dollars in his pocket.

He wouldn't be greedy, he promised himself. He'd

double his money, maybe go a little more if the action was good, then head back. With a ten-grand stake in his pocket, he'd be in good shape...

The blow he'd tooted was wearing off, and his head was pounding. There was a tight ball in the center of his gut.

"Sir?"

"Oh, yeah. Hold on," Tony told the dealer, fumbling in the inside pocket of his jacket. It couldn't be, but it was: he'd gone through all the money except for six hundred bucks. Only a few hours in Atlantic City, and it was nearly all gone.

"I'm gonna make it now," he told the dealer, taking out three of the six bills.

"Quarters?" the man asked.

"No," Tony decided, feeling a spurt of confidence. His luck *had* to change.

"Three hundred," the dealer said over his shoulder to the pit boss. The blonde got a blackjack; Tony had a pair of sixes to the eight the dealer showed.

"Split 'em," he said, his fingers tapping the felt.

"Sixteen," the dealer announced, giving him a jack.

Tony scratched for another hit.

"Over," the dealer said, laying down a seven. He took the cards and three hundred dollars away.

"Jesus, not again!" Tony cursed, as a ten covered the remaining six. He waved the dealer away, deciding to stand on sixteen.

"Eighteen," the dealer said, flipping over a ten. He turned his head toward the pit boss. "Shuffle."

"A new deal'll straighten things out..."

The blonde's voice faded as Tony left the table.

He was broke, busted, wiped out—more than four grand in a couple of hours. *Why?* he wanted to know. Why had he been so sure that he was ripe for a killing? Why had he blown the only money he had in the world? *Why?* It was a question he'd asked himself countless times over the years, and as usual there was no answer.

Hoping against hope, he searched his pockets, finding a couple of crumpled singles and a few coins.

"Chump change," he told himself.

"Jackpot!" a blue-haired woman cried joyously as her slot machine lit up and rang. "I hit a jackpot!"

It's always somebody else, Tony thought, putting a quarter into a machine near hers. He pulled the handle. Three $7.50's came up on the center line, and the money rolled out. Feeling like a sucker, he put the quarters into one of the paper cups left by the machine for the purpose.

"Good for you!" the blue-haired lady said.

"Yeah, great," Tony answered. It wasn't much of a jackpot, but at least it was bus fare back to New York.

What am I doing here? Sandy asked herself, pausing at the door of the suite.

Finally, after so many years of imagining it, it had happened. She'd been with Dennis again, but instead of staying with him (Bobby wouldn't have expected her for another hour or two), she'd felt she had to come back. Now that she was back, listening to the muffled sound of the TV set, she wondered what had impelled her to return so quickly.

Guilt? That didn't make sense. It was 1978, the era of the "new morality." Back in Houston, over half the people they knew had either been divorced or were talking about it. Even their friends who were married had affairs that everyone knew about but politely ignored. Besides, it wasn't as if she'd slept with some stranger for the sake of a thrill—maybe, when she stopped and thought about it, that would be easier... simpler, anyway. An anonymous, intense hour of sex with no repercussions.

Not once in all their years together, Sandy realized in amazement, had she ever considered going to bed with any of the men she'd known or seen in Houston. She'd been faithful to Bobby, except in her memories and imagination. Even then it hadn't been with any unknown fantasy figure—there had only been Dennis...

She smoothed her hair with her hand and ran her tongue over her lips, then opened the door. "... And the score is tied with a little over eight minutes left on the official Ranger clock in this exciting third period!"

"Good game?" she asked.

"It's great. Did you have fun?"

She nodded. "That Connie can still crack me up."

For a second, Sandy panicked. What if he'd learned somehow that she wasn't with Connie? Then, as quickly as it had come, the fear subsided. He wouldn't ask. It would never in a million years occur to Bobby that she'd tell him anything but the truth.

"Did you eat?" he asked her.

"I'm not hungry. I think I'll take a bath."

He stood to kiss her cheek as she passed him. "Hey—I love you."

"Me too," she said quickly, turning away so that he wouldn't be able to see the uncertainty in her eyes.

After her bath, Sandy wondered what her husband would say if she told him the truth about where she'd been. He wouldn't get angry—probably he'd assume that she and Dennis had simply had a drink together, and ask if she'd had a nice time.

"Guess who's on the phone?" Bobby called out. "The pride of Texas A and M."

She couldn't get there fast enough. "Don't rush, honey. He'll hold on."

"Hello, dear," Sandy said, lifting the receiver. "I was just thinking of you..."

He'd seen a TV spot plugging the special, Bobby, Jr. told her. He and his friends were making up a party to watch it.

Yes, she said, they were having fun and getting a kick out of seeing the old gang. Tomorrow, they'd practice the disco number they'd worked up for the show.

"Take care of yourself," she told him. "Remember that your father and I love you very much."

It was only when she hung up the phone that Sandy realized that Bobby, Jr.'s real father hadn't even asked her if his child was alive.

5.

"MR. PALMER WILL BE WITH YOU IN A MOment, Miss Duvane," the secretary said.

"Thank you," Kay answered mechanically, wondering if the girl was bright enough to know what was going on. Being sent for on the spot like some messenger was one thing, but this time Mike Palmer had taken it a step further. Summoning her to his office and then making her wait was yet another way of trying to humiliate her. Telling herself that she'd be goddamned if she'd give the little bastard the satisfaction of getting upset, Kay smiled at the young blonde.

"Dear, would you mind buzzing Mr. Palmer? Tell him that if something more important has come up, I'll go back to my office and wait for a more convenient—"

"Hello, Kay," he said, opening the door to his private office and stepping outside. "Sorry for the delay."

"Mike. I was just telling your secretary that I could come back—"

"No, no—come in, won't you?" He stepped back, the

perfect gentleman, letting her go in first. Kay thanked him, smiling sweetly. *I've played this game before, hotshot, and with better players than you*, she thought, determined to match her adversary move for move.

"How are things going in your department?" he asked.

"Fine, thanks. Didn't you get a copy of my report?"

He cleared his throat. "Of course, of course. I've been reading all your reports with great interest. Naturally, we're looking for some big numbers next week—"

"And I think we have the specials that will deliver them," she said with assurance, refusing to be intimidated.

"Yes, we do," he agreed grudgingly. "But there is one problem."

"Oh? What's that?"

He slid a manilla folder across his desk. "It's *her*. A guest on your *Dancetime* special."

Kay saw an opportunity and seized it: he'd made it clear that he didn't like her, and there was nothing to lose by making him like her a little less. "Thank you for the compliment, Mike, but I really can't take the credit. It's Lee Dean's special, and Sheila Granger is responsible for pulling it together. Of course it's *our* special in the corporate sense—"

"But you supervised it."

"Yes, I did that."

"I'm a little surprised, frankly, that a veteran like you would let a thing like this slip by." He tapped the folder, and Kay opened it.

The clippings were familiar enough, and so were the photographs. For some weeks, Alice Lane had been getting increasing amounts of press coverage. It began with her recording of "Glad To Be A Woman." The feminist groups had wasted no time in reacting, and Alice had taken them on. There'd been statements and interviews, and then, a few weeks before, CBS had profiled Alice on *60 Minutes*.

The interview had been controversial. Not only did Alice adopt a firm anti-ERA stance, she also gave her opinions on a number of issues, opposing affirmative action hiring policies, gay rights, and a proposed increase in the California welfare system. She defended the "appropriateness" of a performer's taking hard-line political positions, and went so far as to say that she was "seriously considering" running for office in California.

The reaction to her media appearances and pronouncements was heated—she had her supporters, and she provoked the anger of those who opposed the conservative views she was increasingly coming to represent. She had arrived in New York early in the week, and pursued a busy schedule of interviews promoting Alice Lane.

Sifting through the clippings, Kay looked up at Mike Palmer with a puzzled expression on her face. "I'm afraid I don't get the point of all this."

"The point is that Alice Lane is controversial, Kay. She's trouble. I can see her on a magazine-format news program, or with Phil Donahue. What I don't see is how she fits in with an entertainment special—particularly one we're counting on so heavily."

Kay didn't miss a beat. "She fits in, Mike, because she had one of the top three hits exactly twenty years ago. That was part of the concept Lee Dean brought us—and we bought it. If you look at Alice's contract, there's a specific clause that says we're hiring her as an entertainer. She's going to sing, she's going to talk a little about the fifties, and she's *not* going to talk about politics. We're covered on that."

"On a live show, nothing is covered, Kay. You know that. There are other considerations, however. We've got to face the possibility that a lot of potential viewers are going to be turned off by the fact that Alice Lane is even *on* the special. We stand to lose a hell of lot of households—"

"That," Kay said tersely, "is a matter of opinion. Granted, some people won't watch the show because they don't like Alice. Some won't watch because they don't like Tommy Del or The Fantastiks. We're in New York, Mike, and New York isn't Alice Lane territory. I don't think the number of people who won't watch as some kind of protest will be significant. But I do think we'll pick up a lot of viewers in the midwest—and all over the country, for that matter—who think she's the greatest thing since sliced bread."

He shook his head. "It's still trouble, Kay. It's a headache—"

"Look, Mike... this thing was set months ago. *Before* she made that record and the publicity started to snowball."

"I understand that. But it airs on Sunday, and that's what matters. We've had calls, Kay—lots of them. And letters. One of the women's groups is going to picket the studio on Sunday. I'm sure the gay activists will be there, and the pro-welfare people. It's trouble."

Kay sighed. "Okay, it's not exactly a dream scene. But it's nothing we can't deal with. The picketing, when you think about it, will be good for last-minute PR for the show. Some extra security will keep it all under control—"

"If we go with Alice," he said.

"I beg your pardon."

"I said, '*If* we go with Alice.' Some people here think the best thing to do would be to cancel her out and avoid the whole problem."

The matter, Kay realized, must have been discussed at the top level, and she hadn't even been consulted. For the moment, though, she let it pass. "That would be ridiculous—and you know it! All we'd do is exchange one problem for another. I don't think I have to tell you that Alice Lane's side is a lot better organized than the opposition. You talk about letters? Dump Alice Lane, and I guarantee you the calls and the mail will be like an avalanche. Every conservative paper in the country will be out to get us—and Alice herself will have another issue to talk about. What it comes down to, Mike, is that you can't please everyone."

"No. And I don't see why we have to antagonize any segment of our audience—"

Kay's anger was mounting. "If that's the way you feel, why don't we take off all the Anita Bryant commercials? Let's not rerun any of the old John Wayne pictures, and of course we'll have to forget about Jane Fonda and Vanessa Redgrave, too. Maybe we can get some cartoons from children's programming and run them in prime time: that way, we'll avoid controversial themes—"

"Kay, come on! What the hell are you getting so worked up for?"

She stood, her body tense. "Why? Because I've been through this song and dance one time too many! I'm supposed to come up with specials that are interesting, but not so interesting that anyone will be offended. I've learned to live with that one, and I've passed on some damn good ideas. But here's a special that's pure entertainment, that tugs at the heart, and now you're as much as telling me that my ass is in a sling because Alice Lane decides to shoot her mouth off!"

"Kay, Kay! You're overreacting. Personally, I agree with you. I think it would be a mistake to drop Alice. We're married to her, for better or for worse. I'm simply saying that there's some concern, and that I feel you should be aware of it for your own good."

"Thanks. I'll keep that in mind," she snapped, hurrying toward the door. Abruptly, she turned. "But you tell me about it on Monday morning, Mike. Wait till the overnights are in, and then we'll see just how much concern there is!"

Seething, she rushed to her office, ignoring the sheaf of phone messages her secretary held out.

"Damn him!" Kay said aloud, once she slammed the door. Who did Mike Palmer think he was? Why the hell was he out to get her? She was no threat to him. He didn't have to like her, Kay thought, but once the final numbers were in on the sweep, he'd at least have to respect her. She tried to think of the pleasure she'd feel when he was forced to compliment her on the lineup of specials TBS would be running during the Nielsen sweep. The local affiliates had prescreened a sampling of the programming and the response had been tremendous. Wait till the numbers were in...

Then the tiny pinprick of satisfaction she felt vanished. There were no guarantees. She knew that. The quality of the programming was only one factor. Just like TBS, the other networks were loading their schedules with specials and movies. The competition would be keen.

"And what do you get if you win?" Kay said to nobody in particular. At best, if the numbers were right, she'd get a reprieve. She'd be safe and secure again, but only until the next time. If Mike Palmer didn't go after her, someone like him would—someone waiting for a chance to clean house and bring in his own people. Even if she managed to survive the next several generations of men like Mike, the only thing she could look forward to for all her troubles was a pension.

I'll be one of those sad little ladies living on the memory of the good old days, she thought. She'd seen them, trotted out every now and again and hailed as "dedicated pioneers" of the industry. They were honored at luncheons (more for still being alive than anything else—except perhaps a chance for everyone in the room to feel like a do-gooder). Then, when the luncheons were over, they were shepherded back to their little studio apartments. One day, you looked on the obituary page of the *Times*, and learned that they'd died alone "at home."

Maybe not! Kay thought. *Maybe it doesn't have to be that way for me!*

The last thing she had expected was a rekindled romance with Lee, but it had happened. And this time, *this time*, she knew so much more. He hadn't yet asked her to marry him, as he'd done years before, but if she gave him the slightest hint, the least bit of encouragement—

"Yes?" Kay barked, annoyed at the ringing of the intercom.

"I'm sorry to disturb you, Miss Duvane, but it's Mr. Dean—"

"Fine. Thank you." Her spirits soared. She'd just been thinking about him. It had to be a sign. He'd ask her, and she'd accept. She'd get out while the getting was good, stopping only long enough to tell Mike Palmer where he could put his copy of the latest Nielsen survey...

"Lee! How are you?" she asked. They'd been together the night before—it was only a matter of hours since she'd seen him.

"I'm terrific, Kay. I've been trying to get you. Guess who I had lunch with today?"

"Jackie Onassis?" she teased.

"No. Nat Gallin—"

"Is he still upset about your getting the commitment from Sylvia behind his back?"

"He didn't even mention it. He wanted to talk about something else. He had a couple of calls—I guess people must remember that he used to handle me way back when—and there's an offer for me to take a 1950's show out. Not the tank towns this time around, Kay, but London for starters. Then Europe, Japan, and Australia, of course—isn't it great? Of course it's just in the talk stage, but look at how well *Beatlemania* has done..."

Kay sank into her chair, feeling every bit her age and then some. *I've been thinking of making a home, a life with him, and he's thinking of leaving.*

"Are you there, Kay?" he asked. "It's like a second chance."

"Yes, a second chance," she said in a monotone. "I'm thrilled for you."

"I knew you would be. You're a real sport. We'll celebrate later. I'll fill you in on all the details. I've got to get back to the rehearsal now. 'Bye!"

"Good-bye," Kay Duvane said, slowly replacing the receiver. *Second chances*, she thought: *it was a shame there weren't enough of the damn things to go around.*

"Here," Tommy said, ceremoniously handing her the brown paper bag. "It's a naive little tuna salad on rye, but I think its presumption will amuse you. The guy at the deli swore it was fresh, but he didn't say when." He leaned across the row of seats to kiss her cheek, and to his surprise Sheila clung to him.

"I'm sorry about this morning—" she began, but he leaped over the seats, silencing her.

"Forget it. Eat. Lady producers have to eat, you know."

Smiling, Sheila took the sandwich out of the bag, along with the container of milk. Her stomach had been acting up, and when she'd gone to the doctor at Tommy's insistence, he talked about incipient ulcers and put her on a bland diet.

"I thought the producer was supposed to make sure the stars ate," she said, taking a bite. "Did you eat, Tommy?"

He nodded. "On the way over. Two greasy eggs."

"I should have fixed breakfast for you," she apologized. "I was such a dragon—"

"Sheila, come on. You've got a million and one things on your mind. I understand, really."

"That's good," she said. "Because I don't."

Admitting it, after all she'd put him through, was the least she could do. That he was so patient was a source of amazement to Sheila. More and more, particularly this final week before the show, she found herself short-tempered. It wasn't just the sound of her own voice snapping at someone that bothered her. She hadn't dared to admit it to anyone, not even Tommy, but the most frightening thing was that she felt she'd been cast in some play or movie she'd seen before.

From the start of her career, she'd loathed the way some producers treated the staffs of their shows—like dirt. She'd wondered why people—talented artists and technicians let such men and women demean them. The money was part of it, she realized, and then too, there was the matter of credits. Being associated with a hit show or special helped you advance to other good jobs when that one was over: you had to swallow your pride, at times, to be able to afford success.

I'll never be like that, Sheila had vowed. It seemed like ages ago instead of a few years, and in spite of her promise to herself, she found herself turning into the very thing she loathed. The puzzling part of it all was that nobody called her on it. If she'd been rude and abrupt back when she was only Kay Duvane's assistant, the complaints would have come in fast and furiously.

But with her new stature, everyone acted as if her rudeness was acceptable, even normal. Only that morning, there'd been a squabble about a mixup of some of the stills that would be used on the show. After a few moments of listening to buck-passing, her nerves had snapped.

"I don't care who misplaced them!" she'd said. "Find them, and get this silly mess straightened out."

"Lady producers," someone said, loud enough so Sheila heard it as she left—though she pretended not to.

The unions were encouraging women to pursue technical jobs that had traditionally been all male: still, most of the women who responded were young and inexperienced. It would be years before they really competed with men, in spite of the policy directives from personnel that said women were to be "significantly represented" in the production of all TBS programs. The special was staffed technically by men who had, for the most part, years of experience and impressive credits. They were polite (some of them grudgingly so) but at times Sheila felt that they resented her not so much for being young as for being female.

Magazines devoted countless articles to the question of whether it was possible to be a "person" on the job and a "woman" in personal life. Nearly all of them assured the readers that it was—the lawyers, doctors, and corporate executives used as case histories found it relatively easy.

But for Sheila, it was different.

At Tommy's place in Agawam, she was able to turn off part of her mind, the part that was involved with her job, and the tension that went with it. Cooking meals, playing with Jessica, working or relaxing around the house... they were unexpected pleasures. She assumed, when Tommy came to town for weekends, that it would be the same in Manhattan. She was lucky, she told herself, that she had a chance to enjoy the best of both her worlds.

But again and again, she caught herself ordering Tommy around the apartment as if he was a servant instead of the man she loved and a guest. She'd apologize quickly and profusely, and rush to do whatever task or chore she'd asked him to do. He didn't mind helping—he enjoyed doing things for her, he said—and he treated her little outbursts as a joke, in an effort to make things easier for her. But if he was able to ignore them (only that morning she'd snapped that she didn't have time to "waste" making him breakfast, when all he'd asked for was a cup of coffee), she couldn't.

She liked having him with her: the pressure of the week was so hectic that she needed comforting and coddling at the end of the day. Part of her, some stubborn part she didn't understand, refused to accept the very things she wanted most. Was she trying to scare him off, Sheila wondered? Was there some self-destructive monster inside her, hellbent on destroying the happiness they'd found?

"Earth to Sheila," Tommy said, mimicking *Star Trek*, pulling her away from her thoughts and back to him.

"I'm sorry."

He squeezed her hand. "Don't be. You're too pretty."

"I'll be sorry when the show is over, Tommy," she told him, surprising herself. "When you go back for good, that is. I've been so horrid you'll probably be glad—"

"No," he told her, not smiling any longer. "I'm not looking forward to it at all. It'll be like I feel when you leave the house on Sundays and come down here. Worse, really, because the more time we spend together, the more I love you. Sheila? Maybe neither of us has to be sorry. Not if you come with me."

Holding his hand, she closed her eyes. The easy, unpressured atmosphere of the house he lived in struck her as a luxury. It tempted her, but she wasn't sure if she could afford it... not at the expense of everything she'd worked so hard for. But she told herself she finally *had* what she'd been working for, and somehow it wasn't enough.

"I'll think about it," she said. His quick kiss surprised her. "What was that for?"

"For luck. I think I'm making progress."

> ...*A love that's right*
> *Won't last for just a night.*
> *It's a symphony, not a song...*
> *And I'll know from the start,*
> *Yes, I'll know in my heart,*
> *When the right kind of love comes along.*

She held the last note, and with it the sincere, reverent half-smile, as the strings coming from the pre-recorded tape gave her a big finish.

"Brother!" some man snickered, but if Alice Lane heard him, she gave no indication.

"Lovely. That was very nice, Alice," the director said, hurrying toward her. "We'll pick you up right here and do the number, then we'll go into a commercial."

"Lee?" he called, looking across the stage to the podium and bleachers, "When we come back, you and Alice will be in the first row over there." He motioned for someone to take the mike Alice was still holding, then guided her across the set. "Now, the interviews are going to be nice and nostaligic...lots of warmth is what we want. Memories of the fifties, what it felt like when you had your first hit, when you did *Dancetime*. That kind of thing."

Out of the corner of his eye, the director glanced at Sheila, who was sitting in the first row of seats, listening intently. The mood in the studio, on the surface at least, was calm, but beneath it the tension was almost electric. Alice Lane, everyone knew, had to be handled with kid gloves.

"I see what you mean," Alice replied sweetly.

"Of course we'll want the interviews to sound spontaneous, but we'd like to run through it if you don't mind, just to get a check on the time..."

"That would be fine," she answered. "I have a pretty good idea of what I'm going to say."

"You do?" the director asked, knowing he was showing his nervousness, then trying to recover. "That's great— fine. Let's go through it then, okay?"

"You did a nice job with the number, Alice," Lee said as the director positioned them.

"Why, thank you, Lee—"

"Okay," the director told them. "We're coming back in five, four, three..."

"'The Right Kind of Love'," Lee Dean said. His face filled the monitor. As he spoke, the camera pulled back, revealing the album cover he was holding.

"Oh, no!" Alice laughed.

Lee smiled. "Remember the girl in this picture?" he asked. The camera came in close for a shot of the cover photograph—a teenage Alice Lane. She was dressed in a blue felt circle skirt with a pink appliquéd poodle. A white cardigan was fastened over her shoulders with a sweater clip, and she was smiling.

"Just barely," Alice told him. "But I do remember a girl who looked like her and was very nervous about singing on *Dancetime, USA!*."

"Really? Why was that, Alice?"

"Well, Lee, on most of the other television shows, the variety programs, I was the youngest performer. There'd be comedians, jugglers, and a Perry Como or Bing Crosby or someone who'd had years of experience in the business. A young performer was safe—the atmosphere was 'give the little girl a big hand.'"

"And here?" Lee asked.

"On *Dancetime*, you were performing for an audience of your peers. I was terrified!" She laughed.

"But you came out, did that song and, as I remember it, 'The Right Kind of Love' was the number-three hit in the country twenty years ago this week."

"Yes, Lee, it was."

"Hey, tell me—we hear a lot of talk about nostalgia today. All of a sudden, the 1950's are 'the good old days,' do you remember them that way?"

Alice paused. "I do. But I think that whatever period you grow up in looks good in hindsight. When we look at the fifties, those of us who were teenagers back then, we're remembering a way of feeling as much as the time itself."

The director gave Lee the signal to wind it up.

"That's a good point, Alice. Gee, I'm glad you could be with us tonight—"

"My pleasure."

"We're going to have lots more looking back at the good old days," he said, facing the cameras. "With Alice

Lane, Tommy Del, and The Fantastiks—right after these words. Stay with us."

The director took Alice's hand, pumping it in relief. "Great," he said. "That was beautiful. Do it just like that on Sunday night, and we'll be fine."

"Thank you," she said. "Will you be needing me any more today?"

"No, no, that's fine."

Alice nodded and turned to Lee. "I've got an appointment. Good luck with everything, Lee."

"Thanks. You're going to be great on the show, Alice."

She waved and walked across the set toward the stage door, and the waiting limousine.

It had been easy to fool them, she thought, as the driver pulled away from the curb. They'd been waiting for her to say the wrong thing, probably looking for an excuse to get rid of her. Playing it their way had been a good idea.

But the special itself would be different. For weeks, the publicity and press coverage had been building—and she had no intention of letting it stop. Her agent had told her that the network was worried about protesters picketing the studio. If she came on the *Dancetime* special and simply sang a song and said a few words about the good old days, it would look as if she'd backed down, bowed to the pressure.

Besides, it would mean blowing what just might be the biggest PR opportunity of them all. And that, Alice Lane told herself, was the very last thing she intended to do.

6.

"TRY TO RELAX, WILL YOU?" CARL ASKED.

Connie stared at her husband. "Relax? How can I relax? Jimmy's in the hospital, and you tell me to relax?"

He was pulling his shoes on, seated at the edge of the bed, but he got up and went to her.

"He's not *in* the hospital—he's at the hospital. You heard what happened, Connie. He was climbing a tree and he fell. It happens to kids all the time."

"Not my kids. Not *ours*. I'm going with you, Carl—"

"You can't. It's Sunday, remember? You have to be at the studio in a couple of hours. I'll call you from the hospital, I promise. Right from the emergency room."

"And you'll tell me the truth?"

"Don't I always?" he asked.

"Oh, I hope he's all right," she said, clinging to her husband.

"He'll be okay. I'm sure of it. I'll probably be back before you even leave." Kissing her, he started for the door.

"You'll call me? I'll be right here—"

"I'll call you the minute I see what's going on," he told her again. "You relax. And if I'm not back, I'll meet you at the studio."

She nodded, and he was gone.

There was no point in even thinking of going back to bed, Connie knew. The call from her daughter had shattered any thoughts she had about a leisurely Sunday morning breakfast in bed with Carl. She was probably overreacting, she knew: Carl was right. Kids fell out of trees all the time, and it wasn't as if Jimmy had been unconscious. But a mother, she told herself, is a mother—and worrying was part of motherhood.

All week long, she'd had the feeling in the back of her mind that something was going to happen... Getting together with the old gang, she'd thought—until it actually happened, would be a lot of laughs. But the laughs were strained somehow, and after the initial greetings, there'd been surprisingly little left for them to say to one another. Bobby and Sandy had kept to themselves for the past few days; maybe, she thought, they were making the most of the trip and the hotel. Dennis had been aloof, just like he'd been in the old days. Cathy... well, who could figure out her problem? Whatever it was, those pills she kept taking when she thought nobody was looking didn't help—she was "spaced out," as the kids would say. Don was as handsome and pleasant as he'd been twenty years ago, but pretty much of a loner, preferring to spend most of his free time with that friend of his...

So what did I expect?, Connie asked herself, trying not to think of her son's injury. They had never really been the kind of friends that the kids who watched *Dancetime* thought they were. Sure, they posed for the magazines as if they were the best of buddies, but about the only thing they had in common was being on the show. She'd known it back then, but it hadn't struck her as important. Over the years, with the old clippings to trigger her memory, she'd almost forgotten it. The past week, in its way, had been a sharp reminder—

Jimmy! she thought, grabbing the telephone before it could ring a second time. *Something had happened at the hospital...*

"Hello?"

"Connie? Where are you two?"

It took her a moment to place the voice as Tony's, and another few seconds to remember that they'd mentioned something about getting together for a Bloody Mary that morning.

"Oh hi, Tony. I'm all screwed up. We got a call from home. One of the kids had an accident. Carl went to the emergency room—"

"Is it serious?"

She sighed. "Probably not as serious as I'm making it. He was climbing a tree and he fell. Hurt his arm. Carl's going to call me as soon as he sees what's happening. I'm supposed to 'relax,' pardon the expression."

"Want to have a drink? That'll help."

"I don't want to leave the room, Tony. I'm waiting for the call—"

"I'll be right there," he said, hanging up.

Five minutes later, giving her just enough time to brush her hair and put a robe over her "silk-look" pajamas, there was a knock on the door. She opened it, and doubled over laughing. "No! It isn't true," Connie said, barely able to get the words out. "This can't be happening."

"It is," Tony assured her, wheeling a huge serving cart into the room. It was loaded with serving dishes, and he ceremoniously uncovered them. "Scrambled eggs and bacon, courtesy of the friendly folks in 804—"

"What friendly folks?" Connie asked.

He shrugged. "I stole the food from outside their door. Think I stayed around long enough to get acquainted?"

"You're too much—"

"Let's see what else we got. One pitcher of orange juice from that nice couple in 723...one bottle of ginger ale...four tomato juices...toast—"

"Stop, I'm going to get sick!" she begged him.

"And one bottle of vodka, courtesy of—"

"Don't tell me—tell your priest," she said, laughing. "Oh, Tony, thanks. I needed a joke."

"Who's joking? Want to eat or drink?"

"A drink sounds good. A screwdriver."

"Here's a little shortcut I learned," he announced, opening the bottle of vodka and pouring a third of it into the pitcher. "They're easier by the bunch."

"What'll we drink to?" she asked, as he handed her a glass. "The good old days?"

"Sure, the good old days," he said. He finished the drink in a single swallow and poured himself another.

"Yuck!" she said, making a face. "I could feel that. Isn't it a little early in the day to be knocking them back?"

"Nope. Not too early for me, anyway. I've been up most of the night."

"Why?"

He didn't take a seat, but walked back and forth. "I dunno. The jitters, I guess. You, doing the show—"

"The jitters? You? Come on, Tony! You're not the type."

He drained his glass and poured another refill. "Sure I am," he said, totally without the forced joviality of a few moments before. "You know it, Connie. I guess you kind of always did."

"Think you're special? We all had the jitters about being Regulars back then. You should have seen what went on in the girls' dressing room. It was better than the show."

"Yeah? I wonder if the other guys felt like I did. They never let on."

"Guys never let on about things like that—at least they never used to."

He stared at her so hard and long that Connie felt

uncomfortable. "I did," he said at last. "Remember? Remember how I used to talk your head off? You used to be so good about that. You'd listen and listen, and then you'd act like it never happened at all."

"Everybody needs someone to listen, Tony. I suppose I was just the one you opened up to—"

"*Just? Just?* Hey, I was crazy about you. Not in the usual way—but don't think for a minute it didn't cross my mind. You were special, Connie. Different from the rest of them. I used to say to myself, 'Hey, jerk, what're you messing around with a bunch of bimbos for when you could be with Connie?' I'd think about asking you to go out."

"Why didn't you?"

He shrugged and went back for another screwdriver. "I was afraid you'd turn me down. At first, anyway. Then, by the time I had the nerve, we were more like . . . I loved you like a sister or something. Know what I mean?"

She nodded, smiling. "I do, and it's nice to hear. And for the record, Tony, it's good to see you again. Looking so good, dressed so sharp, doing well . . . you're a real . . ."

His hands were trembling. He turned away so she wouldn't see it, but it was too late.

"What is it?" Connie asked, tugging at his sleeve. "Tony, what's wrong?"

"It's me!" he cried. "*I'm* wrong. Me—the one who everybody said was gonna go all the way. The sure winner! The guy with all the chances. I had 'em, Connie. More than I deserved, maybe. And I blew 'em all. Every fuckin' one—"

"No," she said gently, as if she were speaking to one of her children, comforting him after a bad dream. She made Tony turn to face her. "Don't say that. It's not that bad—"

"It's worse. I'm a fake! A washout. This suit came off a hot check. I don't have a goddamn dime, and I don't know where the hell I'm gonna go after this thing is over." He tried not to cry, but couldn't stop himself. "I'm—I'm scared, Connie!

"I dunno what I used to think. Maybe that I'd be a kid forever, or like a kid. That it was all good times. Now, it's like I wake up, and I know all that time is gone. Too much time is gone. I got nothin', and I'm so goddamn scared—"

Her arms opened, and he cried on her shoulder, his body shaking. "That's it," she encouraged him softly. "Get it out of your system, Tony. It's the only way." Slowly, he began to steady himself; the wild sobbing became more controlled. Connie led him to a chair, and he offered no resistance.

"Don't you see?" he asked. "I'm never gonna get it out. It's me. It's what I am. A waste and a fuckup."

For his sake, she'd tried to be strong, but it was too heart-rending. "I'm—I'll get a washcloth," she said, rushing to the bathroom. She turned the cold water on full blast and leaned her forehead against the cool tiles. She had actually prayed in church that Tony had changed. She'd longed to see him make something of himself. All week, she'd been careful not to take more than a quick look, careful not to ask too many questions. He had the clothes and the cool—if it was still the same Tony playing the same old part, she didn't want to know. But now the image had finally crumbled, and the truth and the tragedy were there, naked and unavoidable.

There has to be something, she thought, soaking the cloth and wringing it out, trying to stop her own tears. *Dear God, please! Let me find something to say, something to give him!*

"Look what you did," she said, wiping her eyes as she came back into the room. "Talking about the old days got my waterworks started." He tried to push her hand away as she pressed the cloth to his forehead. "Come on, it'll feel good. Take my word."

"I'm doing it again, huh?" he asked, embarrassed. "Laying my shit on you, making you listen and cry—"

"Is that so? Well, listen, bigshot," she said, summoning the last of her false bravado, "who told you I was crying for you? I happen to be crying for myself."

There were tremors in her voice as she grabbed his hand. Connie knelt on the carpet, leaning against his chair.

"Know what made me cry, Tony?" she asked softly. "More of those memories. Memories... boy, they're something, huh? I was thinking, there in the bathroom, about what it used to be like. Not what we wore or did, even, but what it really *felt* like. And what I remember most is how proud I used to be dancing with you—"

"Huh?"

"Yup," she said, chuckling through her own tears. "You heard me. I was so proud to be your partner, I could've burst. You were the best, Tony. The very best. Dennis, Don, Hank, even Bobby—there wasn't one of them that even came close."

They looked in each other's eyes, as if searching for something that had happened a long, long time ago.

"When I look at you, Tony, that's what I see. That's what I'll always see. Tonight on the show, make me feel that way again. Feel the way you used to feel back then. Try. Be the best you can be, Tony—what the hell else can we do?"

He tried to say something, but the words wouldn't come. Then he tried again. "You never lost it, lady. You always had class. You always knew how to make a guy feel good..."

The jarring sound of the phone broke the mood. Connie ran to it.

"Carl? How is he?... Really? You're not leaving anything out? Yes—yes, put him on. Jimmy? Honey, are you all right? Are you sure?... What do you mean, 'upset?' Who's upset? Just because you're dumb enough to fall out of a tree, you think I'm going to get upset? Gimme Daddy... Okay, right, take him home and I'll meet you back here or over at the studio. I love you too, Carl. Hey, kiss the kids! Tell them I'll call them after the show, when I'm a big TV star." Hanging up, she gave a silent prayer of thanks, then she smiled at Tony. "See the way life is? Sometimes you think a part of you—or a part of somebody you love so much it's the same as a part of you—is broken. Sometimes it is, Tony. But there are times when it turns out like it just did with that kid of mine. Though it hurts like hell... it's only a bad sprain."

The day before, she told Bobby she wanted to treat herself to a facial, and the day before that, she used shopping as an excuse. This morning, though, there was no need to invent a convenient out—Bobby had wanted to go to mass at his old parish in Brooklyn, and to have an look at the old neighborhood.

"Wonderful!" Dennis exclaimed, when she called after Bobby left. "We'll have breakfast."

As she dressed and put her makeup on, the romance of it had caught her, reminding her of the way she felt when she was a teenager, sneaking out of the apartment on a pretext to meet Dennis and make love.

Once they were together, though, the excitement, like her appetite, faded. Instead, she found herself strangely uncomfortable.

"What's wrong?" Dennis asked, watching as she listlessly pushed the food around her plate. "Don't you like your eggs?"

"I'm not as hungry as I thought I was. Sorry."

He laughed easily. "You were always like that, you know—when we went out, I had to coax you to eat. I'm going to have to keep an eye on you."

"What?"

Reaching across the table, he took her hand. "I said, 'I'm going to have to keep an eye on you—from now on.'"

She looked into his eyes, searching for an answer that wasn't there.

"How are you going to do that?" she asked him. "The show is tonight. I'm going home tomorrow."

"We'll work it out—you'll see. We can get together on

weekends. I'll send you plane tickets. You can come up for a week every now and then. Say you want to shop or visit friends or something."

She shook her head. "There's very good shopping in Houston. My friends—our friends—are mostly there. And there are the classes I teach at the studio. I can't just leave."

He laughed again, walking behind her chair to kiss her neck. "None of that matters, don't you see? We'll work it out."

"It *does* matter," she protested softly. "It's my life, Dennis..."

If he heard her, he gave no sign.

"Kiss me," he said, and she did because it was the easiest thing to do.

"I love you. I love you so much." He was hard—she could feel him through his pants. "Let me make love to you," Dennis whispered, kissing her as he spoke. Sandy let him lead her into the bedroom.

It had been the same since the first night, she realized as she undressed. They talked, but she had the feeling that they were speaking different languages. He heard the things she said, the words, but he acted as if their meaning wasn't important.

"Doesn't that feel good?" Dennis asked, positioning himself behind her and cupping a breast in each hand.

She had to admit that it did. The passion and sensation were still there. As he'd done so many years before, he was able to excite her in ways no other man could...

"What is it?" he asked, amused at her sudden spurt of laughter.

"It's me," she said. "I was just thinking of something. I've only know two men in my life—you and Bobby. Isn't that funny... the way things work out, I mean?" He didn't answer, but kept massaging and squeezing her breasts. "Dennis, have you had a lot of women?"

"Why do you ask?" He sounded annoyed.

"Because I'd like to know."

"There've been some these past few years. But nobody as important as you. There's never been anyone I loved the way I love you—"

"There's your wife," she said, turning to face him.

"She doesn't matter. Nothing matters now except our being together. My Sandy, with the soft skin and the streak in her hair—"

"Dennis, for God's sake, look at me!" she told him, suddenly annoyed.

"What is it? What's wrong?"

"Can't you see?" She raised the window shades, then stood in the light. "Look at me! I haven't had that damn streak in my hair for twenty years."

He chuckled nervously as he came toward her. "It doesn't matter, does it? It's because you haven't changed—you look the same to me. You're still my girl. And this time we won't hurt each other..." He reached to embrace her, but Sandy pulled back.

"Listen to yourself! For God's sake, *hear* what you're saying. We *have* changed, both of us. I'm not a girl any more. I'm a woman...a wife. And hurt *each other*? You were the one who hurt me, Dennis. The only thing I did was love you—and believe you."

"But we'll make it different this time. I promise."

"No," she said, shaking her head slowly. "Our time is almost over. I'll be going home—"

"You belong with me!"

She looked at Dennis without answering for a time. "I thought I did, once," she said at last.

"You still do! It doesn't have to be over! I'll—I'll get a divorce from Buffie. We'll get married..."

Sandy felt the tears gliding down her cheeks.

"Why are you crying?" Dennis asked.

"Because things have all turned around. You sound like I sounded...back then. Remember? I was going to decorate a house and cook for you. I was going to come and see you at school on weekends. Everything was going to work out—"

"Why do you have to keep going back to all that?" he asked, anger in his voice. "That's the past. This is now!"

"But all we have now *is* the past."

"What do you mean? I still make you feel good, don't I?"

"You do," she said, because it was true.

"Well then, what is it?"

"It's only that... feeling good—sex—isn't enough."

"It used to be!" His face showed the hurt he felt.

"Maybe it did, Dennis. When you're a kid, so many things are different. How something feels, moment to moment—those are the things that count."

"It doesn't have to be different—"

"It does. It *is* different! What happens in bed, no matter how good it is, is only a little piece of time out of a day. I don't know. Maybe it's different for a man... for some men, anyway. But talking, *really* talking... listening to each other and caring. Even knowing how somebody feels when they don't talk. Those are the things that count."

"I wouldn't know about that," he said, spitting the words out. "Unfortunately, I never enjoyed that kind of relationship."

In spite of his tone, his words touched her. "I'm sorry for you." She stroked his face, or started to, but he pulled away.

"I don't want your pity, damn it. I want you!"

"No," she said gently. "You want what you remember—me, the way I was. The girl with the streak in her hair. She's gone, Dennis. She's been gone a long, long time." For the first time, she seemed to notice his age.

"But you—I thought you wanted the same thing."

"I did. I wanted to feel... well, young again. In love with you, the way I was."

He looked hurt, stricken. "And you didn't? Not at all?"

She smiled "I did. When we went to bed, it was like the

old times. *Like* them, Dennis." She picked up her clothes and began to dress.

"Then why can't we have that? Why are you leaving?"

"Because I need other things. And because what it costs to feel that way is too expensive. It's this whole week—this reunion. It stirs around memories and gets everything all mixed up. I have a life, a better one than I thought I did. Now, I have to get back to it."

"What are you going to do? Tell Bobby everything? Ask for his forgiveness?"

"No. Not that I wouldn't like to have it. But what good would telling him do? It would only hurt him. I'm the one who went to bed with you, and I'm a grownup. If anybody's going to forgive me, I guess I'll have to forgive myself."

He watched silently as she finished dressing, and at first he didn't even follow as she went to the door. Then, when her hand was on the knob, he called her name.

"Sandy!" he stopped a few feet away from her. "Is this how it ends? Are you saying it's over?"

"Oh, Dennis, don't you see? It was over a long, long time ago."

"How about this one, huh?" Al Hartley asked, beaming with pride. "You look great, honey. My little girl, looking like a million bucks!"

With a pair of scissors, he carefully snipped the article out of the newspaper, tossing the Sunday News to the floor.

"Hey, here's another one," he told her. "Look at this!"

Cathy tried to smile, but she couldn't. The moment the stack of Sunday papers—not just the New York papers, but the out-of-town ones as well—had been sent up by the TBS publicity department, Al had gone to work. The pictures and articles thrilled him, but Cathy only pretended to look at them.

The sight of herself "then and now" was too painful,

too final. It was a matter of record now, there for everyone to see: she was old, *old*...

"I'm so proud of you, Cathy," Al was saying. "My little girl on a TV special and in the papers. Wow!"

He didn't mean it, she knew. He was only being nice, trying to make her feel good. He could see the terrible changes and so could everyone else—she was old and dried up, inside and out. The special would let everyone see it. They'd all know and laugh at her. Even the other Regulars knew it: they tried to hide it, but they hadn't fooled her. She'd seen them looking at her with pity in their eyes, searching for the girl who'd once been so beautiful.

Al cut out another picture and looked at his watch. "Almost time to leave," he told her. "Better hurry and get ready, sweetheart. I'm going to call home, I want to make sure everyone watches you—"

"I won't do it," she said.

"What did you say?"

She swallowed hard: the pills had made her mouth dry. "I'm not doing the special," she repeated.

"Huh?" His amazement turned to laughter. "Oh, I get it. You're kidding me—"

"No."

"Come on, sweetheart. You're joking. You know how proud I'm going to be to see my little girl—"

"I'm not your little girl!" The fear and anger pent up inside her was exploding. "I'm old. I'm ugly!" she wailed.

He froze, stunned by her outburst. Then he tried to calm her, holding her in his arms. "What is it, honey? What's the matter? Tell me—"

"You know!" she cried, breaking away. She couldn't stand for him to pretend any longer. "You can see it. Everybody can see it. I'm old..."

Slowly, treating her as if she were a crazed animal that had to be approached with caution, he tried to move closer. "Come on. You're tense, that's all. Who wouldn't be? Going on TV—"

"I'm not! I won't, I won't!"

"Sure you will, honey. It'll be fun. We've been looking forward to this for months, remember? Your friends—"

"They're not my friends! They... they feel sorry for me. Just like you do. I won't let everybody see me like this! I won't..."

Her purse was on the dresser. Grabbing it, she fumbled for the bottle of pills.

"Hey, Cathy... look, I'll call someone. That Sheila Granger. You can talk to her. Or Lee, huh?"

She whirled on him, panic etched in her face. "You can't make me! Nobody can make me!"

"Okay, it's all right," he said, moving toward her again.

But it wasn't, she knew. She couldn't trust him—not even Al. He lied to her. He told her she was beautiful. Al and all of them wanted to trick and hurt her. She backed away toward the bathroom. They'd try to trick her into going on the show and making a fool of herself. Even if Al promised to take her home, she couldn't believe him. He wanted to make her go to the studio, where there would be lights and cameras, and everyone would see...

"Come on," Al pleaded. "Whatever you say, honey. We'll call a doctor, how about that? We'll go home right now—"

See? She knew he'd say that. The voice inside her was getting louder and louder. Now it was hurting her ears. She held the pills so tightly the edge of the bottle cut into her skin, but she didn't feel the pain. *The pills,* the voice said. *If you take the pills, you won't have to do it. They won't be able to make you do it...*

"The bottle," Al was saying. "Give it to me, Cathy. We'll forget the whole thing." His hand reached out, just a few feet away from her. "Give me the bottle, Cathy—"

"No," she whispered, shaking her head. *If you give him*

the pills, he'll make you do it. And they'll see you. They'll all see you...

"Cathy!" he lunged for her, but she was quicker, pulling away. Once in the bathroom, she slammed the door and quickly turned the lock.

"Cathy!" She heard him say over and over, pounding on the door. But as if she were in a trance, she slowly turned on the water in the tub. Then, carefully placing the pills on the edge of the sink, she looked into the mirror and smiled...

Through the film of steamy mist, she was beautiful again.

7.

"...IN THE BATHROOM! PLEASE! DO SOMEthing. Say something to her. You and Sandy, you're friends."

"I'll try, Al," Connie told him, still trying to make sense out of what was going on. She'd been dressed and waiting, hoping that Carl would get back in time to go to the studio with her, when Al found her.

"Please!" he begged her.

"Al, I called Sandy's room, but there was no answer. They must have left already. Maybe you should call a doctor."

"Doctor? But she's not sick—"

"She's been out of it all week long. She's been taking those pills she carries around like they're going out of style... But never mind that now." She motioned for him to sit down and went to the bathroom door.

"Cathy? It's me, Connie." There was no answer. "Cathy? Please let me in, just for a minute. I'm alone—I swear to God I am. I just want to talk to you."

A muffled voice answered. "You're tricking me."

Thank God, Connie thought. "No. I want to talk. Like the old days, remember? No boys allowed. Open up, then we'll both be inside and we can close the door again. Come on... please? For old time's sake?"

There was the sound of the lock being turned. Slowly, Connie turned the knob.

"Boy, is it hot!" She fanned her hand in front of her face, forcing a false lightness into her voice. "See, I'm locking the door."

The woman seated on the edge of the tub didn't answer. Connie turned from her stare to look at the bottle of pills on the sink. In a flash, Cathy reached out and grabbed it, holding the bottle tight to her as if it was a precious gem.

"What did you do that for?" Connie asked.

"You—you wanted to take them away."

"No, no, I didn't. But you don't need any more pills, Cathy."

"I do!"

"Why? You can tell me, can't you?"

"You know already! You can see it! I'm old!"

Connie ignored the twinge in her heart and made herself laugh. "Old? *That's* what's wrong with you? Well, welcome to the club."

"But you don't understand," Cathy told her, "It's different for you."

"Is it?"

"You—you don't care. It doesn't matter to you. It never did."

"That's what *you* think!" Connie said. "I remember being so jealous of Lorraine I could have killed her. That hair of hers was so straight and soft, and I was stuck with Brillo. Hey, remember the time we ironed my hair? That terrible smell? My mother thought we were burning the house up!"

Cathy nodded, not smiling, but relaxing her face a bit.

"And you! If you hadn't been so nice, I could have

hated you. You looked just like the girls in the magazine ads. The worst thing was, you never had a pimple. It wasn't fair."

Sighing, Cathy looked at her wistfully. "You could always do that. Make jokes..."

"What else can you do? It's better than dwelling on things you can't change. Laugh, and the time goes by. Cry, and it's the same old thing."

Cathy leaned forward. "But don't you care?"

"Of course I care. Sometimes I look in the mirror and it's like—well, like somebody snuck in during the night and painted an old woman's face on me. It's like... like when we were kids on the show and we'd get together and fool around with makeup. Remember that? We'd put tons of junk on and tell each other how gorgeous we looked—when we really looked like Eighth Avenue whores!"

Cathy smiled. "The beauty marks—with an eyebrow pencil."

"Right! And dying our eyelashes! Remember the time I was doing it for Sandy and I practically blinded her?"

Cathy extended her index finger, pressing it against her face, cupping her elbow with her left hand.

"The poses! I almost forgot about them. We'd copy the models in *Vogue*. Suzy Parker and Dovima were going to eat their hearts out. Hey, how about this one?" Sucking her cheeks in to emphasize her bones, she splayed the fingers of both hands in front of her eyes. She burst out laughing. "Buying all that cheap makeup at the five and ten? It's a miracle we didn't get a skin disease!"

Cathy giggled, but only for a moment. "But now it's not like it was," she said plaintively. "Now it's no fun. The lines won't wash off."

"No, they won't."

"And when I look in the mirror... it hurts..."

Connie sighed. "I know. Believe me, I know. Sometimes I want to break the damn glass. But there are other ways of seeing yourself, Cathy. Me, I'm lucky enough to have a husband who doesn't care how I look as long as I have dinner ready when he gets home. And five kids who wouldn't notice if I turned into a witch as long as I had a box of Band-Aids and a shoulder to lean on."

Cathy began to cry softly. "You have a family. It's different..."

"And what's Al, I'd like to know? He's *your* family. He's crazy about you, Cathy—anyone can see that—"

"He's not!" she insisted. "He loved my looks, and I'm losing them. I'm too old to be his 'little girl.'"

"You'll *always* be his little girl. Maybe you're partly right—people fall in love for lots of reasons. But looks don't keep love going. They don't keep a marriage working or love alive. Cathy, don't you see? It's not just how you look that Al loves. It's who you are. Now he's out there in the other room, scared to death. You could come out with a faceful of wrinkles and he wouldn't notice—"

"Oh, Connie! I'm so...so scared!" the bottle of pills dropped to the floor and rolled under the sink as the two women fell into each other's arms.

"I know," Connie said. "This whole week, the show, seeing everyone again...it makes you think too much. You start to wonder where the time went, how it got away."

"And how it *was*, Connie."

"How we remember it—"

"Maybe it was different. Was it?"

Connie helped the other woman to her feet, then she started to laugh. "Search me. Now, what's it going to be? Want to rest for a while? Want to go home?"

Cathy bit her lip. "If you'll help me, I want to do the show—"

"Good," Connie said, hugging her. "Once a ham, always a ham." She opened the bathroom window, then drained the tub. "Come on, let's get out of this hothouse before we melt." She opened the door and led Cathy through the bedroom. "Hey, if you feel shaky, think about this one: the kids who used to watch us and write all those letters? Well, tonight they're just as old as we are. Hey, Al!" she called. "Let's step on it, huh? You've got a couple of TV stars to take to the studio."

The red-eye special hadn't even left LA on time: for three excruciating hours, the attendants had promised that the "slight mechanical problem" would be fixed in a matter of minutes. Then, when the plane had finally taken off, Sylvia had been so exhausted from a day on the set that had begun at 6:00 a.m. that she hadn't been able to sleep.

Laura Chesnay, the unit publicist on the picture, had set up a luncheon interview with the *Times*; they'd have a story in the entertainment section the following Sunday. The suite at the Sherry Netherland had been filled with fruit and flowers, but there hadn't ever been time to read the cards, much less sleep.

"How you guys keeping?" Sylvia asked.

"No complaints," Libby said, sitting beside her in the car. Not only had she insisted on coming, but when Sylvia told her that she ought to stay at the hotel and rest, she'd actually bristled. "When I get so old I got to take to my bed, I ain't gonna need you to tell me!" she insisted.

"I hope the photographer is on time," Laura said. The opportunity to photograph Sylvia being reunited with the other two Fantastiks was a PR gold mine.

"I'm *dead*!" Pierre announced dramatically, from the jump seat opposite Laura's. For emphasis, he pretended to swoon.

"Watch some man come by shakin' his business and you'll be rarin' to go," Libby observed.

Sylvia laughed. "Oh, Lord!"

"Getting edgy? 'Bout the girls?" Libby asked.

"Who, me?" Sylvia asked. "Course not! It'll be fun... Damn, I never could lie to you, could I? It's kind of heavy, I guess—oowie! Will you look at that crowd!"

The sidewalk and much of the street in front of the stage entrance to the theater was packed with people. Some carried signs and placards.

"GO HOME, ALICE!" Pierre read. "ALICE LANE IS A SEXIST PIGLETTE!" "GAYS FOR EQUALITY—AND AGAINST ALICE!" He turned to Sylvia. "It's not your fan club, Miss Girl!"

"That crowd looks like trouble," Laura Chesnay observed. "Driver, we'll go to the front entrance."

As the car stopped, Sylvia pulled her full-length lynx coat tightly around her, turning up the collar. Libby handed her a pair of sunglasses. Already, a number of people without tickets had lined up in the hope of being admitted to the broadcast. They murmured and pointed as Pierre and Laura stepped from the car, then cheered and called out to Sylvia. She waved, blowing a kiss before vanishing inside. When they were safely in the theater, Pierre went back to the car to pick up Sylvia's costume, the makeup case, and the wig box.

"Gimme that," Libby insisted, reaching for the garmet bag.

"Mama, you're too *old* to be totin'," he teased.

"Ain't too old to slap you where the sun don't shine!" she snapped, grabbing the wig box instead. They made their way down the aisle, past the rows of empty seats.

"Hey, y'all!" Sylvia called. All conversation on the set stopped as she climbed up the steps, followed by her entourage.

"How nice to meet you," a young woman said. "I'm Sheila Granger..."

They were immediately joined by Kay and the director, then by Lee Dean.

"Told you I'd be here, didn't I?" Sylvia said. "Didn't say I'd look like hell, but those are the breaks."

"Thanks a million," he told her as they trouped

through the wings toward her dressing room. "The girls are waiting to see you."

Hooking her arm through his, Sylvia looked at him wide-eyed. "Virgie got a gun?" she asked in a stage whisper.

"You're too much!" he answered, slipping his arm around her waist.

Suddenly she stopped. "Where *have* I seen that good-lookin' white boy before?" she asked in a loud voice.

"Hey, Sylvia!"

"Tommy!" she laughed, hugging him. "Hey, this is old home week for sure, huh?"

"You look good. You haven't changed since—well, whenever it was."

"You're mighty fine-lookin' yourself," she observed, stepping back to study him. "You've changed, but it sure looks good. Catch you later on, huh? I want to get settled in."

"Sure. It's great to see you."

The moment they reached her dressing room, Libby hung the garment bag and began to unzip it, and Pierre began setting up his tubes and bottles and brushes.

"I want to give you a deep cleansing mask," he told her. "The change of climate is *terrible* for your skin—"

"Ms. Chesnay? We spoke on the phone. I'm the unit publicist, Maxine—"

"Oh yes, how nice to meet you. We'll want to get some pictures—*if* that photographer of mine shows up . . ."

"When you're settled, we'd like to just run over your portion of the show, Sylvia . . ."

"Okay, honey. Just give me a minute," she said, sinking into a chair. She stretched her legs out and closed her eyes tightly. But there was so much noise, so many different voices, that resting was impossible.

"No rest for the weary, like they say . . . *Dee*!" She suddenly bolted from the chair, her fatigue gone at the sight of the woman in the doorway. "Dee!" she cried out happily, pulling her into the throng. "Look who's here, Libby. Pierre! It's Dee! How you doin'? How's that husband of yours—and those kids? Oo, I got so much to ask you girls! Hey, where's Virgie?"

Dee laughed. "I'm doing fine and so's the family, thank you, and Virgie's in our dressing room down the hall."

"Well, what's she waitin' for? Libby, see if you can find us something to drink, huh?"

"There's a bar in the green room," a production assistant offered.

"Ought to rest," Libby muttered pointedly, "and party later on!"

Sylvia ignored her. "How did the dresses work out?" she asked Dee.

"Sylvie, they're gorgeous. I should've thanked you—"

"Forget it. Where's that Virgie?" She started for the door, but Dee stopped her.

"You wait here—I'll get her." She hurried out, and a moment later, the sound of a raised voice cut through the noise in Sylvie's dressing room. Pierre and Libby gave each other a silent look that meant "trouble!"

"... You come on and be nice, hear?" Dee was saying in the hallway. Sylvia pretended she hadn't heard as Dee returned with the third Fantastik in tow.

"Virgie!"

Virgie stood still and silent. Her body tensed at Sylvia's hug, and she made no move to return the gesture of affection.

Determinedly, Sylvia maintained her smile. "You look so fine!"

Instead of answering, Virgie's eyes darted around the room, taking in the flowers and the space itself.

"Something wrong, honey?" Sylvia asked.

"No," Virgie said bitterly. "Ain't nothin' wrong. You got the big, fancy dressing room, didn't you? Things are pretty much the same, I'd say."

"Don't the girls have the same kind of dressing room?"

Sylvia asked the production assistant.

"We did the best we could," the young woman apologized, "but this is a very old theater—"

"We're doin' fine without your help!" Virgie snapped. "Don't worry yourself about 'the girls,' *Miss* Sylvie—"

"Now you stop that!" Dee cautioned her.

"Sure! I better stop! We can't have anything upset the big movie star—"

"Virgie, I didn't know about the dressing room," Sylvia told her.

"And you didn't know about walking out on us either, huh? It just kind of happened, right? Seems everything has a way of working out so's it's good for you, don't it!"

"We'd better go," Dee suggested, taking her arm, but Virgie pulled away.

"Why? Suppose I don't want to go nowhere? Sylvie wanted to go once, didn't she? Nobody stopped her. She went! She walked right out and left us high and dry!"

Her patience and good humor were leaving Sylvia quickly. "That's not the way it happened—and you know it!"

"Hell I do. And hell it didn't!" Virgie snapped. They were face to face, so close that they could feel each other's breath. Neither of them backed off. "You looked out for your own damn self. That was all that ever mattered to you... you bitch!"

With her fist clenched, she pounded Sylvia's shoulder. Sylvia, taken by surprise, needed only an instant to recover. She drew her arm back and slapped Virgie's face.

"I'll kill you!" Virgie vowed, as they pummeled each other. The fracas lasted only a few seconds. Pierre forced himself between the two women. Dee grabbed Virgie while Libby, surprisingly strong and agile, restrained Sylvia.

"Get her out of here!" Pierre ordered Dee. Virgie and Sylvia were glaring at each other, both struggling to catch their breath. Sylvia was leaning forward from her waist, her shoulders and arms hanging loosely. With a deep breath, she pulled herself up straight.

"No!" Sylvia said. "She's gonna stay. We had this coming for a long time, and we're gonna settle it now. Pierre, Libby go on out. Everybody but Dee and Virgie—"

"She's crazy! She'll go at you again," Pierre warned.

"I grew up taking care of myself," Sylvia told him, not taking her eyes from Virgie. "And I still know how."

Then the room was empty except for the three Fantastiks. Sylvia backed toward the open door and slammed it shut.

"All right!" she challenged, "you got something to say, huh, Virgie? Had it eatin' at you for a long time? Then say it now! For once and for all, say it."

"You know damn well what I got to say! You know what you did—"

"Okay!" Sylvia roared. "I did it! I left the act! There—are you happy?"

"See?" Virgie asked Dee. "She doesn't even care! She didn't care then, and she don't care now—"

"Bullshit!" Sylvia interrupted. "I cared plenty! I saw the writing on the wall—you didn't even want to look."

"What writing? What wall?" Virgie demanded. "We were the hottest act in the business!"

"And the business was changing, damn it! Like it always is. People were getting tired of three colored girls singing together. It wasn't *new* any more—"

"So *you* changed," Virgie said, spitting the words at her. "Little Sylvie, goin' to parties, posing for the fashion magazines. You were a toy for them. A freak! A little nigger babydoll they could dress up and show off—"

"And I let them! You think I didn't know? I saw it for what it was, all right. And I saw how I could use it. Maybe I was in on a pass, but I made my own place. I smiled and went along with whatever the program was until I could do what I wanted to do. Where were you, Virgie? Do you remember? You were buyin' this, and bitchin' about work—you thought it was one big damn party, and you were the guest of honor!"

"You were a schemer! You still are, Sylvie!"

"Damn straight, I am! And so were you and you too, Dee. How the hell else did we get out of Harlem? I schemed and when I could; when I got a chance, I took it. *I* was the one that went to the parties when we were asked, so *I* was the one they asked back. *I* was the one they came to with the offers. *I* was the one they wanted to hear, and put in movies.

"Think it's been easy? I been workin' so long and so hard I don't know what it's like *not* to work. I was born hungry and I stayed hungry. Maybe back then when I left you I was scared... I was young, that's for sure. I coulda done it better or nicer. I'm sorry I didn't."

"Sorry, my ass!"

Sylvia glared at Virgie. Dee stood off to one side, silent, "Then tell me! Virgie, here and now, you tell me. If it had been you—if it had been *your* chance—would you have done it any different?"

The sudden quiet hung in the room, already heavy with tension. As if the air were electricity and she'd been shocked, the muscles of Virgie's face, clenched and set, began to quiver. The hatred and hardness began to melt in her eyes. Tears rolled down her cheeks.

"But it *wasn't* me," she said. "It was you."

Tentatively, hesitantly Sylvia reached out, touching Virgie's shoulder. "It's me for now, but don't you see? It'll be somebody else soon enough. Nothin' lasts in the business. You know that. You get a chance—you got to take it. That's what I did. That's *all* I did, Virgie. If I had to leave you to do for myself, well, I'm sorry. I did it the only way I knew how..." She could taste her own tears.

"I'll tell you this," Sylvia continued, "it's nothin' like old times. The fun we had... the way it felt when it was new, gettin' out there and hearin' 'em applaud—"

"Scared to death they wouldn't," Dee observed, chuckling.

"Damn, the rows and rows of faces. I used to get so scared I'd grab on to you," Virgie recalled.

Sylvia sniffled and smiled. "Tell me 'bout it. My hand still don't work right." Suddenly they were smiling at each other. Sylvia spoke softly. "Used to be, we was close as sisters. Closer, maybe, on account of we picked ourselves up, we made it that way. For tonight—for all that time that used to be—can't we at least be friends?"

"Thanks for letting me ride over with you," Carl Schmidt said as they got out of the limousine and pushed their way through the crowd. "I must've just missed Connie."

"She'll be inside," Don told him, following Gary. "I'm glad your son is all right."

"He's more shaken up than hurt. You know how it is with kids..."

As if a current had swept through the sea of bodies surrounding them, people began pushing and turning.

"Don!" Gary called. A sudden surge of people had separated them, and he was already in the doorway.

"Be right there!" Don answered. But the tide was against him. A car had come to a stop where the TBS limo had let three men out, and the onlookers were waving their signs and calling out to the passenger inside.

"What the hell?" Carl said. Like Don, he knew it was useless to try to fight the crush of bodies. The two men watched the scene, feeling the movement as the crowd stirred in response to the restraining check of the several policemen in the street.

"It's Alice Lane," Don said. "I wonder what she thinks of her welcoming committee?"

"GO BACK TO CALIFORNIA!"
"YOU DON'T KNOW SHIT ABOUT WELFARE!"
"HEY, ALICE! GO BACK TO WONDERLAND!"

Some of the voices were mocking and taunting: others were bitter to the point of hatred. The woman who stepped out of the back seat of the car was obviously upset, and not even the protective barrier of policemen put her at ease. Arms out, the cops cleared a path. Reluctantly, the crowd parted, giving her a few feet of space at a time.

"Who are you gonna hate next week?"

"Did you ever try to raise four kids on your own?"

"Bitch!"

She shielded her eyes with her hand, unable to confront the angry faces and the shaking fists.

Don and Carl stepped back as she came closer.

An egg crashed against the side of the building. Those who saw it began to laugh.

"Too bad you missed her!" someone called out.

"*I* won't miss her!" another voice promised. A broad-shouldered man lunged at Alice. Before he realized what he was doing, Don drew his arm back and shot it forward, his fist connecting with the would-be attacker's chin. Then Alice Lane was pressing herself against the protective safety of his shoulder. Carl closed in on the other side of her, and the two men rushed her toward the door. The guard who'd been watching, his hand only a fraction of a second away from the gun at his hip, closed and bolted the door the moment they were inside.

"It's okay," Carl told the quivering woman. "They won't come in."

"They... they hate me!" she whined. "Why?"

Carl shrugged. "What'dya expect, lady? You say things on television, you get 'em all stirred up."

"I talk about issues," she said.

She tried to compose herself. She looked up at Don. "At least not everyone hates me. I can't thank you enough for helping me."

At first Don didn't know how to respond. He wasn't the type of man to make his life public on a TV special, much as he loved Gary. But here was a chance to at least confront one of the people who made him wish he was.

"You're welcome," he said. "But for the record, I hate every narrow-minded, bigoted thing you stand for just as much as those people out there. I don't want to see you become a martyr. That's not the way to fight you."

Alice's face dropped.

"I'm gay," he said. "I'm one of those dangerous 'menaces to American life' you're always talking about. For your sake, I hope another 'dangerous menace' will help you the next time somebody tries to attack."

Carl looked at Don in surprise, then laughed and slapped him on the back. "Buddy, I don't care what the hell you are. You sure pack a mean right. Come on, let's find Connie and the others."

Gary fell into step, a firm squeeze to Don's arm conveying his pride and approval. And without a backward glance, the three men walked away from Alice Lane.

8.

"READY?" KAY ASKED.

Sheila looked out at the audience. Every seat was filled, and several hundred people had been turned away.

"No," she answered, hearing her own heart pounding above the backstage noise.

"Too bad," Kay said, checking her watch, "but it's 8:50. In other words, my dear, see you after the warmup." She gave Sheila a playful push.

It's silly to be nervous, Sheila thought, as she walked onstage. Somebody had to do the warmup, after all. Lee's impact would be diminished if he came out before the show. Somehow, though, it was easier to think of the millions of unseen viewers at home than the hundreds in the studio audience whose eyes watched her as she made her way past the cameras and crew members. A small microphone was clipped to the lapel of her jacket, and she found herself wondering if it would leave a permanent mark: the rust silk suit had cost nearly four hundred dollars.

Clearing her throat, she wished she'd brought a clipboard or some other prop. There was a smattering of applause as she stood in the center of the stage. Embarrassed, she held her hands up to stop it.

"Thank you," she said, "but please save your applause for the show. I'm Sheila Granger, and I'm producing what you're going to see tonight. I'd like to thank you all for coming..." Once she had their attention, her confidence grew.

"I'd particularly like to welcome the students from NYU, Columbia, and Hofstra who are here tonight—"

"And Visual Arts!" someone called out.

"*And* Visual Arts," she added. "More than two decades ago, *Dancetime, USA!* went on the air on TBS. I'd tell you that it was an innovative and unique concept, except most of us probably know that ABC was already running Dick Clark's *American Bandstand*. So let's say that it was one of *two* innovative concepts at the time—and of course any similarity between the two shows was purely coincidental."

The audience laughed, and she continued.

"Hosted by Lee Dean, *Dancetime* was more than just a program. It quickly became both a mirror and an image, reflecting styles and shaping trends for millions of teenagers. It helped to launch the careers of dozens of stars. You'll be seeing some of them in film clips during the show, and you'll be seeing, live, the stars who had the top three records in the *Dancetime, USA!* survey: Tommy Del, Alice Lane—"

The chorus of boos surprised her and she decided to depart from the speech she'd prepared.

"Look... I know that Alice Lane has expressed some controversial views, but tonight she's here strictly as an entertainer. I can't *tell* you what to do, but I can ask: we'd all appreciate it, since we want to entertain you tonight, if you could put personal politics aside and just enjoy the show. We'll also be seeing the fabulous Fantastiks, singing together for the first time in about fifteen years."

The applause was deafening.

"Besides Lee Dean and his guests, you'll be meeting seven of the original *Dancetime, USA!* Regulars—the kids who danced on the show every day. It's been twenty years since the last time they sat in those bleachers behind me. We'll be finding out what it felt like to be on the show back then, what they've been doing since—and what it feels like for them to be together again.

"In keeping with the original format of the show, the *Dancetime* reunion will be going out live. We'll be recording 'live on tape' for the West Coast. There are monitors in the studio to help you see what's going on, and there's an applause sign—" she paused, and it flashed—"to show you when we'd appreciate your applause. Most of all, we'd like you to sit back, relax, and have a good time."

They applauded as she walked off the right side of the stage, where Lee was standing with one of the two assistant stage managers who would make sure that the right talent was in the right place at the right time.

"A star is born!" Kay proclaimed dramatically.

"Tough act to follow," Lee teased.

Sheila chuckled, as much in relief as amusement. "I think you can handle it," she told him.

"Do I look all right?" Lee asked, as the wardrobe man straightened his tie.

"You look sensational," Sheila assured him. In the old days, Lee Dean's trademark outfit had been a narrow-lapelled blue blazer, white chinos, and white bucks. For the special, he was dressed in an updated version of the look. The blazer had a tailored, European look; the slacks were pleated; and instead of white bucks, he wore white leather loafers.

"I don't know," Kay interjected, surveying him

critically. "The eyebrows look a little crooked—"

"Ready with Lee?" the stage manager said, answering the query of the director. He listened intently to his headset.

Years before, when the theatre had originally been turned into a TBS studio, a control booth had been built in the front of the mezzanine. Over the years, it had been enlarged and modified in accordance with technological advances. The director wouldn't be looking at the live action through the window, but rather on the monitors. The "program" monitor would show what shot the director was taking at the moment, the "preview" monitor would show the next planned shot. Four smaller screens would reflect the images the four cameras were picking up, each monitor corresponding to a camera number. The "film" monitor would roll the black and white clips that would be used throughout the show. As the director picked his shot, a red light would go on above the monitor giving him that feed. Finally, an "On Air" monitor would show exactly what the network was sending out.

The associate director would follow the script, telling the director what was coming up and what shots had been planned in rehearsal. It was the production assistant's job to keep precise track of time; to tell the director how much time there was before going into and coming out of commercial breaks; and to cue the film clips, slides and pre-recorded music.

The technical director, seated at a board with so many buttons that Sheila was always reminded of something out of a science fiction film, would execute and regulate the technological mechanics of choices the director made. Following his annotated script and the snap of the director's fingers that indicated the shot changes, the technical director switched the feed from camera to camera.

Producers were an unwelcome presence in the control

room. With the special being done live, Sheila had wisely decided to stay on the floor.

A makeup man hurried over as the set was fully lit, dabbing some last-minute powder on Lee's forehead.

"Bringing Lee on," the stage manager said into the miniaturized mike of his headset.

Kay darted forward, kissing Lee's lips lightly. "For luck," she said. "And old times' sake."

On the other side of the stage, an assistant stage manager was readying The Regulars.

As Lee took his place at the podium, the stage manager announced, "Thirty seconds."

"Hold my hand?" Sheila whispered, reaching for Kay. The stage manager's hands were up, a finger going down with each of the last ten seconds.

"This is your baby, Sheila," Kay said—her eyes like Sheila's, fixed on the monitor in the wings. "Enjoy it—"

"Four... three... two..."

The opening shot from one of the old *Dancetime, USA!* kinescopes filled the screen, as the old theme song played.

> *Rockin' on Dancetime,*
> *Where the beat rolls on and on—and on...*

The audio man brought the music down to background level.

"Here it is!" the announcer on the floor said. "the big music show with the big-city beat. One more time, it's time for *Dancetime, USA!*. And here's that real cool guy from up north, Lee Dean."

The black and white image of Lee twenty years earlier, surrounded by dancing teenagers, was replaced by a color shot of Lee in the same place, but with the set empty.

The studio audience clapped and cheered wildly.

"Good evening," Lee said. "Or as we used to

say—'Hey, cats and chicks, get ready for some kicks! Your troubles won't matter when we spin a platter...'" Chuckling as if he could hardly believe it, Lee made his way down from the podium.

"I guess that dates me...right back to 1958. Those were the 'good old days'—only nobody knew it then. Then, it was simply the time of our life. To help you get a fix on exactly how long ago 1958 was, let me try it this way.

"It was two years after everybody's favorite comedians, Dean Martin and Jerry Lewis, split up—and a year after the Russians launched Sputnik. At the movies, Elvis Presley was starring in *King Creole*, Cary Grant and Ingrid Bergman were *Indiscreet*, and Liz Taylor was the *Cat on a Hot Tin Roof*.

"If you had a television set, and more and more families did, you could check out the new programs—*Naked City* and *Peter Gunn*; *Yancy Derringer* and *Wanted: Dead or Alive!*; *Sea Hunt*, *77 Sunset Strip*, and *The Donna Reed Show*. Oh yes—there was another program, too. It was on every weekday afternoon, and if you were a 'teen on the scene,' you might have tuned in yourself."

The music came up, and a film clip, put together from old newsreel footage, rolled on the monitors. It showed screaming teenagers lining up outside the studio, with Lee at record hops, and on the show itself. As it ran, Lee talked about the history of *Dancetime, USA!* and the search for the "lucky guys and gals" who were selected as Regulars.

"In a moment," he said, "we'll take a look back at just who The Regulars were. Right after these announcements."

They went into the first commercial break. The assistant stage manager brought The Regulars onto the set: the comedy troupe was waiting in the wings. Flashing a smile at Lee, oblivious now to the studio audience, Sheila approached Sandy and Connie and the others.

"You all look wonderful," she said. "Remember—the main thing to do is relax, okay? You're old pros at doing this show. I know you'll be terrific."

"Ten...four...three...two," the stage manager counted.

"They were called 'The Regulars,'" Lee said, the camera tight on him, "but they were special. Hundreds of teenagers—thousands of them—entered the competition. Only a handful were chosen. The biggest teen idols of the day made guest appearances, but The Regulars were the real stars of the show. Viewers at home copied their dance steps and their hairdos. Each of them received hundreds of letters each week. The fan magazines wrote articles about them and took their pictures, and the nicest thing about them, I think, was that they weren't professional entertainers, but average kids having a good time...kids who remained nice kids, unchanged by the attention and publicity. Let's look at some old pictures."

Cathy...Tony...Dennis...Bobby...Sandy...Don ...Connie...The old publicity shots, sent to the fans who wrote in, were shown, and their names given. Other slides showed magazine covers and layouts on The Regulars, as Lee read composite sketches of them.

"It's been a long time—too long, I sometimes feel—but I still remember those kids," he said. "You know, when I look at those bleachers, I can almost see them now..."

The shot panned his line of sight. Lee did a double take and joined them. One by one, they introduced themselves. Lee led them through several minutes of talk about the old days. Meanwhile, Tommy Del was positioned in front of a midnight-blue backdrop.

"What do you remember the most about *Dancetime*?" Lee asked The Regulars. "What was the most exciting part of the show?"

"The dance contests," Bobby O'Brian said.

"And the spotlight dances," Sandy added.

"Having all the people you knew watching," Tony said.

Lee turned to Cathy: they'd rehearsed her answer during the week. "The guest stars," she said, to Connie's relief.

"When it came to guest stars," Lee said, as still photographs of various entertainers who had appeared on the show filled the screen, "we had the biggest and the best. Fabian, Tommy Sands, Ricky Nelson... and tonight, we're pleased to have one of the nicest. Singing the song that was a chart-busting hit twenty years ago—Mr. Tommy Del!"

Watching him, Sheila Granger was impressed. By any standard, "A Teenage Tragedy," hadn't aged well—every line was packed with the clichés that were the substance of dozens of songs like it. If he'd come out and done the number too seriously, Tommy would have risked looking foolish. Instead of trying to recreate his 1958 performance and look, he wore a wine velour sweatshirt and a pair of off-white jeans and adopted a casual ease to go with them. He didn't push the lyric too hard, nor did he play it for laughs.

In a strong, clear voice, he sang the song and came across as just what he was—a man reliving a pleasant memory. Sheila had worried that after so much time out of the business, Tommy might be nervous. His ability to turn the old professonalism on so easily surprised her. It was like a switch inside him, she thought: he'd been able to walk away from the business without a backward glance and now, with the same ease, he was able to return to it for a night.

The fame, the name, the allure of being a personality—he'd had them all, and there onstage he had them again. But he'd gladly exchanged them to become a husband and father. He felt free when he got out of the business, he'd explained, liberated. Watching him from the wings,

Sheila wondered if she really knew what being a "liberated" woman meant. Kay, standing beside her, was liberated by any definition, but in spite of her career and her professional achievements, she herself felt restricted. Maybe, she told herself, feeling liberated meant being free to be yourself in the way that felt best... the way she felt in Tommy's arms—

"Tommy Del!" Lee was saying, joining the performer. "Boy, they don't make songs like that any more, do they?"

Tommy laughed. "I think someone must've passed a law."

"And you're not singing songs like that any more, are you?"

"I do my singing in the shower these days, Lee..." They talked for a few minutes, then Lee introduced The Amateurs doing a skit about teenage crushes. There was another commercial, and then Lee was back in the bleachers.

"One of the most popular couples on *Dancetime*," he began, "was this pair right here—Connie Donati, now Mrs. Carl Schmidt, and Tony Merino."

They smiled at each other.

"Of course they've changed a little bit. Let's see if this film clip triggers some memories for you two."

"Oh, no!" Connie moaned, as the film began. It was a sequence of shots in which she was dancing with Tony. "Look at that!" she exclaimed, as the camera picked them up during a slow number. Her right arm was hooked around Tony's neck. Her left and his right were extended straight down, hands joined alongside their hips.

"What were we doing?" Connie asked, providing the voice-over. "Dancing or pumping for oil? We look like midnight at the dance marathon."

"*You* do," Tony teased affectionately. "I look tough."

"You always thought you looked tough," she answered. The audience laughed with her.

"Now we're picking up the tempo a bit," Lee observed.

On the monitor, they were bopping. Tony spun and whirled Connie across the floor.

"Isn't that a riot?" she asked. "I'm moving forty miles an hour, but my hair doesn't even bounce. I must've supported the whole hair-spray industry."

"Look at Tony's hair," Lee said.

In the film, Tony's dark hair was slicked back and glistened.

"Those were the days when it was cool to use the 'greasy kid stuff,'" Tony offered in defense.

"Do you remember what you used to think about when you knew the camera was on you?" Lee asked.

Connie laughed. "I used to worry about my skirt. See it there? If you were a really tough chick—and my mother wasn't about to let me be a tough chick—you pegged your skirt. That black skirt I'm wearing was one I used to keep in the lockers we had here in the studio. My mother would've killed me if she saw it. I kept thinking, today I'm gonna go home and she's going to catch on about the skirt, but she never did. And I used to worry that it would split when I did a turn..."

As the clip ended, Lee continued the conversation.

"Connie, you were going to go into show business, weren't you? Did you ever have that career you wanted?"

Connie smiled easily. "I went into the business—the baby business. I have the greatest kids and the greatest husband in the world. I have to say that, Lee. Otherwise they won't let me back into the house."

"But you wanted to be an entertainer at one point," Lee said. "Did the show point you in that direction?"

Connie nodded. "I loved being a Regular, and I'm glad you showed those old pictures. Now my next door neighbor will *have* to believe I used to be slim. Because I came from a big family, being a Regular on *Dancetime* made me feel...well, special. I thought that in show business, I could continue to feel that way. I tried it but it didn't work. And the funny thing is, what really makes me feel special now is my family."

Lee gave her a hug as the audience applauded. He turned to Tony. "And you Tony. Folks, this guy was known as The SWAK Kid. That was the way all his fan letters came in: Sealed With A Kiss. Tony, you were a heartbreaker! How did it feel getting all those letters from girls in every part of the country?"

"It didn't exactly hurt, I can tell you that," Tony answered, getting a laugh. "The thing of it is, when you're a kid, you don't appreciate things enough. You try to act tough and older than you are because you can't wait to grow up. Then you turn around and it's twenty years later. Instead of wanting it to, you know, speed up, you discover it's going too fast..."

"Okay," Lee said brightly, changing the mood and turning to Connie. "Back in April, 1958, we introduced a record on *Dancetime* that you were crazy about, Connie. Over the years, it went on to be a big hit for two other groups besides the original artists, who were The Five Royales. What was that song?"

She thought for a second. "I can't remember—"

"Maybe this will remind you," Lee said.

A black and white clip from the old days came onscreen. Lee was at the podium, and Connie and Tony were standing with him.

"You've heard the record," Lee was saying, "now let's see what two of our most popular Regulars, Connie Donati and Tony Merino, think of it. How do you rate it?"

"Well, Lee," Tony answered, "it wasn't my kinda tune, you know? So I'll give a fifty-five—"

"Come on!" Connie protested. "It's a great song."

"You two don't seem to be in agreement," Lee told her.

Connie made a face at Tony. "When it comes to picking hits, he can be a real dip!" she said.

"How do you rate it?"

"I thought it was real romantic, and I liked the beat. So I'm going to give it a ninety-nine."

"That's what our two Regulars think of The Five Royales' new release," Lee told the home audience. "It's called 'Dedicated to the One I Love.' Will it be a hit or a miss? That's up to you..."

The clip ended. "Tony, I think Connie called that one a little better than you did."

Tony shrugged his shoulders and smiled. "You can't win them all, Lee."

"Guess not! The other groups, of course, were the Shirelles and The Mamas and The Papas, both of which had big hits on the song. But the last time you two heard it on *Dancetime*, you just listened. How about dancing to it now in a *Dancetime, USA!* Spotlight Dance?"

The audience cheered, the music began, and Tony and Connie started to dance. At first, they slumped together in a parody of the film clip shown earlier. After a few moments, though, and after the laugh, they straightened up. Her eyes closed, Connie leaned against Tony's shoulder. Confidently, he led her across the floor.

"Stay with us," Lee was telling the audience. "We'll be back after these words with The Amateurs, our *Dancetime, USA!* Regulars, and more guests and surprises."

"It's like old times," Connie whispered to Tony. "Like no time at all has passed..."

After the station break, The Amateurs did a piece of material about a slumber party. The references to boys who were "nerds" or "cool cats," and girls who were "shanks" or had "bad reps" got a good response.

The montage of scenes from the big films of the decade was shown.

Then Lee talked about mishaps that had happened on the air. A clip showed several of the more memorable such moments—records getting stuck as guest stars lip-synched their hits, dancers falling down, Lee himself mispronouncing names. When it was over, Don was standing beside him.

"When we selected the people—'groovy guys and gals,' we called them back then—who were our Regulars, we didn't realize it but we were putting together a kind of cross-section of types. Tony was our fifties version of The Fonze. And this fellow, Don Simpson, had a different image. Remember what it was, Don?"

A series of stills, shots from the show and from the magazines, made it clear that Don had been *Dancetime*'s all-American boy. Looking at the old photographs, Don had to laugh.

"Tell me," Lee asked, "was that the real you? Your old bio says that you were an honor student and an athlete. Were you what we used to call a 'goody-goody,' or did you sometimes raise a little hell?"

Don considered the question. "I think I was what was known as this," Don said. With the index fingers of both hands, he traced the figure of a square in the air.

"Come on, not really—"

"You know, Lee, things have changed so much in twenty years. Not only for me, but in the world. Today, it's more than acceptable to talk about your feelings and insecurities—it's fashionable. But back then, a lot of people—and I'm one of them—used to hide behind an image."

"How do you mean?"

"You know—the black leather jacket and the shades, the short-cropped hair and the button-down shirts in my case. It was like it was some kind of play, and there were only a few parts to pick from."

"Do you think it's different for kids today? Easier, maybe?"

"I can't speak from experience, because I've never been married or had children of my own. But from what I see, and what a psychologist friend of mine tells me, I think that even if the problems of being a teenager are the same—the looking for identity and all that—people talk about them and acknowledge them more easily than we did. It took me a long time to find out who I really am. I think kids growing up today will learn to live with themselves a lot sooner."

"Interesting," Lee observed. "When you stop to think about it, popular music has always reflected a lot of the problems and emotional questions of teenagers. In the 1950's some things seemed very clearcut. Boys, as you said, Don, were 'rebels,' or nice guys. Girls, depending on how far they went with their rebels—or their nice guys—were good or bad. And if a girl had trouble deciding how far to go, there were songs that helped her make up her mind. Here, singing one of those songs and one of her biggest hits, is Miss Alice Lane!"

There was no booing this time, but the applause from the studio audience was little more than polite as Alice began her number. When it ended, the response was only a bit more enthusiastic.

Lee stood as Alice joined him and The Regulars in the bleachers. They went through the lines they'd rehearsed about the old album cover, and Alice pretended to be surprised. But instead of talking about being nervous when she appeared on *Dancetime*, she headed in another direction.

"That picture and those clothes remind me just how much things have changed since the old days, Lee," she said sweetly.

There was nothing for Lee to do but go along with her. "That's right," he agreed. "Clothes, styles, music—"

"And people," Alice added. She was delighted—it was just the kind of lead-in she'd been looking for. From the moment she'd been asked to do the show, she'd had an idea of what she'd say, how she could use it for her own purposes. Now, her time was at hand. "The way we live and the things that concern us are changing all the time. I was listening backstage before I came on. What was said about things—values, a sense of right and wrong—being very fixed and set back in the 1950's was very interesting. People are a lot more confused today about good and bad..."

She was sitting next to Lee, but she glanced at the upper tiers of the bleachers as she spoke, including all The Regulars. They were watching and listening with varying degrees of interest. Her eyes met Don Simpson's. He was watching her intently.

A confusion of thoughts suddenly filled her mind. She remembered the angry faces of the mob outside the studio, and the fear she'd felt. Don, by his own admission, was a symbol of everything she opposed. But he was also the man who'd saved her, in spite of her convictions. She heard herself making speeches and statements against the "menace" of people like him, but there he was, not one of a faceless and unseen number, but a man to whom she owed gratitude and, more than that, respect...

"But... but in a way," she continued, "I think the confusion is good. It—it shows that we're thinking. That we're continually reexamining our ideas. We... we make up our own minds, and we're not afraid to say what we think or to change our ideas. And that's what makes our country so great."

It wasn't at all what she'd planned to say: she had memorized a brief, fiery statement about the decline of decency and self-reliance in American society. To her surprise, though, the audience applauded.

Lee was faced with an immediate choice. Alice hadn't pushed herself or her causes; her statement was more surprising, considering her politics, than anything else. If he now cut her off, he'd make his fear that she might say the wrong thing obvious. If he pressed on, it was a risk...

"Tell me," he asked, deciding to plunge ahead, "do you ever get nostalgic for the good old days? That time when life seemed so much easier, so much more simple?"

"I think we all do," she answered. "But for all the problems we face today, both as individuals and as a country, I think that in twenty years we'll probably look back and think of these as the 'good old days.' And I think that if we're... we're not afraid to get involved, to listen to each other's viewpoints and problems, the days that are to come will be the best ever."

Again, the audience responded, led by The Regulars this time.

"Alice Lane, ladies and gentlemen. Stay with us. We'll be right back..."

"What the fuck is going on?" the director screamed, freaking in the booth. "She knows she's not supposed to be doing this shit!"

Looking at the monitor, Kay Duvane shook her head. "Was that for *real*? What the hell got into her? For a minute there, it sounded like she was getting ready to give her version of the call to arms!"

A production assistant rushed up. "Miss Granger? A couple of local stations just called. They want a tape on Alice Lane for the news—"

"Tell them to call the network," Sheila said. Their break was over, and Lee was back.

"Right now," he said, "I'd like to introduce two more Regulars. Cathy—now Mrs. Al Hartley—and Dennis Bradshaw. Here's how they looked in the old days."

The clips showed the two Regulars being interviewed by Lee Dean. Cathy, a beautiful seventeen-year-old then, told him that her future plans included modeling and a career in fashion. Dennis, then eighteen, said that he wanted to go to law school after college.

"And here they are today," Lee said, when the clips were finished. They opened with a wide three-shot. "Well, you both did it, didn't you? Cathy, you modeled and had a career in merchandising before getting married. And Dennis, you're a partner in a top law firm. When you look back, do you get a feeling of satisfaction? At a time when a lot of young people were very confused about their futures, you both made your plans and followed through."

Dennis cleared his throat, then answered, slowly. "The thing of it is, Lee, that when you're young and looking ahead, you only see part of what's in store for you. You think that everything is possible. It's only when you get older that you realize there are some things you can't accomplish, things you never thought about.

"You can look back at the way things were, as we're doing tonight. But you can't go back. And that's a goddamn shame..."

In the wings, Sheila turned to Kay. "Did I hear that right?"

"You and who knows how many millions of the folks at home, my dear. See why live TV is dead?"

On camera, Lee turned his attention to Cathy. "Hey, if my memory is right, you were always the girl who gave the beauty advice, Cathy. The magazines used to run stories about how you did your hair and makeup, and tonight you're still gorgeous. Do you have any secrets to share?"

Cathy looked up to where Connie was sitting with Tony and smiled. "I learned one today, as a matter of fact. You have to start by not being afraid to change. Because it's going to happen anyway. We all... all of us get older. And how you think about that makes a big difference. I guess I'm lucky. I have a wonderful husband. He thinks I'm beautiful. When you feel beautiful, you are—no matter how old you happen to be."

"Good advice," Lee commented. "And speaking of looking good and keeping in shape, let's take a look at some of the dances that our Regulars used to do...

"The Bop, the Hop, and the Bristol Stomp," he began, narrating the piece of film that featured some of the best moments of dancing from the *Dancetime* kinescopes. "The New Continental, the Calypso, and the Shuffle. The Popeye, the Duck, the Monkey, and the Dog... The steps changed as the beat went on. All over the country, teenagers tuned in to watch the kids on *Dancetime, USA!* and to copy the latest dances."

The studio audience cheered the more extravagant steps and moves, applauding at the end of the three-minute clip.

"You probably recognized two of those dancers as two of our most popular Regulars—the couple that was always first with the latest steps. They were partners on *Dancetime, USA!* and they went on to become man and wife. Here they are to prove that nobody can keep up with the times like our Regulars. In a Spotlight Dance, still dancing, Sandy and Bobby O'Brian!"

The familiar sound of the disco version of the *Dancetime* theme began. A hand-held camera on the floor cut to Sandy striking a pose. Her tangerine disco dress swirled around her legs. Bobby, in a white suit—the jacket, like the tan silk shirt he wore under it, open—reached for her as the beat picked up. Looking only at each other, they dipped and whirled and spun toward one another as the colored lights that backlit them broke into prisms shot through the star filters mounted in the cameras. More than simple practice, the perfect unison of their movements reflected the years they'd danced together and the total knowledge of each other's bodies.

As the number ended, Bobby spun Sandy to his side. Together, they took a bow.

The applause wouldn't stop—not even when half the studio audience was on its feet.

"Come over here!" Lee called, clapping with The Regulars. They joined him, bowing again, then hugging each other. Finally the excitement died down. "Just a little something you improvised, huh?" Lee asked.

"Right," Bobby said. "We kind of threw it together."

Lee shook his head. "You two are too much. You still keep up with the new dances?"

"More than that," Sandy said, "We teach them. We have a dance studio in Houston, Texas."

"Hey—you're the storybook romance of *Dancetime, USA!*. Millions of kids used to follow you on the show. Why don't you fill us in on the last twenty years?"

"I'll try," Bobby said. "Let's see... After *Dancetime* went off the air, Sandy and I decided we still wanted to be partners. We got married—"

"—and we moved to Houston. It's a wonderful place. We love it," Sandy added.

"We opened a dance studio, and we—"

"Not right away we didn't!" Sandy interrupted. "We had a son, remember?"

"We still do, don't we?" Bobby asked.

"Oh, you!" she said, laughing. "We have a wonderful son, Lee. Bobby, Jr. He's in college now."

"That's great," Lee said, beaming. "I feel like a matchmaker—and it looks like a pretty good match."

"The best," Bobby said, putting his arm around his wife.

"Twenty years," Lee said. "Let me ask you this: you were partners on the show, and you teach dancing now. Do you ever get just a little bit tired of dancing together? Do you ever get an urge to... well, change partners?"

"Never," Bobby answered. "Not once."

Oblivious to the cameras and the audience and Lee Dean, Sandy turned to her husband. "I love you," she told him. The audience cheered as they kissed.

"Stay tuned," Lee advised, above the noise. "We'll be right back."

"Nice," the director said over the PA. "Thanks."

"Did you plan that?" Kay asked Sheila. "My God, you didn't! It really got to you—"

"I'm keyed up, that's all," Sheila insisted, pulling a tissue from her bag and dabbing at her eyes.

"Sure," Kay said dryly, "and I'm Queen Marie of

Romania—nice to meet you. Admit it, Sheila—you're a big softie at heart."

"No, I'm not!"

This time, Kay's voice was soft and gentle. "It isn't the worst thing in the world, you know. Especially not if the person who makes you feel that way loves you..."

Sheila didn't answer, but opened her bag for another Kleenex.

In the bleachers, Bobby and Sandy were talking with Lee when Sandy felt someone tap her on the shoulder. She turned and found Dennis leaning close.

"Tell me," he whispered. "I have to know. I have the *right* to know, Sandy. That son of yours—is he mine?"

All week long she'd waited for him to ask about the baby, and when he hadn't, she'd waited for the right moment to tell him. It hadn't come, not even as he asked the question.

"No," she said, in a final, necessary deception. "I—I never had that baby. My son—*our* son—is Bobby's."

The stage manager pointed at Lee.

"Okay, we're back!" Lee Dean said. "We've just seen what they call in the business 'a tough act to follow,' but *Dancetime, USA!* presented some of the biggest acts going, not only in the fabulous fifties, but in the history of music. Some of them were already big stars when they came on the show. Others were just starting out, but they had stardom written all over them. Take a look at these three ladies, as they made their first appearance on national television."

The film rolled, showing The Fantastiks as they'd looked and sounded in 1958. When they finished their song, Lee had joined them for a quick interview.

"That was great, just great!" he said. "Everybody says we're going to be hearing a lot from you girls, and I think they're right."

"Thank you," they said, giggling nervously.

"We know you as The Fantastiks. Why don't you tell us your names and a little about yourselves?"

He extended the mike to the girl on the left. "My name is Dee Phillips," she said.

"And how long have you three been singing together?"

"Oh, since way back when," she answered. "We've always been singing."

"Uh huh," Lee said, moving over. "And on this side, we have—"

"I'm Virgie Kendrick."

"And I guess it must feel pretty good, having your first hit record?"

Virgie nodded. "It's like a dream for us."

"And in the middle we have—"

"My name is Sylvia, but everybody calls me Sylvie."

"What are your plans now that you've made it?" Lee asked.

She thought for a second, then grinned. "To just keep on goin' as long and as far as we can."

The audience, packed with Fantastiks' fans who'd written for tickets months before, went wild.

"That was back in 1958," Lee said. "If we had another hour or so, I could read you the long list of just how far those three ladies went—the list of hits they recorded, the records they broke in their club and concert appearances. But instead, I'll just say that here they are again, and we're truly honored to present them tonight. Together for the first time in a long time, the fabulous Fantastiks!"

Everyone involved with the show had known that there would be no controlling the studio audience when the trio came onstage. The audience stood, screamed, and cheered for the matching sequin gowns, and for the sight of the three singers reunited. The audio tape with the accompaniment wouldn't start until the audience settled down. Meanwhile the three Fantastiks looked at each other and laughed.

"Thank you," Sylvia kept saying. "We thank you so very much..."

They'd always kidded and clowned between songs. It came back naturally.

"Who's gonna tell them what we're singing?" Sylvia asked.

"Don't look at me!" Virgie answered, remembering the old routine. "What *are* we singing?" She and Sylvia stared at Dee, who turned around as if looking for someone else to ask.

"We're gonna have to see what comes up, I guess," Sylvia said, smiling. "But before we do, I want to say something. I should have said it a long time ago. It's not a big something, and I don't know why I didn't say it before, unless maybe I was in too much of a hurry.

"Virgie? Dee? I want to say thank you," she told her former partners. "Thank you for all those good years. Because if it wasn't for you two, I could never have been me... Now, where's that music?"

The track for their medley began. The reaction at the end of the song was so intense that they were already into "Mama Made Do" before the audience quieted down.

"The fabulous Fantastiks and the one and only Sylvia!" Lee said, standing with them when the song was over.

"No, Lee," Sylvia corrected him. "That was just the fabulous Fantastiks."

They waited for the audience to quiet down. "How did it feel to sing together again?" Automatically, he asked Sylvia, but she stepped aside, waiting for Virgie to answer first.

"It was a lot of fun. Like old times, maybe even better."

"The same goes for me," Dee added.

Only then did Sylvia speak. "It was so good," she said, smiling at her former partners, "that I don't know why we waited so long. But I do know that it won't be that long till we do it again. A lot of good songs have come along since the trio stopped working. I haven't asked Virgie and Dee yet because the idea just came to me, but it might be fun to record some of them on an album..."

The audience signified its approval.

During the commercial that followed, The Regulars, joined by Al Hartley and Carl Schmidt, gathered in front of the podium along with the guest stars. Lee stood behind it, above them.

"If you remember the old days," he said when they were back on the air, "you know that when we talked with the kids on our show, we always gave them a gift—something to help them remember us. I hope it won't be another twenty years before we're together again, but until then, our Regulars can relive some of their favorite memories on their new video cassette recorders—our way of thanking them for being with us tonight. Our thanks, too, to Tommy Del, Alice Lane, The Amateurs, The Fantastiks... and to you, for watching and for remembering. Now, if you're looking at your clock and thinking that it's a couple of minutes too early for us to say good night, you're right. Because we're not done yet! This is *Dancetime, USA!* and we're going to dance!"

A tape of The Diamonds singing "The Stroll" began. Two lines formed, the men next to Bobby and the women standing beside Sandy, directly across from them.

"Ready?" Bobby asked his wife.

"Whenever you are," she answered. "If you remember how to do it after all these years."

"I remember," he said. His right foot brushed the floor in a semi-circular movement. Sandy matched the step, and down both lines the others followed suit. Lee Dean watched from the podium, smiling into the cameras.

"Hey," Tommy Del called to him. "What are you waiting for? Another reunion? Come down here or I'll come and get you!" He took a few steps as he spoke, indicating that he was serious. Lee joined him, playfully punching Tommy in the arm as the music played.

At the head of the line, Sandy and Bobby began to "Stroll" down the aisle between the sexes.

The screen was filled with a long shot from a camera mounted on top of the control booth. The viewing audience saw the dancers, but heard the pre-recorded music track, and some of them wondered what the dancers were saying to each other as their lips moved silently.

"Having a good time?" Bobby asked.

"For twenty years, it's been a good time," Sandy answered. "Even when I didn't know it."

"I don't know what I'm supposed to do," Carl Schmidt told his wife, as they took Sandy and Bobby's place.

"Don't worry about it," Connie said, pulling him along. "All we have to do is get from this end to that end."

"Connie?" he asked. "Are you ever sorry you didn't keep up with this? The show-business stuff?"

She looked at him as if he was crazy. "Are you nuts? Come on, move a little faster, will you? I want to go home."

"Like this?" Al Hartley asked Cathy, trying to follow her steps.

"That's right," she told him, as they danced by the others.

"You know," he said, "you were the most beautiful girl—no, make that the most beautiful woman—on the show."

"Oh, Al..."

The audience was applauding, and in millions of homes, the credits began to roll over the images of the dancers as the three Fantastiks danced down the space between the two lines together, joined by Tony, Lee, and Tommy.

Alice Lane found herself at the head of the girls' line, facing Don Simpson.

"That was nice, what you said to Lee," he told her, as

they danced together. He wondered if she'd meant it or if she'd just been intimidated.

"It was—nice of you to help me," she answered.

"The Stroll" ended, and another song began. It was the rock waltz version of "Auld Lang Syne" that had signaled the end of a million record hops. The lines became couples, and they were joined by others from the audience.

"Come on." Lee said, pulling Kay from the wings.

"I'll never forgive you for this!" she vowed.

"You, too," Tommy said, grabbing Sheila.

"Hey," Lee Dean said, waltzing Kay through the maze of couples, "I was talking to Tony. He's looking for a job, and I was thinking maybe he'd work with me on that show."

"Oh yes, that show. I'd almost forgotten."

"It won't be for a while, Kay. I'll be around. And sooner or later, I'll be back..."

Beyond them, the stage manager was counting down the final seconds of the program.

"Congratulations, lady producer," Tommy Del said. "You did a really fine job."

"Is that a professional judgment or a personal opinion?" Sheila asked, smiling.

"It's the unbiased opinion of the man who loves you," he answered. "I'm not sure how to take on a TV network, but I'm going to fight for you—and I'm going to win."

She smiled to herself, running her fingers through his hair as he held her in his arms. Lifting her head, Sheila looked up into his eyes. "You won't have to fight too hard, Tommy."

The set was crowded as more and more couples came up from the audience. Most of them stayed in place, moving only a few steps in any direction. One man and woman, though, had a style all their own, moving easily and expertly in spite of the crowded floor. They seemed unaware of everyone else... as if they were the only ones on the floor. They moved with the ease of two people whose bodies—whose lives—had been made to fit together, as though they'd be partners for a long time to come.

They made a pretty picture. Camera number two took it. The director picked it from all the choices before him. The technical director punched a button. From the studio, the image went out through cables to the transmitter, then over the air. In millions of homes, the video signal was picked up and translated back into a medium closeup of the two dancers as the music played.

Viewers saw the woman observe something over the man's shoulder and look surprised. When she called his attention to it, he smiled.

"Look," Sandy O'Brian said.

"Look at what?" Bobby asked.

She guided him into a semi-turn. "See? On the monitor. It's us—"

"It's *television*," he told her.

"Bobby," Sandy asked, "Did we ever really have the times we remember?"

"What do you mean?"

"What—what were we really like?"

He smiled at her again. "Damned if I know, honey. Ask me in another twenty years."

"Oh, you!" she said, laughing, holding tighter to him.

"That's a wrap," the stage manager announced. The show was over.

But the dancers ignored him as they moved in time to the old familiar tune, swaying to the beat, steady... and regular.

STEPHEN LEWIS

With *The Regulars*, Stephen Lewis returns to the show business setting of *The Love Merchants*, the 2,000,000 copy bestseller that established him as one of today's most popular novelists. His other novels include *The Club, Natural Victims, Beach House, Something In The Blood,* and *The Best Sellers,* for which he received a Gold Medal Award from "The West Coast Review Of Books."

Born in Springfield, Massachusetts, Lewis began writing after working as a model while in his teens. After establishing himself as a successful gossip columnist and interviewer covering entertainment personalities, he turned to investigative reportage in a series of books concentrating on aspects of the new morality before his transition to fiction.

A total of 15 million copies of his books have been sold, with translations in eleven languages.

In his own words an extremely "private person," Stephen Lewis lives in Los Angeles, where he is currently at work on a new novel.